ULTERIOR OBJECTIVES

A

LILLIAN

SAXTON

THRILLER

SCOTT DENNIS PARKER

QUADRANT FICTION STUDIO

2016

Ulterior Objectives

A Lillian Saxton Thriller

ISBN-13: 978-0692793466
ISBN-10: 0692793461

Cover design by Scott Dennis Parker
Photo Credit:
Top Photo: OSORIOartist
Bottom Art: B&J

www.ScottDennisParker.com

Give feedback on the book at:

scott@scottdennisparker.com

Twitter: @sdparker7

Second Edition

Printed in the U.S.A

To Dad,
who helped me envision this story
from the beginning

CLOSE QUARTERS FIGHT!

The door opened a crack. Half a face peered out. Lillian made eye contact and the person's eye widened in surprise. He grunted and tried to close the door quickly. She rammed her shoe in the space and prevented it. Next, she slammed her shoulder into the door. Taking the other person by surprise, she flung the door open, banging him in the face.

Lillian stormed into the room. A distinct odor, a new one, met her. She recognized it but had no time to determine what it was. The man had quickly recovered and was moving towards her.

She recognized him as Brown Suit in the instant before his fist flew at her. It came from her right side. She raised her right arm to deflect the blow while, at the same time, pivoting on her right foot. She used his momentum in her favor. His fist met air and he momentarily lost his balance. That gave her time to crash her left fist on his face.

Years ago, when Lillian had joined the Army, she knew her size and weight would never prevail for long in a fist fight. Lillian felt confident in her abilities if her opponent was a woman. When fighting a man, however, she knew her size and weight meant she needed to end it as quickly as possible. Speed and dexterity were her greatest allies. Her blows couldn't end fights with a single thrust, so she honed her ability to rain multiple blows on her opponents.

Her left fist landed on Brown Suit's jaw. She brought her knee up a second later and smashed his chest. Finally, with her right arm now free from deflecting his one swing, she placed her hand on the back of his neck and shoved him downward.

Brown Suit toppled to the floor on his hands and knees. He held his head at such an angle that Lillian knew she had stunned him good. She took a step back to regain a proper fighting stance.

His hand shot out and clipped her ankle. She lost her balance and stumbled backward. She reached out for something to stop her movement and found only air. Lillian backpedaled a few more steps, her thick heels clogging on the wooden floor. A few more feet and she hit the back of a couch. This stopped her backward movement and gave Brown Suit time to stand.

He charged.

1

"Sergeant Saxton, what do you think of when you hear the word 'treason'?"

Lillian Saxton stood at attention and frowned. She wore her assigned brown uniform, belted at the waist, tie neatly knotted, with a skirt that hung just at the knees. Since she was inside Houston's Rice Hotel, her garrison cap was folded over the belt. Her red hair was pulled up behind her ears.

"I'm sorry, sir, I don't understand what you mean." Her voice was curious but deferential.

"Treason, Sergeant. It's a simple concept. What does it mean to you?"

The man who snapped at her she didn't know, but his brown uniform displayed the rank of colonel. He stood to the side of a table in one of the upper suites of the famous Rice Hotel. The man who sat at the table, littered with stacks of paper and a typewriter, she knew. He was Captain Ernest Donnelly, her commanding officer. She looked at him for clarification.

"I'm the one speaking to you, Sergeant," the colonel spat. "If there's ever a situation where you think you need to look elsewhere for help, then we've got a bigger problem than I imagined."

Donnelly, dressed in his brown uniform but with the tie loosened around his collar, leaned back in his chair. "Honeywell, why don't you just…"

"Don't tell me what I should do, Captain," Honeywell blurted. "I've asked the sergeant a question. I expect an answer directly from her and not from her superior officer or anyone else she thinks can help her."

A little fire burst into existence deep within Lillian's gut. She hated what many of the men in the United States Army thought of her: weak, not as good as a man, only good for typing up reports. She was none of that, and she strove every day to prove wrong that kind of thinking.

"Treason," Lillian began, speaking evenly but with force, "is the active betrayal of one's country. In most cases, especially in war time, it is punishable by death."

Honeywell regarded her for a moment. His short cropped hair was receding across the top of his head. The gray flecks caught the lamp light and seemed to glow.

"That is pretty much the letter of the law, Sergeant. Now, even though we're not at war, what do you think should be done about someone who may commit treason?"

"May commit, colonel?"

A small twitch along the corner of his mouth might have grown into a smile, but Honeywell didn't give it the chance. "Yes, Sergeant. Would you trust anyone whom you suspect of committing treason?"

Lillian pondered the question for a few heartbeats. "It would depend on the circumstances, Colonel. If the person was only suspected, I would seek out additional information, either to clear the individual or convict him."

Another twitch, this time along Honeywell's eyebrows. Lillian had to admire a person like the colonel who could so easily contain his outward emotions. She made a note never to play the colonel in poker although that likelihood would probably never come to pass.

"So you would investigate?"

"Yes, sir."

"Undercover?"

"If necessary, yes."

"What if you knew the person? Would that cloud your judgment?"

Another few heartbeats. "No, sir. This is the United States of America. All citizens, military or civilian, are assumed innocent until proven guilty. Same goes with someone suspected of treason. You investigate, gather evidence, and, if the evidence points to treason, you arrest the individual. You bring him to trial and, if he is found guilty, you inflict punishment."

"Back to my second question: what if you knew the person? Would you hide evidence, alter testimony, or do anything to sway the arresting officer or jury?"

"No, sir. Treason is treason, and if the evidence indicates that, there is no other recourse." She glanced to Donnelly, then back up to Honeywell. "I would, of course, be upset, but that's a personal matter, not a military one."

In the intervening silence, Donnelly spoke. "Well, Colonel, I think that should satisfy you."

Honeywell narrowed his eyes. "I'll let you know when I'm satisfied."

"Of course." To Lillian, Donnelly asked, "Have you contacted Wade to get his report on your brother?"

Donnelly was referring to the assignment recently completed. Samuel Saxton, Lillian's brother, was lost in Europe. She feared the worst, especially with the Nazi army threatening to strike. A reporter, Wendell Rosenblatt, had information about Samuel. He was due to land in Houston, but had vanished. Lillian had hired private investigator Benjamin Wade to locate Rosenblatt. He did, but it was too late. Rosenblatt was dead, but Wade found the reporter's notes complete with all the details about Samuel's whereabouts.

Lillian had been waiting for Wade to deliver his report when Donnelly summoned her to his room in the Rice Hotel.

"No, sir."

Donnelly gestured with his head to the next room. "Why don't you give him a call?"

Lillian nodded once and left the room.

***

"I think she passes your muster, Colonel," Donnelly said.

"You're just too close to her and the rest of your little squad."

Honeywell walked over to a bureau where a single bottle of Jack Daniels whiskey rested. He poured himself a couple of fingers and downed half in one gulp. He held the glass in his hands and mulled over something in his head. "But the communique was to her personally. Do you think Monroe is trying to recruit her?"

"Don't be silly," Donnelly blurted. He realized he was addressing a senior officer and stood. He poured his own glass of whiskey. "As far as I know, Frank Monroe is only an investment banker. His job takes him all over the U.S. and Europe. He has contacts everywhere. Sure, he's been over to Germany since they invaded Poland last year, but there's no cause to think he's turned traitor."

"Why else would he insist on seeing her? You think he knows she works for the Army?"

"Lillian Saxton's job is no secret. What she does for the Army is. Look, they're old friends from back when they attended college in Europe in the '30s. He says he has vital information about the war, but will only talk to her. And the meet's in D.C. They're not even leaving American soil. What's to lose?"

"I don't trust anyone who has business dealings with the Nazis and then turns around and asks to meet with one of my soldiers."

Donnelly did not have time to respond. The adjoining door opened and Lillian Saxton walked in the room. She must have tried to mask her emotions, but Donnelly noticed the red rimming her eyes.

"Is everything okay, Sergeant?" Donnelly asked.

Saxton merely nodded.

"You find out about your brother?"

"He's dead."

The two senior officers gave the revelation a few moments of silence. "I'm sorry," Donnelly said. He reached into his pocket and held out a handkerchief. She walked over and took it.

"Thank you, sir." She dabbed at her eyes. She stood straighter and pulled herself together. She handed the handkerchief back to the captain. "What's the next assignment? It's why you brought me here, isn't it?"

Donnelly said, "Sergeant, this is Colonel Clive Honeywell. He will explain the situation."

Honeywell stepped forward. "Sergeant, do you know a Frank Monroe?"

Donnelly watched the emotions cross Saxton's face. He prided himself on not just being a commanding officer to his squad, but to know his officers as real people. Saxton had a circuitous route to the United States Army, but she had acquitted herself beyond even his expectations. The name "Frank Monroe" hit a nerve.

After a moment, Saxton said, "Yes, sir. He's from a prominent family in Boston. He and I went to the university back in 1934. He's some sort of banker now, I think."

Honeywell narrowed his eyes. "You hesitated. Why?"

"The name came out of left field, Colonel. We haven't even seen each other in years. It just wasn't a name I expected you to say."

Pursing his lips, Honeywell said, "He's asked to meet you."

For the second time, Donnelly noted Saxton's surprise.

"Me?"

"Yes. Personally."

"Where?"

"Washington."

Saxton frowned. "Why?"

Honeywell raised his glass and pointed a finger at her. "That's what you're going to find out."

2

The place where Frank Monroe suggested he meet with Lillian was on the National Mall near the Washington Monument. On the flight from Houston to the nation's capital, Donnelly had filled Lillian in on all the details of the mission. Banker Frank Monroe, while at the London branch of his bank, had contacted the American Embassy and requested a meeting with Lillian Saxton, sergeant US Army, in Washington. The reason he gave was top secret—even Donnelly didn't know the truth—and might help the coming war effort.

The message had been passed up the chain of command of the diplomatic corps, over to the military, and back down to Colonel Honeywell. He, in turn, had contacted Donnelly and met in Houston on the tail end of Lillian's mission. Since the nature of the message from Monroe was secretive, Honeywell immediately didn't trust him. Or Lillian, who had been serving under his command for nearly two years. It was all Donnelly could do to persuade Honeywell not to post watchers along the perimeter of the National Mall.

But Lillian pretty much knew they were there. If she were in charge, she'd do the same thing.

She sat on one of the north benches that faced the tall obelisk. Against Donnelly's judgement, Lillian wore a nice professional business suit, the kind worn by any civilian working woman. She told the captain it wasn't a good idea to walk around in an Army uniform—thus announcing her identify—if the reason for all the secrecy was to meet clandestinely. Tourists milled about the entire area, enjoying the late spring temperatures before Washington became an insufferable city in the depths of summer. Families with children mixed with citizens who worked in the city. The sun shone down on all. The flags that ringed the monument flapped in the breeze. It was a scene such as this that reminded Lillian why she did what she did.

A man approached and sat next to her. "I'm glad you got my message."

She turned. A huge grin spread across her face. If any of Honeywell's spies questioned that, she'd just have to explain her physical reaction to seeing an old friend after so many years. She reached over and threw her arms around Frank Monroe's neck.

"Well, if that's the kind of reaction I had coming, I would have contacted you much earlier."

She pulled back and gave him a pouty stare. "Then why haven't you?"

"Business. And your job isn't one that keeps regular office hours. What is it you do for Uncle Sam?"

Doubt immediately flashed through her. Was Honeywell right to cast this meeting under a cloud of suspicion?

"I could say it's classified but you'd keep asking. So I'll just say that I do whatever the Army needs me to do." She sat there a moment and just looked at him.

When she had last set eyes on Monroe, it was on a celebration vacation in Paris after their graduation from Oxford. She, Frank, and a few other friends had all crossed the Channel and celebrated their freedom from academics. Frank, born in Boston to a family that could trace its lineage back to the Mayflower, was always the richest of the bunch. He often spotted their little gang of Americans a few rounds in the pubs. His father had paid for a week's vacation to Paris as a reward to his son before the younger Monroe started his professional life.

Even during the trip, Lillian had known about Frank's ulterior motivation. She and another member of their cadre, James Geiger, had split as a couple. He wanted to stay in Europe, preferably Germany, and use his mathematical talents as an engineer. She did not. That caused an irrevocable split between them. Frank, always the third wheel, saw his opportunity.

But Frank was never one to recognize good timing. Her

heart was still raw from the breakup and she had had to tell Frank "no" to his proposal of marriage. He had accepted her answer magnanimously but she had also cut short her vacation and left Paris ahead of her friends.

Now Frank Monroe sat next to her. He had lost none of his charming good looks. His blond hair still remained radiant under his gray fedora. The only wrinkles that marred his face were on the corners of his eyes and around his mouth. He must laugh quite a bit, she thought. As it was back in the day, his gray suit was immaculate. Even his shoes were shined to perfection. Knowing her life since she left Paris, Lillian wondered what it would have been like had she accepted the offer.

"Penny for your thoughts" Frank's smile showed perfect teeth that were perfectly white.

She patted his arm. "It's really good to see you."

He put his hand over hers. "You, too."

They sat silent a moment before Lillian broke the spell. "Now, what is so important that you had me fly halfway across the country just to meet you?"

Some of Frank's joviality eroded from his face. "It's about James."

***

The man in the brown suit acted like a tourist. He walked around the Washington Monument gazing up at the tall structure. He admired the Americans for erecting a monument to a soldier even if Washington himself was known more for retreating than actively fighting. There was also the dastardly sneak attack on the Hessians in New Jersey. Was that the only offensive role Washington had ever successfully attempted?

Around the man's neck was slung a camera. He snapped some pictures he wouldn't even bother to develop. He also snapped pictures of his mark, a man named Frank Monroe. The man in the brown suit had followed Monroe from the train station all the way to the Mall. The mission was simple: find out who he talked to and, if possible, the subject. When Monroe sat on the bench next to a red-haired woman, the camera in the brown-suited man's hand clicked. He watched as Monroe and the woman hugged each other. The smiles on their faces revealed they knew each other. Old friends, perhaps. The way they held each other's hands indicated something more.

Click.

The man in the brown suit swept his eyes around the perimeter of the monument. He wanted to see if there were others watching Monroe and the woman. He saw tourists freely walking around, not a care in the world. The Americans had that luxury. Their oceans had protected them for their entire history. No one dared attacked shores hundreds of miles away. But with superior German air power, the Americans would soon learn that their precious oceans would no longer protect them.

There. That officer in uniform loitering under the trees. He pretended to read a newspaper but his eyes rarely reached the page. Instead, he stared at Monroe and the woman.

Click.

The man in the brown suit captured the officer's image. That picture might prove useful in the growing dossier of known military personnel.

Monroe stood. So did the woman. They made their way to the curb of the nearest street. The officer under the trees folded his unread newspaper under his arm and followed at a discreet distance. That answered that question.

Monroe hailed a cab and he and the woman climbed in. From down the street, a parked car eased away from the curb and pulled up next to the officer. He climbed in and the dark sedan zoomed after the cab.

The man in the brown suit hailed his own cab. He opened the door and sat in the back seat. "Do you see that car a block away? Follow it."

The man in the brown suit spoke perfect English. He smiled at himself. He had worked long and hard to remove all vestiges of his German accent before being stationed in America.

3

Frank directed the cab driver to a nice upscale eatery a few blocks away from the National Archives. Situated on the Dupont Circle, the Hoffsteader Restaurant was hopping with the noontime crowd.

Lillian wasn't sure what Frank said to the head waiter, but they quickly found themselves at a nice table in the center of the floor. Large paned windows bordered three sides of the structure, giving the patrons a wide panorama of the Circle and the cars, buses, cabs, and pedestrians moving about. The fourth wall led to the kitchen, but above it was a large mirror, giving the room an even grander feel.

Frank ordered for them: two pastrami sandwiches and coffee. Lillian also asked for water. Giving the room another once-over, Frank finally settled his eyes on Lillian.

"Yes, it's about James."

"What about him? I'll admit that six months after Paris, I stopped looking for details on his life."

Frank grinned. "Six months, huh?' He folded his hands together and leaned on his elbows. "That's a rather peculiar date."

Lillian just gave him her eyes. She sipped her coffee.

"You take it black?" Frank asked. "You used to take cream and sugar, two teaspoons if I remember correctly."

"You remember correctly. I decided to change the way I drink coffee in the years since we were at Oxford."

"Let me guess: did that change also happen around six months after Paris?"

Heartbroken at the breakup with James and shocked to have had Frank propose marriage in that aftermath, Lillian had returned to England and was adrift. Unlike Frank or James who had their professional lives lined up before they left college—

one might even say they had their lives lined up before college—Lillian was at Oxford to broaden her mind. A California girl who grew up in San Diego, Lillian wanted to put as much distance from her upbringing as possible. It wasn't that she didn't love her parents and family, but she wanted to see the world, and the only way to do that was to get out of San Diego. Education was the key, and she earned a scholarship to U.C.L.A. and then on to Oxford. She studied philosophy and history, the subjects that were great in school but had little real-world value. She also had a knack for mathematics. That's how she met and fell in love with James Geiger who was also studying math at Oxford. But after his desire to remain in Europe and Germany, an irrevocable split emerged and nothing, not even the love of math, could mend it.

Six months after they broke up, James Geiger married Elsa Schmidt.

She gave Frank a wan smile. "There were lots of things I changed at that time."

"Well," Frank said, reaching over and grasping her hand, "some things never change. You still look as radiant as ever."

Lillian chuckled, effectively dismissing the comment even though she inwardly like the compliment. "Let's get down to it. What's the story about James. And why in hell should I care?"

Another quick scan of the room. Frank reached into his suit coat and withdrew a small package. He put it on the table and slid it to Lillian.

The package was wrapped in brown paper and sealed with tape. On one side, her name was handwritten in a script she recognized. James had written it. He had even included the fancy tail he always applied to the "S" in her last name. It had been so long since she last set eyes on this style that her heart skipped a beat.

The sensation surprised her. After all the years of tending to her own happiness and trying to forget James, she didn't think something as insignificant as seeing his handwriting would do that to her. She was at once happy and angry with herself.

She picked it up and held it up to the light to examine the

tape.

"No, I didn't open it," Frank said. He smirked. "Thanks for trusting me."

She curled half her mouth at him. With a fingernail, she sliced open the tape and unwrapped the object.

It was a small book, hardback, that could easily fit inside trouser or jacket pockets. The exterior was a turquoise blue. Her heart skipped another beat. She already knew what this book was. She turned it over and opened the cover.

There, on the fly leaf, was the inscription James had written to her over five years ago: "To Lillian, may we grow old together reading these poems to each other. Always yours, James."

The sting of a tear stabbed her eyes. She turned her face away from Frank. She bit her inner cheek and tried her meditation techniques to stem the coming tide of emotions. It took her a few moments, but she succeeded. When she looked up, he was giving her a meaningful look.

"I'm sorry about that. I didn't know what it was."

Lillian cleared her throat. "You weren't supposed to. It was to me. But what does this have to do with James?"

Frank gazed at her. "When I saw James a week ago, he gave me that package. He also gave me this message." He looked at the ceiling, clearly recalling the words. "You are to remember that time in London when you both went to see Romeo and Juliet. From there, do the calculations."

Lillian frowned. "Do the calculations?"

Frank shrugged. "That's what he said. Heck if I know what it means. It wasn't directed to me."

Lillian started mouthing the message over and over again. She thought about the time she and James took the train down to London. It was a weekend fling to get away from the drudgery of their studies. They stayed in adjoining rooms at one of the fancier hotels in the city, and quickly opened the common door. It remained open the rest of the weekend. They took in two plays, ate great meals, and generally forgot about the world for two glorious days. It was during that trip that he had bought this book for her. They had repeatedly checked out a similar copy at the library, but hated having to return it. They wanted their own copy so that they could write in it.

Realization dawned on Lillian. She flipped through the pages. There, in the margins, were all the annotations they had made. Some passages were underlined, others had hearts and designs surrounding them. It was a mixture of her handwriting and James's. But what made these annotations particularly personal were the dates. Every trip they had taken together resulted in a new favorite poem. They had begun to write the dates of their trips and the towns visited. In a sense, this small book was a history of their relationship.

And James had kept it. Now he had sent it to Lillian.

The more pages she flipped, the more she started to mouth the words to the message. "Meet" appeared first. Then "in Belgium." "Will deliver" followed. The next word puzzled her.

"Codebook?" Lillian said.

Frank gave her a curious look. "What did you say?"

"Codebook. What codebook?"

The blood in Frank's face lightened one shade. He quickly sipped his coffee to hide.

"Frank, what is it?"

He kept drinking. He drained his cup and clattered it down on the saucer. "I didn't know."

"Know what?"

Frank signaled the waitress. He held up his empty cup. She came over and refilled his cup and Lillian's.

Once the waitress had left, Lillian leaned forward and whispered, "What didn't you know?"

"The nature of James's message."

"Of course you didn't. You just told me that."

"That's not what I mean." He paused and adjusted himself in the chair. "You said you haven't kept up with him, right?"

She nodded.

"Do you know what he does now?"

Lillian shrugged. "Other than being married?" Her tone was

dismissive. "Or his job?"

"His job."

"I haven't the slightest idea. He majored in mathematics back in Oxford with a minor in engineering."

Frank nodded. "Since he stayed in Europe and married Elsa"—he glanced at her to gauge her reaction—"he got himself some rather influential and powerful friends and family."

Lillian narrowed her eyes. The only influential people in Germany nowadays were likely to be Nazis. "How influential?"

"Very. We're talking just about as high as an American-born man can get. Elsa's family is rich and well-connected. James used those connections to make more connections. He is entrenched in what's going on over there."

Lillian thought about what that meant. Here in late April 1940, they were in what the press dubbed The Phony War. Germany had invaded Poland back in September 1939, prompting Britain and France to honor their treaty and come to Poland's aid. It hadn't amounted to anything, for the country fell in a matter of weeks. Then the Nazis did a most unusual thing for a war: they stopped. No one quite knew why but it had happened and it had gone on for months. Long enough to make everyone in Europe on edge. Chances were good Hitler wasn't completely satisfied, but no one knew where he'd strike next. He had already invaded Norway at the beginning of the month. The western front was probably going to come next.

But when?

Frank continued. "Don't you see? What codebook might James have that you'd want? I'm talking 'you' as in 'your job' you."

Lillian knew what he meant and it puzzled her yet again. While she had stopped keeping up with James years ago, clearly James hadn't stopped knowing about her. That meant he knew she worked for the U.S. Army.

She gasped as the ramifications slammed into her. She sat up straight, blinking. She looked at Frank. His eyes met hers with a steadiness that meant he had figured it out as well. She broke off her gaze with him and scanned the room. Her back was to the front door and windows so she looked up in the mirror to scan the rest of the room.

And she stopped. There, in the reflection, she could see a man waiting outside at the bus stop. He looked familiar. He wore a brown suit with a camera slung across his neck. She had seen a man dressed exactly the same at the Washington Monument. She had taken every person there for a tourist. But what were the chances that a tourist from the monument would come to this coffee house and be standing right outside the window within sight of her and Frank?

Possible, but unlikely.

She closed the book of poetry and slipped it into her pocket. She picked up her coffee cup but didn't drink. She talked from behind it.

"Frank, you see that man outside at the bus stop? Brown suit. Camera. No, don't stare at him. Just sweep your gaze around. That's better. He was at the monument when we first met."

His eyes got wider. "Are you sure?"

"You remember who I work for, what I do? I'm trained to notice things like this. It could be coincidence but I'm betting not. Here's the thing: he's probably following you."

Frank frowned deeply. "Surely not. You're the one in the Army."

"But I'm not dressed like I'm in the Army. And the last few assignments have all been here in America. You, on the other hand, just arrived from Europe." She patted her pocket. "And you just delivered something to me."

It was Frank's turn to lift his coffee cup and talk from behind it. "You sure?"

She gave him a pitying look. "Would I ever question you regarding banking activities? So don't question me on this. Listen, I'm going to buy a paper from the newsboy over there near the bus stop. I'll get a better look at him."

He reached out a hand and grasped her arm. "Let me."

Lillian plucked each one of his fingers off her arm and

stood. "I'm not the way I was back at Oxford. I don't need some handsome hero to look out for me."

She folded her napkin and turned to the front door.

***

The man in the brown suit had gambled when a bus arrived at the stop and he didn't get on. He was pretty sure Monroe and the woman hadn't noticed him. It helped that the cafe had windows on three sides. It enabled him to walk on any of the three sides and still keep an eye on the Americans.

He noted they ate pastrami sandwiches with sauerkraut. He gave them points for eating good food. The sight of it made him want a sandwich. Or sausage links and sauerkraut. His mouth watered. He also noted when Monroe had delivered a package to the woman. A new focus came over him. What his superior officer suspected proved to be true: Frank Monroe was a spy.

The man in the brown suit now stood next to the bus stop. He glanced into the cafe.

The woman was gone. Probably went to powder her nose. No matter. He'd follow her when she left, see where she lived and where she worked.

Amid the screeching brakes of the approaching bus, a woman's voice said, "Excuse me."

The man in the brown suit turned and came face to face with the woman Frank Monroe had met. Up close, a part of his mind noted the details of her face. Her lips were full with red lipstick giving them a glossy sheen. Her red hair, pulled up over her ears, caught the sunlight. Her skin seemed flawless except for delicate wrinkles under her eyes. He wondered what had put them there.

"Can I help you?" the woman asked. "You seem lost."

"No, thank you, madam," the man in the brown suit stammered. "I know perfectly well where I am."

"Care to tell me why you're so interested in me and my friend?" She stepped closer to him. "And why you're taking pictures?"

The man in the brown suit had been trained well, but this was his first mission. He had internalized all the scenarios and the appropriate responses. One dictum stated "when approached by an officer of the law, stick to the cover story. So he did. "I am a tourist from Indiana. I'm in town to visit the sights. It appears that we are both seeing the same sights and eating at the same restaurants."

"Then why haven't you come in and ordered?"

"The cafe is crowded. I was merely waiting for the line to thin."

The woman looked at him with clear suspicion. He read it on her face. He also could read she had nothing other than suspicion. He tried to change the subject. "What do you recommend?"

"The Reuben."

Frank Monroe arrived and stood next to the woman. She looked up at him and smiled wanly.

"Are you ready?" Monroe asked the woman.

She nodded. "Sure."

Monroe offered her his arm. She took it. Together, they walked down the street.

The man in the brown suit breathed a sigh of relief. The intersection was way too public for any sort of altercation. He was confident he would prevail, however. The training he had undertaken was extensive. There were few who would emerge unscathed.

Turning, the man in the brown suit hopped onto the bus. He didn't care about its destination. He just wanted to put as much distance between himself and the couple. Once safely away, he'd get to his apartment and the dark room therein. He needed to develop his photographs as soon as possible so he could make his report to Herr Colonel.

4

"Hail a cab," Lillian blurted.

"What?"

Lillian broke off from Frank's arm and stepped into the street. A car swerved to avoid her. She paid it little mind. Her focus was on the cab halfway down the block. She waved her arm and the yellow car veered to meet her.

"Get in," Lillian ordered Frank. Mutely, he complied. To the driver, she said, "Follow that bus." The cabbie started the meter.

"What's going on?" Frank asked.

"I want to see where that tourist goes. Something about him I don't trust."

"He looked normal to me."

"Exactly. I don't think he's a tourist."

"Then what is he?"

"Not sure, but we'll find out. Who knew you were coming to meet me?" She thought a moment. "Besides James."

Frank pondered the question. "My boss, of course. I told him I would be taking a few days off and wondered if he needed anything done over here. A few friends. My parents."

Lillian's mind raced. She dared not say anything untoward until she had more evidence. But chances were good Frank had a spy on his tail. But with the U.S. not at war, she wondered who it might be. Germany was obviously a candidate. The Soviet Union as well. She wouldn't put it past France or England to engage in espionage on American soil either. The man had spoken in perfect English so his accent didn't betray him. Maybe his movements now would.

The cabbie followed the bus for two stops. Both times, Lillian had the driver wait until the bus departed, scanning the passengers who disembarked to see if the man in the brown suit was among them. The third time proved a success. She got out of the cab. Frank tried to follow her but she stopped him.

"Listen, you wouldn't want me telling you how to operate a bank. This is what I do. You'd just be in the way. Stay here, but watch where he goes. If things get bad, call the police. Also call Captain Donnelly of the Army." She blew a kiss at him and slammed the door.

The man whom Lillian had come to think of as Brown Suit waited until the bus left and looked around. Lillian found protection behind a newsstand. The cab remained in place. Brown Suit appeared satisfied and walked across the street. Lillian matched his pace on her side of the street.

Brown Suit walked an additional five blocks west, then two north. Lillian turned to verify Frank and his cab were following her. There were half a dozen cabs on the street including Frank's. Chances were Honeywell and his crew were also keeping tabs on them. She felt secure enough to close some of the gap between her and her mark.

At the entrance to a three-story apartment building, Brown Suit turned and entered the lobby. Lillian crossed the street so she could approach without being seen. As she neared the lobby with its bay window facing the street, she slowed to a halt. Cautiously, she peered inside.

The lobby was small. Four chairs bordered a small table littered with ashtrays and wrinkled magazines. A man sat in one of the chairs. He was reading a newspaper. There was no sign of Brown Suit.

Lillian glanced back at the cab. It was half a block away. She scanned the rest of the street. No other cars passed by. If Honeywell's men were anywhere, they were hiding pretty well.

She grasped the handle and walked inside the lobby. The moldering odor of smoke, alcohol, and mildew assaulted her senses. She winced at the smell, not expecting it. At the rear of the lobby was an old elevator, the kind with an Otis scissor door. The door was closed and the car missing. Brown Suit lived somewhere on one of the upper floors.

Lillian turned to the man reading the newspaper. She fingered her red curls and adopted a squeaky voice, the kind one would expect from a love-struck doll.

"Hey, mister?"

He looked over the top of the paper. His eyes were hard and gray. "Yes?"

"Um, the guy who just came through here, the one in the brown suit, do you know which apartment he lives in?"

He displayed no emotion. "Why?"

She assumed a goofy grin. "Well, you see, I saw him at a bookstore today and we got to talking. We talked so much that he accidentally left one of his books at the counter." She pulled out the poetry book and waggled it. "I'd like to return it to him."

He grunted and put the paper back between them. "3C."

"Thanks."

Lillian contemplated the elevator but dismissed it. The noise would have alerted Brown Suit. She chose the stairwell. She winced again. Added to the other odors she already had experienced was now urine.

She ascended the wooden stairs on her toes. The steps made no creak under her weight. The second-floor landing had a bulb that was just about to die, the light was so feeble. She glanced up, just to make sure no one lurked in the shadows. Satisfied, she continued up.

From somewhere within the building, a mechanical sound rumbled. It was the elevator. Hearing how loud it was, Lillian praised herself for taking the stairs.

At the third floor, she reached a door. It was solid. No window. She'd have to open the door with no way of knowing if Brown Suit was wandering the hallway. But why would he? She'd developed quite a good sense on how to follow people. Donnelly and others had commended her for that very thing in multiple reports. She opened the door.

The hallway smelled better than the stairwell. The floor was wood with a long throw rug running down the middle. A light bulb glowed right above her. Another was at the far end of the hallway, about thirty feet away. A third bulb was at the center where the elevator was located. She noted the gate was closed up here.

Four apartments were on each floor, two on the right and two on the left. Lillian moved forward and glanced at the number on her left: 3A. The number on her right read 3B. Odd and even. Apartment 3C was up on her left. The doors had no peepholes. Still walking on tiptoes, she passed the elevator. She could see the cables moving. Whoever was using it was coming up. The sound was quite loud. She used it as camouflage to close the distance between her and apartment 3C.

The elevator wasn't so loud that she couldn't hear footsteps on the other side of the door. She inhaled deeply and set her feet in a fighting stance. She wasn't sure what to expect, but surprise was going to be her weapon. A thought crept into her brain: what if Brown Suit really was a tourist? She dismissed it when the doorknob turned. No tourist would stay here.

The door opened a crack. Half a face peered out. She made eye contact and the person's eye widened in surprise. He grunted and tried to close the door quickly. She rammed her shoe in the space and prevented it. Next, she slammed her shoulder into the door. Taking the other person by surprise, she flung the door open, banging him in the face.

Lillian Saxton stormed into the room. A distinct odor, a new one, met her. She recognized it but had no time to determine what it was. The man had quickly recovered and was moving toward her.

She recognized him as Brown Suit in the instant before his fist flew at her. It came from her right side. She raised her right arm to deflect the blow while, at the same time, pivoting on her right foot. She used his momentum in her favor. His fist met air and he momentarily lost his balance. That gave her time to crash her left fist on his face.

Years ago, when Lillian had joined the Army, she knew her size and weight would never prevail for long in a fist fight. Lillian felt confident in her abilities if her opponent was a woman. When fighting a man, however, she knew her size and weight meant she needed to end it as quickly as possible. Speed and dexterity were her greatest allies. She knew her blows couldn't end fights with a single thrust, so she honed her ability to rain multiple blows on her opponents.

Her left fist landed on Brown Suit's jaw. She brought her knee up a second later and smashed his chest. Finally, with her right arm now free from deflecting his one swing, she placed her hand on the back of his neck and shoved him downward.

Brown Suit toppled to the floor on his hands and knees. He held his head at such an angle that Lillian knew she had stunned him good. She took a step back to regain a proper fighting stance.

His hand shot out and clipped her ankle. She lost her balance and stumbled backward. She reached out for something to stop her movement and found only air. Lillian backpedaled a few more steps, her thick heels clogging on the wooden floor. A few more feet and she hit the back of a couch. This stopped her backward movement and gave Brown Suit time to stand.

He charged.

Still not quite on perfect balance, Lillian gambled. Brown Suit expected to body slam her. In response, she fell to the floor, landing on her back. A few puffs of air escaped her lungs but she was rewarded by the surprised look on his face as he sailed over her, arms outstretched.

Lillian rolled over and got to her feet. Brown Suit hit the wooden back of the couch and fell to the floor again. A grunt of rage erupted from him but she didn't press him nor did she move closer. His hitting her ankle told her he knew how to fight. Better to get a good handle on her surroundings than to risk another swipe at close quarters.

The interior of the apartment was spare. The couch she had met. Only a coffee table fronted it. The large room had a small kitchen off to her left. A modest wooden table and chairs were to her immediate left. On the far wall was a door that likely led to the bedroom.

Lillian looked around for a weapon. She found none. Not

even a plate or a knife on the counter. Only a radio. She judged it too heavy for effective use.

Brown Suit now stood opposite her. His hair had fallen in his face and he swiped at it. A stream of blood coursed from his lip. The red spot left by her fist was already starting to bruise.

"You're an interesting one," he said. "How did we miss you?"

We? Lillian didn't have time to think about that now. She studied his face, watching his eyes and his body for the next move. What she saw took exactly one second to process. It was a subtle change in his expression. A relaxing of his grimace. And a slight shift of his eyes to a spot behind her.

She ducked. In the same moment, she swept her leg out behind her. It met something solid. Another person's leg. She heard a cry of surprise from that person—a man. She hoped her action might give her a precious few seconds to readjust to this new scenario. Two to one. Not good.

The other person lost his balance and fell. He landed almost directly on the seat of one of the kitchen chairs. The momentum and his weight cracked the wood. It gave way and splintered into pieces.

It also gave her a weapon.

She reached out and grasped one of the broken chair legs. Out of the corner of her eye, she noted Brown Suit was reaching his hand into his suit pocket. Chances were good he wasn't trying to be gentlemanly and offer her a tissue.

Holding the chair leg like a baseball bat, she swung. With his hand buried deep in his suit, there was nothing he could do. The wood connected with Brown Suit's face. He crumpled to the floor.

Not waiting a second, Lillian pressed her advantage. The other man was now on his knees. She recognized him as the man reading the newspaper in the lobby. Unfortunately for her, Newspaper Reader had already drawn a pistol and was bringing it to bear on her.

She shifted her grip on the chair leg from a baseball bat to a fencer's grip. She extended her arm and jabbed at the gun hand.

Newspaper Reader, having just witnessed Lillian swing with two hands, was momentarily surprised at her action.

He swatted away the chair leg. That was exactly what she had hoped for. She wanted him to think that was her only move.

It wasn't.

Lillian let the shattered chair leg leave her grip. She leapt into the air and brought her leg around in a roundhouse kick. The thick heel of her shoe found its mark. Already on his knees, the man huffed in pain and crashed to the floor.

She landed on both feet. In a single movement, she kicked the pistol across the room. She pivoted and assumed another fighting stance just in case either man had more fight in him.

They didn't.

And that's how Honeywell's men found the situation when they stormed into the room, guns drawn.

5

"We have to go to Belgium." Lillian Saxton repeated.

She stood in the office of Colonel Honeywell in Washington, D.C. It was two hours after her altercation with the two men in the apartment. Scattered across an ornate table of dark mahogany were black and white pictures of people in various stages of life. They were clandestinely clearly taken.

The odor Lillian had detected upon entering the apartment was developing fluid. The second room was a darkroom. Brown Suit was a spy.

"Out of the question" Honeywell stood behind his desk, glowering. Donnelly kept his silence near the table with the photographs.

"Why?" Lillian asked.

"Let's start with we're not at war," the colonel snapped. "And we can end it there."

"War is coming. You know it. I know it. Blast it, the whole world knows it. This so-called Phoney War is merely the calm before the storm. If we can get our hands on a Nazi codebook, we can have the upper hand."

"We're not at war with Germany. Besides, how do you know those men are German spies? They spoke perfect English."

"Exactly. It's too perfect. And regarding our using the book, why not deliver it to Britain or France? They'll certainly be fighting Hitler before we will."

Honeywell looked at Donnelly. The junior officer merely shrugged. Honeywell continued. "And this friend of yours, James Geiger. Why do you think he's doing this?"

Lillian shook her head. "I'm not sure. But there has to be a good reason he's willing to deliver a top secret Nazi codebook to me."

"You don't think it's just so he can get you over there?"

"To what end?" Lillian said, exasperation settling into her voice. They had been at this for nearly an hour.

Donnelly, for his part, stayed out of it. The colonel let the silence say what he didn't want to voice.

Lillian shook her head, exasperated. "James is married."

"Since when has that ever stopped anyone?" The colonel arched an eyebrow.

"It's enough to stop me. Besides, we ended things a long time ago."

"Not so long that he didn't contact you, of all people, to make this offer. If he wanted to smuggle out a codebook, why not just give it to your other friend in the outer office?" He was referring to Frank who had accompanied her to Honeywell's office building but was refused admittance into this meeting. "There's something else going on here."

"I don't know what it is, sir, but I'd like permission to find out. What's the worse thing that could happen?"

Honeywell walked to the mahogany table. Lillian watched his fingers run over the images. She knew some of the subjects. They all worked for Honeywell. Curiously, her picture was not in the mix. Likely it was in the camera they had seized at the apartment. Honeywell's team was developing the pictures as they argued.

A knock sounded at the door and Honeywell's adjutant entered. He wore the same brown uniform that everyone wore except Lillian. "Sir, there's a gentleman to see you."

"Not now, Private. Can't you see I'm in a meeting?"

"He said it pertains to the meeting."

Lillian glanced out of Honeywell's office and locked her gaze with Frank. He raised his eyebrows in a silent question. She shook her head.

Honeywell frowned. "Who is it?" He ran a tight, closed ship and few people outside the military knew his business. And, as he had yet to report to his senior officer, no one knew the nature of this meeting.

"The name's Reginald Nevins." A man with a British accent

strode into the office uninvited. He was tall, dressed in a fine gray suit complete with vest, and carried a black cane. Of all things, he wore a derby. He removed his hat with a flourish and bowed at the neck. "My friends call me Reggie. If you hear what I have to say, you can do the same."

No one spoke for a few moments. Lillian was surprised to discover her mouth hung open. Honeywell was not the type of Army officer who suffered his authority lightly. Indeed, he recovered first. "Who the hell are you?"

"Reginald Nevins. I believe I said that already." He turned to Lillian. "And this is the lovely lady who took on two Nazis with scarcely a scratch on her." He reached for her hand, scooped it up in his, and shook it. "Impressive work, my dear. We couldn't make heads or tails of what was happening until your boys stormed into the room."

Lillian smiled at Nevins, still unsure what was going on.

"How the hell do you know what happened?" Honeywell demanded.

"Oh, we have the room bugged." Nevins's tone was offhand and dismissive.

"Who's 'we'?" Honeywell asked but Lillian already knew the answer.

"British intelligence. MI-5. And you boys owe us."

***

"What the hell are y'all doing spying on American soil?" Colonel Honeywell demanded of Nevins after the British spy had detailed his group's activities regarding the two men Lillian had bested. It turned out Brown Suit's name was Dieter Hous and his companion was Kurt von Himmel. Both were Nazi spies that Nevins's team had been keeping tabs on since the invasion of Poland eight months ago.

"Trying to guarantee we win," Nevins replied.

Nevins had strolled into the room like it was his own office. He examined the photographs on the table and began naming the ones he knew. Honeywell stood in shock.

Inwardly, Lillian enjoyed the sight.

"Okay." Honeywell finally broke out of his stupor. "I understand spying over here. What do you know about this?"

"Trying to determine if that banker out in your waiting room is helping the Nazis." Nevins spoke the words as a statement.

"What?" Lillian moved next to Nevins. "Frank? Helping the Nazis?"

Nevins shrugged. "Why else would someone like him meet with a known Nazi collaborator?" He let the words hang in the air. In the meantime, he withdrew a pouch of tobacco and a short pipe. He filled the bowl, put the pouch back in his pocket, and put a lighter to the dried leaves. The pungent aroma of the burning tobacco filled the room.

Lillian's mind raced. *Nazi collaborator? Whom could Nevins mean?* The answer zeroed itself out of the blue. "Do you mean James Geiger?"

"Precisely, my dear." He pointed to the wall on the other side of which sat Frank Monroe. "A week ago, that man travelled to Berlin ostensibly on business. He met with the same James Geiger you mentioned. Tall man, broad-shouldered, dark brown hair, flecks of gray along the temples?"

Lillian tried to image the young man she had last seen four years ago with gray in his hair. She couldn't. They were both still twenty-nine and she had no gray hair despite the life she had chosen.

"I don't remember the gray part, but yes, that's James."

"You know he's working for the Nazis?"

All eyes turned to Lillian. She straightened her back. "As I've already told my commanding officer, I've had no contact with James Geiger for over four years. It been just about that long for Frank Monroe. And if you think either one is helping the Nazis, you're crazy."

Nevins cleared his throat. "I admire your loyalty to your friends, but in the case of Geiger, he is helping the Nazis. He manages a factory that manufactures barrels for large artillery."

Lillian nodded. "That makes sense. He majored in math."

"He also helps the Nazis create their codes."

A thunderclap of silence filled the room. In the pregnant pause, Honeywell spoke to Lillian. "Tell him."

Lillian moistened her suddenly dry mouth and told Nevins about the true nature of Frank's mission back to America. She showed him the book of poetry and explained how the code worked. Lastly, she vouched for Frank as being unaware of James's request until she told him herself.

"Your friend, Frank," Nevins said after she finished. "You sure he's not in on it?"

"Unlikely. It makes no sense if he was. Besides, what would be the outcome? Why request the two of us to return to Belgium and meet James in person next week?"

Nevins sucked on his pipe. His eyes were focused on one of the trophies on the shelf. "Why indeed?" Plumes of smoke wafted in the air. On a dime, he turned. "Colonel, might I have a word with you? In private."

Honeywell indicated the door with his chin. Lillian and Donnelly took the hint and left the room. Donnelly closed the door behind them. Frank stood expectantly. Even the adjutant stopping typing a report.

"Well?" Frank asked.

Lillian shrugged. "Not sure yet. You know the man who just arrived here?"

"No."

"Ever seen him before?"

"No."

"How did James contact you? I mean, was it out of the blue or do you have regular contact?"

Frank seemed to be taken aback by the line of questioning. "Have I done something wrong?"

"Just tell me, Frank."

He furrowed his brow at her. "We have regular contact. Well, we did up until last fall. Normally, we'd get together every time I had to go to the Continent. Especially when I went to Germany.

Didn't matter the town, he'd make a point to meet me, even if it was just for supper."

Donnelly found his voice. "Why'd he do that?"

"We're friends, sir. That's what friends do."

"What would you talk about?"

Frank cocked his head. "What's going on?"

"Tell me what you talked about," Lillian said.

"The old times." Frank spoke the words slowly. "College times, mainly. He told me once it was good to speak to someone he knew that also spoke English. He didn't mind German but he liked speaking in his native Texas tongue."

"Do you know what James does? His job?" Lillian asked.

"Sure. Manages a factory that builds barrels for all the big artillery. Told me he gets to use his math skills to help design improved ways to shoot the bombs and make them more accurate."

Lillian changed tactics. "What happened last fall?"

"How do you mean?"

"If you had regular contact up until last fall, why'd you stop meeting?"

"The war started." He paused. "My bank stopped going over to Germany. Froze many of their assets. But after Poland and this Phoney War business, things kind of got back to normal."

"Last week," Donnelly said, "who initiated the meeting? You or Geiger?"

"He did."

Lillian and Donnelly exchanged a look. "You think it strange, his contacting you?" Donnelly asked.

"Not really. It was a good time. We met in Berlin, had supper, good beer, took in a show. Even got to see the apartment he lives in there." He paused. "Saw Elsa, too."

A wave of emotion coursed through Lillian. She hated her feelings at that moment and buried them. Deep within her. "And that's when he gave you the book and the message to me?"

Frank nodded.

Lillian chewed her inner lip.

The door to Honeywell's office opened. The colonel beckoned them inside. Frank, too. He closed the door and walked around to his desk. He sat in the chair. Nevins sat in a chair next to the desk, smoke pluming from his pipe.

"Sergeant, Captain," Honeywell began, "we've come to a decision. Upon consultation with Mr. Nevins here, we feel it is in the best interest of America as well as Britain that you go to Belgium. Meet with James Geiger. Obtain the codebook and bring it back to London."

"Why not Washington, sir?" Donnelly asked.

"Because we're not at war with Germany yet. They are." The colonel pointed at Frank. "Are you going as well. If the message from Sergeant Saxton is correct, Geiger is expecting both of you, not just her."

He folded his hands and spoke the next words carefully. "Sergeant, you are going as an American citizen, not as a member of the United States Army. You are not to wear your uniform or any insignia. You will travel by air but using commercial aircraft."

Reginald Nevins puffed on his pipe. "Just because you'll be operating undercover and away from the U.S. military, our assets will be at your disposal, should you need them. But I caution you to refrain, as much as possible, from contact with my agency in London. There are no doubt Nazi spies in London. Despite all our efforts, they've probably marked some of my people as spies as well. We'd like to minimize contact to avoid outing any of my people."

He blew a ring of smoke into the air. "Nevertheless, I've arranged for the two of you to report to my office in London when you arrive and before you disembark to Belgium. The ferries are still running to the Continent. Planes as well. Make whatever travel arrangements you like, but let us know so we can at least monitor your activities. Mr. Monroe, that'll be your job. It'll look better anyhow."

Frank nodded.

Lillian nodded.

Honeywell leaned back in his chair. "If those photographs

over there are any indication, the Nazis have spies everywhere. Curiously, Sergeant Saxton, your image is not a part of the collection. There's a possibility they don't know who you are. Let's keep it that way." He folded his hands across his stomach. "For all intents and purposes, the two of you are merely meeting an old college friend in Belgium."

6

Johannes Bauer sat at the port and waited. He wore a blue suit with a red tie. His black shoes were in the process of being shined by the boy at his feet. His hat was on his lap as was a folded newspaper. He liked getting his shoes shined. It enabled him to watch the people milling about without the subterfuge of holding a newspaper.

He again thanked his seniority that enabled him to be deployed in England rather than Africa. It suited him better, especially since there was a larger pro-Nazi community in Liverpool, London, than elsewhere in the country.

He pulled out his small notebook and opened to a page marked with a business card. A small photo slipped into his hands and he looked at it. The man he was to follow was named Frank Monroe. The American was a banker who worked for Lloyd's of London. He was due on the RMS *Queen Mary* this evening. The ocean liner now rested on the dock. The only thing remaining was for the passengers to disembark.

In a communique from Herr Colonel, Bauer had learned of the debacle in Washington. Two agents arrested and exposed as German spies. Bauer didn't know them but felt confident they'd never betray *der Führer*. None of Herr Colonel's soldiers would ever do that. Bauer knew he'd die before revealing anything, no matter how much pain he might endure.

The precise nature of how the agents were apprehended remained a mystery. The message stated the American Army had something to do with it. That made no sense to Bauer considering Monroe wasn't a member of the Army. Nor was America at war with Germany. Perhaps he really was a spy as Herr Colonel suspected. Fellow agents in New York reported that Monroe was traveling with a woman with red hair. Nothing more was known about her. Bauer was to report any information to Herr Colonel whenever possible.

And get some sort of book Monroe or the woman carried. He didn't know why it was important, just that it was. A good word from Herr Colonel, and Bauer might get a plum assignment in America. There, he would truly be at home. He might even visit his parents' graves.

A whistle sounded. The passengers began to disembark. First-class customers led the way over the gangway and onto the dock proper. Bauer kept his eyes peeled for the blond Monroe, yet nearly every man wore a hat. Frustrated, Bauer paid the shoe shine boy and hurried closer to the gangway.

Proximity didn't help. Without getting right up next to these men, Bauer wasn't going to be able to spot Monroe.

The women, however, were a different matter. Not all of them sported hats. He recalled the woman traveling with Monroe had red hair. Bauer perched himself next to a lamppost and eyed the departing ladies.

Monroe's banking salary must be modest for no red-haired woman exited the ship in the first wave. Neither for the second wave. Bauer began to sweat. Was his information incorrect? Or had he misinterpreted it? Herr Colonel would have his head—literally—if Bauer missed his mark.

Finally, walking next to a tall man, was a red-headed woman. He wore a snappy dark gray suit. She wore a green dress, belted at the waist. Bauer squinted and was fairly confident that the man was Monroe. The redhead leaned on Monroe's shoulder. She walked feebly.

Then, without any warning, she lunged toward the edge of the gangway and threw up over the side.

***

Lillian Saxton fully believed she had never been as sick as she was on that trans-Atlantic voyage. Planes were not a problem.

Fast cars or buses. Zero issues. Trains. Loved trains. It was her preferred means of travel.

Ocean voyages. She'd like to vow 'never again' but she knew there would always be ocean crossings. Ever since the start of the war last fall, civilian air travel in Britain had halted. When Honeywell ordered her to travel to Britain as a middle stop ahead of Belgium, Lillian had immediately pictured herself in a fancy plane and landing in London within two days.

It had taken the *Queen Mary* five days to cross the choppy Atlantic Ocean. The liner might have made better time if it hadn't been required to steer a course that wouldn't enable German U-boats to get a bead on her. Numerous ships and boats had been torpedoed in the intervening eight months. Halfway through the passage, Lillian had made a vow to herself: the return trip was going to be by plane or she was going to obtain some sort of prescription that would knock her out for the entire trip.

She wiped her mouth with the back of her hand. A thin line of drool snaked from her mouth and wafted in the breeze.

Frank leaned over her, his strong hands gripping her shoulders. It had been a while since she had dated anyone. The nature of her job and its undercover missions pretty much meant personal relationships were a luxury, if they even existed. She enjoyed her work, enjoyed making a difference, but she had also resigned herself to leaving anything romantic to the future. Whenever that happened.

"Are you better now?" Monroe asked.

Lillian glared at him. "This is the third time today I've been sick. I've been sick every damn day since we left New York. It doesn't get better." She inhaled deeply. "It just is." Her voice sounded guttural to her ears.

Frank patted her shoulders. "Listen, I'm going to make new arrangements. Let's avoid the train tonight. The Adelphi is just down the street. I've stayed there many times. We can rest there tonight and get a fresh start tomorrow."

"Does it move?"

"I'm sorry."

"I just want dry land and a walkable surface that doesn't move." Lillian leaned on him. She welcomed his arms around her shoulders. Surprisingly for a woman in her profession, she actually felt protected.

"It's a good thing, too," she muttered. "Unpredictability. Anyone that might be following you will have to improvise."

Frank chuckled. "I don't think anyone's following us here. How could they know we got on the *Queen Mary* and sailed here?"

"Believe me, Frank, they'll know." A dry heave coursed through her. She swallowed hard and stifled the urge. "Now, get me to this hotel of yours so I can lie down for a while."

7

The Adelphi Hotel turned out to be one of the most luxurious hotels Lillian had ever seen. In her line of work, she had been in plenty of hotels, a few of them fancy, but the Adelphi put them all to shame.

The exterior was Edwardian in architecture. White limestone formed the outer facade of eleven stories of rooms. Columns were installed on the upper floors as well as Roman style arches.

Lillian literally gasped as they entered the foyer, despite her queasy stomach. The marble floor positively sparkled in the late afternoon sun. After Frank made the arrangements, they walked through the spacious sitting lobby that spanned nearly the entire first story. Tables, chairs, and couches dotted the area, many clustered in small groups for intimate conversation. The ceiling was at least two stories above them. Chandeliers beamed cascades of light. High, arched windows looked out onto the street and into the equally spacious restaurant.

Lillian stared open-mouthed at the spectacle. That actually helped her feel better as she delivered more oxygen to her lungs. The old feeling resurface, that she had made a mistake in refusing Frank's offer of marriage those many years ago. In that first year after she had left Paris and come to terms with her decision, she had tried to imagine what life might have been like with Frank as her husband. The images she conjured were nothing compared to this. The ease with which Frank interacted with the concierge, the elevator man, the bell boy who carried their bags surprised her. When she had last seen him, Frank was just a college kid who played at being a fancy person. In the intervening years, he had grown into the type of man for whom this kind of life was normal.

Involuntarily, she gripped Frank's arm a little tighter.

Still, Frank's timing those years ago had been bad. Her heart had still been raw from James's abrupt breakup with her. For all the elegance and panache Frank displayed now, it wasn't there back in their college days. Had Frank waited just a few months before he popped the question, Lillian might have said "yes."

The elevator took them up. By the time it opened onto the seventh floor, Lillian found she could walk easily. Some of her strength was returning. She righted herself but still held onto Frank's arm.

If he noticed, he was gentlemanly enough not to say anything.

The bellboy led them to Room 718 and produced a key. He opened the door with reserved flourish and stayed in the hall while Lillian and Frank entered the room. For a split second, as they rounded the door frame, Lillian worried about the sleeping arrangements. While there may have been some chemistry between them back at Oxford, she had always been with James. They had never done more than dance a few slow songs at a few parties. She had recognized the chemistry back then. Perhaps he did, too. But with her heart firmly belonging to James, they never got a chance to find out.

She needn't have worried. Two beds occupied the room, each with sheets and blankets crisply drawn. Changing times might be a tad awkward, but at least the sleeping would be fine.

A distant part of her was sad, however. Here they were, years away from their younger selves, meeting again as adults in the real world. The reason for their being here was serious, but for the next few hours here at the Adelphi, the outside world could just go take a hike.

"Frank, this room is gorgeous," Lillian murmured.

"I agree. I've stayed here numerous times on my trips to and from the States. Granted, someone like James would stay on the top floors, but I've discovered over the years that I'm well suited for the upper middle floors."

The bellboy stowed both their suitcases in the closet. He walked to the bathroom and flipped on the switch. He turned on the lamp between the two beds and moved to the window.

"Please keep the curtains closed," Lillian said.

The bellboy stopped. His uniform was tight, the skin of his neck chafing along the high collar. The tag on his suit read "Cedric."

"As you wish, ma'am." He turned to Frank. "Is there anything else you need, sir?"

Frank looked at Lillian, eyes raised. "Supper?"

She grinned. "In a place like this, I'd be happy with broth. Of course, let's go to supper."

Frank smiled and nodded. "When is dinner served?" he asked the bellboy.

"It's already started."

"Very good." Frank tipped the young man and walked him to the door.

Lillian looked around the room, awed. No matter how much she was dazzled by the opulence of the Adelphi, this was still an assignment. Two Nazi spies had followed them back in Washington. They already knew Frank and what he looked like. There was also a chance they knew her, despite what Honeywell had said. No matter how clever she and her agency tried to be or what kind of false names they used, when agents traveled commercially, they were able to be seen. It was an illusion to think that the two spies she had beaten were the only two in America. No, there would be others. It was best to be prepared.

She sat on the bed near the door.

"I see you've made your choice."

"Yes. I need to be nearest the door." Lillian rose and walked to the closet. She opened her suitcase and rummaged through the top layer of clothes. She brought out a small pistol. She ejected the magazine and cocked the weapon to discharge the remaining shell. The bullet landed on the pristine sheets. Next, she examined the weapon under the light next to the bed. Satisfied, she thumbed the extra shell into the magazine, slid the magazine back into the grip, and cocked the gun again.

Lillian caught Frank's curious gaze. "It's a Browning Hi-Power, .9 mm. Holds thirteen shells."

"I thought your colonel said to travel unarmed."

"He's not here. And I don't go on any mission unarmed. He knows that. I'm just not going to carry it on my hip for all to see." She reached over to her purse and slipped the gun inside.

Frank stood there, slowing shaking his head, a beaming smile etched across his face. "Lillian Saxton, what a remarkable woman you've become." He gestured to the lavatory. "Would you like to freshen up before we go downstairs?"

Lillian stood and sashayed by him on the way back to the closet. She ran a finger across his chest. "Why, Frank Monroe, I'd love to. And I'll also tell you about the other message James sent."

***

Johannes Bauer had to be careful. Standing alongside a boat dock full of a mix of different people, he didn't stand out. Tailing Monroe and the redhead into the Adelphi Hotel was something else entirely. For one, he wasn't sure his attire was good enough. It was more than passable on the docks. Now, he barely reached concierge attire. He considered heading back to his apartment flat, the safe house, but rejected it. He wasn't entirely sure what Monroe was going to do tonight. He thought the American and his lady friend would board the train bound for London. Bauer had already purchased a ticket. But when the redhead vomited over the side of the gangway, even Bauer knew the plans were going to change.

He stood outside on the street opposite the Adelphi's front doors. The woman was clearly sick so the chances she and Monroe would visit the restaurant were small. Besides, he wasn't sure of the state of the romance. If they were in love, they might not even leave the room even if she was well. That meant he was going to need to determine their room number in a manner that would arouse no suspicion.

Involuntarily, he reached over and pressed the comforting weight of his Sig Sauer nestled in its shoulder holster. He never went anywhere without it. He wasn't sure if he would need it tonight, but he had other means to obtain what he needed.

He crossed the street and entered the Adelphi. At this hour of the evening, the lobby was a tizzy of movement. Locals were out on the town for a fancy meal. Passengers embarking on and disembarking from ocean liners caused general havoc around the concierge. It was a contained frenzy, something Bauer determined to use to his advantage.

He sauntered over to the bellboy row and assumed an exasperated, confused look. "Good evening," Bauer said in his best American accent—not a problem considering he was born in America—"I was wondering if you could help me?"

A bellboy, stocky with hair cut short and little in the way of a neck, said, "Yes, sir?"

"I'm meeting my friend, Frank Monroe, here tonight. He's just come in from America and I'm going back. We need to meet to discuss banking business. Could you tell me what room he's staying in so I can go up and see him?" He held out his hand. A blue five-pound British note rested in his palm.

The bellboy eyed Bauer, then grabbed the bill and slipped it into his pocket. Turning on his heel, he walked over to the main desk and came around the back. He craned his neck and studied the register. Satisfied, he returned to Bauer.

"7D."

Bauer tipped his hat. "Much obliged." The German spy crossed the lobby and ascended the stairs. Reaching the seventh floor, he peered out into the hall. He saw no one. The stairwell was on the opposite side from Monroe's room so Bauer walked across the entire floor and put an ear to the door of 7D.

Inside, he heard rustling and moving around. His nose picked up perfume. Perhaps this really was Monroe's girlfriend. Bauer made a mental note to add that to his report.

He gave serious consideration to the idea of barging in, gun drawn, and demanding the book and the identity of the redhead. In his mind, he saw himself like a gangster in one of those films Hollywood churned out every year. Bauer didn't always have to inflict pain on those he followed, but when he did, he found he had a knack for the job. And an enjoyment of it.

He took a few moments to play out what results he might get if he took that action. He would certainly get the element of surprise. He could use the gun coercively to get Monroe and the woman to do his bidding. He'd be less inclined to shoot them outright at first, but he would, noise be damned. The silencer for his pistol was in his suit pocket. As long as he had the time to make them stand down, he'd have time to screw it on before he shot them.

The rustling from inside the room got closer. A hand gripped the doorknob. Bauer had to make a split-second decision: shoot or not.

8

Lillian Saxton discovered that a shower went a great deal to making her feel better. The warm water flowing over her skin seemed to relax her clenching stomach muscles. The soap refreshed her skin after all the miles traveled. By the time she stepped out of the tub, towel wrapped around her, she felt pretty good.

She ran a brush through her hair. She wiped the condensation off the mirror and looked at herself. Typically, on a mission, there was a hardness to her eyes. She needed that strength when she did her job. But this assignment was unlike any she had undertaken for the Army. Outside that door was a man she could find herself loving. They had history. They were already friends. Could they conceivably take the next step? In the long hours on the liner when she wasn't confined in the bathroom throwing up, she had learned more about Frank in the intervening years. He was still a bachelor, having not found any woman he loved deep enough to ask the question he had asked Lillian years ago. Honestly, Lillian liked hearing that.

Her hair combed, she unwrapped herself and toweled dry. She stood there, naked, looking at herself in the mirror. She liked what she saw. She had a positive outlook on her physical appearance. On the liner, she had caught Frank's eyes lingering on her more than once. If she opened that door right now and went to him, she knew what would happen.

But could she give up this job and the work she did?

Frank rapped on the door. "You fall in?"

Shaken out of her fantasies, she said, "No. I'm just getting ready." She reached over and started dressing. Five minutes later, she opened the door and walked back into the room.

Frank Monroe's mouth hung open. He inhaled the air. "Your perfume smells great. And you look even better."

Lillian walked into the room and did a twirl. She ended up directly in front of him. She looked up at him. "Thank you. Do you need the lavatory?"

"Already cleaned up." He gazed down at her and deep into her eyes.

Her stomach flipped at the attention. She sniffed the air. "You smell good, too. And you're pretty easy on the eyes as well."

"I'll take that as high praise from a woman who carries a gun."

And there it was. Frank's knack for saying the wrong thing at the wrong time was still in place.

The moment dead, she smiled wanly. She picked up her purse, opened it to verify both the gun and the book were inside, and snapped it closed. "I'm ready."

Frank figured out he did wrong. He hid it by slipping on his suit coat and walking to the door. He patted his pocket for the room key and opened the door. He held out his arm and let Lillian into the hallway first.

The first thing she noticed was a man in a blue suit. He stood next to a door two rooms down. He let go of the doorknob and sauntered in their direction.

"Good evening, folks." His accent pegged him as a New Yorker. "Heading down to the restaurant?"

"We are," Frank said. "Been there yet?"

He shook his head. "Just got in on the *Queen Mary*. I'm pretty tired, but I'm famished."

Lillian examined the man head to toe. He was nearly six feet tall. His hair was neatly coiffed in the latest style. His suit looked well tailored. His shirt was neatly pressed. Almost perfectly pressed. She glanced at Frank. He had changed shirts but travel wrinkles were visible on his clothes.

The man in the blue suit didn't have any of them. And he carried his left arm just slightly away from his body. Her eyes travelled to his chest. If she were asked to bet, she'd say this man wore a shoulder holster.

Lillian doubled over, holding her stomach. She let a small moan escape. She leaned against Frank. "We're going to need to stop at the pharmacy before we get down there."

Frank put his arm around her. To the man, he said, "She had a bad trip. Seasick almost the entire time. Catch you downstairs, then?"

The man looked concerned. "Sure. Hope she feels better." Pausing an additional moment or two, the man began walking to the elevator. He pushed the button. "Going down?"

"Yes." Frank started moving to the elevator. Lillian tried to hold back, but he half carried her. There was no way she could warn him and not tip off the mystery man. She relented, but kept a wary eye on the potential adversary.

Frank and the man talked business while the elevator descended. They got in, the elevator man opening and closing the door. On the lobby level, Lillian asked if the hotel had a pharmacy. He directed her and she thanked him.

"Save you a seat?" the man in the blue suit asked. "It'd be great to talk to another Yankee."

"Sure thing." Frank and the man shook hands and the man walked to the restaurant.

"You feeling that bad?" Frank asked.

"I'm fine, but that man is wearing a gun."

He looked at her skeptically. "Are you sure?"

She arched an eyebrow at him. "It's my job to be sure. Yes, I'm sure. Trust me, Frank. I know what I'm doing. Let's eat, but stay away from him. Okay?" She turned his face to hers with her finger on his chin. "Remember, we're on a mission here. You've already been spotted back in Washington. We can't trust anyone here. No one. That man may be exactly who he says he is, or he may be trying to kill us. Or question us. In my line of work, you want to face off against the ones who only want to kill you. It's much easier that way."

"Why?"

Lillian sighed, thinking back to earlier assignments. "Because questioning can get messy." She slid her arm around his. "Now,

Mr. Monroe," she said, a little of her earlier excitement returning to her voice, "will you please take me to supper?"

9

Johannes Bauer watched from a concealed area as Monroe and the woman walked across the lobby. They stopped and talked. When they moved again, they did not go to the pharmacy. They went to the restaurant.

That meant the woman had lied. Who was she? Bauer thought there might be answers in their room.

He doubled back and went up the stairs to the seventh floor. As before, no other person walked the hallway. He slipped up to the door of 7D. It was locked, of course, but locked doors were no problem for Bauer.

He pulled out a small case full of tools. He extracted a couple and, within seconds, had the door open. He slipped inside and put his tools away. Now, in the room, he found both travel bags. He started with the woman's.

It was full of her clothes and toiletries, of course, but the zipped leather case at the bottom of the case surprised him. He pretty much knew what it was but opened it to verify. It was a gun-cleaning kit complete with a spare clip. He ejected one of the shells and examined it. Nine millimeter. He ejected the remaining shells, counting each one. Thirteen. His mind went through all the guns that held a thirteen-shell clip. There were a few, but it didn't matter what kind of gun she carried. What mattered was that she was carrying a gun at all. The questions about this woman deepened, but Bauer now assumed she was not the delicate flower she pretended to be.

The kind of woman who carried a gun that held thirteen shells was also the kind of woman who knew how to use it. Bauer thought through possibilities as he searched the rest of her bag and then onto Monroe's bag. Surprisingly, he found no name tag anywhere on her belongings. Monroe's accouterments revealed no information on her either. On a hunch, he dumped the contents of the trash can onto the made bed. He sorted and sifted through the crumpled papers, unwrapping each one.

A grin formed on his face when he read a name on the ocean liner ticket: Lillian Saxton.

"Bingo." Bauer slipped the ticket into his pocket. Not wanting to wait any longer, he picked up the phone in the room and asked for an outside line.

"What listing?" the operator asked.

"Buckley's Antique Shop."

***

It turned out Lillian's stomach wasn't nearly as well as she hoped. Frank had slipped the maitred' a little extra to secure a secluded corner of the restaurant. The room itself was massive. Easily fifty tables were arranged on the floor. Each one had a black tablecloth with an angled white cloth on top of that. A lit candle sat in the center of each. The shiniest silver, the most dazzling wine and water glasses, and the most delicate china were placed at their precise positions.

Lillian was impressed. She was also unhappy that the odor of all the food made her stomach start to flip for all the bad reasons. All the food looked and smelled scrumptious. Lillian knew, even as she took a menu from the waiter, she was not going to have any of it.

She latched onto a roll and gnawed on it. She had tasted few rolls as good as that one, so she savored what might be her only food for the night.

After encouragement from her, Frank ordered shepherd's pie, a red wine, and a salad. She asked the waiter if there was any soup or broth. He said yes and she ordered some. She hoped it would be the best soup she ever tasted because that was her supper for the evening.

Frank's face, lit by the low lights of the restaurant and the candle, looked so good to Lillian. Again, thoughts of a life with Frank flashed into her mind. A life like that would bring many more meals like this one.

"So, tell me this other secret you mentioned," Frank said.

Inwardly, Lillian sighed. Frank Monroe could teach a class on saying the wrong things at the wrong times. Outwardly, she leaned forward.

"So, you know about the message that got us here. James actually wrote me two messages. I just decided to keep the other one to myself since it has no bearing on the mission."

Frank gave her a curious look. "That doesn't seem like you, deliberately misleading your commanding officers."

"It's not misleading if you never mention it."

"Sure it is. That's like insider trading. It's illegal in my field. Isn't there something similar in yours?"

In some cases, Lillian might agree. In this one, however, she didn't. "It's about Samuel."

"Samuel?"

"My brother. Remember I told you about him. He was killed a few weeks ago. That's why I was in Houston when I got your message. I was supposed to rendezvous with a reporter who had information on what had happened to Sam. The reporter was killed, but the private investigator I hired on the Army's behalf found the truth."

Frank sipped his wine. "What does that have to do with James's other message?"

She lowered her voice so much he had to lean in to hear. "James knows who killed Sam. He's going to tell me."

"Are you kidding me?" Frank blurted. He looked around, then lowered his voice. "What are you planning on doing with that information?"

"I'm not sure. Our mission here is very tight: in and out in a matter of hours. A day or two at the most. After it's over...." Her voice trailed off.

"What?" Frank persisted. "What will happen after it's over?"

Lillian shrugged. "Depending on the type of intelligence James gives me, I might ask for some time off."

"To do what? Hunt this guy? Kill him?" He downed another

large drink of wine. He stared at her, studying her.

No, she thought. *Frank was judging me.* The realization stung her. She sloughed it off. What the hell did he know about her world anyway? Dealing with enemies in a final manner was what you had to do sometimes. The alternative—keeping them alive—could prove too dangerous.

"Whoever this person is who killed my brother. That kind of thing shouldn't go unpunished."

"And you're the judge, jury, and executioner?"

"If need be, yes." She roughly tore off a hunk of the roll and ate. The taste had evaporated. Her appetite withered as well.

The waiter arrived bearing a large tray. He set Frank's shepherd's pie in front of him. For Lillian, a steaming bowl of nearly clear broth. She thanked the waiter but made no move to pick up her spoon. She gazed away from Frank and out the window.

Frank, on the other hand, actually rubbed his hands together. He gripped his fork and plunged it into the mashed potatoes that topped his savory dish. Steam visibly rose from the food on his fork. He blew on it and gingerly ate the bite.

He inhaled rapidly, trying to get air to cool his scorched tongue. He waved his hand in front of his mouth to help out the cause.

Lillian smirked at him. "Next time, blow longer." The next thing he did surprised her.

Frank Monroe's hand went to his throat. His brow furrowed in concentration, then concern, then outright panic. His eyes bulged. The food from his mouth popped out and landed on the table.

Lillian's senses went on alert. "Frank? Are you choking?"

He nodded. Both hands clutched his throat. His movements brought the attention of other diners.

Lillian dropped her roll and moved to stand behind Frank. She motioned for him to stand up. She wanted to try to force the lodged piece of food out of him. The part of her brain that processed situations like this told her something: the food had fallen out of his mouth. It lay there on the table.

Panic driving her actions, Lillian knelt next to him. She grabbed his face and turned it. His eyes continued to bulge. His skin took on a bluish hue. Foam had formed around the corners of his mouth.

Frank Monroe looked at Lillian Saxton one last time before he fell forward. His head slammed on the table, bounced once, and fell over the side. His body followed suit. Lillian had to stand quickly to avoid having his body land on hers.

The shock of the moment had already begun the transition to sadness. Tears stung her eyes as she touched her fingers to his neck to determine his pulse. She knew the action was futile. She had seen dead bodies before. She already knew the truth: Frank Monroe was dead.

10

The part of Lillian Saxton that was an old friend and potential future lover of Frank Monroe stood frozen in place looking down at the body. The part of Lillian Saxton that was a sergeant in the United States Army on a clandestine mission took over.

She turned, scanning the entire restaurant. Nearly every person stared in her direction. Waiters had stopped moving between the tables. The maitred' leaned on the doorway, wondering what had happened. The only sounds, other than a few gasps, came from the kitchen where the chefs and cooks continued their jobs unaware that a man had died.

One person seemed out of place. He stood off to the side, near the kitchen door. She recognized him. The man in the blue suit, the one they had seen up on the seventh floor. The one with the gun.

She made a leap of a decision: Blue Suit had poisoned Frank. Maybe her food was poisoned as well. Surprisingly, her seasickness had saved her.

Hot rage flared within Lillian Saxton. She pointed at the man in the blue suit. "Stop that man!"

He turned and slipped inside the kitchen.

Lillian snatched her purse from the table. She opened it and jammed her hand inside. When she withdrew her gun, screams and more gasps erupted among the patrons. She ignored them all. She slung the purse across her shoulder and ran after Blue Suit.

She got lucky. The diners, already shocked at the death of a fellow patron, remained riveted to their seats at the sight of the red-haired woman running with the gun in her hand. She had enough presence of mind to wipe her eyes to clear her vision. She knew one thing: when she caught up with Blue Suit, she was going to find out who he was working for and why he had poisoned them.

And then she was going to kill him.

She hit the swinging door to the kitchen with her shoulder and slowed long enough to ask, "Which way?"

Almost as one, all the cooks pointed to the rear of the kitchen. It was spacious for a kitchen. The better to match the spaciousness of the Adelphi.

"Call the police," she called over her shoulder. No doubt they had already been alerted, but she felt compelled to follow standard protocol.

She charged through the kitchen, heedless of turns and twists. If Blue Suit was a typical spy, he would choose flight over fight. When she caught up with him, he would no longer have a choice.

Lillian glanced around every corner, but quickly found herself at the back door. It was unlocked. She stopped for a quick moment, steadied the purse on her shoulder, gripped the knob, and threw open the door. It swung completely open. No one behind the door.

She continued her pursuit. The narrow alley behind the hotel was dirty and smelled of trash and rotting fish. Light bulbs hung over each door into the hotel, but the other side of the alley was dark. She reached another corner and halted. She listened.

Up ahead and to the left were footsteps. They moved fast and the sound began to fade. Whoever it was—Blue Suit most likely—was running away. Having no mental view of the street layout, she estimated. She veered on the nearest alley leading to the left. It was a short one that ended on another alley leading right. She stopped and listened again.

Sirens approached. And more footsteps. She examined her options and wondered how she could catch Blue Suit. The monotony of the running had enabled her to think past the blind hatred and be logical.

Blue Suit was bound to hit an actual street soon. If he did, she would likely lose him completely. He knew the area. She didn't. She was going to have to even the odds. Or catch a break.

She got the break.

A woman screamed. The sound came from straight ahead. Had Blue Suit doubled back?

Lillian tore down the alley. Her purse slammed on her shoulder. Sweat coated the palm that held her gun. Nearing the edge of the alley, she saw a figure run across the opening. It was Blue Suit. Lillian poured on more speed.

Emerging out of the alley, Lillian turned in the direction Blue Suit went. She laid eyes on him, half a block ahead. Their position was on the east side of the Adelphi. Blue and red lights bounced off the facade from the police cars parked haphazardly in front of the hotel.

Blue Suit was running in that direction. Lillian couldn't figure out why Frank's killer would run to the police. It wouldn't matter. She was gaining ground and would overtake him before he reached them.

Blue Suit made a fatal error. He looked over his shoulder to see how close Lillian was to him. That slowed him down. She reached out to him with her empty hand and snagged the back of his collar. She brought the pistol down in a high swinging arc and slammed it down upon his head.

Blue Suit stumbled upon the impact. His knees buckled and he fell to the ground. Lillian caromed over him. She had enough presence of mind to let go of his collar, but she was off balance. She pivoted on her heels, but they got tangled underneath her. She landed on her side. Her body met concrete and hot pain knifed through her. She grunted, but held onto her gun. She rolled with the momentum and quickly came to a halt. She got to her feet and brought her gun to bear.

Blue Suit lay crumpled on the sidewalk. He lay still. Other people were moving. Bystanders looked on as Lillian approached Blue Suit's body. She held the gun in a two-handed grip, elbows locked in place. She nudged the body with her shoe. Nothing.

"Put the gun down, ma'am!"

Lillian turned. Three police officers stood in the street, guns aimed at her. Another approached her from the sidewalk.

She looked down at the man who had poisoned Frank. Sure, she was glad retribution had come to him and that she was the one who had delivered it, but she wanted—needed—answers to questions. Now, she wouldn't get them. And it looked like she wasn't going to do anything else for the time being.

She noted the officers slowly walking to her. Remembering what Honeywell had told her—the Army would disavow her if anything happened since the U.S. wasn't at war—Lillian was pretty sure she couldn't play that card. But she could still appeal to their sense of law and order.

Lillian dropped her gun and raised her hands. To the first officer, she said, "This man killed my friend by poisoning him at the Adelphi Hotel. I pursued him. In the effort to stop him, it appears he needs medical attention. Call an ambulance."

"You shut your mouth." The officer cuffed Lillian's hands behind her.

"Call an ambulance," she repeated. "This man is likely a Nazi spy. He has answers I need."

The officer who had cuffed her brought his mouth right next to her ear. "Shut your mouth about Nazi spies," he hissed, "or I'll shut it for you." He jerked the cuffs to make his point.

"Contact Reginald Nevins, British intelligence. He'll explain everything." Lillian hoped he would.

11

Twelve hours later, sitting in a jail cell, Lillian Saxton knew the officer had not made any effort to contact British intelligence. In the intervening hours, with time to think, she allowed herself time to cry for Frank Monroe. She remembered all the good memories, the college years at Oxford and the late night talks that kept them up past midnight. Even the potential future she had imagined with him played in her mind. The more she thought of it, the more the anger burned within her about Blue Suit and the people who had ordered him to poison Frank.

That led Lillian to mull over all the events of the previous night and week. Nazi agents knew enough about Frank to tail him back in Washington. In all likelihood, he had been followed longer than just in Washington. He was a banker, not a particularly notable one, so why was he being followed? The only answer that fit the events was that the Nazis thought Frank Monroe was a spy.

But was Blue Suit a spy? Clearly yes, but for whom? He spoke perfect New York English, but so did the man in the brown suit back in America. Blue Suit, however, had an accent. A scary possibility crossed her mind: had she killed—she assumed he was dead—an American agent? Surely not. Americans don't go around poisoning other Americans while abroad.

On the other hand, could she be one hundred percent sure Blue Suit was the man responsible for the poisoning? After Frank died, he was the one she zeroed in on and called out. Even if he wasn't involved, he might have felt compelled to slip out the kitchen to avoid all the eyes that turned his way. If it was a misunderstanding, a case of mistaken identity, he could have just explained it away.

But he ran. *No*, Lillian reminded herself, *he ran when you told the entire room he was the murderer.* Wouldn't you have run?

Probably.

The door to the cells opened and a man entered. The police station had six jail cells in this one room. Currently, Lillian was the only resident.

The man stopped in front of her cell. She remained seated on the small bunk. He carried a cup of steaming coffee. The aroma reminded her that it had nearly been twelve hours since she had eaten anything, and then, it was only the roll. The roll that had saved her life.

"Good morning, Miss Lillian Saxton." The stripes on the man's uniform indicated he was a captain. "My name is David Bratton. I am in command of this precinct. I understand you had quite an evening last night."

Lillian cleared her throat. She didn't want her first impression to be that of a squeaky voice. "The man I pursued. Is he dead?"

Bratton held up a finger. "If you don't mind, I'd like to ask the questions and have you answer them. Sound good?"

Lillian demurred. "Yes, sir."

"Good." He sipped the coffee. "First of all, what's an American girl like you doing running around in my town with a gun in your hand?"

Lillian weighed her options. Bratton seemed like a reasonable man, so he could probably understand her predicament. "My name is Lillian Saxton. I'm a sergeant in the U.S. Army. I'm on a..."

"Wait. You're military?"

"I am."

"Why are you here?"

"I'm on a mission, undercover, on behalf of Reginald Nevins, a member of British intelligence. MI-5 I believe."

He nodded.

"We received a secret coded message that my friend and I were to travel to Belgium by way of England to meet an old friend who would deliver something that your government can use to help fight the Nazis."

Bratton raised an eyebrow at that. "Really? Sounds like one

of your Hollywood movies."

"I assure you, it's very real. And my traveling companion, another old friend of mine, is now dead. Poisoned."

"That he was." Bratton stepped closer to the bars. "And the room you both shared was completely trashed."

"What?" Lillian now stood.

Bratton nodded. "Any idea what someone might be looking for?" He took another sip of his coffee.

"Yes. My book of poetry."

Bratton choked on his drink. "All of this disaster was on account of a book of poetry? I find that hard to believe. Sounds like a lover's quarrel more than some secret mission."

"I assure you, it's true. And I need to get out of here as soon as possible so I can continue my mission." She grew quiet. "Although it'll be more difficult without Frank."

Bratton tapped the bars. "You won't be going anywhere for a while, Miss Saxton. Not until we figure out the truth."

Lillian lunged and grabbed the bars. "It is the truth. And I'm on a time schedule. Look, just contact Reginald Nevins. He'll tell you everything."

Bratton turned on his heel and strolled to the exit.

Lillian cried out, "The man I chased. Is he dead?"

Stopping, Bratton rested a hand on the knob. He didn't face her. "He is." He opened the door and exited the room.

Lillian slumped onto the bunk. At least that news brought some semblance of satisfaction. Now, she needed to get out of this jail.

12

Another few hours found Lillian tired, famished, and not a little angry. She had tried yelling but the cement walls didn't respond. Exhausted, she lay on the bunk and surprised herself by sleeping.

Jangling keys woke her. She sat up and stared bleary eyed at the cell door.

Two men stood outside the cell. Bratton had the keys jammed into the lock. He opened the door and beckoned her out.

Lillian didn't waste a moment. She stood, adjusted her balance and her dress, and walked out of the jail cell.

The other man wore a dark suit with, of all things, a bow tie. His round spectacles reflected the dim light. He extended his hand. "Good morning, Sergeant Saxton. My name is George Ludlow. I work with Reggie Nevins."

Lillian grasped his hand and broke into a huge grin. "Mr. Ludlow, I'm so glad to meet you." She threw a sharp glance at Bratton. He returned her gaze impassively.

"And I, you." He possessed a high voice, the kind that would be at home on the stage. "Forgive the incarceration, but, as you can imagine, we don't get a lot of poisoning deaths or foot chases resulting in deaths."

"My apologies. Frank Monroe was an old friend. When he died, I wanted answers. I didn't think I hit the man I was chasing that hard, but the captain tells me he died as well."

Ludlow nodded gravely. "The people I answer to need answers as well. Let's discuss it over a meal."

The meal proved to be at a small restaurant down the street from the Adelphi. Overnight, while Lillian whiled away the hours in her jail cell, the local police had swarmed the hotel. They had confiscated all her belongings as well as Frank's. Everything had been gone through. Damning evidence for Lillian was her gun kit. That had kept her locked up longer than necessary. What had turned the trick was Bratton's hitting a wall, when he tried to explain away the incident to his superiors and the press. He had made some calls and, within a few short hours, Ludlow had arrived.

One of the first things Lillian asked, her mouth full of toast and eggs, had to do with Frank's body. Bratton told her it was at the morgue awaiting an inquest. She said she would contact his family and they would make arrangements to bring their son home. She hid the sting of her tears behind a steaming cup of hot tea.

Next she asked about Blue Suit. Papers in his suit listed his name as Theodore Montgomery and an address across town. Bratton's men raided the apartment, but it was empty. Now, they had begun to wonder if Montgomery was truly his name.

"Probably isn't," Lillian muttered.

Bratton smirked at her. "Of course not. There is one clue you can help us out with. Why did your friend Mr. Monroe ask for an outside line and call a local antique shop?"

Lillian stopped chewing. "He didn't. We were together the entire time. Well, the only time we were apart was when I showered. What time was the call?"

"A little after nine forty five."

Lillian shook her head. "We were at the restaurant at that time." She swallowed her food. "You don't think it could have been Blue Suit, er, Montgomery?"

Bratton shrugged. "It was probably him or someone who worked with him."

"He probably acted alone," Ludlow stated. "Often, spies who only watch do their jobs alone and report in at regular intervals."

"Wait," Lillian said. Her plate was empty so she put her fork and knife down. "Are you telling me someone made a call from our room to some antique store?"

Both men nodded.

She frowned, then realization slammed into her. "That's where we need to go." She wiped her mouth with her napkin and made to stand.

"Why?" Bratton asked.

"You said our room was tossed, right? Yes, well, Frank was a known person by these spies. I wasn't. There's a good chance they were looking for the book and for who I was. The book was with me." She patted her purse that Bratton had reluctantly returned to her, including her gun and the book. "I carry my ID on my person." She thought back to the past five days. The only other thing that would have her name on it that she didn't keep was...

"The ticket. Frank held onto the tickets. I'm not sure what he did with them. Were they on his person?"

"There were train tickets," Bratton said. "But Montgomery had your liner tickets in his pocket."

Lillian's eyes widened in certainty. "He found out who I was. And the phone call was his report." She set her jaw hard and stood. "C'mon. Let's go see what's at the other end of that call."

13

The other end of the call proved to be Buckley's Antique Shop. A squat little building a few miles north of the Adelphi and the docks, Buckley's sported two large paned windows behind which were Victorian furniture and china. The door was made of solid wood, painted green, with a shiny brass door handle.

Upon a brief consultation among the three of them, it was agreed that Lillian and Ludlow would go into the antique shop together while Bratton and a few of his men stationed themselves at both corners and the block behind. The police captain didn't particularly like it, but he won a concession: both Ludlow and Lillian now carried whistles in their pockets.

Lillian had retrieved her suitcase from police storage and changed her clothes. Now she wore a travel suit, khaki, belted at the waist. Her shoes were the same she wore last night during her pursuit of the man she now knew as Theodore Montgomery. She still carried her purse on her shoulder. Her pistol was comfortably inside.

Together, Lillian and Ludlow strolled down the street, appearing to anyone watching to be window shopping. They arrived at Buckley's and entered. The interior smelled musty, but all the collectibles showed no dust. Tight, close shelves housed small pieces of Victorian knickknacks. One wall displayed china, while another featured glassware.

No other patron shopped at Buckley's. Lillian and Ludlow had the place to themselves. Not optimal for a scouting mission since they would not have anything else with which to distract the shop owner.

He was a blond-haired man who sat behind the counter reading a newspaper. He wore a tie, loosened, and his shirt sleeves were rolled up to the elbows to help alleviate the stagnant heat. He lowered the paper when they walked in. "Can I help you find anything in particular?"

Lillian put on her best deflect-the-annoying salesperson smile. "No thanks. We're just browsing." She affected a British accent. It occurred to her in the split second before she spoke. Depending on who was here, having an American walk into this shop would prove conspicuous.

The shopkeeper didn't return to his paper. He turned his attention to Ludlow. "Sir, what kinds of antiques do you prefer?"

"Well, my boy, let me tell you. I'm partial to late Victorian clocks and glassware. Would you be so kind as to show me what you have?"

The shopkeeper beckoned Lillian to join them, but Ludlow interrupted.

"Don't worry about her. She can't stand glassware except to drink her martinis out of." Ludlow chuckled. He slapped the shopkeeper on the arm and gave him a knowing wink, man to man.

Lillian shrugged when the shopkeeper turned to confirm Ludlow's story.

"Now," Ludlow continued, "let's talk shop."

He led the shopkeeper around one of the freestanding shelves, thus enabling Lillian to sweep her professional eyes over the rest of the store without attracting any undue attention.

The majority of the shop consisted of shelves and shelves of stuff. The stuffiness of it all made her feel somewhat claustrophobic. She kept her Washington apartment clean, almost Spartan. It was a direct result of her time with a Japanese-American monk in the months immediately after her breakup with James and her fleeing Paris after Frank's ill-advised proposal.

***

In those early months, her heart broken, she literally wandered the world. It wasn't an easy thing to do as a single woman, but she made it work. She ended up back in San Diego, having nowhere else to go. She hated being back home. Absolutely hated it. Her parents loved having her being back under their roof, but Lillian looked for any reason, even the most flimsy, to get out of the house. That's how she ended up stranded in the mountains east of Los Angeles one summer's day.

Lillian had taken a bus out to the country with the intent of climbing a mountain for no other reason than to see if she could. She hadn't brought the proper supplies and burned through her remaining money buying what she needed. Having conquered the mountain, she felt exhilarated but empty. The thrill of the climb filled the hole in her soul only as long as she was on the mountain. Once back on level ground, the hole was there again. She considered climbing the mountain again, but decided against it, knowing she'd need something to fill the void in her life.

She decided to hitchhike down the mountain roads and make her way back to San Diego. Being an attractive red-haired woman meant she didn't lack for cars that stopped. She fought off one man who tried to take advantage of her. His response was literally to throw her out of the car. Dirty and disheveled, Lillian was walking when an old black Model A Ford slowed to a halt next to her. Inside, an old man gazed at her. She shielded her eyes from the sun and approached the car. Lillian was surprised to discover the man was Oriental. He introduced himself as Kenji Tanaka and offered to drive her all the way back to her home in San Diego. She didn't think the Ford could make it that far, but she climbed in nonetheless. There was a comfort level she immediately felt, so much so that she started to talk. She talked and talked and told this old stranger everything. By the time they pulled up to her childhood home hours after dark, he knew her entire story.

"Thank you for driving me and listening me ramble on," the young Lillian had said.

"It was a pleasure, Miss Saxton." He smiled warmly. "If you wouldn't mind a piece of advice, I might have the answer for you."

"What is it?"

"Would you meet me tomorrow at this address and you can determine if what I have to offer is for you." He scribbled on a piece of paper and handed it to her.

The location turned out to be an academy for martial arts and Zen teachings. Lillian tried it. Six months later, she found herself content and longing for a new mission in life: to give back. She joined the Army the following spring and quickly found herself a member of a group that looked out for American interests at home.

And abroad, she thought to herself now, standing in the antiques shop. The academy had brought her a sense of contentment with the world; her time in the Army, working secret missions, had trained her to find the odd thing in a given situation.

She let her eyes move across everything inside Buckley's. Nothing seemed out of place, really. Glass cabinets showcased jewelry. A mirror on the wall allowed potential buyers to see themselves with the new jewelry. The china had little cards with typed descriptions of locations and origins. To the casual observer, this was a normal antique shop in Liverpool.

But Theodore Montgomery had placed a call here last night. Montgomery was a spy and a murderer. Something was here. And she was damn well going to find it.

Lillian glanced at Ludlow. He had the shopkeeper discussing something on a far shelf. They faced away from her. She took that opportunity to slip behind the counter. Again, nothing seemed out of place. All looked normal.

Her eyes found the closed door that led to the rear of the store. Another glance at Ludlow to confirm he still had the shopkeeper enthralled and she opened the door and slipped inside.

A short hall was lit only by a single bulb located in the center of the ceiling. Two doors, on opposite sides of the hallway, were the only things to see here. The floor was covered by a long rug that ran the length of the hall. Waste-high wainscoting ran along all the walls.

She heard something faint. The sound came from down the hall. On tiptoe, she walked deeper into the antique shop. The sound grew louder. It was talking, but she couldn't make out any words. She moved to the door on the right and put an ear to it. She frowned. The sounds were not any clearer.

Something caught her eye on the floor. It was a sliver of light. For some reason, it ran the length of the wall. On a hunch, she stepped forward and put her ear to the wooden paneling.

Here, the sound was much clearer. It was talking, but she couldn't make out what she heard. There was little doubt about where this talking emanated from: a secret room. It was the only conclusion to be drawn from the current facts.

A shiver of fear coursed through her body when she realized why she couldn't make out what she heard: the person inside this secret room was not speaking English.

He was speaking German.

Involuntarily, Lillian's upper lip curled into a snarl. Her jaws clenched. Now, she had a decision to make: leave this hallway, alert Ludlow, exit the store, and return with all of Bratton's men. In this scenario, the shopkeeper might get suspicious and destroy any evidence behind this wall.

Or she could find the secret switch and go in alone.

It was an easy decision. She pulled out her pistol, checked the clip, and secured her purse over her shoulder.

She knelt on the floor and pulled up the rug. No scratches appeared on the floor, which meant the door swung inward. Standing, she felt around the wall for some sort of hidden lever or knob. The walls above and below the wainscoting were perfectly smooth. She ran her fingers along the wainscoting and found a break in the wood. She discovered another one about a foot away. Was this the handle?

From out in the shop, she heard the shopkeeper speaking loudly. He was asking about where she was. Any moment, he would barge through that door and discover her. Granted, she had a gun, but she preferred the element of surprise to be on her side.

Holding her pistol up, her arm at a ninety-degree angle, Lillian Saxton turned the length of wainscoting. A click from within the wall sounded. She pushed the wall, at once feeling foolish and ready. The wall swung inward at the same time as the door from the shop burst open.

14

Lillian Saxton risked a glance at the shop door. The shopkeeper filled the door frame. Ludlow stood behind him, moving to her position. She had to have faith that Ludlow could handle himself. Of that, she wasn't one hundred percent sure, considering his slight size.

Her eyes shifted to the visage before her. Inside the wall was a room she considered too large, considering her mental image of this small antique shop. A part of her mind wondered if this was a false wall to the neighboring store. Immediately in front of her were two wooden desks butted up against each other like the police stations in America. On the far side, facing away from her, a man wearing a brown shirt sat at a table. On top of this table was a radio receiver and transmitter. To her immediate right, the wall stopped and a larger interior revealed itself.

"Ludlow, take him!" Lillian raised her gun to the man at the radio. The sound of scuffling emanated from the direction of the main shop. She, however, did not take her eyes off the radio man.

He whirled, his eyes wide with fear. A split second later, he reached out the pistol—a Luger—lying on the table.

Lillian squeezed the trigger twice. Two short bursts erupted in the small room. Lead slugs bit into the wooden table, one of them knocking the Luger to the floor.

"Don't move!" she shouted at Radio Man. Her arms extended, she stepped into the room to cover him.

A third, previously unseen person lunged at her from the right. Lillian saw it coming, but could do nothing to prevent the person's body from slamming into hers. They both fell to the floor. Her martial arts training had prepared her for situations such as this. She pivoted in mid-fall, enabling her to land on her shoulder and fling her assailant off balance and, more important, off her. It was a he, she noted. He smacked into the left wall.

Radio Man, taking the opportunity his co-conspirator gave him, bent down and snatched up his Luger. He turned and brought the firearm to aim at her.

Lillian had not lost her grip. She saw what was about to happen and fired off three more rounds. The bullets chunked into Radio Man's body, sending streams of blood from his body, splattering the walls.

"No!" The cry came from the man who had tackled her. He lay behind her.

Lillian rolled away from him. Her thinking was to scare him enough to surrender. She still had many questions she wanted answered. Ludlow also would need any potential spies captured alive. He had made that point abundantly clear when he allowed her to join him. It was his only condition.

In the heat of the moment, orders and intentions could get muddled. That was not the case here. Her assailant saw her bringing her gun to face him, having gotten to his feet. She didn't think she'd have any problem curtailing him.

He lashed out with his foot. His shoe caught her pistol. She lost her grip and her gun skittered across the floor. The force knocked her to her knees.

She looked up at him to assess if he had any weapons. Seeing none, she thought her skills might win the day. If only she could get her feet under her.

The man didn't give her a chance. He kicked at her face. Lillian moved. The heavy boot missed her face, but passed so close she felt the breeze.

Lying on her right side, she replied to the missed kick by bringing her knee up. It caught him on his ankle. Her blow along with the spent momentum of his strike caused him to lose his balance. He crashed on his back right in front of her.

She threw a punch directly into his side, hoping to land a blow to the kidney. He was already moving and her hand crunched on his ribs. Sharp pain shot up her arm. She cried out despite herself.

The man was rising to his feet. Lillian saw no good opportunity to smack him, so she did the next best thing: she scrambled to her feet and moved to the opposite side of the room. She positioned the two wooden desks between them, needing a few seconds to get her bearings and devise a plan.

The man stood and crouched into a fighting stance. His dark hair was disheveled, his red shirt untucked. A line of blood trickled from the corner of his mouth. As he grinned, she saw blood coating his front teeth.

"Your move," he grunted, gesturing with his finger to rejoin the fight.

Lillian grinned back at him. "Not today."

"Scared?" His voice dripped contempt.

"Not in the least. I could easily take you, but why bother when the cavalry's here?" Her eyes flicked to the doorway. Her opponent's did likewise.

George Ludlow stood there, barely ruffled from his skirmish with the shopkeeper. He aimed a pistol at the man. "Funny you should say that. I never learned to ride a horse."

15

Much like Lillian Saxton imagined the police did the previous night at the Adelphi Hotel, Bratton's men quickly swooped in and secured the antique shop. They slapped cuffs on the man whom Lillian had fought. Curiously, when they walked him out the front door, he started speaking German until he was loaded into a police car and driven away.

Ludlow made some calls and within a half hour, some of his fellow spies descended on the shop. They allowed Lillian to remain, especially when she showed them transcripts in German and proved to them that she could not only read the language but speak it as well. They let her scour the papers while they went about the task of discovering the true nature of this enterprise.

All afternoon Lillian, Ludlow, his men, and the police investigated Buckley's Antique Shop. They found a good number of communiques to and from England, Wales, France, Belgium, and, of course, Berlin. Lillian compiled a list, complete with dates and destination cities of each communication. Naturally, the messages Radio Man was working on when she barged in were the most recent. As she categorized the messages from the previous evening: she read her own name. The communique requested information about her. She found her name on two separate messages. One went to Boston. The other went to Berlin.

It was plain that her mission was known by the enemy and not just because of Frank. Now someone in Germany knew her name, knew she had accompanied Frank and, if her room at the hotel was any indication, knew she carried something secret, probably the book of poetry.

The mission. Late in the afternoon as the sun set, Lillian remembered what had brought her to Liverpool in the first place. It had never really left her conscious mind, but she had been so focused on reading the German communiques that she had pushed it aside. Now it returned. How did the enemy know about Frank and Lillian and their mission?

She knew one way to find out.

Lillian hitched a ride back to the main police station where they had taken Radio Man. The shop keeper was the contingency plan. Maybe he knew nothing about the secret organization behind him, although that was highly unlikely. No, the person she'd start interrogating on was the man who had fought her.

Ludlow had left the antique shop earlier in the afternoon. She wanted to touch base with him and see if he had learned anything from the spy. Upon reaching the police station, some of the pure exhaustion that adrenaline had kept at bay returned. She got a cup of hot tea. Holding it in both hands, she walked down the hallway to the interrogation room where Ludlow's men had set up headquarters. She opened the door and her mouth hung open in astonishment.

Sitting at the table, wrists uncuffed, all cleaned up—and looking rather handsome, she had to admit—eating a plate of food, was the man she had fought.

Ludlow turned and beamed at her. "Ah, Sergeant Saxton, welcome. We've been waiting for you to arrive."

***

The man Johannes Bauer called Herr Colonel sat in his well appointed office and read through the daily communiques from all regions. His large oak desk was roomy enough to accommodate different stacks. He had a system. He visualized his desk like the map of Europe. Reports from the Soviet Union were stacked on the far right while reports from England sat on the far left. Everything else was in between. The messages from America, while slim, were on a smaller table that stood next to his main desk.

Herr Colonel sipped French cognac as he read. A cigarette smoldered in the overflowing ashtray. He glanced at his watch and noted he needed to eat supper shortly. He wondered what his wife had cooked for them.

The sheer number of messages that crossed his desk in a day was staggering. No human could keep up with it all. Yet someone had to be accountable, and it fell to Herr Colonel. He had devised his own system, hand-picked his own staff, and assigned them specific regions to monitor. Their orders were simple: read everything from their assigned region, make a summary report, and flag anything that appeared out of the ordinary. These reports Herr Colonel read daily, just before supper over cognac. If he found anything of note, he would follow up after his meal.

With the so-called Phoney War in effect, Herr Colonel knew it was only a matter of days before the invasion of Western Europe began. The number of messages from his agents in the Low Countries and France was mountainous. Most of the spies had been recruited before and during the invasion of Poland last fall. Now, it was time for those assets to come out into the open and show themselves.

The last stack that evening was the one from England. Not that there wasn't important news from the island, it was just that the British Expeditionary Force was deployed on the Continent. Not a lot was happening on their home shores.

Which was why Herr Colonel was somewhat reluctant to review the British communiques. If anything unusual had occurred, he would have already known about it.

He lit another cigarette and polished off the cognac. Of all spirits, he admired French cognac the most. After the successful invasion, he would make it a point to acquire some for his personal bar. He poured just a little more, picked up the top paper from Britain and read the summary. Again, Herr Colonel insisted his officers be as concise yet as thorough as possible. If reports warranted two pages or more, so be it. But if the daily activities could be summarized in one page, so much the better.

The most recent report from Britain was notable for a blank line next to Liverpool. Herr Colonel preferred his daily reports to be on his desk by 6:00 p.m. local time. All units needed to account for the time differences and send messages accordingly. England was an hour behind Berlin so the 6:00 p.m. report needed to be sent by 5:00 p.m. from England.

Herr Colonel had a temper that he worked daily to control. Little errors and mistakes in the chain of command really got under his skin. Immediately, his anger toward Alfred Wilhelm, his officer in charge of England, was profound. He picked up the receiver on his desk and jammed his finger on a button. When the operator answered the line, Herr Colonel all but hissed the order to summon Wilhelm. Less than a minute later, breathing heavily because he had to climb four flights of stairs, Wilhelm stood at attention.

"Where's today's report from Liverpool?"

"It hasn't arrived yet, Herr Colonel."

"Do you know what time it is?"

"Yes, sir. I am actively trying to locate the radio man in Liverpool and determine why the report is late."

"Why haven't you already done so? That's the kind of thing that demands a special note and not just a blank entry." Herr Colonel leaned on his desk. "There are others who would kill to take your spot on my team. Would you like to fight one of them?"

"No, Herr Colonel," Wilhelm stammered.

"In our business, the absence of a report is often a signal that something is wrong," Herr Colonel snapped. "Was there anything of note from yesterday's report from Liverpool?" He asked the question to cover the fact that he had not yet read the communiques from England, so preoccupied was he about the invasion.

Wilhelm stepped closer to the desk. "It's in my summary, Herr Colonel."

"I'm asking you to tell me yourself!"

"Yes, Herr Colonel. Our activities in Liverpool are going along normally based on last report, which was yesterday. If something happened last night, we don't know about it yet. The only thing our assets in Liverpool were expecting was the arrival of the *Queen Mary*. It was due last night. Yesterday's report indicated it had arrived on time. On board was an American our agents followed in Washington. He and his traveling companion arrived just as the report was sent yesterday."

"And there is no news since then?"

"No, Herr Colonel."

"Who was this American?"

"I'm not sure. He wasn't yet in my jurisdiction."

Herr Colonel jabbed a finger at Wilhelm. "Find out and report to me as soon as possible." When Wilhelm didn't move in a split second, Herr Colonel snapped his fingers.

The younger officer saluted and exited the room.

Sighing, Herr Colonel drained the rest of the cognac. He lit another cigarette and picked up the telephone. In a matter of moments, his wife answered.

"Good evening, my dear." Herr Colonel's voice took on a new timbre, one that his underlings would never have guessed he possessed. He poured another glass of cognac. "I'm afraid I won't be home for supper right away."

16

Lillian stepped into the room. She performed a quick once-over. No, Ludlow did not seem to be in distress. Yes, the man she fought was not manacled. No, there were no other guards in the room. Her brows furrowed, trying to determine what was going on.

"What the hell is he doing?"

Ludlow gestured to an empty spot at the table. "Please, Sergeant, sit down. I'll get you a plate and you can join us." He stood and held his chair out for her. "There you go, dear."

Dumbly, Lillian moved to the chair and sat, all the while staring at the other man. For his part, he had stopped eating and bore his eyes into hers. Anger flashed behind them.

Noticing the man's anger, Ludlow said, "On second thought, I'd better stay and explain."

"That would be a good idea," the other man snarled. "Otherwise, I might have to take out my frustration on her!"

Getting fire in her backbone, Lillian leaned on the table. "You can try. You won't win."

Ludlow stepped to the table and placed his hands on the shoulder of both people at the table. "Calm down. There's no reason for any of this."

Lillian jammed a finger at the man's direction. "His people killed my friend."

The man retorted, "She screwed up months of undercover work with her reckless invasion of the antique shop."

His words processed in Lillian's mind quickly. She cocked her head and glanced up at Ludlow. "Undercover?"

Ludlow nodded.

"He works for you?"

Another nod. "Us. British intelligence."

"You were gathering intelligence?" she said to the man.

"Key word there: 'were.' Until you had to stick your nose in there."

"What about you?" Lillian asked Ludlow. "If this was your operation, didn't you know he was in there? Why the hell did we even stage all that?"

Ludlow held up a finger to halt any further conversation. He stuck his head out the door and yelled down the hall. A disgruntled police officer answered his call. Ludlow asked that the officer bring another plate of food, water, and tea. The officer shuffled away, clearly upset to be playing waiter in his own police station. Ludlow, satisfied, sat back at the table.

"Now, Sergeant, please understand that, while I work for British intelligence, I'm not privy to every operation in existence. I was unaware of Henry's involvement until I began to question him here at the station."

Ludlow took out his pipe and worked tobacco into the bowl as he continued to speak. "Be that as it may, there are always eyes watching everyone and everywhere. It's true: Buckley's Antique Shop was a front for a local Nazi spy ring. You'll be glad to know the man you shot and killed really was a German."

That didn't bring any happiness to Lillian. She had a job to do here in Britain: get to Belgium, get the codebook, and get back. If she could do that without any loss of life, that would be just fine with her. She knew, understood, and accepted that part of her job involved violence and bloodshed. She didn't particularly enjoy it, but she was good at it. She comforted herself with the belief that deaths by her hand and others of her team prevented even more deaths later on. This philosophy won her harsh stares and derision from her fellow American soldiers—mostly men— so she held back speaking. She needed to know how these two felt about their jobs.

Instead, she merely nodded.

"The shop owner is a British citizen. He has some rather unfortunate beliefs about our government and that of Germany. He'd be perfectly fine with Hitler's setting up shop at Ten Downing Street. He thinks the country would be better off with a little national discipline and order. Obviously he knew about the secret room. Turns out he actively sought a role like that among like-minded British citizens. He got his wish. Now, he'll get a cell."

"Or a firing squad," Henry mumbled. At a glance by Ludlow, he said, "It's what traitors like him deserve."

"Maybe." Ludlow puffed on his pipe. "But we have the luxury of holding off on that for the time being. Perhaps he'll talk, and that's far more valuable than a corpse."

"Give me a go at him," Henry said. "I can still play my part, get him to talk."

"Maybe," Ludlow conceded through a plume of pungent pipe smoke, "but we have a more pressing issue."

"What?" Henry said.

"Miss Saxton's mission."

Henry stared at Ludlow, then at Lillian. "What's so bloody important that she takes priority?"

Until that very moment, Lillian hadn't realized the predicament she was in. She gasped at the realization.

"It's Frank."

"Who?" Henry blurted.

"My friend who's dead," Lillian snapped at him. She turned to Ludlow. "James is expecting the both of us in Belgium. Now, without Frank, the mission is in jeopardy."

"Not any more," Ludlow said, grinning his teeth around the pipe stem in his mouth.

"What do you mean?" Lillian said.

With a flourish that would make a used car salesman proud, Ludlow said, "Lillian Saxton, meet Henry Clark. He's your new partner."

***

Herr Colonel gnawed on a link of dried beef he kept in his office for times such as this: working late and unable to get home to his wife's wonderful meal. It infuriated him when this happened. He knew his wife was a steadying influence on him and he cherished it. Herr Colonel sighed. Considering how long it was taking Wilhelm to locate the information and return, Herr Colonel could have just gone home and enjoyed the meal.

Herr Colonel rubbed his eyes. His reading glasses rose and fell with the movements. Reading. All he did was read reports and offer suggestions to his commanding officer and others. That was what the German army generals considered best for Herr Colonel. With a civilian job as a university professor of history, Herr Colonel was used to dealing with higher-ups not as smart as he was. Politics and inter-office squabbles always got in the way of the important things: research and teaching.

The students weren't much better than the other professors in the university. So focused were the young people that they often regurgitated the answers they knew Herr Colonel wanted to hear rather than actually thinking for themselves. That kind of lock-step thinking manifested itself in the German Army and his current position. Herr Colonel's junior officers and staff modified their behavior and thinking to accommodate him. He didn't want that. He wanted them to think on their feet. He expected someone like Wilhelm, two decades younger than Herr Colonel's fifty years, to notice the report from Liverpool was missing and find out ahead of time, not just leave a blank on a daily report.

It's what Herr Colonel would have done.

He heard shuffling footsteps hurrying to his door, then three short knocks.

"Come in."

Wilhelm entered the office. He had forgotten to wipe off the beads of sweat on his forehead. They ringed his face, looking like a beauty pageant crown. The younger man passed some papers to Herr Colonel, who ignored them.

"Report." Herr Colonel took a cigarette out of the gunmetal case on his desk and lit it.

Wilhelm cleared his throat. His eyes darted to the papers on the desk.

"Please tell me you don't need to read the report to me." Herr Colonel kept his voice even instead of blasting Wilhelm. His wife would be proud.

"No, Herr Colonel. I cross-referenced our latest reports from America and Liverpool. We've been keeping an eye on him since he landed in Belgium a few weeks ago."

"What did he do in Belgium?"

"Apparently, on a business trip, he met with another American who now lives in Berlin and is married to a German woman."

Herr Colonel grew thoughtful as he smoked his cigarette. He knew some Americans had chosen *das Vaterland* over their ancestral home, but not many. There were famous ones who thought what Germany was doing was not wrong, namely Charles Lindbergh. If he kept talking, Germany might not have to face off against the United States. Despite what *der Führer* and his high command thought of their prospects against America, Herr Colonel would rather not put the confrontation to a test.

"What did these two Americans do?"

"Have supper."

Herr Colonel's eyebrows rose. "Supper?"

"Yes, Herr Colonel. From what I have gathered, they met in Amsterdam, spent the night, and departed."

"Why?"

"Sir?"

"Why did they meet?"

"Apparently, they are old friends."

Herr Colonel waved his hand. "I understand. Who ordered that the American from Berlin be followed?"

"General Siegfried."

Herr Colonel grunted. General Hans Siegfried was two rungs above him in the chain of command. He had a temperament that made Herr Colonel seem downright pleasant. "Any idea why Siegfried wants the American in Berlin followed?"

Wilhelm shrugged. "Not sure. He's mentioned he doesn't trust any foreigners, even ones who are actively helping our cause."

Herr Colonel had heard sentiments such as that through his time in the military. He didn't always agree with that opinion, but understood why the thought persisted. "What's he do?"

"He helps out with our codes."

Herr Colonel pulled the paper report to him and glanced at it. He frowned. "Is this report from Liverpool accurate?"

"Yes, Herr Colonel. Frank Monroe is the American we've been following. He's a banker. Travels to multiple countries."

"Who is the man we're following who lives in Berlin?"

"His name is James Geiger."

Herr Colonel set the report on his desk. He picked up the receiver again to call his wife. To Wilhelm, he said, "Have the secretary make a pot of coffee. We're in for a long night."

17

"Are you out of your mind?" Lillian Saxton blurted to Ludlow. "His people killed Frank."

"Hey, they weren't my people," Henry retorted. "I was undercover. It was my job."

"Well your *job* got my friend killed and basically has killed the mission." To Ludlow, she said, "James is expecting me and Frank, not me and some other man. It can't work."

"It can and it must. What's the alternative?"

Lillian thought about that. It was true that most of the mission had been compromised, but there was always a contingency plan. She wasn't sure why James wanted both her and Frank, but that was out of the question now. Perhaps this could work.

The other issue still existed, the one about her brother's killer. Lillian had kept Frank in the dark about that part of the message. She had never told Donnelly or Honeywell and she was certainly not going to tell Ludlow. Henry, on the other hand, would be a problem. How would she be able to get the information she needed without tipping him off?

"Sergeant," Ludlow said, "I hope your silence doesn't mean you're trying to wiggle your way out. The solution to our problem is simple. And, if I might remind you, your commanding officer basically lent you to us. For better or worse, that makes me your commanding officer."

Lillian bristled. "You don't have to get ugly about it. I'm not wavering. I'm merely thinking through the situation. I'm not sure Pretty Boy here is my best option."

"'Pretty boy?'" Henry said. "I could have bested you."

"You didn't. And, believe me, you couldn't."

Henry opened and closed his mouth. No words came out. He turned to Ludlow. "Sir, despite what this American thinks,"— he let clear derision drip from his words—"I don't think accompanying her is the best option for me." He put his fork down and slid the plate aside. "I'm in deep here in Liverpool. The Nazis and Nazi sympathizers here in England trust me. They think I'm one of them. It's why I spoke German when the police arrested me. They don't know what's going on here, with all this nice food and a shower." He leaned forward. "Sir, let me go back to them. I was this close"—he put his thumb and forefinger a millimeter apart—"to learning the name of the person on the other end who is coordinating these subversive activities here in this country."

Ludlow puffed on his pipe in silence for a few moments, long enough that the silence became pregnant with possibility. "Henry, first let me say you've been a keen asset in our war against the Nazis and subversives. And even before that with all the business down in the Caribbean. Excellent work. Your record is spotless. But you've been under for too long. You've lost sight of the bigger picture."

He gestured to Lillian. "Take the sergeant here. Her friend, may he rest in peace, was a civilian. Granted, this James person in Belgium is expecting Mr. Monroe to arrive with Lillian, and while we don't know why right now, it's clear there's a reason. Now, we are faced with filling his vacancy. And we can fill it with a man trained in combat and espionage. That way, the both of you, both trained, both looking for the cracks in the enemy's armor, both looking in the shadows, are, frankly, a better option than we had before. No offense, Sergeant."

Lillian kept her mouth shut to avoid saying anything impertinent.

Henry grabbed his fork and shoved another mouthful of food into his mouth.

"So, it's settled. Henry, you will accompany Sergeant Saxton to Brussels, retrieve that codebook, and return it to me or other members of British intelligence. Since you've been undercover for so long, I'm not too sure you need a cover. We'll just let you go as yourself." To Lillian, he said, "You have the tickets?"

"They're with Frank," she mumbled. "They're not in either

name, just basic tickets."

"What tickets?" Henry asked.

"The ferry that crosses the Channel," Lillian replied.

Henry shook his head. "Look, my pop's down in Dover. Let's just get him to take us across."

Ludlow demurred. "No. This is an out-in-the-open operation. While the mission itself is clandestine, the fact that you and the sergeant are traveling to Belgium to see an old friend of hers is your best cover because it's the truth."

Ludlow made to stand but Lillian cut in. "Who's in charge?"

"I'm sorry?" Ludlow said, sitting back down.

"Who is in command?" Lillian persisted. "I think it should be me."

"Like hell it should," Henry blurted. "This is a British operation. I should be in charge."

Lillian leaned forward toward Henry and tapped her chest. "But the message was to me. Not you or any British person. When it was Frank and I, it was an easy call: I was in charge because I was the military person. Now, with two of us, I need to know who's in charge."

Ludlow blew air out of his mouth. His lips flapped in a rather comical way. No one laughed. "I see your point, Sergeant. How much field experience have you had?"

"Enough. More than enough."

Henry shook his head.

Ludlow looked at both of them. "Why don't you both share command? Sergeant, you can be in charge of talking with your friend and getting the codebook. Henry, you can be in charge of operations, getting to and from Brussels. Does that satisfy you both?"

"No," they said in unison.

"Good." Ludlow stood. "Sergeant, you will need a place to sleep tonight. I'm not sure the Adelphi will want you back, so we'll find a place for you. Henry, you need to go home and pack. You're both leaving in the morning."

"Sir," Lillian said, standing next to Ludlow, "would it be

possible to see Frank, pay my respects to him?"

Ludlow nodded. "He's already in the morgue. You can see him there."

"Sir," Henry said, "since we're in the business of granting personal requests"—he sneered at Lillian—"might I have some time to visit my father on the way to Belgium? My mum, well, she passed on while I was undercover and I've not been able to visit her grave."

Ludlow nodded again. "Granted. But don't be too long about it. And don't be too maudlin. You're on the clock now. You're on His Majesty's time. See to what you need and get on with it. The sooner we have that codebook, the sooner we might be able to learn when the Nazis are going to invade. God help us when they do."

***

The room was small and smelled of disinfectant. The odor tickled Lillian's nose. After last seeing and smelling Frank the previous night—when the world felt vastly different—this new smell proved jarring.

The medical man in charge of the morgue had been alerted she was on her way. Graciously, he had made the sterile room as palatable as possible. The table on which Frank's corpse lay couldn't be moved, but the other tables and trays were covered with cloths. The lights were dimmed, even the center light over the main table. The doctor had gone the extra mile and arranged Frank's clothing to resemble something approaching normal. As a result, he almost appeared to be sleeping.

Except his neck. The strain of the poison gripped his neck into a rictus so bad it made him look like he was straining to lift something heavy. Lillian noticed it but didn't dwell on that part of him. She reached out and took his hand. The feeling of his cold skin bit into her. Tears filled her eyes, then rolled down her cheeks. They splashed on the white sheet covering the lower half of his body. She didn't let go of his hand.

"Oh, Frank," Lillian whispered. She smoothed his mussed hair along the hairline. Thoughts of the previous evening, standing in the shower, flooded back to her now. If she had opened that door, both literally as well as figuratively, maybe Frank would still be alive. They certainly wouldn't have gone downstairs. She didn't mistake her feelings now for outright love, but she conceded they could have developed in that direction.

"I'm sorry," she whispered. More tears, this time, they landed on his cheeks. "I'm so sorry. I don't know why James wanted you to come with me, but I'll be sure to tell him you died for it."

Her thoughts replayed that moment back in Paris, 1934. Early June. Bright sun. Warm air that carried the scent of grass and flowers. In her mind, the images kaleidoscoped like an impressionistic painting. She wore a long dress, light blue, her hair kept in place by a scarf. She walked in the grass, barefoot and alone in the park.

And then Frank Monroe was there, with her. His shadow crossed hers before she knew who it belonged to.

"Penny for your thoughts." Immediately, he snapped his fingers and checked himself. "Strike that from the ledger. I know your thoughts."

That was Frank. Always just a little behind. She curled a strand of her red hair around her ear. It immediately escaped again. She gave up and sat on a nearby bench. Frank sat next to her albeit on the far side.

"Why would James do that?" Lillian said. It was more of a whisper.

The rustle of fabric told her Frank shrugged. "Because he's an idiot."

A smirk of laughter erupted from within her. Was that the most timely thing Frank had ever said? The smirk became actual laughter. A honest-to-goodness smile emerged. More laughter, then Frank, tentatively, joined in. Lillian turned to face him. Three feet separated them.

The sun caught his face. His gregarious smile beamed brighter than the sun. His blond hair glowed under his hat. He removed it and set it between them.

"Well, he is," Frank continued. "I mean, really. Just look at you. You're beautiful. Look, there, when you really laugh and smile, those little dimples appear on your cheeks. They never show unless you're really laughing or smiling. Think he noticed that?"

Actually, Lillian thought, *James had noticed*. For all that the world and his upbringing had bestowed on him, James possessed a certain sense of entitlement. She understood it and, coming from a poor background like hers, she craved it. Some people who grow up in that entitled environment got dulled by the world, not seeing the little nuances that make life worth living. James wasn't like that. He strove to push the boundaries of his family heritage. Not that he'd ever break free entirely, but he wanted to see the world for what it was, not just behind the fancy walls and windows of high society.

For Frank's sake, Lillian shook her head. "Thanks."

"I bet he noticed your eyes. How could anyone not? The green in them is like..." he paused, trying to complete his metaphor. Lillian prayed the future banker didn't land on "money" as his example.

"...The fresh grass here in this park. Is there anything more lovely than Paris in spring? Yes, there is. The spring of your eyes is like Paris all year round."

Where had that come from?

"But for all your outer beauty," Frank went on, "it's that brain of yours that's your best feature. You're brilliant, Lillian. Brilliant. I could barely keep up in some of our classes. Even James noticed that. He kind of hated it at times, your being smarter than he is, but it's true. Old Professor Potter knew it. That's why he was so hard on you." He gave her a conspiratorial grin. "You showed him, didn't you?"

Lillian smiled with pride. "I did, didn't I?"

"Yes, you did. You very much did. I think students will be talking about that when we all meet up in ten years for our reunion."

They both laughed. Thoughts of 1944 and where she'd be in ten years entered Lillian's mind. Interestingly, nothing truly emerged. The thought saddened her.

Frank picked up on it. "Hey, that's not meant to be a sad thing. Lil, the world is at our fingertips. It's ours for the taking."

"It is if your life's already planned out like yours is." Her countenance dropped and she sighed. "You've had your life mapped out since you were growing up. James, too. Me? My life's like a book that's being written as I go along. Poor girl escapes her old life only to find out that the only thing left is her old life. That's not exactly the type of story I figured I'd be living. It's why I left San Diego. It's why I worked longer and harder to get into school, get over here. I want to do something with my life, not just go back to California and live out meaningless days." Her voice cracked with anger, then tears welled in her eyes.

Frank scooted nearer to her. He put his hat behind him. Now, only a foot separated them. He reached out and touched her shoulder. "Hey," he said. With his other hand, he reached out and touched her chin. With gentleness, he raised her face to meet his eyes. They were calm eyes, gentle eyes, eyes that saw into her.

Lillian's anger subsided. *Frank Monroe*, she thought. *You are one classy guy.*

Who was one minute away from ruining it all.

"You don't have to go back to California. Like I said, the world's at our fingertips. This is 1934. Whatever it is you want to do, you can."

At that moment, Lillian wanted to go back in time and tell James she'd stay with him. It didn't matter that they'd live in Germany. That way, she could avoid the broken heart he had dealt her.

No. That's not true. She didn't want to live in Germany, not with what the new Nazi government was doing. Power consolidated into one political party controlled by one person was unhealthful to modern civilization. Might as well just go back in time to Rome and their emperor. It all adds up to the same thing.

There was nowhere to go. At least not now. She said as much to Frank.

"Of course there's a place for you in this world."

"Where?"

He paused and lowered his voice. "With me."

Lillian Saxton sat there, on that bench in the middle of Paris, and tried to make sense of what she had just heard. Surely it wasn't what she thought it was, right? *He didn't just propose to me, did he? Please tell me he isn't so dense as to think this was the optimal time to broach that subject.*

A voice inside her told her the answer to all her questions was yes.

The broken heart of Lillian Saxton shattered. She was furious and confused that her other best friend could be so stupid as to propose marriage to her at this time, in this place.

Anger rapidly overwhelmed her heart at that moment. She stood and grabbed her shoes. She whirled at him. Tears welled in her eyes. Her lower lip trembled. At any moment, she was going to lose it. A million things she wanted to say flooded her mind, most of them not nice. In a supreme effort of will, nothing left her mouth. Instead, she stormed away. She packed her bags within the hour and was on a train to the coast in two. That image of Frank's confused face was the last one she had for six years.

Until last week when he popped back into her life.

And now, standing in a morgue, looking down at Frank's dead face, she had another. More tears blurred her vision.

In the years since she had met and studied with Kenji Tanaka, she had come to know what it takes to master her emotions in nearly any circumstance. It had served her well in her missions.

This was not one of those times. Lillian cried. She didn't care if anyone heard her. This was a human moment. She cried for the kind person Frank was, his trying to help her those years ago in his own befuddled way. She cried for the potential future she'd never have now. Most of all, she cried for her friend. He had gotten himself mixed up in espionage and murder, things for which his life as a banker had never prepared him.

But Lillian was prepared. She knew the risks. She also knew justice. And retribution. She had killed the man directly responsible for Frank's death. But Bauer took orders from someone else. She would find that person and make him pay.

Frank's voice sounded in her head. "Are you to be judge, jury, and executioner?"

She knew what he'd say were he alive.

But he was dead.

She wondered if the spirit of Frank Monroe had anything to add.

Lillian answered him in a suddenly calm, serious, and determined voice. "In this case, yes I am."

18

Rolf Klein rode his motorcycle at top speed and felt the warm air in his face. The rushing wind exhilarated him, gave him a nice antidote to the bloody business up in Glasgow. Traitors. He just couldn't stomach them. When he had been told by his commanding officer, General Hans Siegfried, to investigate the apparent tip-off to the local police of the presence of a secret pro-German group, Klein didn't relish the assignment. He preferred his time in Liverpool where he knew the streets and alleys intimately rather than a strange city. But he had orders and follow them he did.

It was a rather easy job, all things considered. Traitors, by and large, were a cowardly lot. It was why they betrayed their countries and causes in the first place. The man named Jones was a recruit, a local, who wanted Hitler to rule Europe. But he was lured by the promise of easy money. The way Klein left Jones's body was meant to send a message not only to the local police but also to the other members of the ring: talk and this will happen to you. Klein made sure the gruesomeness created an absolutely clear message.

Driving through the streets of Liverpool, Klein was ready to rest for the night. His friend, Otto Fuchs, was the radio man here in the city. Together, they lived in an apartment with Peter Becker, another pro-German man here in the UK. Klein had picked up a little souvenir: a pint of beer. They were going to share it that night.

His route to the apartment took him along the road where the antique shop was located. To his great shock, he saw lights and people milling around in the streets. Blue lights of police cars flashed on the building facades.

"*Sheisse*," Klein muttered. He slowed his motorcycle. In a quick decision, he turned onto a side street. Why would there be police in front of the shop? The only reason he could discern was that they were found out.

Klein had no way of knowing if that was the case. Liverpool was a big city and there were dozens of reasons why the police could be on that stretch of road. Klein, for his part, could think of only one.

He parked his motorcycle on a parallel street. Adjusting his bag over his shoulder, he strolled through a small alley. The halo of lights grew brighter the closer he got. Klein considered it a stroke of good luck when he saw a bystander leaning against a building at the edge of the alley. Klein came to a halt next to the man.

"What's going on?" He altered his speaking pattern slightly from what he had been using.

The man, arms folded across his chest, didn't look Klein's way. "Found a nest of Nazis in there."

"Really?" Klein said with mock horror. "What happened?"

"Coppers showed up. Had a couple go in first, scope out the place. Then we all heard gunshots."

Despite himself, Klein's heart skipped a beat. Gunshots? If the police were here, that meant bad news. "Anyone killed?"

The man nodded. "One of 'em. Seen him around here. Never had a clue he was a Jerry. They hauled Buckley away to the station."

"Bloody hell," Klein swore. He hated the next question, but he had to ask. "Which one got killed?"

"That Otto fella. Becker was gibbering out in German when they arrested him." The man unfolded his arms and turned to Klein. In the light that shined on half his face, Klein could tell the man recognized him. Klein also recognized the man. It was Bill Jacobson. He worked at the butcher's just down the road. They had chatted more than once while Bill was carving meat Klein took home to his friends.

Bill continued. "Hey, you're that other one who works in the shop. That means you're a…"

His words died in his throat when Klein slid the knife he

carried at the small of his back into Bill's side. Klein, an expert at ways to kill without sound, had brought the blade upward just below Bill's right rib cage. The six-inch blade pierced the skin, carved through muscle, nicked a kidney, and punctured Bill's right lung. Blood and bodily fluid were already pouring into the lung, preventing Bill from uttering another word.

Klein's strength prevailed here as well. He grabbed Bill by the collar and hauled him back into the darkness of the alley. Bill's legs only took him about a dozen steps before they gave way. He slumped to his knees. Klein bent down with him. The knife was still in Bill's side.

"Sorry, mate." Klein allowed his true German-inflected accent to come out. "But I can't have you talking anymore." He twisted the knife and then yanked it out. The thin wound now widened. Blood gushed out of Bill. Klein, not wanting to attract any undue attention, eased Bill to the ground. He was almost nurse-like. He took Bill's shirt and wiped blood from his blade. Keeping a watch at the end of the alley, Klein was satisfied enough with the cleaning job to put the knife back into its sheath.

Klein looked down at Bill. "We had some good talks, mate. Sorry about your widow. I liked her, too. She'll get on without you. Won't be easy, but then, what the hell in this life is supposed to be easy?" He patted Bill's face.

A few trash bins sat nearby. Gingerly, Klein lifted each one and covered Bill's body from view. Good enough.

Quickly, Klein hurried back to his motorcycle. No way to avoid the sound when he started the engine, but he resisted the urge to gun the engine by merely puttering away.

He drove through the streets, passing many businesses that were dark. Made sense. Everyone was home now. Time for him to get to the apartment, get his stuff, and get away. He also needed to send word back to Berlin about Liverpool. Klein couldn't be sure when the raid had happened, but his commanding officers in Berlin would know something was amiss when the nightly report didn't appear.

On high alert, Klein actually passed his building twice before stopping. If Becker had been arrested, he might have already talked. Then again, Klein didn't think Becker would willingly divulge any information. Still, Becker was a local recruit and Klein couldn't trust him one hundred percent.

He parked his motorcycle a block away and approached his apartment building from the rear. Only Lucy the landlady used the back door for deliveries and trash. She wanted all her tenants to come in via the front door. Not tonight. The back door was unlocked and Klein slipped inside.

He let his eyes adjust to the dimness. The back door faced the lobby and front door. There was a low-wattage bulb in the foyer but no other light until one reached each landing. It was part of the campaign to make Liverpool as dark as possible in case the Luftwaffe decided to start bombing.

On tiptoe, Klein climbed the cement stairs, thankful they were not made of wood. No one was in the second-floor hallway nor the third, where his flat was. It was the rearmost room on the floor. If worse came to worst, Klein could slip out the window, land on the second floor's awning, and escape.

He opened his door, walked inside, and closed it again. On a hunch, he locked it. Becker might not spill any secrets but the coppers could easily take his keys and search the place. Come to think of it, Klein wondered why they weren't already here. Maybe Becker was making them work for it. He smiled in the darkness. Perhaps Becker wasn't as bad as he thought.

Klein stepped through the common room which consisted only of a couch, throw rug, coffee table, and card table that doubled as a kitchen table. The remains of the last gin rummy game from two nights ago were still there.

Stepping into his room, Klein grabbed his one leather bag and began throwing his clothes into it. He wasn't loud, but the rustle of fabric against leather was loud enough that he didn't realize the front door had opened until he heard it close.

***

Henry sat and watched as Ludlow and the American woman left the briefing room. His muscles ached from the fight earlier that evening. He flexed his jaw muscles, trying to come to terms with his new situation.

His undercover identity of Peter Becker had been well-established. It had taken him over a year to work up his bona fides with the pro-Nazi movement here in Britain. That work had led to some heated arguments—arguments he mostly hated, truth be told—but he kept his cover and got in deeper. He earned the trust of Klein, Fuchs, and others who, slowly but surely, let Henry into their little circle.

And Henry knew that with the upswing of the war imminent, it was only a matter of time before they introduced him to other members of the Nazi spy ring, perhaps even taking him back to Germany where some real intelligence might be gathered. It had been the thing Ludlow and his ilk had wanted from Henry.

All that planning, all that time, all those words Henry was forced to utter had amounted to nothing. Henry tried hard to keep his emotions under control. He failed.

He lashed out. The plate of unfinished food sailed off the table and smashed into the far wall. Moments later, a policeman stuck his head through the open door.

"Everything okay, sir?"

Henry stood. His chair toppled backwards. "I dropped the plate. Get someone to clean it up." He stormed out of the room, bumping shoulders with the befuddled officer.

If there was one thing that could cheer him up, it was a drink. He needed an anonymous bar. The police station was across town from the antique shop so any of them around here would do the trick. He walked four blocks, passing the first few, knowing they'd be full of coppers and folks who liked coppers.

He recognized a car parked in front of a pub. He opened the door and saw the driver hunched over the bar. The driver looked up, saw Henry, and motioned him inside. Henry walked in and took the stool next to Ludlow.

The bartender asked, "What will it be?"

"Same as him." Henry gestured to the four glasses in front of the spy chief. Three were empty. The last contained something brown. Something wonderful.

Within moments, four empty shot glasses were lined up in front of Henry. The bartender took a bottle of Scotch and filled the four glasses. Henry downed the first one before the bartender had even filled the fourth. He tapped the first glass to indicate it needed to be filled again. The bartender complied then melted away.

"This is bollocks," Henry muttered. "All that time I spent undercover, all that work, and some Yank comes in and blows it to hell."

"It's part of war," Ludlow demurred. "Sometimes, the best laid plans fall flat and get blown to hell. For you, my boy, this is one of those times."

Henry drank the first glass again, then turned it over on the bar. "But why this mission? Why not just send me back in? I'm so close. And with Otto dead, Klein will be in the wind. I can contact Berlin and get in. I can be their top man here in Liverpool. Imagine the intelligence I can get for us. Imagine the counterintelligence I can generate. It's a win for us all."

Ludlow pursed his lips and nodded. This late in the night, his hair, graying throughout, had lost some of its shape. "You're right."

"Then why not try? We can concoct any story we want. They'll bring me in, maybe even reveal who the primary is here in Britain. That's something we need to know before Hitler starts up again."

"On that note, no word from Berlin about when that might be?"

Henry shook his head. He downed the second glass and turned over. "No. It's all just reports over and over again. Daily reports by five. They will already be alerted that something's happened here when we haven't reported in. We can still salvage this operation."

Ludlow stared into the middle distance. "It was a good plan, your going undercover. You gave us lots to work with." He sipped half of the Scotch in the last glass. He swirled the liquid. "But this codebook opportunity trumps it."

Henry slammed his palm on the bar. The glasses jingled. Some of the Scotch from glass number three sloshed onto the bar. The eyes of the other patrons caromed their way. The bartender looked over, eyebrows raised. Henry shook them all off. He emptied glass number three into his gut and turned over the glass.

"Why a lady?" he muttered. "Why'd it have to be a woman?"

Ludlow shrugged. "She's quite attractive."

"Bollocks."

"How'd you do against her today?"

Henry grew reflective. He shrugged. "It was close quarters. I could have taken her."

Ludlow smiled. "When I arrived, I remember you were the one bleeding."

"Luck."

"Or skill. Nevins tells me she's quite the fighter. She's one of the best the Americans have."

"I'd just like one more go at her."

"Why? You're both on the same mission now."

"Maybe," Henry snarled. "But the mission will end sometime." He wheeled at Ludlow and held up a finger. "So help me, if I think she's failing in the mission, I'm taking her out. You understand me?"

Ludlow put a calming hand on Henry's arm. "Not before you get the codebook. Once you have that..." He paused, trying to form the proper words. "Once you have that, well, the codebook becomes the mission. The only mission. Do you understand?"

A grin creased Henry face. "Yes, sir." He downed the last glass of Scotch and turned it to match the others. "I'll contact you if I can. Now," he slid off the stool, "I have to go pack."

"Be careful, my boy," Ludlow said. "Come back in one piece."

"I always do."

Henry left the pub and walked a few more blocks. He hailed a cab and directed him to stop two blocks away from the flat he shared with Klein and Fuchs. He paid the cabby and waited until he rounded the corner. Then Henry walked to the apartment building.

He came in the front door, but quietly. He ascended the stairs and eased the key into the lock of his flat. Opening the door, he stepped inside.

And smelled something. It was an odor he knew well. It was Klein's favorite cologne. If Henry smelled that now, it meant Klein was here.

That thought entered Henry's mind at the split second a body slammed into him.

19

With a strong hand grabbing Henry's shirt, Klein slammed Henry into the wall. Henry had heard enough stories about Klein and his methods to know what came next: a knife. Klein always bragged that he came in low and stabbed upward. Henry swung his left arm down and caught the upswing of Klein's right arm. The blade snagged on Henry's long sleeves and the trajectory was altered. The tip of the knife scraped across Henry's forearm. He swore. The voice surprised Klein who paused for only a second.

That was all the time Henry needed. He grabbed Klein's left wrist and squeezed hard, digging his fingernails into the soft underside of Klein's wrist. At the same time, Henry punched Klein in the face with his left hand. Finally, Henry brought up his knee and caught Klein in the crotch. The three counterattacks did the trick. Klein backed up a few steps. His grip on Henry's shirt loosened. Henry yanked the hand and pushed the German away. Klein stumbled backward, hitting the coffee table with the backs of his knees. He crashed onto the table and it surprisingly held his weight.

"Klein," Henry whispered harshly in German, "it's me. Becker." He reached over and switched on the light.

Klein blinked up at Henry. "Becker? Where have you been?"

Henry's mind whirled. Klein wasn't supposed to have returned until tomorrow. That he was here indicated the side mission he had driven up to Glasgow to conduct was already over. Over beers and late-night talks, Klein had regaled Henry and Otto with all the hideous deeds performed for *der Führer*. The sense of pride he displayed, while admirable, was also disgusting. Nevertheless, Henry had no way of knowing how much Klein knew about the raid on the antique shop. Henry gambled at a plausible story.

"Avoiding arrest," Henry muttered. "You heard what

happened at the shop?"

Klein got his balance and stood. The knife didn't leave his hand, although he kept his arm hanging loosely at his side. "Where's Otto?"

"Otto's dead. Buckley's in jail."

"What happened?"

"There was a raid. Police surrounded the shop. They stormed in, discovered the back room. Shut it all down." Henry rearranged his shirt, tucking the tail back into his pants. He walked over to the small sink and filled a glass of water. He had expected to sleep through the night. He had a good expectation sleep wasn't going to come soon. The effects of the five Scotch shots, which had evaporated with the adrenaline rush of the fight, now started to reassert themselves. Henry downed one glass, then filled another.

"Where were you?"

Henry's mind concocted a story on the fly. "Out for errands. Getting food. Sending mail. I was in Bill's butcher shop when the coppers showed up."

The look Klein gave Henry served as an early warning sign. Something was wrong. The German cocked his head to the side, the corners of his mouth curled up slightly. "That's not what he said."

"Who?"

"Bill. I questioned him." Klein held out his knife arm. The ends of his sleeve were dark red. "I came back. The business up in Glasgow was done. I even brought back a local ale for you, me, and Otto to split. I rode up to the shop and Bill was there. I asked him what happened. He told me. Said Otto was shot, Buckley arrested." He took a few steps toward the sink. "But he also said you were arrested as well."

The kitchen in the flat barely earned the name. The area was shaped like an "L" with the sink in the middle of the long side. On the short side was the stove. A few cabinets and drawers lined the long side. The only silverware the three of them possessed was in a drawer next to the sink. Henry knew any move on his part to that drawer would tell Klein all he needed to know. On the other hand, Klein still held his knife at his side. Henry, keeping eye contact with Klein, used his peripheral vision to scan for anything he could use as a weapon.

"Who are you?" Klein pointed the knife at Henry.

"Rolf, buddy, I'm one of you."

Slowly, Klein shook his head. "I don't think you are." He took another step. Now his position blocked Henry from a quick dash to the front door.

"C'mon, pal," Henry said. "What do you think's going on here?"

Klein raised his eyebrows in surprise. "Me? What do I think is going on here? Let me see. Our base in Liverpool is raided. Buckley's in jail. Otto's dead. That just leaves you and me. You tell me you sneaked away. Bill, with his dying words, tells me you were arrested. One of you is lying. I'm willing to believe it wasn't Bill. You'd be surprised how truthful a person can be at death's door."

He moved one step closer. The area in which Henry could successfully operate or defend himself continued to shrink.

"But let's say Bill's correct and you were arrested. The police would have searched you and found the key to this flat." Klein looked around, mimicking an actor searching for something. "Where are they? Why aren't the police storming down this door? Why aren't they already here?" Another step. "I'll tell you why. You're working with them. That, my friend, makes you a traitor." His lip snarled in derision. "And if there's one thing I hate most of all, it's a traitor."

Henry had heard enough. This situation was getting ugly fast. He flung the glass at Klein. The German anticipated it and sidestepped. The glass flew through the air, shattering on the floor.

Klein lunged at Henry. In his only defense, Henry grabbed the dish towel and swung it at the oncoming blade. The sharpened metal pierced the fabric and got snagged. Henry twisted the fabric and further ensnared the knife. Then he pulled with all his might in an effort to dislodge the blade from Klein's grip.

That didn't work, but it made Klein lose his balance. Henry helped by grabbing a handful of Klein's shirt and flinging them both toward the floor. The German crashed into the kitchen table. Unlike the coffee table, the kitchen table cracked under Klein's weight. Wood splintered and snapped. A second later, Klein was on the floor, the table falling inward.

Henry wasted no time. He threw open the drawer with the silverware and grabbed the only cutting knife they owned. The small blade was half the six inches of Klein's knife, but it would have to do.

In the time it took Henry to acquire his weapon, Klein was already on his feet. Henry narrowly missed a vicious lash from Klein. Henry ducked the swing and turned. His back now faced the wider part of the room. The spare furniture still afforded him little in the way of a weapon. This was going to be an old-fashioned brawl.

Bloody hell.

Klein grinned. Henry hadn't seen him like that. He imagined this was what Klein looked like when on a job that involved killing.

"You British intelligence?" Klein mocked.

Henry didn't want to talk at all. He wanted to bash Klein against a wall and eliminate him. All those months of undercover work, Klein's stories and holier-than-thou attitudes about the world had churned enough bile for a lifetime. Now, it all came out.

Henry picked up one of the couch cushions and threw it at Klein. He knew the German would easily deflect it, but that was the point. Instead of charging Klein, Henry hurried over to the small counter where they kept the food items. It was also where they kept the liquor. He grasped the half-empty bottle of whiskey at the base and smashed the neck.

Klein barely moved as he knocked the cushion aside. He wasn't so lucky when the broken bottle hurtled in the air to him. He held up a hand for defense. The jagged top of the bottle caught on a finger, cutting it. The trajectory of the bottle and liquid changed. Not all of it fell on Klein's body, but most of it did.

Henry continued throwing everything on the counter at Klein. In his heart, he knew this was a sissy way to fight, but he wanted the distraction more than style points.

Klein moved forward.

Good enough thought Henry. He plunged his hand into his pocket and pulled out his lighter. He flicked the flint. A yellow flame burst to life. Henry tossed it at Klein.

The German tried to knock the lighter out of the air. He missed. The lighter and its flame landed on his shirt. The alcohol immediately ignited. The fire spread rapidly up Klein's shirt and over onto his sleeve. He didn't yell out.

Henry pressed his advantage. He took two steps toward Klein. With one backhanded swing, Henry hit the hand with the knife. The blade fell to the floor. Henry followed with a savage kick to the ribs.

Klein hoofed and grunted.

Ironically, some of the alcohol-infused fire found a home on Henry's pant leg. He patted it out. The same was not happening to Klein. The fire now had spread over his left side and arm. Now, he screamed.

"Enjoy the fire, you bastard. You're going straight to hell."

Henry left the fire to do its work. The screams would bring the attention of the neighbors and, soon, the police. He gave a split second's thought to rushing into his room to grab his clothes and other things. He decided against it. Those items could be replaced.

He risked a last glance down at Klein. The German was rolling on the floor, trying to put out the fire. What he also did was spread the flames.

Henry tore through the front door and closed it behind him. It was then that he saw his neighbors on the third floor all standing in doorways looking in his direction. The fire would consume the dried wood of this building and they'd lose everything.

Damn, he hated his conscience.

"Call the fire brigade!" Henry shouted. "There's a fire in my flat!"

Just because Henry had a conscience didn't mean he was going to stand around and help. He ran to the back stairs and took them two at a time to the ground floor. He burst out the back door and ran. He didn't have time to spare. He glanced up to his third-floor window. The fire from within flickered.

Henry turned and ran into the night.

20

The place where Lillian Saxton finally lay down to rest turned out to be the room Ludlow had rented. It was a two-room flat, with a common room in the middle. The Victorian furniture and generally old decor reminded her of the Sidney Paget illustrations of Sherlock Holmes in The Strand magazine. Upon entering the room at Ludlow's behest, the warmth and comfortable nature of the flat made her feel a little better. He had given her a key and sent her away by taxi. He had arrived a couple of hours later smelling like tobacco and Scotch.

They had talked, mainly about things other than the mission. Ludlow, it turned out, was a veteran of the first war. He moved up from a signalman to artillery to intelligence when he single-handedly deceived an entire German platoon into thinking they were going to raid a defenseless French farmhouse only to discover a squad of British soldiers ready to capture them. No shots were fired and Ludlow earned himself a new job.

In the years since, his devotion to duty manifested itself in moving higher and higher up the ranks of British intelligence. His imaginative genius at coming up with schemes led him to teach others his thought process. Henry was one of his top disciples. There were others, Ludlow had said over brandy as the two of them sat in matching arm chairs, but Henry was probably the best.

When the subject of her own country arose, they both conceded America needed to be a player. "It was only a matter of time," Lillian said.

"I hope it's as soon as possible."

Lillian held her own glass of brandy. "But with Hitler not actively doing anything, it's going to take a lot to get America in the war."

Ludlow sighed. "I just wish he'd move so we could get this

blasted war going again."

Lillian stood, stretched, and excused herself. She cleaned up in the small bathroom adjoining her room and lay down. The mattress was harder than she preferred but felt like clouds compared to the jailhouse bunk of the previous night. She began to run through the events of the past day and a half, but didn't get far. All-consuming sleep enveloped her.

The front door slamming open startled her awake. She checked her watch. She had been asleep for a little more than an hour. She reached over to the bedside table and grabbed her pistol. Standing, she pulled on a robe and opened her door.

Henry stood in the middle of the room talking with Ludlow. Henry's sleeve was bloody and his clothes disheveled. She caught a strong odor of alcohol and fire.

"What's going on?" Lillian asked.

"I'm afraid," Ludlow began, "the timetable for your journey to Belgium and Dover has been moved up. You're leaving now."

"Why? What happened?"

Henry turned to her. "Just following orders, yeah?"

She bristled, then ignored him. "What happened?" she asked Ludlow.

"Henry had a run-in with the last member of the German spy ring. There was an altercation. Henry came out on top, but left things in a rather sordid state."

"Look," Henry said, "I had no choice. It was him or me."

"True, my boy, but your emotions prompted you to take Klein out in a rather gruesome way."

Henry stopped pacing. "Don't tell me about emotions. I have had to stifle them for months! I've hated listening to him brag about all the people he's killed and tortured. You weren't there. So don't you damn well tell me what I should have done."

"But your actions will bring undue attention to our operation," Ludlow persisted. "I can assuage the locals, but if the building burns to the ground, we're going to have to reimburse all the new homeless."

Lillian put her gun in the robe's pocket. "You burned down

a building?"

"Casualty of war," Henry grunted. "Get dressed and pack your bags. We're leaving as fast as possible." When she didn't snap to it, Henry said, "Come on!"

Ludlow turned his head and smiled apologetically. "I'm afraid he's right, Sergeant. The authorities will be asking questions. Those questions will lead directly back to me. If you both are gone, it'll just be easier all around. Take my car. I'll catch the train down to London and get another."

"I need some money," Henry blurted. "I had to leave everything in the flat."

Ludlow pulled out his wallet and forked over everything he had. "Sergeant, on the jump!"

Still bristling at being ordered around by both of them, Lillian complied. Within a few minutes, she had changed into a brown traveling suit. All her belongings were in her leather valise. Her pistol was in the pocket of her jacket.

Henry gave her the once-over and cocked an eyebrow. "Always dress up for spy work?"

"You always burn down buildings?" she retorted.

"Touché to the both of you," Ludlow said. "Now, be on your way. Let me know when you get to Dover. I'd advise you to keep your homecoming as short as possible."

"Will do." Henry stopped in front of Ludlow and extended his hand. "Sir, thank you."

Ludlow grasped the proffered hand and shook it. "Always, my boy."

With a curt nod, Henry beckoned Lillian to follow him. They descended the stairs and hurried to the street. Ludlow's car turned out to be a four-door Armstrong Siddeley. Lillian didn't have a clue what kind of car it was until Henry mumbled the name out loud.

"Guess your boss likes to travel in style." Lillian threw her valise in the back seat.

"And he likes to drive fast, which'll help us now."

They both slid into the front seats. Henry started the car and gunned the engine. A grin creased his face. "I'm dog-tired but I'm gonna love driving this thing." Henry checked his rearview mirror and pulled out into the street. Neither one of them said anything while Henry concentrated on getting out of town.

When the lights of Liverpool dimmed along their rear horizon, Lillian asked, "How long a drive do we have?"

"Five hours."

Lillian turned and rummaged in her valise. She sat back in her seat. In her hands was a small alarm clock. She checked her watch, set the time, and then set the alarm. Finally, she placed the clock on the floorboard.

"I'll relieve you in two hours." Lillian said. "But for now, please drive with as few bumps as possible. I need to get some shuteye."

With that, Lillian Saxton eased herself lower in the seat and promptly fell asleep.

21

George Ludlow watched his prized Armstrong Siddeley drive away under Henry's strong hands. He loved that car. It took quite a few strings to pull in order for MI-5 to allow Ludlow to drive a private car for government business. But he had done it. And he was the talk of the bureau for it. His car was known among the diplomatic corps. The mere sight of it was enough to announce Ludlow's arrival. It was just like being the king.

He chuckled. Wide awake now, he moseyed across the room to the phone. He picked it up and asked for a line to London, the home office. While he waited, he poured another glass of brandy. Outside his windows, shadows overwhelmed all light.

There was a sound at the door. A rasping of metal on metal. It came from the doorknob and its lock. *Dear God*, Ludlow thought. *Someone was breaking into the house.*

Ludlow placed the phone on the table. He purposefully didn't end the call. He sipped the brandy, then placed the empty glass on the table. Opening a drawer, he slipped a snub-nosed revolver into his hand.

The rasping stopped when the lock clicked open. Ludlow considered rushing across the room and slamming the deadbolt back into place, but it would ultimately do no good. Whoever was out there would just pick the lock again and again. Better to make a stand now.

Ludlow settled into one of the wing chairs and doused the light. The movement outside the door stopped. A cough, then a groan. Then, the knob began to turn.

Ludlow pulled the hammer back. He waited.

The knob fully turned. The door whooshed open.

Ludlow fired. His bullet thunked into the far wall across the hallway. He was an excellent shot. He aimed where a man's body should be.

No person appeared in the doorway.

A dark shape darted across the open door. Ludlow fired again. He hit only air. Frustrated, Ludlow violated a cardinal rule in warfare: don't give up a secure position. He stood and walked to the door. He held the gun at the ready. Whoever was playing this game was going to lose.

Ludlow didn't see the object that flew through the air and hit him in the face. He only felt the searing pain of the thing as it struck his cheek. He grunted and staggered backward. The object rolled on the floor.

The person in the hall took that opportunity to surge into the room. The silhouette appeared odd to Ludlow. He couldn't put his finger on what was wrong. Nevertheless, he brought his pistol up to shoot the intruder.

The other person's foot connected with Ludlow's hand and sent the pistol skittering across the floor. The pain of the blow numbed Ludlow's arm for a moment.

The intruder bent down and grabbed handfuls of Ludlow's suit and shirt. He hauled the intelligence officer's body to his feet. Ludlow's shoes met only air.

Ludlow didn't wait long. He kicked out with one foot; it only glanced off the intruder's shin. Ludlow tried to knee the stranger. Surprisingly, the man—Ludlow knew it was a man; who else could lift him up?—pivoted and the knee missed.

In retaliation, the intruder slammed his forehead into Ludlow's face. Ludlow saw stars just after he heard his nose crack. Darkness met him. He blacked out.

***

George Ludlow woke. He didn't know where he was. His face was wet so he tried to raise his hand to wipe it. His hand wouldn't move. Within seconds, he determined he was tied to one of his wooden chairs. The lights in the flat were on and he angled his head to see how bad the bindings were.

They were bad. Both wrists and ankles were secured to

the chair arms and legs. The attacker had used Ludlow's own belts, drilling new, ragged holes for the belt pin. Ludlow felt no clearance in the bonds.

He frowned. Over in the corner, sitting on the floor, was a grenade. The pin was still in place. That must have been the object that had struck him in the face.

"Good," the stranger said, "you're awake."

Ludlow spun his head and wished he hadn't. Waves of nausea flipped his stomach. All the brandy and food he had consumed flooded up and out of him. The sickness landed on his lap and down his shirt.

"That's disgusting." The intruder stepped into Ludlow's field of vision.

If he hadn't already vomited, chances were he'd have done it at that moment. The other man's left side was burned. The wound was fresh. Blood and pus seeped from the other man's cheeks. The eyes weren't affected, but the lower half of the left side of the face appeared melted.

"Dear God," Ludlow muttered. "You're hideous."

"Do I look that bad? There wasn't anything I could do. Your man did this to me. I knew him as Becker. What's his real name?" The stranger stood in front of Ludlow.

The intelligence man frowned. "Are you wearing my clothes?"

The other man shrugged. "Turns out, we're almost the same size."

Ludlow gazed up at the man and studied the undamaged side. In his mind, he ran through photographs of men he had been watching until he found a match. "You're Klein."

"You know me. That's wonderful. It'll help our chat." He reached into his back pocket and pulled out a wallet. Ludlow recognized it as his own. "You would be George Ludlow. British intelligence. That means the man I knew as Becker is British intelligence as well. I had already figured that, but confirmation is always good."

Klein walked across the room, grabbed a chair, and returned. Sitting at Ludlow's side. The German made sure to keep his burned side close to the Briton.

"That's a bad burn," Ludlow said. "You should put something on that."

"Hurts like hell, but we've got something to discuss. What is Becker's mission?"

Ludlow found his inner strength. He sat up straighter in the chair and stared straight ahead. "You will get nothing from me."

"We'll see about that."

Ludlow put as much anger in his voice as possible. "You forget: I have been through the last war. I can resist."

Klein smacked Ludlow across the face. "You arrogant Brits. You haven't figured out this is a new war." From past Ludlow's field of vision, Klein picked up something and showed it to Ludlow.

It was the brandy decanter.

Klein opened the lid and threw it across the room. He sniffed the liquor. He put his lips to the rim and drank deep. Some of the alcohol ran up and over his lips and down his burned cheeks. The German sucked air through his teeth at the pain.

"Damn, that hurts."

With nonchalance, Klein poured some of the brandy on Ludlow's thigh. "Do you want to know how your man did this to me?" He poured enough to soak the pants fabric. "We were fighting. I was going to best him and he knew it. So he cheated." Klein pulled Ludlow's handkerchief from Ludlow's breast pocket and shoved it into Ludlow's mouth. "Let me show you."

He took a matchbook from the writing desk. He lit one match and dropped it onto Ludlow's leg.

The heat was almost instantaneous. The fabric caught fire up and down his thigh. Some of the brandy soaked up to his groin. The flame followed where the brandy was.

Ludlow screamed like he had never screamed before in his life. It seemed like forever, but it was only seconds. Before he knew it, Klein had taken a towel and tamped out the fire.

Breathing heavily through his nose, Ludlow moaned. The next thing he knew, Klein poured some of the brandy on the burned leg.

The stinging seared though him. He yelled again.

Klein waited for Ludlow to regain his composure.

"Now, Mr. Ludlow, how much more of this can you endure?" Klein leaned forward and lit another match with his fingernail. "Tell me what Becker's real name is and his mission. And who was that woman he left with?"

***

Herr Colonel finally arrived at his house after midnight. He opened the door with his key. The door creaked like a clarion call. He cursed. He had been meaning to take care of that squeak for days now, but work always interfered. He made a mental note to tend to the hinges first thing in the morning before the day's activities.

Unfortunately for him, the squeak woke up his wife. Even here, in the entry foyer to his house, he heard the stirrings and the springs creak. He sighed. She was a light sleeper. Chances were he'd fall asleep faster than she would.

In a concession for quiet, he sat and removed his boots and socks. His feet ached from being cramped all day. He enjoyed being a part of the military organization here in Berlin. He didn't particularly enjoy having to wear a proper uniform all the time. Give him the traditional professor's uniform of a suit, tie, and loafers and he could go all day and never be uncomfortable.

Herr Colonel padded his way down the main hall. His reading room appeared ghostly in the dim light. He noted the little table next to his favorite chair. A small stack of books remained unread, waiting for him to return. With the impending invasion, he had been working longer hours than before. Whatever free time he earned he spent with Wilma. Reading was what he had to give up for *der Führer*.

Walking down the hall, Herr Colonel unbuttoned his uniform coat and removed it. The waft of stress sweat met his nose and he grimaced. He detoured to the bathroom. Without turning on the light, he wetted a washcloth and wiped his face, neck, and armpits. He brushed his teeth, making sure to get the little tendrils of beef out from between his teeth. Satisfied, he continued his walk to his bedroom. He hoped his wife had fallen back asleep.

"Long night," Wilma said when he silently opened the bedroom door. He had already made sure to fix those hinges.

He sighed deeply. "*Ja*." He draped his uniform jacket over a chair and unbuckled his pants.

"Can you tell me about it?"

He sighed again. "*Nein*." He peeled off his undershirt and boxers. He sauntered over to his dresser to retrieve a fresh pair of underwear.

"You won't need those," his wife said.

The next thing he knew, he felt her touch on his arm. It was light but firm, pulling him to bed. He didn't resist. He slid into the warm sheets and felt his wife's soft skin all along his body. Despite the hour, his excitement grew.

His lips found hers. Long hours had kept him away from her. She had complained, quietly, but always understood. The needs of the government sometimes outweighed the needs of the individual.

Not tonight. Tonight, the needs of two individuals would be met.

After they finished, they lay together. They had thrown the sheets off them. Their breathing calmed. Wilma turned on her side and put her arm over her husband's chest. Her lips whispered in his ear, "I love you."

"I love you, too."

Herr Colonel drifted off to a peaceful sleep.

That was broken an hour later by a ringing phone.

He jumped awake. The arm that was under his wife's neck felt numb.

Wilma cursed and sat up.

Herr Colonel retrieved his numb arm, all tingling with pins and needles, and stumbled across the room to the phone stand.

He snatched the receiver.

"What is it?" With so little sleep, he made no attempt to mask his anger.

"Herr Colonel, sir, my apologies for waking you, but it's urgent."

"Then get on with it."

"We've got a message from England. Liverpool in particular."

Anger vanished from him. "Tell me."

"He's still on the line."

"Who?"

"Our agent in Liverpool. Rolf Klein."

Herr Colonel sat at the table. He flicked on the small lamp.

Wilma groaned. She turned over and put a pillow over her head.

Herr Colonel pulled a pad and pencil over. "Go."

There were a few moments of static and rustling. Then, a voice. "Herr Colonel?"

"*Ja.*"

"This is Klein. We have a problem in Liverpool."

"Tell me."

Herr Colonel jotted notes as fast as Klein talked. The operation in Liverpool had been compromised. Otto was dead. Buckley was arrested. Becker wasn't who he said he was. He was a man named Henry Clark. He worked for British intelligence. He left with a woman.

"Who was she?"

"Don't know yet."

"Any clue as to Clark's mission?"

"The man I questioned gave up some information, but not that." The note of frustration in his voice sounded real.

A chill ran down Herr Colonel's spine. He knew men such as Klein were an integral part of intelligence work and the methods deployed were sometimes necessary, but he didn't like it. He knew Klein only through reports, but other members of the organization spoke highly of the field agent. Over beers in pubs, those other men, all military, laughed at what Klein would do to get what he wanted.

"Well, he gave up some information, but I'm not sure I trust it," Klein went on.

"What is it?"

"He said Clark was heading down to London for further instructions."

That seemed a blanket misdirect. On a whim, Herr Colonel asked about the American, Frank Monroe.

"The subject didn't come up. I didn't know to ask."

Of course he wouldn't. If the reports were accurate, Klein had been temporarily deployed up to Glasgow to take care of a traitor who had revealed sensitive information to the local police. His memory wasn't as sharp at this time of night, but Herr Colonel thought the mission was supposed to last another day. He asked Klein about it.

"The mission went better than expected. I finished early."

Another chill coursed through Herr Colonel.

Thoughts raced in Herr Colonel's mind. He tried to put some of the pieces in a logical order. Frank Monroe, an American banker, was being followed all the way from the United States. He landed in Liverpool with a traveling companion, a woman. Word from higher up in the chain of command had instructed an agent named Johannes Bauer to acquire a book Frank Monroe carried. In addition, the daily report from Liverpool was empty. Herr Colonel chalked that up to the raid.

But Bauer would have reported in before that. He was to pick up Monroe's tail two nights ago. His activities should have been in that earlier report. They weren't. That indicated something had gone wrong.

"Klein, listen. Our task was to follow the American, Monroe, and see where he was going. He is carrying a book we need. It might lead us to figure out why Monroe met with another American down in Belgium last month." He told Klein what he knew about the meeting.

"I know you don't always know how we operate," Klein began—Herr Colonel bristled at the insult—"but I would say that Monroe and the other American are spies. Something was passed between them and it's in that book." He paused. "Would you like to have me to look around, find out what happened to Bauer? And locate Monroe?"

Herr Colonel thought about it. He didn't like not knowing where Monroe was. He didn't relish delivering the news to his commanding officer that an agent was missing. He needed to know.

"Yes. See what you can find and report back to me."

"Yes, Herr Colonel." Klein hung up.

Herr Colonel put the phone back on its cradle. He scanned his notes. Liverpool station down. Otto dead. Becker a British agent undercover. Buckley arrested. No word from Bauer. No known location of Monroe. Klein still active. Soon, he knew Klein would have answers for him.

"Turn off the light if you're done," Wilma mumbled from under the pillow.

"Apologies, my dear." Herr Colonel complied. He slid back into bed next to his wife. He pulled the sheet up to cover them both. He stared at the ceiling and the shadows of the window panes. Sleep did not come soon.

22

Lillian Saxton awoke to the sight of headlights coming straight for her.

She screamed. The lorry's driver blared his horn.

Henry Clark started. He noted the situation and swerved. The automobile caromed off the paved road and into the adjoining field. He brought the car to a halt. Dust motes swirled in the headlight's glare.

"What the hell were you doing?" Lillian yelled. Henry stammered a response but Lillian cut him off. "You were sleeping." She pointed back at the lorry which had stopped. The driver was hustling over to them. "We can't complete this mission if you keep slacking off."

Henry held up a finger. "I wasn't slacking off."

"You fell asleep while driving!" She shoved him. "Get out. I'm driving."

"Like hell you are."

The lorry driver arrived. His scruffy face and jowly cheeks made him look like a bulldog. "Everything okay here?"

"No." Lillian reached over and snagged the keys from the ignition. "My friend here just fell asleep at the wheel. Can you help me trade places?"

"Sure thing." The lorry driver opened the driver's door. "C'mon, mate. Let the lady drive."

In the semi-darkness, Henry glared at her.

Lillian met his gaze evenly. "Get out."

Henry shook off the lorry driver's attempts to help him. He stormed around the rear of the car.

Lillian got out and walked around the front. Her heart thudded in her chest.

"Are you okay to drive, miss?"

"I'm fine," she said. "Are you okay?"

"As rain, miss. Thanks for asking."

"Good. My apologies for my traveling companion. Maybe he needs some remedial driving courses." She and the lorry driver chuckled. They shook hands and Lillian climbed behind the wheel. She glanced at Henry.

He glared at her.

Lillian ignored him. She started the engine and familiarized herself with the controls. "If we're going to meet your dad, don't you think it would be better in this car than in a morgue?"

Henry grunted.

"Suit yourself."

"I bet you don't even know how to handle a car like this," Henry challenged.

Lillian placed her hands on her chin and imitated a damsel in distress from a Hollywood movie. "Oh my, this is a car and I'm just a lady. How could I ever hope to drive this thing?" She arched an eyebrow and threw the car into gear. Dirt flew up behind them as she guided the Armstrong Siddeley back onto the road.

Henry grunted again, this time, not as deep. He made to sleep.

"No way, mister." She elbowed his side. "You have to stay awake and make sure I stay awake." She indicated the alarm clock on the floorboard. "That never went off. If we're going to do this mission, we at least need to help each other. Right now, let's chat."

"About what?"

"Anything you'd like. Tell me about your undercover work. How long were you with them?"

Henry settled into the seat and began talking. He had volunteered for the undercover mission because he spoke fluent German. When he said that, Lillian, who also spoke German, tested him. After a few minutes, she had to admit he was good.

But so was she.

Henry had infiltrated the spy ring eleven months ago, just before the Nazis invaded Poland. Ever since then, he had been relaying information back to the home office via coded messages at the local grocery store. It was the one place Henry could convincingly go alone. None of the other members of the spy ring liked the drudgery of buying food and cooking. Henry became that man.

"You cook?" Lillian put a false mocking tone in her voice.

"Yeah. You're a spy?" He mimicked her tone.

"Yes, I am."

"How many other lady spies in your government?"

"Not sure. We like to keep secrets. I know a few. None like me."

"Oh yeah? Why's that?"

"Detached in Britain. Near the front lines. Most of the other women I know are not part of the Army. They're all attached to the State Department. That makes me unique."

Henry continued his story. Every three days, he would stock up on food items. When Otto had asked why he didn't just buy more food, Henry had told him about spoilage and reminded the German that he, Henry, was the cook. In the grocery store, Henry always bought fresh bread. While standing in line, waiting, he would surreptitiously pass a report to another patron. Always one of two men so any onlookers wouldn't get suspicious. In exchange, Henry's contact would deliver new instructions from the home office. That was how Henry came to know about Frank Monroe. "He was your friend?"

Lillian loosened her grip on the steering wheel. "Yes. He and I attended Oxford together."

"You came over here for school?"

"I did. It was as far away from California as I could get."

"Bad memories there?" Henry asked.

"You could say that. Anyway, he and I were part of a tight group of friends. The man we're going to meet, James Geiger, was also a member of the group. James and I were an item."

"Hold on a minute," Henry cut in. "The man we're meeting is an old flame?"

Lillian nodded.

"That puts a whole new spin on things. Why'd he ask you to come?"

Lillian shrugged.

"Gonna get back together with him?"

"Not at all. He's married."

"That doesn't always mean anything."

"It does with me." She put a lot of emphasis on her words. "I don't know why he asked for me," she lied. In her mind, she re-read the second coded message from James: "I know who killed Samuel." She remained mum on that subject to Henry. All James was going to provide was a name. It would be up to her to do something about it.

But now she had a second ulterior motive: she wanted to see if she could find out who ordered Frank killed. And her, for that matter. The man, Bauer, she had taken out in Liverpool was only following orders. There was a higher authority involved. And she damn well was going to find out who.

And make him pay.

Frank's voice drifted into her mind. "Judge, jury, and executioner?"

She shook her head to clear that voice.

"So," Henry said, "we're going to see your old lover with his new wife?"

"I don't think she'll be there. He didn't say anything about her."

Henry barked out a laugh. "Of course not. Why would he tell his wife he was to meet an old girlfriend?"

Lillian had no comment on that subject. She had never even thought James's wife—what was her name?—would be there. All she expected from him was the delivery of the codebook and the name. Then they'd part ways again, likely never to see each other again. If it hadn't been for the second coded message, Lillian might not have even been going to Belgium.

No, check that. She would. It was now a military mission. She was in the Army. She followed orders, no matter her personal feelings. Except this time, orders and personal feelings merged.

They continued talking and chatting until they saw the dim line of dawn peek over the horizon. Just before they reached the outskirts of London, they switched positions. This allowed Lillian to get a sense of the great city she had never seen. Henry steered them around the capital, regaling her with interesting tidbits about the landmarks and his upbringing.

Soon, London faded into the distance and the gentle green countryside of southwest England emerged. By the brightness of early morning, they arrived in the coast city of Dover. Henry skirted the coastline and drove north. The English Channel was a gorgeous blue that reflected the sun's rays. Before Lillian knew it, Henry slowed the car and pulled into a small neighborhood. The houses were old but well maintained. He came to the end of one street and pulled up in front of the last house. He killed the engine.

"This is it." He opened the door and got out.

Lillian gazed at the little bungalow. Flowers in the beds were in full bloom. The yard was neatly maintained. Even the house itself appeared to have a new coat of paint. She got out.

An older man emerged from the side of the house. He carried a bag full of garden tools. He wore brown work pants and a work shirt dirty with soil.

The old man took one look at Henry and dropped his bag of tools. "As I live and breathe."

Henry walked to the old man. Lillian heard the word "Pop" emerge from Henry's mouth before the two embraced.

***

By noon, Herr Colonel was in a foul mood. He noticed his underlings going out of their way to avoid him. He didn't care. He had had precious little sleep the night before and, despite the romantic detour, still felt restless.

He waited all morning for any news from England. The lead agent in England, a man named Erwin stationed in London, had scoured all the available newspapers and listened to all broadcasts. Finally, just as he was leaving for lunch, Herr Colonel received a special message. According to news reports, an American had died of food poisoning at the Adelphi Hotel. The name was withheld pending a formal inquiry. Local police were also investigating the beating death of another man outside the hotel.

Herr Colonel read the message in disbelief. He didn't dare jump to the conclusion that this American was Monroe. He had no data to go on. But something in his gut told him it was true. Bauer had been assigned to intercept Monroe and get the book by any means. Would he have been so brazen as to poison a foreign national in the middle of a restaurant?

The food Herr Colonel ate for lunch was tasteless and uninspiring. He consumed it only because his body needed nourishment. He ate at his desk, reading report after report but not the one he truly wanted. He barked at all his subordinates who disturbed him if they didn't bring what he wanted. He longed to find the notes so he could figure out what to do next.

It wasn't until late afternoon that the message he wanted finally arrived. Wilhelm delivered it. He wore a grin on his face. "I think this is what you've been waiting on, Herr Colonel."

"I'll be the judge of that." He snatched the printed paper out of Wilhelm's hand and read.

"Monroe dead by Bauer. Bauer dead by Monroe's friend. Monroe's friend gone. Murder of Ludlow discovered. Assume Monroe's friend is same woman I saw leaving with Clark. Orders?"

Herr Colonel re-read the communique three times. The implications startled him. Frank Monroe was dead, but the book was unrecovered. It was clear that this woman with whom he traveled was part of this. Last month, Monroe and Geiger met in Belgium. Monroe went to America then returned to Europe, this time with a woman. The obvious conclusion was that Monroe and Geiger were going to meet again, perhaps in Belgium.

And yet Monroe and this mystery woman were intercepted

by Bauer in Liverpool. Monroe was killed but the woman took out Bauer before he could deliver a report to Berlin. Now, Monroe's friend was traveling with Henry Clark, a known British intelligence agent, presumably to complete the meeting with Geiger.

Why?

Herr Colonel stood. "Get me a meeting with General Siegfried. I need to alert him of a new development."

Wilhelm saluted and scurried to comply.

Herr Colonel pulled a cigarette out of his desk case and lit it. With what he knew about James Geiger, Herr Colonel couldn't be positive the American was delivering secrets to their enemies, but the likelihood was there. Frank Monroe was called in to help. Now Monroe was dead, but his friend—a woman no less—was carrying on the mission.

He buzzed the intercom. "Come." An adjutant entered the office.

"Yes, Herr Colonel?"

"I need everything we have on an American, James Geiger. He's living in Berlin and working for *der Führer*. On the jump!"

The adjutant saluted and left.

The wheels were turning, Herr Colonel thought.

He only wished he knew who was driving.

23

One of the talents Lillian Saxton had learned in her stint in the Army involved the ability to sleep anywhere. Anywhere, on this day, turned out to be a small guest room in the house of Henry's father, Simon. He and his late wife, Mary, were part of big families. Cousins, uncles, aunts, and grandparents all came to visit this home by the sea. Simon had built the add-on to accommodate the constant flow of people. Lillian was just the latest to arrive.

When Henry had introduced Lillian to Simon, the older man smiled warmly. Simon's hand was dry and leathery, but he held hers delicately, as if she might break. He gave his son a questioning look, to which Henry shook his head. "She's a work colleague."

"A woman?"

"An *American* woman, Pop." Henry added emphasis to the word American.

Simon then gave Lillian new appreciation. "Love Americans. They saved us in the last war. You'll probably have to do it again."

They had gone inside and eaten a hearty breakfast of eggs, bacon, and bread. The coffee was hot and stout. The kitchen was small and still possessed the womanly touches with which Mary had adorned her domain. The three talked about the war, when the Nazis might make their next move, and London's response. Simon didn't think Prime Minister Neville Chamberlain was going to do anything worthwhile.

"There's another up there, named Churchill. He'd be a good one." Simon's accent sounded distinctly English to Lillian's ears.

"But he's not the PM, Pop."

"He should be. The speeches he's given make me think he sees the world as it is, not how folks want it to be."

The conversation grew quiet. Henry circled a finger around

his coffee cup, gazing down at it. "Pop, I'm sorry I wasn't able to come down when Mom died." His voice was small, apologetic, and childlike.

Simon's lower lip quivered. He inhaled deeply and put on the best smile he could. "That's okay, son. I know you were working for the king. That kind of service always gets in the way of personal lives."

"My condolences, as well," Lillian said.

Simon reached over and patted her arm. "Thank you, miss." He looked up at a photograph of him and his wife on their wedding day. "My Mary was a remarkable woman. Cancer took her too soon from me. The last war took one of my nephews. Do you know I pray every day that my boy only goes to sleep at night, that he doesn't sleep with the Lord? I'm not sure what I'd do if I lost you, son."

The two men, stoic up until that moment, wept together. Lillian, as quiet as possible, eased out of her chair and walked outside. She made her way down the street. Her thoughts traveled back to California. It was true her parents loved her, but they never understood her. They didn't understand why she wanted to go to college, get away from their homely life, and do something grand. They especially didn't understand when Lillian moved out of their home and started living at the estate of Kenji Tanaka. The day that happened was an ugly day for the Saxton family. Her father, Todd, showed his true colors by making racist slurs against Tanaka. Lillian, young and impetuous, still recovering from the double broken heart delivered by Frank and James in Paris, lashed out verbally.

It was the kind of phrase that resonated long past its utterance and hearing. She had seen her parents sporadically since then, and the after effects of that day still dominated the silences between them.

Henry Clark, on the other hand, seemed to come from a happy family. Well, sad without Mary, but a family that loved each other and wasn't afraid to show it. What a way to grow up.

She reached a small rise. The view over the hill was

breathtaking. The famous cliffs of Dover down to the south gleamed in the morning sunlight. Boats and people worked the waters and the ports down below. The grass in the nearby fields was as green as she'd ever seen. It was a beautiful sight. She breathed deeply the lush fragrance of peace.

Henry ambled up to stand beside her. "Sorry for all that crying back there." He sniffed and tried to pass it off as allergies.

"It's perfectly fine. You grew up here?"

"All my life until I left for the service."

"It's magnificent."

He shook his head as he took it all in. "I don't get down here much, and not at all since the last assignment. But I love it here. Reminds me of why I do what I do. To protect this, these people, this land, this way of life. Hitler's version of life is a prison. You seem to know it. Wonder why it's taking your country so long to see it."

Lillian blew out a long gust of air. "Hell if I know. Well, no, I do know. We're safe with both oceans surrounding us. Germany's certainly not going to mount an invasion of New York and Japan's so far away, they'd never invade L.A. Mexico's on our side, or, at least, not with the Nazis. It's a tranquil paradise."

"Wonder what it'll take to get you in?"

"Not sure I want to find out."

Henry motioned with his head back to his house. "C'mon. I told Pop we both need some sleep. Then, later on, before we head on over to London, I'd like to show you where my mom is."

"That'd be nice."

Lillian and Henry walked back to the house. Once inside, Lillian took the guest room while Henry retreated to the room in which he had grown up. She wondered what it would be like for her to return to her house in San Diego. Would she be able to sleep in the room that brought not only joy but heartache? This room, on the other hand, was wonderful. She pulled the shades and curtains, but a little light still intruded into the room. It didn't matter. Within five minutes of laying her head on the pillow, Lillian Saxton was sound asleep.

***

"General Siegfried requests your presence," Wilhelm informed his superior officer.

Herr Colonel looked up from the stacks of paper on his desk. Reading glasses were perched on his nose. "Why?"

"He didn't say. Just to come get you."

Herr Colonel's heart beat a little faster. He had a nice position in the hierarchy, with enough independence to do what he wanted. But General Siegfried, veteran of the first war, could tug Herr Colonel's leash whenever it suited him. He didn't do it often, but when he did, Herr Colonel's days grew markedly worse.

Herr Colonel stood and straightened his uniform. He grabbed a pad of paper and pencil and strode out of his office, chin held high. The outer office was ablaze with activity. Rows of desks were populated by uniformed men and women dutifully toiling at their tasks. Like Herr Colonel, each one had a gift for espionage and a keen sense they were among the lucky ones not to be out in the field.

The general's secretary smiled without humor at Herr Colonel. She rose and, without a word, opened the door. Herr Colonel walked in and saluted.

General Hans Siegfried sat behind his desk, a cigarette dangling from his lips. His gray hair was cut in proper military fashion. His uniform looked impeccably pressed. Herr Colonel subtly straightened his tunic.

Siegfried didn't look up. "Sit."

Herr Colonel sat. The secretary closed the door.

"You have been asking questions about one of my operations." He made the comment as a statement. He dropped the file he had been reading on his desk and folded his hands. "Why?"

Herr Colonel spoke clearly. "Herr General, my operation has

been following an American banker, Frank Monroe. He arrived in Belgium last month and met with another American, James Geiger. Geiger lives in Berlin with his German wife, Elsa. He also helps with the codes based on his mathematics degree. I feared some secrets might be passed between them."

"I know." Siegfried's lips appeared parched and dry.

Herr Colonel was momentarily speechless. He recovered quickly. "With Monroe dead by our hand, yet the mission continuing, I wanted to learn more about Geiger and determine if he was a person who would betray us or if it is a big misunderstanding."

Herr General wetted his lips. "How do you know the mission is continuing?"

"There's a book Geiger supposedly gave to Monroe. He took it to America with him. The next thing we knew, Monroe was returning to Europe with the book and a woman. When he was removed in Liverpool, our assets there were unable to locate the book. Presumably the woman, accompanied by a British intelligence officer who infiltrated our operation..."

"*Your* operation," Herr General blurted.

"Yes, Herr General, my operation." He paused when Siegfried grunted with derision. "This man, named Clark, is now missing. So is the woman."

"Any idea who the woman is?"

"None, Herr General."

"How do you know the British man is an agent?" Siegfried stubbed out his cigarette. He lit another.

"One of our agents, a man named Klein, obtained the information from a reliable source." He let the words hang in the air, their meaning perfectly clear.

"I know. Klein is one of our best in Britain. He gets results. He questioned a high-ranking British intelligence officer. The man's name was Ludlow. He was a veteran of the first war. If he gave up any information, it should be regarded as questionable. A man of his stature, knowing death was imminent at the hands of a foreign agent, would at best give up a misdirect. At worst, an outright lie." His eyes bore into Herr Colonel. "True military minds would know that."

Herr Colonel straightened his back. "I do know that, Herr General. That is one of the reasons I ordered my staff to create a dossier on Geiger. I wanted to see if he was leaking any secrets. It's also the reason I had my staff scour British phone records and addresses, looking for all the Henry Clarks in the country. Turns out there were quite a lot."

The smugness on Siegfried's face irked Herr Colonel but he continued. "But then I thought about Clark. He's been undercover for months. Yes, sir, I know he infiltrated our organization. We can tighten our ranks. But the point is that Henry Clark likely had no direct communication with the outside world during his time with us. Sure, he talked with other British agents, but he probably never called home."

"Your point, Herr Colonel?" Siegfried had already smoked the new cigarette down to a nub. He jammed it into the ashtray and folded his hands.

The general wasn't always talked to this way. Herr Colonel knew it and inwardly liked it.

"With all the Henry Clarks in the country, it is an impossible task with the time we have remaining to us. But if we scour obituaries, we might have a clue."

Herr Colonel was proud of himself for making Siegfried speechless. He tried his best to keep the grin threatening to burst onto his face from showing itself as Herr General caught up with Herr Colonel's line of reasoning. Finally, the superior officer nodded.

"Good thinking, Herr Colonel."

"Thank you, Herr General."

"Did you find any records of recent deaths of a person named Clark?"

"We did." Now the grin broke free. "And it's on the way to Belgium."

"Where?"

"Dover."

"Have you assigned any assets?"

"Yes, Herr General. They are already on the way."

24

The final resting place for Mary Clark was in Ramsgate, a half-hour's drive up the coast. Some gravestones in Ramsgate Cemetery have been there longer than America has been a country. At first, it took Lillian's breath away. Soon, however, she became fascinated and studied the names and dates, imagining the lives these people led.

She held back while Henry walked with his father to his mother's gravesite. Out of earshot, she didn't need any sound to note Henry's slumped shoulders. They shook. Simon put his arm around his son's shoulders and held tight.

How Lillian longed for that type of closeness with her parents. She was sure her choice to leave home and stay with Kenji Tanaka had severed ties like that. One day, she might have to find out.

After a while, Henry walked back to her. He tried his best to hide the evidence of his tears and sadness. She acted like he had succeeded.

"It's a lovely place, this cemetery. She'll rest well here." Lillian angled her head up at him. "I'm sorry you weren't here when she died."

"King and country, right?" A sniffle escaped.

They had slept for the better part of the day. It was too short, but enough to regenerate them both. After a late lunch of beef, cheese, and bread, they had come out here. As nice as it was, Lillian was itching to get moving, get back on the mission. It was her perfect way to avoid thinking about the family relationship Henry had that she did not.

"You have a nice family. Are you the only child?"

"No. I have an older brother who's already in the RAF and a younger sister. She's away at university up in Cambridge. You?"

"Youngest of three. The other two are my brothers. Only

girl. Lots of expectations there." She let the implications die. He didn't pick them up. She didn't know if he was being nice or didn't have a clue.

"Expectations. They're a bitch, aren't they?"

Lillian chuckled. Maybe he did pick up on things.

Simon strolled up. Unlike his son, he didn't bother hiding his grief. His eyes were red-rimmed. "Thank you for coming."

"I'm sorry about your wife." Lillian gripped Simon's hand and squeezed. "She sounds like a wonderful woman."

"One in a million." Simon stood straighter and inhaled deeply. "But she also wouldn't want us to be all weepy. You have a job to do. How do you plan on getting over the Channel?"

"That's what we're going to figure out once we get to London."

"London?" his father said. "Why you going to London?"

"We've got to check in with the home office. They're the ones who will tell us how to get over the Channel. I phoned them this morning, told them where we were. They're sending out a car."

Lillian didn't like the idea of a phone call to the home office. They were on the clock. James had told her to meet in Belgium by May 9. He was specific with that request.

From over the rise, a car puttered up to the church at the center of the cemetery. It was a black convertible, the top pulled down. In the back seat, leaning at a angle, was a golf bag. The clubs rattled around.

The driver all but leaped out of the car. He wore knickers, an argyle sweater vest, and a tweed driving cap. He looked exactly like Lillian would expect a golfer to look.

The driver looked around, saw the three of them, and sauntered over. He carried a bouquet of flowers and placed them at the gravesite next to which they stood. He crossed himself. "It's a shame she had to die like that."

"She had so much promise," Henry responded.

Lillian frowned, then realized it was a code. This driver was their man from London.

"Tobias Monk." The driver made no motion to acknowledge Henry. "I'll be your driver to London."

"Golf clubs?" Henry said.

Monk shrugged. "I got in nine holes before I came here."

Henry arched an eyebrow at Lillian. She smirked with humor.

"My pop's car is on the west side. Meet us there in five minutes."

Monk nodded and departed. He started the car. The engine roared to life. He executed a large U-turn and exited the way he had arrived.

Henry put his arm around his father and the three of them walked down the hill to the west side of the cemetery. Henry told his father nothing about the mission, other than it was important. Simon understood, but Lillian, who walked a few paces behind the pair, noticed the older man's slumped shoulders. He appeared to carry the weight of a man who hoped and prayed to see his son again, but feared the worst.

Henry pulled his own bag, stocked with old clothes from his closet, from his father's car. He took Lillian's bag for her.

Lillian reached out her hand, but he left it empty. *Odd*, she thought. *Why would he do that?*

Monk's little black convertible was a four-seater. Lillian couldn't place the model, but if Ludlow's Armstrong Siddeley was any indication, the agent of British intelligence certainly drove in style.

Monk hopped out of the car and came around to the trunk. He opened it and placed both their bags inside. "Ready?"

Lillian nodded with her chin. "You need to put up the top." When Henry looked at her askance, she pointed to her hair. "No scarf."

Henry and Monk looked at each other. Monk shrugged, Henry shrugged, and Lillian rolled her eyes. "Do you need help?"

"Nope, we got it." Both men set about pulling the cover over the passenger area of the car.

Simon took Lillian's hand in his. "It was a pleasure to meet you." He hugged her. "Please take care of my boy." His voice choked with emotion. He hugged her a little tighter.

Surprised, Lillian hugged him back. "We'll take care of each other. It's a short mission. Low key. We'll be back within a week."

They pulled apart. Simon looked at her and smiled.

"Ready?" Monk's voice was entirely too cheery.

Henry and Simon hugged each other. Then, Lillian, Henry, and Monk piled into the car. Monk put the car in gear and peeled out.

"Sit back and enjoy the ride." Monk settled back behind the wheel and started the ninety-minute ride to London.

Lillian, somewhat cramped in the back seat with the golf clubs, decided she much preferred the roominess of the Armstrong Siddeley. To compensate, she rested her back on the side of her seat. This not only gave her a view of the front, she could also see out the back.

That meant she was the first one to notice the black car and two motorcycles that started following them a few miles outside of Dover.

25

"Hey," Lillian Saxton said to the two men in the front seat, "take a look at what's behind us."

Henry turned in the seat to stare out the rear window. He frowned.

"I've seen them for the past few miles," Monk said.

"They're riding your tail," Lillian commented.

"I'll pull over, let them pass."

Lillian and Henry exchanged a glance. Henry continued to watch as Monk, while not slowing, eased the convertible to the shoulder of the road.

The black car sped up and made to pass. The motorcycles hung back. Both Lillian and Henry kept their eyes peeled, but the fabric of the convertible top obscured Lillian's line of sight for a few seconds. Instead she turned to watch the motorcycles. She saw the two riders pull guns from their jackets and aim for them.

"Gun!" she and Henry yelled at the same time. The next moment, she noted that the man in the passenger seat of the passing car had also pulled a gun. A shot rang out. The side window she faced shattered.

"Step on it," Henry commanded, but Monk had already jammed his foot on the gas pedal. The convertible jumped ahead.

The black car responded in kind, matching Monk's speed. The motorcyclists opened fire on them. Most of their bullets whizzed by, but one ripped a tear in the fabric of the convertible cover.

In her time with the Army, Lillian had been in a few car chases. She knew how to maneuver, how to veer this way and that, or jam a car into a pursuing car. She waited for Monk to deploy some countermeasures. The young man gripped the wheel with steady determination but was basically driving in a straight line along the road.

That would not do.

Wham!

The black car slammed its front bumper into the side of the convertible. The convertible skidded along the gravel on the shoulder, then Monk righted the convertible.

"Lose them," Henry shouted.

"I'm trying," Monk retorted.

"Try harder. Knock them off the road."

More gunfire from the motorcycle riders.

Lillian pulled her pistol from the pocket of her jacket. She only had thirteen bullets in the chamber. The rest of her ammunition was in her valise trapped in the trunk.

The black car eased forward, then quickly moved behind the convertible as a lorry trundled by on the opposite lane. The black car blocked the approach of the motorcycles which had to fall back to avoid being smashed. With a lurch of speed, the black car sped up and matched Monk's driving speed.

"Head down!" Henry aimed his gun at the approaching car. He didn't get a shot off before their assailant let loose a volley of gunfire. The rear windshield blew out in a thousand pieces.

Lillian found herself with a lapful of broken glass.

The flying bullets found a victim. One moment, Tobias Monk was driving the car on a steady pace. The next moment, a bullet blasted its way into his brain. He was dead almost instantly.

"Bloody hell!" Henry shouted.

Lillian glanced forward. The convertible maintained the same momentum for a few moments before slowly edging across the road.

"Move him! I'll cover." Lillian sat up and aimed her pistol through the shattered window. She let off three quick shots. All three thudded into the side of the black car. One bullet spider-webbed the front windshield. As a result, the black car veered wide, away from the convertible.

Behind them, the motorcyclists sped up and continued their

barrage.

Lillian heard the sounds of hot lead thunking into the trunk.

She risked a glance over the front seat. The convertible, with Monk's dead foot only halfway on the gas pedal, began to lose speed. Henry couldn't properly slide under or over Monk's corpse and get behind the wheel.

"Hurry up!" she shouted. "They're getting closer."

Henry made a decision. He reached over to the door. He pulled the latch and opened the driver's side door. With a mighty shove, he pushed Monk's dead body out of the car. The convertible slowed even more as Henry positioned himself behind the wheel. Gripping the wheel with both hands, he slammed his foot on the gas. The convertible got its second wind and sped up.

Monk's body, after it was tossed from the car, flopped on the pavement. It wasn't a pretty sight, Lillian thought to herself, but the young driver performed one last act to help them. One of the two motorcyclists had no time to react to the presence of a corpse on the road. He smashed into Monk's body. The sudden jolt of a stop sent the motorcycle driver high over the handle bars. He pinwheeled into the air and landed with sickening finality on the pavement. The machine flipped into the air and crashed almost on top of the driver.

One down. Two to go.

More bullets lashed through the convertible from the black car. It had swerved away from Lillian's fire. The windshield she had shattered but not broken was gone. The driver and the gunner had broken it, giving them a clear line of sight to Lillian and Henry, albeit with a face full of wind.

Whenever she had been in battles or skirmishes before, a subconscious part of her noted particular features of her enemies while her conscious mind performed whatever task needed to be done at the time. Her conscious mind busied itself with how she was going to take out the motorcyclist. She'd leave the car, even though it was closer, to Henry. Her subconscious mind noted something strange about the driver of the black car. He had bandages on the right side of his face, almost as if he had been recently injured. It was an interesting fact, one she might think about later, but it meant nothing to her at the present. All that mattered was that these people were trying to kill them.

Lillian turned her attention to the remaining motorcyclist. He was gaining on them, but driving in a zigzag line. She let off a few shots, but all missed their mark. She tried again. Still missed.

She swore and looked forward.

Henry was driving like a professional. He edged all across the road, making it difficult for the black car to gain any advantage. She had to admit he was doing a remarkable job. He had closed the driver's side door so the wind swirling inside the convertible and rattling the canvas top came only through the shattered window.

Lillian got an idea.

She shoved her gun back into her jacket pocket. Reaching around to the bottom of the passenger seat, she pulled a lever and the back of the seat fell forward. She dove to the front passenger seat, extending herself along the entire passenger side of the car.

"What the hell are you doing?" Henry demanded.

Lillian reached up and put her fingers around the fastener that held the top in place. "Grab the release. Slow down and let the motorcycle get closer. On the count of three, release the top."

Henry got what she meant in a second. He eased up on the gas. The motorcyclist closed the gap.

"One, two, three!" Lillian and Henry both yanked on the latch. Henry gunned the engine. The wind caught the underside of the convertible top. Like a sail on a boat, the convertible top plumed and rose into the air. The combination of the wind and the convertible's speed wasn't enough for the rear latches to compensate. The canvas top with its metal frame ripped out of the convertible and flew backward.

Directly onto the second motorcyclist. He didn't even have a chance to swerve. The canvas top slammed into him. Within a second, he was on the pavement.

Two down. One to go.

With the canvas cover gone, Lillian and Henry were completely exposed. Not that canvas offered much in the way of protection, but it forced the shooter to guess at their position.

No more guessing.

A bullet flew by Henry's face. The front windshield on the passenger side blew out. Lillian plunged her hand into her jacket and pulled out her gun. She rose to return fire but ducked just as fast, sliding down to the floorboard in the back seat. The shooter drew a bead on her position and fired.

The sound of metal on metal screeched through the air as the black car rammed into the back quarter panel. Henry adjusted and swerved, creating more space between the cars.

Other automobiles in the oncoming lane blasted their horns. Henry and the enemy driver both maneuvered to avoid a head-on collision. The movement also threw the bag of golf clubs on top of Lillian.

More gunfire erupted from the chasing car. One blew a plume of stuffing and fabric from the leather seat. If something didn't change, they were going to get murdered out here.

Lillian knew it was up to her to even the odds. Henry was doing all he could to keep them on the road. Despite all the gunfire, no one else was coming to their rescue. She needed a distraction. She also needed to take out the shooter. She was good, but the road wasn't perfectly smooth and her accuracy was off. She needed something bigger to aim for.

Or strike with.

Staying below the line of fire, Lillian wrestled the golf bag into a position where she could get a grip on it. She slid the a thick iron out of the bag and got ready.

"Let them get closer," she called to Henry.

"What?"

"Keep your head down and slow a bit. And trust me."

Henry grunted but complied.

The black car edged closer and banged against the convertible's quarter panel. Lillian didn't have to see the gunman to know he was taking aim at Henry. That was what she would have done in his position. In one fluid motion, she heaved the golf bag up and over the side of the car.

The clubs and the bag descended on the hood and into the broken windshield of the black car. Despite the wind, Lillian clearly heard a shouted curse. In German. Not waiting another second, she sat up on the seat. The remaining iron was in her grip. With all her might, she swung. Her target: the gunman's arm.

Metal crunched bone when her blow connected. The gunman's forearm broke. His gun tumbled to the pavement. He pulled his broken arm inside the car. He howled in pain. Lillian was proud of herself as she threw the club at the black car and reached for her gun in her pocket.

But the driver had other plans.

He knocked the convertible's back fender. The collision veered the convertible sideways. Lillian, resting only on her knees and holding her gun, fell forward. The convertible moved the opposite direction. She lost her grip on the gun when it slammed into the side of the seat and tumbled to the floorboard. Unfortunately, her momentum kept her moving to the side of the car. Enough of her was above the side of the car that she caromed over the side.

In a desperate move, Lillian reached out. Her fingers found the channel into which the canvas cover folds. Still, she started sliding over the driver's side. With nothing to break her fall, she was seconds away from certain death.

Whether he noticed her predicament or not, Henry steered the convertible back onto the middle of the road. The change in trajectory enabled Lillian to bang onto the back trunk. Her shoes hung perilous inches above the pavement. She held onto her perch with only one hand. The other flailed helplessly in the air.

The black car's driver saw an advantage. He eased his car directly behind the convertible. He must have gunned the engine because the black car moved inexorably toward the convertible. Lillian saw it and realized the high front of the black car coupled with the low slope of the convertible's trunk meant she was going to be crushed. Yet, she didn't have enough time or strength in one arm to pull herself to safety. Her hair flapping around her face, there was nothing she could do.

Closer and closer the black car came. Lillian screamed at Henry but the wind carried her voice away from him. She was hanging by her right arm, lying on her right side. If she turned onto her stomach, she might be able to get her left hand to hold onto the car and pull herself up. She didn't think she had the time. Besides, she wouldn't have a visual on the approaching car. She certainly wasn't going to lie on her back and hope her left hand found purchase.

The black car forced her hand. It rammed the convertible. At the last moment, Lillian brought her legs up to her chest. Still holding on, she glanced back at the German driver. Both hands were on the steering wheel, a maniacal grimace etching his face. The gunman, still in obvious pain, now held another pistol in his uninjured hand. With no windshield between them, Lillian was a sitting duck.

Without thinking of angle or trajectories, she put her feet down. They landed on the front hood of the car. Using it as leverage, she pushed up with all her strength. At the same time, she pulled with her right arm. All the exercises and drills Tanaka had forced her to conduct paid off. She launched herself up and over the trunk and back down into the backseat floorboard of the convertible.

Her gun shook on the seat in front of her. Her lip curling into a humorless smile, she grabbed it and sat up. With a perfect two-handed grip, she shot the remaining bullets into the driver. She noted his surprised face when her bullets struck him. He jerked violently back. He lost control of the car. The gunman, a pistol in his uninjured hand, could not grab the wheel in time.

The black car skidded, swerved, and ran into a small ditch on the side of the road. It struck something, because it started flipping over and over into an adjacent field.

Lillian slumped back into her seat. Her chest was heaving as she gulped large lungfuls of air. Adrenaline coursed through her. She was ready for the next attack.

But it didn't come. There were no more pursuers. "You okay?" she called up to Henry.

"Yeah. You?"

Lillian sighed. It had been quite some time since she had performed anything remotely close to that kind of activity. She nodded.

Henry slowed the car enough to let her right the passenger seat, climb over, and plop herself next to him. She stared off into the distance. "How much farther?"

"Fifteen miles."

"Sheesh," she muttered. "It's amazing how fast you can get to London when someone's trying to kill you."

26

Max Muller drove his stolen car along the same highway that Clark and the woman had used. He drove the exact speed limit. He didn't want to alert the police he was a spy.

His assignment was simple: follow behind Klein and the other three. Render assistance if possible, but gather intelligence. Above all, do not be outed as a spy.

He knew the route they took as it was the main road that led to London. He didn't need to tail them directly. There was another man in London who would fill him in on the details.

One thing Muller noted as he drove along the road, was the ingenious ways Clark and the woman had dispatched their pursuers. The first casualty was Erich. When Muller passed his fallen comrade lying in a pool of his own blood on the road, local policemen cordoning off the area, he was surprised to see another body. He didn't recognize the corpse, but the dead man wore golf clothes. That was the man who had met Clark and the woman in Dover. A corner of Muller's mouth turned in appreciation that they had managed one casualty.

The policemen had eyed him as he passed along the shoulder, but they eyed everyone. Nothing to see here, the eyes had said. Muller drove on.

Robert was a surprise. The second comrade on a motorcycle appeared to have been hit by…Muller couldn't get a good angle on the black shape resting on the road near Robert's body. Some sort of cloth. With a wire frame. Muller started when he realized it must have been the cover for the convertible in which Clark and the woman had left Dover. How desperate they must have been to use that as a weapon.

And how resourceful. His admiration for Clark grew. Even more, his curiosity about this woman knew no bounds. She had to be military. There was no way Clark could have done all this by himself.

The billow of smoke rising from a burning car in a field gave Muller hope that his comrades had been successful in forcing Clark off the road. His hopes died when he recognized the car as the other one they had stolen with the intent of pursuit.

"Hey, mate," a policeman told Muller, "keep on moving. Don't wanna cause another wreck."

Without realizing it, Muller had slowed to get a better look. The lawman's words startled him and he jerked forward. "Yes, sir," Muller said through his open window.

The policeman had already forgotten him.

Muller hadn't forgotten a detail. It was one of his most prized assets as an agent for *der Führer*: he forgot nothing.

He continued along the road, heading north to London. In his mind, he tried to make sense of what he had seen and what he had been asked to do.

Max Muller considered himself in deep cover. His allegiance to Germany and her cause he kept secret from his friends and family in Ramsgate. He knew the time was fast approaching when he would have to declare his allegiance publicly. He would lose all he had built, but the promise of reward after the Nazis successfully invaded Western Europe and Britain kept him true to his beliefs.

He had been told his services would be needed only after the invasion began. He hadn't been told when that day would be, so he found himself surprised when the call came. It was a coded message from Berlin with instructions to pursue a British agent and his female companion from Dover to London. The agent's name was Clark.

Funny, Max had thought. He knew a Henry Clark. He was Simon's son. All Simon would say about his son's activities was that he was working for the king. He never mentioned Clark was some sort of spy. You never could tell about people.

Max's assignment was reconnaissance. The message from Berlin had stated another team would likely try to capture Clark and the woman. If they failed, Max was to ascertain what went wrong and report. His secrecy was too valuable to risk exposing himself before the invasion.

As such, Max Muller drove all the way to London. Four of his fellow German assets had been killed by Clark and the woman. Strangely, for a service that prided itself on knowing everything, his source in Berlin couldn't tell Max who the woman was. As Max had already surmised, she wasn't some dainty little flower. She had to have been an integral part of the escape. That would go into his report.

The location in London from which his report would commence was a remote house on the outskirts of London, just south of the Thames. He pulled up to the printing office and parked. He walked in.

The man behind the counter looked up. "What can I do for you?"

"I am needing a leaflet for an upcoming church picnic printed. Who do I need to talk to?"

The man behind the counter nodded. His eyes flicked to the doorway, then back to Max. "Right this way, sir."

Max followed the other man to a corner desk. They both sat. The man slid a piece of paper over to Max. "Please write what you need."

Max complied. He had to restrain himself from giving every detail he observed. He could have written multiple pages. Instead, he wrote only one. The man watched him the entire time.

Finished, Max gave the paper back to the man. He read it. "Four?"

Max nodded.

The man nodded. "Okay, we'll get this printed for you. When do you need it?"

"As soon as possible. They're expecting it."

"Understood."

The man stood. Max stood. The man walked Max to the door and held it open. Max exited and got back into his car.

He beamed with pride.

***

Herr Colonel sat in his office and smoked. The daily reports rested on his desk, unread. For all the preparations for the impending invasion, he only wanted one thing: word from Rolf Klein.

It had been hours since his last communication with the field agent. The instructions were simple: get the book, eliminate Clark, determine the identity of the woman and what that might mean. Herr Colonel had all faith in Klein, but things in war often went awry. As a professor of history, he knew that all too well.

His stomach rumbled. A second night in a row without Wilma's cooking. Instead of eating the dried beef, he smoked and felt worse. Resigning himself, he opened his drawer and pulled out the hunk of meat.

His door opened. Wilhelm entered and stood at attention. "Herr Colonel, General Siegfried needs to see you."

Herr Colonel sighed, the knife poised in his hand, ready to cut the meat. "Tell Herr General I'm waiting on word from our field agent, Klein. Once I get word from him…"

From the outer office, General Siegfried barged into Herr Colonel's office. "Klein is dead. Your agents have failed to do what is required." As always, his uniform appeared impeccable.

Colonel Graf jerked to his feet to assume attention. He cut his thumb. He forgot to hide his grimace of pain.

Siegfried sniffed derisively. He remained standing and didn't let Graf relax. He waved his hand at Wilhelm. "Close the door on your way out."

Wilhelm gulped and complied.

"How do you know?" Graf asked.

"You don't think I'd let our organization only rely on people you chose. I have my own people. And you'll never see them." He reached over and snatched up the dried meat. He gnawed off a hunk and chewed.

Graf could hear the chewing sounds.

Siegfried began to pace around the room. "You know the difference between you and me? Practical knowledge. For you, spy craft and espionage are merely academic pursuits. They're something to be studied. You read papers"—he jammed his finger on the piles of paper on Graf's desk—"and write reports. You lack the intrinsic knowledge and understanding to be an effective leader. You seem to excel in administration but not in the field. I, on the other hand, did not have to rely on personal connections to get my position. I earned it in the trenches of Belgium and France."

Graf remembered not to lock his knees or else he might faint. He bent his knees and felt the warm rush of blood to his feet.

"If I understand it correctly, you were not even aware the American banker was being followed. How can you expect to lead if you don't know all the pieces?"

"Herr General, sir, I am aware of all our organization's plans. That was one I had delegated to a subordinate and had not followed up with." He regretted those words as soon as they left his mouth.

Siegfried barked out a laugh. "Not aware? I wonder if others in our organization are aware of your lack of awareness." He let the threat hang in the air.

Graf felt beads of sweat form on his cheeks and forehead. He wanted to sit. He knew now was not the time.

"The British agent Henry Clark and his friend killed four of our men, including Klein. They did it on the road from Dover to London. By now, they will have learned that Ludlow is dead and by whom. You have to thank the heavens Klein is dead or else Clark would certainly come after him. Small treasures, yeah?"

"Yes, Herr General." Graf nearly committed a huge mistake by asking to sit or at least stand at ease. He wanted to wipe the perspiration from his face. A bead of sweat rolled down his forehead and into his eye. The salt stung.

Siegfried continued. "By now, the morons in London are probably determining whether to continue. They might also be thinking the coast is clear." Herr General came to stand in front of Graf. "It's not."

"Yes, Herr General." Another bead of sweat rolled down his cheek. Interestingly, Siegfried watched its progress.

"Where is James Geiger?"

The question threw Graf. It took a moment for his mind to recall the information. "He's in Berlin with his wife. My latest report is that he's preparing to leave and travel to Brussels ostensibly to vacation with his wife."

Siegfried pursed his lips. "On the eve of the invasion?"

Graf shrugged just to move something on his body. There was a reason he had chosen academia over the military. "Yes, Herr General. It is my belief he was to meet Monroe and the woman in Brussels."

"You will meet them there."

Did he hear correctly? "Sir?"

"Clandestinely, of course."

"You want me in the field?"

"Not only me, but other members of the high command. We'd like to see how you handle yourself. It should be a routine mission. The invasion's nigh so if anything goes wrong, the army will be there to bail you out."

"Permission to speak?"

Siegfried stepped back from Graf and waved dismissively. "Granted, but it won't change anything."

Gunter Graf, professor of history, had waded through departmental politics for years and come out on top. It was one of the reasons he was selected for the job he now held. Well, that and connections. He knew when to ruffle feathers and when to keep them in place. This was one of those latter times.

Gunter Graf said nothing.

"Don't have anything to say?" Siegfried said.

"No, Herr General. When do you expect me to leave?"

"Tonight."

"Herr General, if I may, my wife has prepared dinner. Might I have the opportunity to go home and say goodbye to her and eat her wonderful cooking?"

"Of course. Tell her two will be coming to dinner."

27

"George Ludlow is dead."

The words came from the mouth of Charles Hastings, one of the high officers of the Secret Intelligence Service. He sat behind his desk. His tie was loosened, his jacket hung over the back of his chair, and the cup of tea on his desk steamed. Lillian and Henry sat opposite Hastings. They were alone otherwise.

"Sir?" Henry appeared visibly weak and it wasn't from the rush of the car chase.

He had maintained the convertible's fast speed to London, only slowing when they reached the heart of the city. He had driven straight to the SIS offices. The guards at the front gate gave him a wary look, but a brief utterance of a passcode gained them entrance. Henry and Lillian had parked the beat-up convertible in the lot and walked inside. Many eyes stared their way. He was mostly intact. Lillian, on the other hand, with all her extra activity, looked positively disheveled. She excused herself and, carrying her valise, went to the ladies room to freshen up before they met with Henry's supervisor. She emerged a few minutes later with her hair fixed up, all her clothes tucked in appropriately, and her shoes spit-shined. If not for the couple of scratches on her cheeks from falling glass, no one would be the wiser that Lillian Saxton had, that very afternoon, found herself hanging onto the trunk of a moving car.

"I'm afraid it's true, Henry," Hastings said. "When was the last time you saw him?"

Henry had trouble comprehending the news so Lillian spoke up. "Day before yesterday. Up in Liverpool. Mr. Ludlow met with us and gave us his car to come down here."

Hastings turned his attention to Lillian. "You must be the American who caused all of this?"

Lillian frowned. "I don't believe I follow you."

"Ludlow's death, the exposure of Henry as an undercover agent to the Nazis, you know, things like that. And for what?"

"A Nazi codebook," Lillian asserted.

"Sure, and the king's my brother." Hastings blew his tea and sipped. Lillian looked at her cup of tea sitting on the desk. She brought it to her face and enjoyed the steam.

Hastings went on. "Supposedly, the only way we know what this mystery message says in that little book of poetry from your old boyfriend is from what you tell us. Mind showing me?"

Lillian bit her inner cheek to prevent words she couldn't take back from emerging. She opened her valise sitting on the floor next to her and withdrew the book. She stood and came around the desk to stand next to Hastings. Flipping pages and explaining how the code worked, she showed the message in full.

"Your boyfriend was pretty specific on the date," Hastings commented. "Any reason why he picked May ninth?"

"Not that I know of."

"That's not the date of your first kiss or whatever, is it?"

Lillian flexed her jaw muscles and counted to five before responding. "No, sir."

Hastings grunted.

Lillian closed the book and returned to her seat. "Your man in Washington, Reginald Nevins, thought it was credible enough to persuade my government to send me here. My friend has already died in the process. Mr. Ludlow also believed in this mission. He told me so and wished us well."

"So how do you explain the Nazis showing up in Dover after Clark's inexcusable side trip?"

Henry started. "Sir, Mr. Ludlow gave me permission to…"

Lillian silenced him with a hand to his arm. "Mr. Hastings, are you suggesting Ludlow gave up information? How did he die?"

"Burning." Hastings bore his eyes into Lillian, actively challenging her. "And not just one time. He was tied to a chair and burned. In more than one place, I might add, and more than one time."

Inside, Lillian's heart leapt at the knowledge. *What a horrible way to go.* Still, Ludlow was a soldier in His Majesty's intelligence service. Chances were he gave up no information. She said as much to Hastings.

"Then explain how the Nazis found you," he insisted.

Lillian thought a moment. "There must be more of them here in England."

Hastings pounded his fist on the desk, rattling the tea cups and saucers. "Precisely. I know we have assets all throughout Europe. Hitler's got his men over here. It's a given. But that doesn't mean we have to make it easy for them." He started ticking off concepts with his fingers. "Let's say Ludlow said nothing or, if anything, a false lead. I've known the man for a quarter century. He was a good man and I'm positive he said nothing. But I've never been tortured. The brain works differently under torture. Be that as it may, Ludlow likely said nothing. Can we agree on that?"

Henry and Lillian let silence be their acceptance.

"Good. You drive all the way across the country to Dover to see your father and pay your respects to your mum. I understand. I wouldn't have given you permission, but Ludlow was always one who saw the human side. We send a car and driver out there. Good man, too, Monk. It's a shame. I'll have to telephone *his* mum. Think she'll be pleased her son died because of some Nazi scum?" He paused only a second before continuing.

"If we accept Ludlow's silence as a given, then there are more spies out there. We don't know who they are or where they are. But they were good enough to spot you and Henry and try to kill you both, presumably to take that little book of yours. What does that mean? I'll tell you. It means the Nazis think there's something special in that book, but they don't know what it is. They are willing to do anything to get that book. Which brings up the question about the man on the other end of that book. Your old boyfriend."

Lillian grew exasperated. "Mr. Hastings, sir, we went over all this back in Washington with Nevins and my commanding officer. Nevins persuaded my superiors to let me come here and try to obtain the codebook from my old *friend*." She emphasized the word "friend."

"Circumstances have changed." Hastings leaned back in his chair. "What you both are unaware of is the constant chatter across the Channel. Have you wondered why we're not fighting directly with Hitler yet? We have, too. We're waiting for his move. There have been lots of communications from the Continent that the invasion is imminent. It could happen any day now."

"With all due respect, having the codebook would help you plan. You would know what Hitler's up to. We can get that book for you."

"Perhaps you could, but not as a proper British operation. Effective immediately, this operation is over."

28

Gunter Graf had one of the worst dinners in his life. The food was, as always, excellent. The company proved nearly insufferable. The problem was that he wasn't able to tell his wife he had been assigned to the field before Siegfried himself broke the news.

Wilma actually choked on her food. She had prepared *eisbein* with sauerkraut. She grabbed her napkin and hid her mouth behind it. "I'm sorry. You caught me off guard." She turned to look at her husband. "Why didn't you tell me?"

"I only learned about it right before we arrived," Graf said. "I wanted to wait for a good time to tell you."

Wilma harrumphed. "There is never a good time to tell your wife you are heading into a war zone."

"It's not a war zone," Graf said quickly. "It's in Brussels. It's purely a secret mission to apprehend a spy from Britain and ascertain if someone from our side is passing secrets over to our enemies." He smiled, trying to disarm her.

The look in her eyes told him he had failed.

Siegfried chuckled. He swirled his wine and finished it. He then proceeded to pour the rest of the bottle into his glass. "Frau Graf, you should be proud of your husband. He has prepared many reports and done an admirable job at his position. This is more of a promotion. He gets to use his experience and skill on an assignment."

"Herr General." The tone of Wilma's voice indicated a challenge was coming. "My husband is a university professor. His skills are in distilling information gathered from all sources and preparing recommendations. Yes, he is a college professor of history specializing in military history but that does not make him prepared to lead men into battle."

Siegfried waved her off. "Frau Graf, as Gunter said, this is an intelligence-gathering operation. He's going to Brussels, in a fancy hotel no less, to spy on our enemies. He's just gathering the information firsthand."

"Alone?" Wilma had abandoned her food.

"No, there will be a team with him."

"How many?"

"Five others."

"All military?"

"Yes."

"Will he be armed?"

"Of course." Siegfried turned to Gunter. "Perhaps we've employed the wrong Graf." He smiled in a way intended to be kidding.

Gunter returned the smile halfheartedly.

Siegfried said, "Frau Graf, you have nothing to worry about."

"What about the invasion?" Wilma persisted. "It's due to start soon, *ja*?"

Some of the joviality left Siegfried's face. It was verboten to discuss military matters with anyone outside the military, including wives. He eyed Gunter and Wilma who sat to his left and across the table, respectively. "Please tell me, Gunter, you haven't been sharing military secrets here at the house."

"No, sir," Gunter said.

"Herr General," Wilma said, "I assure you my husband is the model of decorum. He has the highest love for *das Vaterland*. He never tells me anything. I only make the observation that the invasion must start sometime. It's spring. We've delayed long enough. You don't stay married to a military historian and not pick up on some of his interests."

Siegfried bowed at the neck. "Understood, Frau Graf. And what do you bring to the table, besides the obvious?"

The silence in the room was thick with derision. Wilma cracked a smile, defusing the moment. "Love. Devotion. Children. Motherhood. And a majesty in the kitchen."

Siegfried laughed. The Grafs tried and failed. "You certainly can back it up, Frau Graf." He wiped his mouth with his napkin and stood. "I'll call for a car, Graf. I expect you back in your office in two hours." He bowed to Wilma. "Frau Graf, I have to say your reputation as a cook is well-deserved. Gunter brags about you all the time. It's too bad it's taken this long for him to invite me."

"Thank you, Herr General." Wilma's fake smile didn't reach her eyes. "You'll have to come again sometime. Perhaps after Gunter has returned."

"Of course." Siegfried looked around the room. "Where is your telephone?"

"Down the hall. In the front room."

"Thank you." Siegfried turned and walked out of the room.

Wilma and Gunter Graf stared at each other. Emotions flooded between them in their gazes. Gunter's stomach was in his throat. His cheeks twitched. He reached out and offered his hand to Wilma.

She didn't take it. Instead, she busied herself with clearing the table.

Ten minutes later, Siegfried was gone. Gunter went upstairs and packed a bag. Given the mission was in a hotel, he decided against packing anything for the field. Into his bag went clothes and toiletries. From his side table, he pulled out his Luger in its holster. He decided he'd wait to strap it on until he returned to the office.

A subtle sound at the door stopped him. He turned, still holding the gun. Wilma stood there. She had put her apron on over her blue dress. A look at her face told Gunter she had been crying. She glanced at the gun.

"When they assigned that to you," she said, "I thought it merely ornamental. Now it'll be part of who you are."

He dropped the Luger in his bag. "No, it's not. I probably won't even wear it. It's not like I get to wear a gun on my hip like the cowboys in the Hollywood movies."

She moved to him, slowly, hesitantly. He wore only his undershirt and trousers, the suspenders hanging down his waist. "I'm scared for you, Gunter."

Since he had just mentioned Hollywood movies, Gunter wanted to be the hero and tell his wife it would all be okay. Most of him thought that was the truth. A part of him was truly scared. The invasion was at hand. Geiger had specifically mentioned May 9 as the meeting date. He was in a position to know the start date of the invasion. That was clearly part of the plan. With that in mind, Gunter was worried.

What would Belgium do when *der Führer's* armies crossed the border? Would it be as swift as Poland or as slow as the first war? Even as well-prepared as he knew the Nazi army to be, Gunter's reading of history told him the fog of war clouded everything. He desperately wanted to tell Wilma all would be fine. He wasn't sure.

"I'm not scared. It'll be a simple mission, with a competent team. We'll assess the situation, decide what to do with our potential traitor, and then come back." He pulled her chin up with his finger.

Wilma looked at him with tears. "Our men are already out there, fighting," she whispered. "I so fear for them every day. But you were always my anchor. Now, you'll be gone, too."

"I'm here now." Gunter pulled his wife close to him in a full-body embrace. He kissed her, tenderly. Their heat grew quickly. She hugged him back with a power he'd never before encountered.

Gradually, he lay down on the bed, bringing her with him. With her on top of him, he felt, then tasted, one of her tears on his face. They separated, looking at each other. Her eyes were glassy. So were his. They smiled at each other.

With a violent thrust of his arm, Gunter shoved his bag off his bed. The next hour consisted of the most passionate lovemaking each of them had ever known.

29

A thousand thoughts flooded Lillian's mind all at once. They all boiled down to one word. "What?"

Even Henry appeared stunned.

Hastings shook out a cigarette from a crumpled pack and lit it. "The invasion's here. We're not sure where or when, but it's all but here. It has to be. We can't risk any military supplies to get you across the Channel."

He held up a finger to stop Lillian from speaking. "In addition, it's too risky. Ludlow, for all his experience and fortitude, might have given up crucial information. I can think of few reasons why the Jerrys caught you off guard on the road from Dover."

"But sir." Henry stopped when Hastings glared at him.

"Then there's the other side."

"The other side?" Lillian asked.

"Yes, the other side. Your old boyfriend—and yes, I'm using that term because it's the truth—what's his game? Why'd he send your other friend all the way to America just to fetch you? Why all the subterfuge? Why not just give Monroe the book and be done with it?"

Lillian pursed her lips. It was true what Hastings said. On the surface, if James had passed the book of poetry to Frank to give to Lillian, he could just as easily have passed the Nazi codebook. Then all of this would be for nothing.

And Frank would be alive.

But there was the other thing, the secret message that she still held close: James was going to name her brother's killer. That was the real reason she was here in London. She desperately wanted that information. And what she did with it was her own business.

In her mind, Frank's voice again asked her the question: "So, you are judge, jury, and executioner?" In her mind, she answered:

I am your avenger. And Samuel's.

But she dared not tell Donnelly or Honeywell back in America so she was surely not going to tell Hastings here in London.

"I'm not sure, sir," Lillian finally responded. "But there must have been a good reason."

"I can think of a few. One in particular involves your linking up with him and causing all sorts of havoc."

Lillian looked at him askance. "Are you seriously suggesting I'm working with James Geiger? To what? Plan something against Britain?"

He looked at her evenly. "The thought has crossed my mind." He blew smoke through his nostrils.

Lillian sat up straighter in the chair and leaned toward the desk. "Let me tell you something, Mr. Hastings. I'm an American. I'm not British. But I know our shared history is linked and forever intertwined. There's a war that's already started, no matter if folks back home call it The Phoney War or not. It's a war. And sooner or later, the United States is going to get involved. It's destined to happen, no matter what the isolationists want. I want us involved. The world *needs* to have us involved. We need to be there in war so we can make the peace."

She pointed out the window. "I've got a friend in Germany whom I've not seen in six years. He's willing to deliver secrets from Germany that might help win this war. For whatever reason he asked me and Frank to come and get it. Frank's dead, so that leaves only me. I'm going to Belgium and I'm going to get that book. And then I'm going to bring it back. And then I will deliver it to you. That's what I was ordered to do. Yes, this isn't an American military mission because we're not at war yet. But it *is* a military mission. If you don't want to help, fine. I'll find my own way across the Channel. But I'm going."

She glanced at Henry who remained mute. The expression on his face surprised her. He was looking at her with admiration.

Hastings stubbed out his cigarette in the ashtray. He scanned the papers on his desk until he found the one he wanted. He picked it up. "Captain Donnelly and Colonel Honeywell thought you might say that."

"Sir?"

"Yes, we called them after the fiasco in Liverpool. Actually, we called the American Embassy here in London and they called your commanding officers. Here's what they said." He passed the paper over to her.

Lillian took it and read it. In all capital letters indicative of a telegram, the message read: "SERGEANT SAXTON MISSION OVER STOP. REMEMBER MCCLELLAN, VIRGINIA STOP RETURN TO US STOP"

She put the paper back on the desk. She had to make sure she didn't give any indication of the coded message she just received.

"What happened in McClellen?" Hastings asked.

Lillian Saxton made up a story. "There's an army base in McClellan, Virginia. We had reason to believe the quartermaster was siphoning gas and other rations and selling them for his own profit. I was sent in, undercover, to infiltrate as a buyer. We needed evidence. Supposedly, there was a ledger that identified the buyers. I was to get it. I found a ledger, but it turned out to be fake. The whole mission crumbled and the quartermaster, who really was selling things on the side, was never punished." She shrugged. "They're reminding me that for everything that might look like a shiny fishing lure, it can hook you and not let go." She sat back in the chair, dejected.

Hastings beamed. "Well, that's that. I thank you for your service here in Britain. And for taking out the Nazi spy ring, even though we had it under control." He said the last with evident meaning. He stood.

Lillian and Henry stood.

Hastings extended his hand and Lillian shook it. She grabbed her bag and left the office. Henry turned to leave but Hastings beckoned him to stay.

She turned in the doorway. "Can I get a car to drive me to the American Embassy or should I take a cab?"

Hastings was still standing behind his desk. "We'll put you in a car and make sure you get to the embassy safely."

"Good." She turned on her heel. "I'll be waiting."

"Oh, and Sergeant?" Hastings called after her.

Lillian stopped and turned to face the British Intelligence officer. "Sir?"

"Don't get any ideas about continuing this little mission of yours. We may be preoccupied with the impending invasion, but that doesn't mean we can't keep our eye on you." He smiled.

Lillian Saxton smiled back. *We'll see about that.*

30

Lillian Saxton had to wait ten minutes on the front steps of the SIS's office before a black car pulled up to the curb. A young man hopped out of the car and approached her. "Sergeant Saxton?"

"Yes."

"My name's John. I've been assigned to drive you to the American Embassy."

Lillian studied the young man. She wasn't sure if he had started shaving yet. His uniform looked a size too large. He wore no side arm.

She gave him one of her radiant smiles, the kind that stopped her fellow soldiers back in America dead in their tracks. This young pup all but melted. "I'm Lillian." She offered him her hand. He took it gingerly, like a knight to his lady fair.

This is going to be easy.

"You're so kind to do this for me," she cooed. She picked up her bag and acted like it was heavy.

John jumped to her aid. "Allow me."

She did.

He put the valise in the back seat of the car. He held the door open for her.

She slipped in and sat. While the young man walked around the car, she slid her skirt up an inch.

John got behind the driver's seat and angled a look at her. He noted the skirt hemline.

She smiled. "Take me away, my English knight."

John cleared his throat. He started the car and pulled away from the curb.

Lillian talked small talk with the young man, lacing her words with enough fawning to have earned her an Academy Award. All the while, she scanned the storefronts, looking for the right spot.

She wasn't sure how far away the embassy was, so she decided quickly.

"John, dear," she said, "before we get to the embassy, I need to stop over there." She pointed at a women's clothing store.

"I'm sorry, ma'am. I was told no unscheduled stops."

"But, John," she said, pouting her lower lip, "I can't show up to the embassy looking like this." She still wore her dirty dress from the car chase. "I need to get some, um, intimate apparel."

She watched John's Adam's apple go up and down over his collar. She placed a hand on his arm. "Please."

He looked at her from the corner of his eye. She leaned closer. The next moment, he pulled off to the side of the road and parked in front of the store.

Lillian pecked him on the cheek. "Thank you. I'll only be a minute."

She got out of the car and walked inside. A few ladies browsed the racks of clothes. None paid her any attention except for the saleswoman. She glided over to Lillian and asked if she needed any help.

"Actually, I do" Lillian used her American accent. "You see that man in the car out there." She pointed. "He's taking me back to Liverpool to catch a boat back to America. But my boyfriend, a British soldier, is stationed here in London. I know I have to go back, but I want one more night with him." She winked at the woman. "Do you think I could slip out the back, catch a cab?"

A thin smile formed on the saleswoman's mouth. "I think I can help you."

"Oh, and if he comes in, make sure to delay him."

The saleswoman pursed her lips. "Why?"

"I don't want him to get into too much trouble. I just want to slip away for a few more hours."

The saleswoman nodded.

Lillian walked to the back of the store and waited. How long before John would come in looking for her? The answer turned out to be fifteen minutes.

John got out of the car and came inside the store. The

jangling bell was Lillian's signal to go out the back. She heard the saleswoman telling John that Lillian was in a dressing room.

Thankfully, the back door did not have a bell. Lillian exited out the back alley, came around the side of the store, and peeked inside. From her vantage point, she couldn't see John. Which meant he couldn't see her. She needed her valise and, preferably, the car. She wondered if he had left the keys in the ignition. More important, she hoped when she got to the car, his line of sight would still be covered.

Lillian crept out from the side of the building and reached the passenger door. She cursed when she had to go around the car, forgetting that this was Britain and the cars were built backward. She opened the door and snatched up her bag. She glanced at the ignition.

No key.

She could hot wire a car; no problem. But would she have the time to do it and get away without being seen?

The traffic kept moving past her while she pondered her situation. She wasn't immediately aware a car had pulled up and stopped next to her until a driver honked in protest.

Henry sat behind the wheel of the other car.

"Going somewhere?" he said. He grinned.

The car behind Henry honked again. Lillian glanced back into the store. She and John locked eyes. She turned back to Henry. "Yes."

He nodded. "Get in."

She did. He pulled away quickly.

Looking behind them, Lillian saw John get in his car and set off in pursuit.

"You can lose him, right?" she asked. "He looks like he's fourteen."

"He's eighteen and an excellent driver. But, yeah, I can lose him."

Lillian watched John's car quickly lose ground to Henry's skillful maneuvering. But she frowned when two other cars, both of the same make and model, veered from side streets and angled in their direction.

"Well," Henry said, "I guess I wasn't the only one who decided to follow you."

Lillian reached into her bag and pulled out her pistol.

"What the hell do you think you're doing?" Henry exclaimed. "Those are my peers. They're just doing their job."

"What are you doing?"

"My job. The one George Ludlow assigned me: get that codebook and bring it back."

"Then why are your friends chasing us?"

Henry grinned. A lock of dark hair fell over his forehead. "Because my bosses and I don't see eye to eye." He executed a hairpin turn down a narrow street and gunned the engine. The car, already moving fast, sped up.

Lillian processed his comment. "Wait, are you saying you're going to help me?"

"Tell me about McClellan, Virginia."

She hesitated a moment, then relented. "Complete fabrication. It's a coded message. In our Civil War, Union General George McClellan found plans for Confederate General Robert E. Lee's marching orders." Lillian had to hang onto the dashboard when Henry blasted out of the narrow street and onto a wider one. Both pursuit cars still tailed them.

"Anyway, McClellan had the plans in his grasp. He beat Lee at Antietam, but failed to end the war conclusively in 1862. He feared it might be counter-espionage. The war dragged on for three more years."

She looked back. Only one car chased them. It was gaining. She found the second one when Henry slammed on the brakes. One of the pursuers had come around and blocked Henry's progress.

"Pardon me," Henry muttered. He threw the car into gear and drove up and onto the sidewalk. Pedestrians dove out of the way. Henry avoided all bystanders and came around the pursuit car that had blocked the street.

"Your gun, please."

Mutely, Lillian handed it to him. He stuck his arm outside the car and sent two bullets into one of the tires of the second pursuit car. The tire blew and air whooshed out. The vehicle visibly slumped. Effectively, he had taken out that car and blocked the passage of the other one.

Henry handed the gun back to her. "Thanks."

"You're welcome."

Not taking anything for granted, Henry pressed his advantage with speed. He zigzagged through traffic.

"We're not going to the American Embassy, are we?" Lillian asked.

"Do you want to? I can certainly make my way there."

"Not on your life. So, what's our next move?"

Henry chuckled dryly. "This is child's play. Getting across the Channel will be the tough part."

"We just pick up a ferry, right?"

Henry shook his head. "Americans. In case you have forgotten, we're already at war. One of the first things we did was to set up a blockade along the Channel. All ships, no matter the country of origin, are subject to a search for contraband and materials the Nazis could use." He angled the car on a highway.

Lillian read the sign; they were leaving London's city limits.

"Every ship has to list its manifest and crew. Royal navy men stop every ship in Channel waters. A team is sent onto the ship and a full inspection is conducted. Wireless radio sends messages back to the Contraband Control. They verify manifests and crew. If a ship passes, she sails on. If not, all contraband is confiscated and the ship's crew is detained." Henry glanced at her sidelong. "If that happens, we're pretty much screwed."

"We?"

"Of course, we. After what I just pulled, the only way I stay out of the stockade or avoid being tried for treason is if I come back with that codebook. Even then, I'll likely be punished. But I'm fine with that provided we get the book and bring it back. Once the thick-headed bosses back at SIS see what we've done, they'll thank us." He paused. "I think."

Lillian smiled. "Okay, Henry. Thanks." At that moment, something in her relaxed about Henry. In fact, she nearly revealed to him the other reason she was so keen on meeting James Geiger.

But she refrained. There would be time enough to tell him once they were in Brussels.

"So, Mr. Traitor," she mocked, "what's your plan for evading the most powerful navy in the world?"

Henry angled his head, acknowledging touche. "I know a guy who owes me a favor."

31

General Siegfried allowed Gunter Graf to select exactly one person for the team. The other four members of the six-person party were supplied by Siegfried himself. Graf wondered why, but only a few moments' thought told him the answer: so Siegfried, via his proxy, could take over the mission.

"You are in complete command of this assignment, Herr Colonel," Siegfried had said. "All the praise will be yours and your team's." What he left unsaid was that all the blame if it went wrong would also be Graf's to bear.

Graf looked around the small squad room in the motor pool of his building. He wore his uniform, tightly buttoned to the top. A slight scent of his wife's perfume permeated the fabric. She had also given him a handkerchief with her perfume. This he had tucked into his pocket.

His aide, Wilhelm Lang, was the one person Graf selected. The young man was in his 20s, blond as *der Führer's* epitome of Aryan breeding, displayed no fear in assembling his road gear. In addition to his uniform, he now wore a side arm in a holster. The flap covered the Luger.

Adolf Richter had the unfortunate luck to be named after *der Führer*. His parents had read *Mein Kampf* and become devoted followers of Hitler. Dieter Wolf and Kurt Schmidt were the other two men. All excelled in small arms combat and hand-to-hand fighting. Each wore a pistol on one side of his waist and a sheathed knife on the other. When Siegfried had told Graf of their credentials, especially in Poland last fall, Graf questioned the general. Both men looked ready for action.

"We're not going into combat."

"Yes, we are. Again, the difference between academia and the real world."

Graf looked at Wolf and Schmidt. Their eyes told him they

had already seen things in this world he never had. It chilled his bones to think what they had done.

Ursula Koch rounded out the small party. Unlike the men on the team, she wore civilian clothes consisting of a long gray dress, with a modest plunge of the neckline. Her blond hair was swept back up and over her ears. Her only concession to the task at hand was the pistol she wore on her waist. If Wolf's and Schmidt's looks were hard, Ursula's was harder. It looked odd for a pretty woman like that to have murder and determination in her eyes.

On her wrist, Ursula wore a black leather bracelet. The watch attached to it was government issue.

"Show Herr Colonel your watch, Ursula," Siegfried said.

She strode over to Graf and held it up in front of his face. She reached up and, with a thumbnail, slid a long, thin, metal wire from inside the watch. She mimed choking Graf.

He was proud of himself for not flinching. He had assumed as much, but wanted to verify.

Verification complete.

"Nice," Graf said. "Let's hope you don't have cause to use it."

"Herr Colonel," Ursula said, "I'm always prepared to do what it takes for *der Führer* and *das Vaterland*."

Siegfried called the team to attention. All but Graf complied. Satisfied, Siegfried deferred to Graf.

Herr Colonel took a step in front of his team and stopped. Ironically, this was the first time since joining the Wehrmacht that he was speaking in front of people. Meetings rarely counted since he only delivered reports and often did it from a seated position. Here, this was like old times, his professorial days when he prided himself on holding students' attention for the full period.

"Gentlemen and Fräulein, our mission is simple: listen and act. We have a situation where one of our own may be secretly trying to deliver secrets of *das Vaterland* to a foreign power in the form of one or two foreign agents. We don't know that for certain. That's what we're going to ascertain. According to my sources, our man, named James Geiger, is to meet these agents in Brussels. We will be there as well. We will act under my authority. If what we fear turns out to be true, we will act. We will detain Geiger, confiscate whatever material he possesses, and deal with the foreign agents as necessary."

Graf glanced at Siegfried. Herr General remained impassive. "Any questions?"

"Herr Colonel, sir," Ursula said. "Request permission to deal with the woman myself."

"Let's hope that isn't necessary."

"Fräulein Koch," Siegfried cut in, "the mission is the priority, not personal glory. However, if the situation arises and the spies need to be dealt with, I think we can all agree that Fräulein Koch can take care of anything our weaker enemies can throw at us."

Graf bit the inside of his cheek to keep from responding.

"Sir?" Dieter Wolf said. "What's your policy on collateral damage?"

Graf hesitated an instant. He knew the date the invasion was to begin, but couldn't be sure if they did. "While a state of war exists between *das Vaterland* and France and Britain—and we believe one of the spies is a British citizen—currently Belgium is neutral. It would be better to keep collateral damage to a minimum unless circumstances change."

"Herr Colonel," Siegfried said, "fall in with your team."

Well, thus ends my leadership of the team. Graf went over and stood next to Ursula Koch.

"Your mission," Siegfried began—he walked along the line of his soldiers—"as Colonel Graf has stated, is one of reconnaissance and recovery. Be that as it may, if it turns out that Geiger is, indeed, trying to pass information to the enemy, he is a traitor. And in wartime, we deal with traitors in only one way: death. There is no trial. There is no innocent until proven guilty. There is only death for traitors." Siegfried came to stand in front of Graf. "Is that understood?"

"Yes, sir," Graf said.

"The same goes for the foreign agents. Understood?"

"Yes, sir."

"Good. Dismissed. Get to your vehicles and go."

The team dispersed, but Siegfried put a restraining hand on Graf's arm. "That order, you won't have any problems following it, will you?"

Colonel Gunter Graf looked at his commanding officer evenly. "Not at all."

32

"Let me get this straight," Captain Matthew Payne said to Henry. "You want me to smuggle you and your lady friend on board the *Gloria Patri* knowing full well it'll be inspected by the brats at the Royal Navy. Then, you want me to take you where?"

They sat in a bar a mile from the port in Weymouth. Soon after the start of the war in September 1939, the British government set up a blockade. They wisely didn't call it a blockade. Rather, it was a contraband inspection. All ships passing through the English Channel had to stop near Weymouth for inspection. British ships or friendly neutrals could expect a delay. Unfriendly ship captains could expect longer delays.

"Antwerp." Lillian Saxton wasn't as confident as Henry was with Payne's willingness to pay up the favor. "That's where you're going, right?"

"Aye, that's where I'm going." Payne was a stocky man. His gut threatened to bulge over his belt. His arms looked like sides of beef, the veins snaking through the thick muscles. His neck was all but nonexistent. He wore a captain's cap, pushed back to reveal a bald head. "How do you know that?"

"It's on the manifest," Henry said.

"You seem to know everything, pretty boy."

"I do." Henry put his hand out to Payne. "You going to help?"

Payne paused.

"We'd be even if you do."

Payne remained silent, thinking. Finally, he said, "You know, if I get caught, I'll lose my ship. The same ship that's been in my family for forty years. My pappy sailed this thing in the last war."

"And you get to sail it in this war," Henry said. "C'mon, pal. You're a British citizen. The Navy doesn't expect you to be smuggling anything, much less a couple of extra souls."

Payne still resisted. "What's so important in Belgium? You running away from something?"

"More like running to something," Lillian said.

Henry looked at her, raised his eyebrows, then turned to Payne. "You want the truth? I'll give it to you."

Lillian started to speak but Henry waved her off.

"Lillian here received a message from an old friend of hers. He now works for Hitler. This friend is offering to pass along to us a copy of the codebook the Nazis are using. All we have to do is get to Belgium, go to Brussels, meet him, get the book, and come back. Then we pass it along to my bosses and we'll know exactly what all the Jerrys are saying to each other. We'll even know the exact date of their next move. Our problem is the Channel. We can't get across on our own. We need someone to take us. This isn't a military operation, per se, so we need to appear to be civilians."

"Why civilians? Why not just send a squad over there?"

"In this case," Henry said, "that's not a viable option. Now, your role in this can't be revealed now, but when they write the history of this war, there'll be a special place for espionage and spycraft." He tapped Payne's chest. "You, my friend, will be in the history books. But now, you'll be helping His Majesty's armed forces defeat that son of a bitch Hitler."

Payne no longer hesitated. "Why the hell didn't you say so in the first place and trust me?" He beamed. "I've got just the place for you. It'll be tight, but you both will get a chance to talk while the inspectors do their thing." He downed his Scotch and signaled the bartender. "You don't mind buying another round, do you, mate?"

33

The hiding place turned out to be a storage locker with a false back. Payne wasn't kidding about close quarters. With the jackets and clothes that remained in place in case some inspector got a wild hair to open each and every one of the lockers, Lillian and Henry were almost touching each other.

The irony of the situation was that it gave Lillian a chance to get a good look at the handsome British agent up close without anyone shooting at them. His jaw was firm and square. Hollywood directors would clamor to cast him in any film. His dark hair was cut short, but a wisp seemed always to have fallen across his forehead. He constantly swept it away only to have it fall back. Why he didn't just break out the Brylcreem, she never knew. Not that she minded. Too often, men with slicked back hair appeared phony.

Another bit that embarrassed her was hygiene. In all the chasing, she had not a chance to shower properly and clean herself. She feared her odor was ripe. Kind of like his.

When Payne promised to keep them safe, he went ahead and closed the locker door. It wasn't solid. It had half-inch holes spaced out in a grid pattern. The design allowed clothes in the locker to get some air. Now, the holes allowed them to breathe and see each other in the dim light.

"Ever been sealed up like a sardine before?" Henry asked.

"A couple of times. Not like this. And not with another person." She adjusted her feet. They scraped his. He moved his feet. He touched hers. They both chuckled at the predicament.

"Listen," Lillian said, "about your friend Payne. I don't think it was a great idea to tell him about our plans."

His expression darkened. "What was the alternative? Not get across? I saw an opportunity and took it. You can thank me later when we're in Belgium."

"Maybe, but I'd like to keep this little mission with as few people in the know as possible."

"Don't forget: you're not the leader. We're co-leaders. Ludlow specifically said I was in charge if things went topsy-turvy. The way this is going, I expect to be in charge pretty soon."

"Hey." Lillian's tone rose. "We wouldn't even be here if it weren't for me."

"And your boyfriend over in Germany." Henry sneered the word "boyfriend." "He's a traitor, you know. Giving us secrets. They'll kill him if they find out."

Lillian had known that ever since Frank delivered the poetry book. But she trusted James that he knew what he was doing and to take into account threats on his life.

"I know. And he's not my boyfriend. He's married now."

Henry grunted.

Outside in the hallway, through the closed door, they heard the sound of voices approaching. The closer the voices got, the better Lillian and Henry could understand what was being said.

"I don't care if you are a British ship," a man said. He had a Scottish brogue in his voice. "I'm on the hook for checking every place a person can hide." Footsteps grew closer.

"But why?" The second voice belonged to Payne. "As captain of this ship, I can tell ye there's only the crew on board."

"Don't matter, Captain. Orders be orders. And as to yer question, word has it from the home office two fugitives, a man and a woman, are trying to get across the Channel. If we spot'em, we are to bring'em back." The footsteps halted. "And woe be the man who harbored them."

Silence thickened the air.

Lillian and Henry looked at each other. Time to see if Payne's little trick would work. Payne had affixed little handles on the backside of the false back, which was a sheet of wood painted to resemble the back of the locker. The idea was that Lillian and Henry would hold the wood in place and make it appear, to a person opening and closing the lockers, that it was merely the back of the locker. With nearly a full rack of clothes in between them and the door, a cursory inspection probably wouldn't reveal the rear wall of the locker was closer to the door than all the others.

That was the plan.

Lillian and Henry had angled the wood to allow air to flow. Now, just as the door to the crew's locker room thudded open, they shoved the false back in place. They were now in virtual complete darkness. The only light was a thin sliver that came in over the top of the false back. Lillian couldn't see Henry at all. But she did hear his breathing. It was fast. She steadied hers.

"I hafta look in all the lockers." The Scot's voice was muffled but clear. He opened and closed the first locker.

"I understand," Payne said. "I don't envy you your job."

"It's the least I can do." He opened and closed the second locker.

The locker in which Lillian and Henry were hiding was the fourth out of ten.

"Who are these fugitives you're looking for?" Payne asked.

"Don't know. One's British. The man." The door to the third locker banged open. A second later, it slammed shut. "The woman's from America. Not sure why they're wanted, but that's who we're looking for. And contraband."

The Scot opened the fourth locker. A slight whoosh of air slipped over the wooden sheet. Lillian held her breath. She heard Henry do likewise.

"What?" the Scot asked. "You got all your heavy coats in one locker?" A hand came into the locker and moved around the winter coats. The hangers scraped on the wooden sheet.

"The men don't like to have those parkas in their lockers during the warm months. So we pile'em in there."

The Scot slammed the door shut. "Good idea."

Lillian and Henry eased out their breaths. They stood and waited for the Scot to complete his inspection of the locker room. The last thing they heard from either man was Payne saying, "Where to next?"

"Bathrooms."

The door to the locker room slammed shut.

Lillian and Henry lowered the wooden sheet. They breathed in the fresh, cool air. Payne had told them not to leave the locker until they were underway. Lillian's legs were killing her. She wondered how long it would be.

34

The answer turned out to be another three hours. Lillian passed the time doing her best to keep her legs from falling asleep. Henry didn't fare much better. When the *Gloria Patri* finally lurched into the Channel, both Lillian and Henry literally fell out of the locker and lay on the floor for a good fifteen minutes. It was long enough for Payne to enter the room and give them both a funny look.

"Shut up," Henry muttered.

"I didn't say a thing," Payne replied. He extended his hand and helped Lillian to her feet. "My apologies, my dear, but it worked."

"Thanks for that," Lillian said. "But the next thing I need is a shower." She motioned her head at the shower stall in the corner.

"Take your time," Payne said. "I'll just drag him to the next room."

An hour later, showered, cleaned, and dressed in a traveling outfit consisting of a blue skirt, tweed close-fitting jacket, and white blouse, Lillian Saxton emerged into the officers' mess. Payne, Henry, and the other men openly gawked at her appearance. She knew she was attractive and could spruce up with the best of them, but it was always nice to have male validation. She plopped her valise on a chair and sat next to Henry.

"You're next. Soap's in the shower. Be sure to use it."

The mild chuckles from the other men made Henry blush. It was Lillian's intended effect. He rose, nodded, and left the room.

Payne placed a cup and saucer in front of Lillian and poured tea in it. "Now, Miss Saxton, why don't you regale us with how you found yourself on our little ship?"

Lillian talked with the mates for nearly the entire voyage

across the Channel. By the time Henry returned, decked out in a dark brown suit and green tie, his hair nicely coiffed, Lillian had run out of story. She didn't let it show, but when Henry cleaned up, he looked downright handsome.

After all the difficulties they had encountered since Liverpool, Lillian found it surprising the crossing was uneventful. Before she knew it, the port city of Antwerp came into view. She and Henry stood on the bow. The sea breeze ruffled her hair. It also ruffled his. The strand of hair fell once more across his forehead.

"What's your plan?" Henry asked.

"Train ride to Brussels. How long does it take?"

"Half an hour in peacetime. Maybe more today. Depends on all the plans the Belgians have made in advance of Hitler's move."

Belgium, to the chagrin of Britain and France, declared itself neutral in 1936. The French hated that stand as it created a hole in the Maginot Line, the fortified line bordering France and Germany. A neutral Belgium, in order to remain in that state, refused to coordinate with the Allies at the outbreak of war in September 1939. If the Germans conducted war the way they had in 1914—that is, if they invaded Belgium—the Allies would have a devil of a time fortifying their left flank.

In lieu of an offensive military, King Leopold III of Belgium ordered his armed forces to operate in a defensive mode. They built up fortifications along the common German/Belgium border in addition to forts around Antwerp and the Albert Canal.

By the time the *Gloria Patri* docked in Antwerp, the signs of a defensive build-up were few and far between. The sun shown brightly down on the largest city in Belgium. Located on the River Scheldt, Antwerp was one of the largest ports in Europe and the host of the 1920 Summer Olympics, the first after the conclusion of the Great War twenty years ago.

Lillian took in the sight of the old city. As an American, her world travels amazed her when she encountered countries and even buildings that were older than the United States. In some cases in Antwerp, structures predated the founding of Jamestown, Virginia, in 1607.

"It's because your country's just a pup," Henry quipped.

"Yeah. I guess so. Still, my pup saved your bacon in the last war."

The Antwerpen-Central train station benefited from architects cognizant of the existing look and feel of the city. The stonework that built up the station made it look right at home with all the other buildings in the area. Lillian and Henry traversed the interior, making their way to the Brussels train. Lillian bought the tickets while Henry kept a keen eye out for anything untoward.

"Excuse me for a moment." Henry eased himself back into the crowd.

Lillian turned and squinted, trying to see where he went. She lost him almost as soon as the crowds enveloped him. Not having any recourse other than to stay where she was, Lillian walked over to a newsstand. She found a French newspaper and bought it. The stories were full of dire warnings about what the Nazis would do next.

If you're so worried about Hitler, Lillian thought, *don't underestimate him.*

The next thing she knew, Henry stood by her side. She looked up at him. A reddening splotch appeared on his cheek.

"What happened?"

"Ran into a friend of mine. Fellow agent. I needed to know if he had received any instructions from the home office."

"Had he?"

"No, but I told him he might. And it would be about you and me. We had a discussion. I wanted to make sure we could conduct our mission without any issues. He, um, saw things differently. Our discussion went, um, in a different direction." He cracked a grin. "I won the argument." He touched his cheek. "But he made some good points."

Lillian examined the growing bruise. "You need some ice on that. Let's get something to drink and then get on the train."

The two of them strolled through the train station. They found a vendor and bought two tall cups of ice water. Henry rubbed a cube on his face. The swelling went down.

A whistle sounded, indicating the impending departure of their train. They hurried through the throng of people and boarded. Finding their seats, they stowed their two bags in the overhead compartment and sat.

As much as she wanted to relax, Lillian remained on alert. The enemies of this mission seemed to materialize out of thin air, when they least expected it. Ironically, now that they were finally in Belgium, nothing happened on the train ride up to Brussels.

Since this route was a major thoroughfare through the country, evidence of military preparations were everywhere. Squads of men, guns, heavy arms, and temporary fortifications dotted both sides of the track. Seeing the map of Belgium in her mind, Lillian wondered how well the Belgian army would hold up against Hitler's seasoned veterans. The poor folks in Poland had barely stood a chance. The army of Denmark barely half a day. She had seen newsreels of the blitzkrieg and read reports from the army. The barricades she now saw appeared to be ready for the first war, not this second one.

The Hotel Le Plaza in Brussels was the designated meeting place. For all of Lillian's defense of the mission, and no matter how much she protested that James was not her current boyfriend, James was not making it easy on her. She and James had spent a weekend in the Hotel Le Plaza back in their college days. It had been Lillian's first true taste of how the other side lived and it marked a turning point in their relationship. After that weekend, the idea of marrying James Geiger hadn't seemed a fantasy, but more like the inevitable future.

When she laid eyes on the building, all those memories and emotions flooded back. Built nearly ten years ago, the Hotel Le Plaza was the finest in all of Brussels. Constructed in a style reminiscent of older hotels in Europe and Paris, Le Plaza sat in the heart of Brussels. The stone facade and structure might have indicated a stolid interior, but the reality was quite the opposite. Natural light was an important feature of the inside of the hotel, with skylights and other windows streaming into the eight-story building. Where the building met the Rue du Progrès and the Rue de Malines, instead of a squared-off edge, the architects rounded the corner, much like the Flatiron building in New York City.

If looked at from a plane, the building was U-shaped with three wings and a rectangular atrium serving as the apex. The carpeted stairways were large, wide, and shaped like squares. To get to the next floor, a patron ascended three flights of stairs with two landings. The corridors and rooms had high ceilings, and paneling along the hallways. Unique among hotels in Belgium was the Le Plaza Theatre. Showing movies and stage concerts, the theatre was housed completely within the hotel itself.

The lobby was just as she remembered. Better, to be honest. Breathing in the air of the hotel was like breathing in splendor. Her heels clacked on the checkerboard marble tiles. She glanced over and noted the couch where she and James had sat waiting for the taxi to take them to the ferry and then back to Oxford.

So many memories.

A flash of anger charged through her. *Why the hell had James chosen this hotel, of all hotels?* She was going to ask him the moment she saw him.

"Everything okay?" Henry was looking down at her.

Lillian stood straighter. "I'm fine. Now, listen, Frank booked our room before he died. You'll just have to go up there and check in for us. I'd do it, but I'm not sure it would be appropriate to have a lady register. Remember what I told you: you are Frank Monroe. You're a banker out of England."

Henry tapped his temple. "Don't you worry about my memory."

He left and approached the desk.

Lillian looked around at the people. No one seemed in a hurry. They milled around, talking with one another, reading newspapers, checking in and out. There didn't seem to be a sense of urgency about them at all.

To conquer her roiling emotions, Lillian decided to sit on the exact same couch as she and James had. She chose James's spot over her own. The fabric was just as soft, even with years of use. She looked at the ornate lobby and remembered.

***

It was November. The late autumn light filtered into the hotel and dispersed into a gentle hue. The hustle and bustle of the people in the lobby was unhurried. Outside, the chilled air foretold the coming of winter.

Lillian Saxton sat on a couch and dreamed. She watched James Geiger, dapper as always in a three-piece suit, settle the bill with the concierge. She wore the new dress he had bought for her on the trip. She had balked at the price, but he insisted. Actually, he gave her no choice. He picked out the dress and made sure the tailor could customize it for Lillian's figure before they left Brussels. A little slipping of cash into the palm and the dress was finished in under an hour.

And it was spectacular. Being a poor girl from California meant that Lillian read the fashion magazines and Hollywood rags and dreamed of wearing a dress like the starlets. Now, she had one. It made her feel special, but not as much as the look on James's face when he saw her in it.

James paid the concierge and returned to her. She stood, and he stopped dead in his tracks. His gaze was one of pure rapture. He opened his mouth. "Okay, we have a room."

Lillian frowned. That's not what James had said. He had told her she looked ravishing. That he loved her. That he wanted to spend the rest of his life with her.

She blinked. James Geiger wasn't standing in front of her. Henry was. He gave her a quizzical look. "We have a room. You okay?"

Lillian shook her head and brushed by him. "I'm fine."

Henry hurried to catch up. "Listen, if something's bothering you, tell me. We're in this together."

Lillian stopped and turned. "It's not mission-critical. It's personal."

"Okay." He held out a sealed envelope between his fingers. "Since your friend is dead, perhaps you ought to open this."

Lillian took the envelope. On the face, written in James's distinctive cursive, were the words "Frank and Lillian." Swallowing another pang of regret for Frank, Lillian used her nail to open the envelope. Inside, on hotel stationery, was a message from James: "I hope your trip was uneventful. Get settled in. Dinner is at 8:00 p.m." Underneath the message was a single cursive capital J.

She blurted out a dry bark of laughter. "Uneventful." She passed the note to Henry. "Looks like we have an afternoon to kill. Let's get up to our room and have a complete look around this place. With all the excitement up in England, I can expect more of the same here."

They walked up the stairs. The room was on the sixth floor. It faced north, overlooking the Rue du Progrès. Henry turned the key and let Lillian into the room first.

The room was one of the modest ones, but a modest room in the Hotel Le Plaza surpassed many other rooms in which Lillian had stayed. The heavy curtains that blocked out the light were drawn up. The sheer curtains underneath diffused the late afternoon sunlight and gave the interior a soft glow. A dressing table and mirror sat on the wall with the window. A larger wardrobe occupied a position opposite the window. To the right was a door that led to the small lavatory.

In the center of the room was the bed. A full-sized bed. Not two beds.

Lillian stared at the bed. Two thoughts swirled in her mind. One, what the hell had Frank been thinking in reserving a room with only one bed. Two, how was she going to convince Henry to sleep on the floor?

"I get the bed." She tossed her valise in the middle of the comforter.

Henry closed the door behind him. "How about we take turns? I get it tonight. You get it tomorrow."

Lillian huffed. "I hope to be gone tomorrow." She checked her watch. "I'll need to freshen up before we eat."

"You look fine." Henry shoved his bag in the wardrobe. He stopped. "Did you pack anything nicer?"

Lillian opened her valise and pulled out a dress she had packed back in Washington. When James's message had arrived and Colonel Honeywell had cleared her to make the journey, Lillian knew exactly which dress she was going to wear upon meeting James Geiger again after all those years.

Not the dress he bought her. Not coincidentally, that dress never made it back to America from Paris those many years ago. No, the dress she picked out specifically to wear the day she again saw James Geiger was the one made just for her. Kanji Tanaka knew a seamstress in the hills of California who could make any dress for any lady. The seamstress, a middle-aged Mexican woman named Aurora, was a genius in seeing a woman's figure and tailoring a dress to accentuate her curves and body structure. Lillian had met Aurora in Tanaka's hermitage and they had become good friends. When Lillian joined the Army, Aurora made a dress for Lillian as a parting gift. Lillian had worn it only once, at a dance the Army threw around Christmas time. Attending alone, Lillian wore the dress, a green one-piece with a modestly plunging neckline, off-the-shoulder sleeves, and a hemline higher than normal. Sergeant Lillian Saxton had been caught unaware by the attention she received. Every non-married officer asked her for a dance. She didn't buy a drink the entire night. In fact, she became the star of the party, something she initially hated, but came to relish. The entire evening was summed up by an old general who wouldn't even make it to Christmas Day. "Sergeant, seeing you in that dress makes me believe Santa Claus is real."

That's the dress she had selected to wear to see James Geiger again. She unfolded the dress and laid it over the comforter. "I'm wearing this."

As a garment, Henry didn't give it the slightest notice. "It's nice."

"Wait until you see it on me." She winked. "Now, will you be a dear and order us some drinks?"

35

Drinks turned out to be gin martinis. By the time Henry had returned with a tray, shaker, ice cubes, the liquor, and two glasses, Lillian had donned her dress. She sat at the dressing table and applied her make-up. She stopped applying her eye liner and watched Henry stand next to the writing table and prepare the martinis. The clatter of the ice in the shaker was loud in the small room. His back was to her so he didn't notice her gaze.

The whole scene made her chuckle. He turned and she began applying the eye liner again.

"What's so funny?"

"You seem so confident mixing drinks. Do you often have cause to prepare cocktails?"

Henry smirked. "I've been undercover for over a year. Those Germans back in Liverpool only preferred beer and whiskey. I'm good with that, mind you, but there's something special and refined about a cocktail. The preparation, the mixing, the presentation." He poured the clear contents into the two martini glasses, giving a little flourish at the end. Not a drop landed on the tray. He plopped two olives into each of the drinks. Taking the glasses in his hands, he glided across the room and placed one on the dressing table. "Don't you agree?"

Even though she wasn't finished preparing her make-up, Lillian stood and took her cup. "I do." She offered a toast. "To our success." They clinked glasses and sipped. The ice-cold liquid burned her throat. She relished the feeling.

Lillian wouldn't admit it to Henry but she was nervous about meeting James again. After six long years, after that horrible breakup, she was going to be in the same room as the man she had loved and with whom she had wanted to spend the rest of her life. That James had picked this hotel was, frankly, a dirty trick. She would make sure to ask him about his choice.

"Penny for your thoughts?" Henry's voice was soft and smooth like the martini.

"I still need to put on my face and you need to freshen up. Do you want some base for your cheek?" The spot where Henry's fellow agent had decked him was much smaller, but still visible.

"Naw. It just helps in the looks department considering we're going to meet your old boyfriend." He winked. "I'm a handsome bloke who'll be escorting you to dinner. I've got a nice suit. The bruise'll just make Geiger wonder about what he left behind." He downed the rest of his drink and put the glass back on the dressing table. "I'm right, yeah?"

Lillian bit the inside of her cheek to keep from saying the wrong thing. Instead, she shrugged.

"I'm right." Henry turned and grabbed his bag. He went into the bathroom and closed the door.

Lillian sat back down and looked at herself in the mirror. With her base and powder on, no lipstick, and eye liner only on one eye, she looked off kilter. Comical even. Henry was right. She had definitely noticed his ruggedly handsome appearance. The closer this meeting got, the more she realized she was glad he was here. Not that she wouldn't have preferred Frank. In fact, if it had been Frank and not Henry, much of the worry would evaporate. The meeting would have been more like a class reunion than what its true purpose was: a military mission.

The more she and Henry talked and participated in this mission, the more she came to appreciate how well he operated. That was to be expected considering he had been good enough to work undercover for nearly a year. No, the simple truth was there for anyone to see: the Nazis knew about her and Frank and their arrival in Liverpool. They had tried to kill them both. Then there was Dover and the spies who had found them there. Clearly, they were being watched and tracked.

But Henry's deft handling of the Channel crossing gave her some hope that they had lost the tails. As Lillian applied rouge and the rest of her eye liner, she had to be honest with herself: she could have done something like that and gotten them across the Channel, but Henry, with his local knowledge, had done it better and smoother. Yes, she was glad he was here with her.

The bathroom door opened and Henry emerged into the room. Lillian was leaning forward, applying her mascara. She stopped and looked at Henry through the mirror. His suit was dark blue, nearly black. The trousers, pleated at the hip, were cuffed at the ankle. The pants touched the top of his black shoes, highly polished. The starched white shirt allowed the brilliant red tie to take all the attention. A pocket square matched the tie. The suit coat was buttoned, giving his physique a sleek, classy look. For his hair, he had swept it back and applied something to it. The strand that seemed perpetually to be falling over his forehead was nowhere to be seen.

In short, he was a knockout.

"Well, don't you clean up nicely!" To hide her admiration, Lillian picked up her glass and downed the rest of her drink. "Got any more?"

Henry put his bag back in the wardrobe. He took her glass and prepared another drink. She finished putting on her make-up. She stood as he approached her. In his hands, he held two more drinks.

"How do I look?" she asked.

"Like someone who's out to prove to an old boyfriend that he was wrong." He smiled.

Lillian smiled. She took the glass. They toasted again.

"You've been trained well. You know just what to say to a lady."

"It's all my mum. And how do I look?"

"Like the perfect man to emphasize the mistake an old boyfriend made."

They sipped their drinks in silence. Henry broke the ice. He unbuttoned his coat and held it open. "I'm carrying. You?"

"In my purse."

Henry hiked his foot onto the bed and lifted a trouser leg. A knife in a sheath affixed to his calf appeared. "Back-up. You?"

"Silly man. You're my back-up. Oh, and I've been trained in

karate. It's a martial art from Japan."

"Well, I guess we have it covered. Shall we?"

Lillian drained her glass. She leaned to look at herself in the mirror and applied her lipstick. Bright red. She blotted her lips on a napkin. "I am now."

She let Henry open the door for her and lead her to the elevator bank. Cognizant of what happened in Liverpool with Bauer following them, Lillian kept a sharp eye out for anyone else. No other person walked the hallway.

The elevator arrived and they rode it down to the ground floor. With her hand inside Henry's arm, Lillian took in all the splendor that was the Hotel Le Plaza. The lobby showcased architecture that reflected a classical approach with marble columns and arches. The grand central staircase spun upward to the second floor. Other guests, all decked out in their finest, seemed to forget there was a war on. The chandelier emitted a soft glow. Lillian felt like a queen.

"We have reservations with James Geiger's table," Henry informed the head waiter. His voice was smooth and debonair.

"Mr. Geiger gave me instructions to show you to the table." The head waiter seemed to have his thin eyebrows in a perpetual arch. "This way, Mr. Monroe."

Lillian stifled a groan at the reminder that Frank was dead. The restaurant proved to be elegant yet muted. The arches and color palette gave the room a Grecian feel. One wall consisted entirely of a mirror. The bar, made of dark wood, showed every bottle of liquor available, each colored bottle sparkling in the light. The head waiter escorted them to a table. Being the professional she was, Lillian noted where the kitchen entrance was as well as the front door. She faced the main entry while Henry, to her immediate left, had eyes on the kitchen.

"Fancy," he murmured.

She smiled. "James's family is generationally rich."

"You ever have second thoughts?"

Lillian paused only a second. In that instant, all she had been feeling about seeing this place again and imaging her life with

James juxtaposed itself with the woman she had become—the woman James had made her—and found she preferred the present. Still, there was something there.

"None."

The wine steward and their waiter both materialized seemingly out of nowhere. Henry scanned the wine list and Lillian deferred to him. He chose a French pinot noir for them both. The wine steward glided away and the waiter presented menus. The prices took Lillian's breath away, but she knew money was no object with James.

"Order whatever you want," she told Henry. She recognized the look on his face. It was the look of a person who worked for the government and was accustomed to the lifestyle that income brought. "James wouldn't have it any other way."

"You sure about that?"

"Positive."

Their wine came and they toasted. "To success," Henry said.

"To success," Lillian echoed. She sipped the wine as her eyes traveled to the entryway.

James Geiger stood in the doorway.

Lillian Saxton audibly gasped.

Henry noticed. He turned to see where she looked.

James Geiger, of course, wore a tuxedo, a black number with black bow tie. The jacket was single-breasted and featured peaked lapels of black silk that caught the light of the chandeliers. His shirt had a winged collar, the points expertly layered behind the bow tie. She noted the French cuffs jutting from the jacket sleeve with cuff links sparkling. His clean face showed no sign of aging. His radiant smile, just like she remembered it, made her stomach do a flip. The dark hair was styled and swept back.

"My God," Lillian whispered.

If being in the Hotel Le Plaza brought back memories, seeing James in person, even from across the room, broke the dam of emotions. Image after image flooded her mind and consciousness. The two of them sneaking around the Oxford library, finding a secluded spot to study each other and kiss. The two of them on the beaches of France on a lazy summer day when Lillian refused to return home and instead spent the warm month living the life of luxury in one of the Geiger family's homes. The two of them on their first date to a performance of Shakespeare's *Much Ado About Nothing*. The two of them on a steamer back to Boston to meet James's parents.

All of these memories and more swept over Lillian as she stared at the man she had loved so passionately, so devotedly, so completely. Her heart began beating faster. Her vision tunneled down to one thing—James Geiger. Everything else, including Henry Clark, faded to nothingness.

This entire time, James talked and laughed with the head waiter. Lillian willed him to find her with his eyes, those gorgeous, perfect hazel eyes. She didn't realize she was holding her breath until her lungs ached and she sent a fresh burst of air down into her body.

James turned his face to scan the room. His expression was one of wonderment. Impassive in its search for Lillian.

Or Frank, she realized. *How in the world am I going to break the news to James that Frank was dead? That Frank was dead basically because of him.*

His eyes went from simple wondering to certitude when his glance locked with hers. His face at once relaxed and beamed. He broke into a wide grin that became an all-out smile as his lips parted to reveal his teeth: white, straight, and radiant. Even from across the room, the smile went all the way up to his eyes. They sparkled.

Lillian's stomach did another flip as she remembered how many times those eyes had turned her insides to butter as he melted her heart with them. How many times those eyes had captivated her. Those eyes, that had seen every inch of her and came away happier in the knowledge. Those eyes that had ravished her, told her they loved her, no matter what the future brought.

Lillian's breath came in short bursts.

Henry said something to her but she didn't hear it or

understand anything. For all she knew, there were only two people in the world: Lillian Saxton and James Geiger.

Then a woman, a blonde woman, sidled up to James. She eased herself next to him and slipped her arm around his. He broke his gaze with Lillian and gave the woman a kiss on the cheek.

All the emotions that had swept up Lillian Saxton and taken her places she hadn't been in six years evaporated in an instant. Her guts turned upside down. The weight that James's eyes had lifted settled itself back onto her shoulders. The world rematerialized around her. It no longer consisted of just James and her and her fantasies. Henry was in it. He was looking at her, a genuine expression of concern plastered across his face. Other patrons were laughing, eating, and enjoying themselves without a care in the world. Waiters were bringing food. The cooks in the kitchen were preparing food. And somewhere in the world, there was a war on.

Lillian finally realized Henry was speaking words at her. She blinked, as if coming out of hypnosis.

"Are you okay?" Henry reached over and grasped her arm.

She noted his touch with nonchalance. She grabbed her wine glass and threw a large amount into her mouth. She pointed with the hand holding her wine. Under her breath, she murmured, "The son of a bitch brought his wife."

36

"How do you know it's his wife?" Henry asked.

"James wasn't the type to step out on a lady," Lillian replied. She didn't need a mirror to know her entire face had changed. She felt it.

"Hey, you never know about a traitor."

Lillian flashed a look at him. "James is no traitor," she hissed.

"Why are we here again?" He cocked an eyebrow at her.

She had no reply.

James Geiger walked and smiled with the ease of a man accustomed to getting everything he wanted. His movements were nonchalant as the head waiter led the couple to the table. It wasn't like Hollywood where all eyes turned to catch a glimpse of a star.

Lillian recognized the look. It was the look of a man in command.

But his countenance changed when he caught sight of Henry. Confusion swept over his face. He looked at Lillian, furrowing his brows in an unspoken question.

Henry must have caught the look as well. He stood when the head waiter, James, and the woman arrived. The woman bowed at the neck at Henry's gentlemanly gesture. "Good evening. My name's Henry Clark."

James appeared charmed. He extended his hand. "James Geiger." The two men clasped hands. "And may I present my wife, Elsa Geiger?"

Now Lillian had a name for her.

With her heels, Elsa and James nearly matched in height. By Lillian's reckoning, that put Elsa a few inches taller than Lillian's five foot eight. The red dress she wore could have been worn by a Hollywood starlet or a princess of a small Mediterranean country. It was form-fitting, showing off all her curves. The plunging neckline revealed just the top of her cleavage. The blonde hair was pulled to the back of her head and then fell gracefully to touch her shoulders. Around her neck sparkled a necklace of gold and gemstones. Matching earrings dangled from her ears. Her blue eyes glittered at the attention Henry was paying to her.

Lillian finished her wine. She placed the empty glass back on the table a little harder than necessary.

James caught the movement. He held out one of his arms. His intention was not to shake Lillian's hand but to hug her. Still sitting, Lillian didn't want to rise and give him that honor.

To accommodate her, James leaned down and pecked her on the cheek. Being this close to him sent shivers down her spine despite her current circumstances. She noted he wore the same cologne she had selected for him back when they vacationed in Paris.

Back when he broke her heart.

"Elsa, may I present Lillian Saxton?"

The blonde must have already known about Lillian's history with James for Elsa appeared nonplussed. She affected the pseudo-genuine smile one dons at parties where all the guests are insufferable.

Elsa extended her hand across the table. In heavily accented English, she said, "Pleased you meet you, Miss Saxton."

She speaks English, too?

Lillian, after a nudge to her foot by Henry's, reciprocated. The two women shook hands. "Hello." The handshake quickly died.

The head waiter, who had stood discreetly to the side during the introductions, now held the chair for Elsa. She sat opposite Lillian. James took the seat immediately to Lillian's right.

James waved off the wine steward. He indicated the glasses already on the table. "We'll have whatever they're having. Oh, and could you bring a refill for the lady here?" The wine steward bowed. He took Lillian's glass and left.

Folding his hands, James gazed at Lillian. "Well, it's certainly been a long time."

Lillian cocked her head. "It certainly has."

"I told Elsa about how we dated in college. Those were good times."

Lillian wished the wine would get there quickly. "Yes, they were." She didn't trust herself to say more than a few words.

James turned to Henry. "And what do you do?"

Lillian stopped short. They had completely neglected to discuss any cover story for Henry. Like James and Elsa, she waited for his response.

He must have realized that the best lie was mostly truth. "I work for the British government."

"Really?" James glanced at Lillian. "In what capacity?"

"Accountant. I keep track of things coming and going. Real dull stuff, to be honest, but the pay's good. And you?"

Their wine arrived. The steward eased away. They all sipped.

Elsa made a face that she quickly tried to hide.

Lillian caught it.

James blanketed the moment by answering Henry's question.

"Munitions. I manage a factory in Berlin that makes ordinance."

Henry nodded once. "Your business must be thriving."

"We're doing well." James turned his attention to Elsa. "My lovely wife helps out in the factory. She comes from a well-respected family that goes back generations, to a time before Germany was Germany."

The waiter arrived to take everyone's order. "Anything you like," James said. "It's on me."

Lillian found she had lost her appetite. To compensate, she found the most expensive item on the menu and ordered it. She caught Elsa's eyebrows as they raised, then lowered.

James, nonplussed, ordered the same thing. Henry and Elsa ordered more modest items. The waiter smiled, asked if there was anything else, and left after James requested a bottle of champagne and four glasses.

"Celebrating something?" Lillian said.

"Actually yes." James reached out and grasped his wife's hand. "It's our anniversary."

Of course it is, Lillian thought. Why the hell did I travel all this distance to see him again?

"I thought it would be a great idea to share it with some of my best old friends from college. Tell me, where is Frank?"

"The morgue. Or maybe already on the way back to America. Either way, Frank's dead."

Henry didn't move.

Elsa's eyes watched her husband's reaction.

James's glass froze halfway to his mouth. He wet his lips and spoke barely above a whisper. "That can't be. I just saw him a month ago."

"I know. He told me."

James wet his mouth with wine. "How?"

Lillian ignored the gentle nudge from Henry's foot. She knew why he wanted to be cautious. They weren't sure how far to trust James. And now that he had brought his wife, who knew what kind of classified material she was privy to? Still, she could tell the truth to a point.

"Food poisoning. In Liverpool. Something didn't agree with him. He fell ill and died soon thereafter." She uttered the words in such a matter-of-fact manner that it surprised even her.

"How dreadful," Elsa said. "James has told me all about your time together in Oxford. You were close to him?"

At that moment, Lillian wanted to know exactly what and how much James had told Elsa about him and Lillian. Instead, she reverted back to good old Frank. "Although we hadn't seen each other in years, Frank was like a comfortable coat. When you put it on, it just fits. Frank was the type of man who always smiled and had a kind word. He always supported you, even if you hadn't seen him in years." Her voice caught and she stopped for a moment.

Henry filled the gap. "It's still raw."

"So," James said to Henry, "how did you two meet?"

Without missing a beat, Henry replied coolly. "I knew Frank.

His bank had dealings with my office from time to time. We got to know each other. I was in Liverpool on business when he and Lillian landed. We ate dinner together before Frank was poisoned. Poor chap. He really was as good as Lillian says he was."

"But why are you here?" James persisted.

Henry shrugged. He reached over and laid a firm hand on Lillian's arm. "After Frank's death, she told me she still had to cross the Channel and come here. I asked her if whatever she and Frank had to do could wait. She said no. I told her I'd be her escort, help her through this." He patted her arm. "Frank was such a good chap."

James sipped his wine. His eyes darted from Lillian to Henry.

Lillian could tell he was weighing what he had heard with what he knew about her. "You're a gentleman to accompany Lillian here to Belgium."

"But?" Lillian said. "I know you well enough to know there's a but coming."

James smiled thinly. "It's just that you had quite an independent streak back at Oxford and in our semester here on the Continent. The Lillian Saxton I knew wouldn't need a man to accompany her on her work."

Lillian simmered with fury at the implication. Aloud, she murmured, "Things change."

"And what do you do?" Elsa asked. "My James has told me all about Oxford but not what it is you do now."

Bristling at the word 'my,' Lillian played it straight. "I'm in the United States Army. A sergeant."

Henry and James didn't react.

Elsa looked as if Lillian's words had just slapped her in the face. "You're a soldier?"

"I am."

"But you're a woman."

"I am that as well."

"Doesn't it bother you to work in a profession where men are naturally superior?"

Whatever Lillian might have said died inside her as the waiter returned with their meal. The four diners were all smiles when they saw the lavish presentation of their food. The wine steward brought a chilled bottle of champagne, four champagne flutes, and an ice bucket. He popped the cork and poured the sparkling liquid into the flutes and departed.

James lifted his flute. "This was supposed to be a toast to old friends seeing each other again and having a gay old time, but let's have the first toast be to Frank Monroe. A steady man in an unsteady world." Lillian, Henry, and Elsa all lifted flutes, clinked them together, and drank.

The quartet ate in silence for a few minutes. The only comments consisted of how good the food was, the niceness of the hotel, and, according to James, how good it was to see Lillian again.

The elephant in the room was brought up by Elsa. "As a soldier, Lillian, do you think America will get into the war?"

Lillian stopped chewing momentarily before resuming. She swallowed. "I certainly hope so. I want to ensure the United States has its rightful place at the peace table."

"I understand. But how do you think your president will react to being the first president to whom terms will be dictated?"

Lillian smiled thinly. "It's not going to happen that way. If anything, it'll be *der Führer* on the opposite end of a victory table."

Elsa frowned and appeared genuinely confused. "Did you not see how we handled Poland? Or Denmark? I think you underestimate how effective our military has become. We will win, of course." She cut another piece of her dinner. "How about Britain, Mr. Clark? Prime Minister Chamberlain is already fluent in giving up."

James interrupted before the discussion could move any further. "My dear, this is a nice meal. These are our friends. Let's not have such talk here."

Lillian wiped her mouth with her napkin and threw it on the table. "Why not talk about it, James? It's why we're here, right? I mean, it's certainly not to see me or Frank, if he were here. You don't really care about me. I know how this sounds, all whiney and such, but I don't care. Not once in six years did you think to write or call to see how I was doing. And I sure as hell wasn't going to call you since I wasn't the one who broke everything off."

Elsa looked shocked for a moment which gave Lillian more evidence that James had not told his wife everything about them.

James smiled at Lillian's outburst. "Come on, Lil. It's not like that."

"Then what is it like, Jay?" Since he had used her nickname, she retaliated by using his. She didn't let him answer. "Forget it. Can we just go to your room so you can deliver both things to us and we can part again? This time forever."

Henry cocked his head at a word Lillian said. "Both? What else is there?"

Lillian waved him off. "It's nothing. No, it's personal."

"Nothing?" Incredulity laced James's voice. "I hardly think it is nothing. Tell me: would you have come all this way just for the codebook? What really got you here?"

"Codebook?" Elsa asked. "What codebook?"

In the back of her mind, Lillian noted Elsa's curious question and determined she didn't know the true purpose of this trip. In the moment, however, Lillian shot back an answer. "You're damn right I would. I'm even here after Frank was poisoned, which, by the way, wasn't from food poisoning. He was murdered by a secret Nazi spy ring in Liverpool." She felt satisfied when a look of shock and worry crossed James's face.

Under the table, Henry kicked her foot. Not softly.

"What?" She turned to him.

"I think you should keep your voice down," Henry murmured. "This isn't the time or place to be discussing this."

Abruptly, James folded his napkin and placed it on the table. "Your friend is correct, Lillian. It would be best if we took this upstairs." He rose and gestured for Elsa to do the same.

"But our food," his wife protested. "We're not finished."

"We are now." James's eyes scanned the room. No one seemed to give them any notice.

"Fine." Lillian stood. On second thought, she reached down and grabbed her wine glass. She downed the contents and slammed it on the table. "Let's go."

Henry rose at that. He put a guiding hand around her waist and leaned in close. "Not here. Mind yourself. And calm down."

His breath tickled her ear. "This isn't my first time in the field."

"But you're acting like it. I noticed at least four people who turned and noticed you while you started off on your rant. After Liverpool and Dover, anything is possible. Lay your head on my shoulder. We might salvage this if they think you're drunk."

"Like hell I am." She moved forward, brushing past James and Elsa, leaving Henry alone next to the table. She strode quickly to the grand central staircase and waited, her arm hooked over the railing.

Henry, James, and Elsa joined her.

"That was a horrible display," James hissed to her. "Don't you realize the situation we're in, that you're in? Who knows how many of those people might be spies?"

Lillian glanced at Henry. He gave her a disapproving look. "He's right."

"Shut up." Lillian whirled on James. "Can we just go to your room and get the damn book and the name?"

Elsa repeated her earlier question. "James, what book is she talking about?"

James narrowed his eyes at Lillian. He pursed his lips, thinking. After a moment, he said, "We're on the top floor. Eight zero nine. Now that we've been seen together, I guess secrecy is irrelevant. Follow us."

He led them all to the elevators. They rode up in tense silence. Henry and Lillian stood in the rear, behind James and Elsa. Deftly, Henry unbuttoned his jacket. With his eyes, he indicated her purse. She nodded once. She snapped it open, holding her fingers over the clasp to avoid making any sound.

They reached the eighth floor. James stepped out and allowed his wife to walk next to him. Lillian and Henry held back a couple of paces. She looked over her shoulder. No one else strolled the hallway. From the open stairway that led to the ground floor, the faint murmur of the restaurant crowd could still be heard. She shifted her purse to her left arm so she could draw with her right.

Arriving at his room, James extracted a key and unlocked the door. His eyes, too, swept the hallway. Satisfied, he opened the door for everyone, then closed and locked it.

"Can I offer you a drink?" He indicated the bottle of whiskey on the desk.

"No, thank you," Lillian said. "Just give us the book and the name and we'll be on our way."

"I'll take that drink." Henry strode across the room to the desk and poured himself a couple of fingers worth. He emptied the glass and pointed to Lillian. "What about this name? This other thing? I thought we were just here for the codebook."

"Not now."

"Yes, now. What are you not telling me?"

"It's a personal thing," Lillian asserted. "Between James and me."

Elsa said, "If there's something you have to say, I'd like to hear it as well." Her tone was icy. "But I'm less interested in that name and more in this book you keep talking about." She turned to her husband. "James, what have you done?"

"Nothing." James poured himself a glass of whiskey and gulped it down. "Yet."

"James." Lillian's tone took on a menacing, somewhat worried tone. "Talk. Where is the book?"

James Geiger inhaled deeply and stood ramrod-straight. "There is no codebook." He tapped his temple. "It's all in here. If you want what I know, you'll have to get me and my wife to England."

37

Lillian Saxton stood rooted to the floor, speechless. Her vision dizzied. She reached out and steadied herself on a chair. She frowned at the floor, studying the weave. *What did James just say?*

Confusion. Anger. Disbelief. All swirled within her and more. She sputtered a few sounds that were supposed to be words, but none came out of her intelligibly.

Henry proved the first one to speak. "Are you telling me there is no codebook?"

James looked up at him. "That's right. It's in my head."

"You can't possibly know the code and how it works."

Lillian's brain and mouth finally teamed up and made sense. She nodded. "Yes, he can." She took a few deep breaths. "James Geiger is a genius in mathematics. That's what he studied at Oxford. A few times he even took the professors to task. Late in our senior year, he was invited to return as a guest lecturer. If he'd wanted to, he could have gone on straight to Ph.D. work. He's that smart."

She turned to James, staring at him in disbelief. "But that's not what he wanted to do. He wanted to stay in Germany. He liked the build-up of arms and the military. He liked German precision. He wanted me to stay with him. I didn't want to." Out of the corner of her eye, Lillian saw Elsa jump with shock. "That's why we broke it off." She moved closer to James. "And now, you present me with this ultimatum? You lied!" Lillian swung an arm and slapped James across the face. The strike sounded loud in the room.

Elsa moved to James. Henry stepped behind Lillian. He reached for her arm but she shrugged it away. "Back off, Henry. I still have questions for him."

"So do I," the British agent said. "James, are you serious

about this? You want us to get you out of Belgium?"

James, a hand to his reddening cheek, nodded. "It's the only way I know we can be safe."

"Safe from whom?" Henry said.

"The Nazi high command. They've never trusted me."

Lillian grunted. "Guess they know you pretty well."

"What makes you think they're after you?" Henry poured himself more whiskey. He poured another glass and gave it to Lillian, who took it.

"I'm an American," James said in a matter-of-fact tone. He smiled sheepishly and shrugged. "It never mattered that I chose to stay in Germany. Chose to work in a munitions factory, using my skills in math to help them build better projectiles. Fell in love with a German girl and married her. None of that mattered to the Germans. It doesn't even matter that I'm from Fredericksburg, Texas, which is like Germany but in Texas. They always had a level of distrust toward me that I could never shake."

He turned to Henry and Lillian and continued. "It started small, so small I never noticed. My bosses at the factory would ask pointed questions of me. As good as I am with math, I'm not always the best in reading people. It took me a little while before I realized the questions they asked me were based on conversations I'd had in the privacy of my own home. They were listening in on me, on Elsa." He paused, then finished. "And us together."

James paced the room. "I started seeing things. Papers I'd left on my desk slightly off. Envelopes of letters with subtle signs of being opened, read, and resealed. For all I knew, I was being followed and photographed. I'd seen how the spy organization in Berlin tracks foreign nationals. I helped them create a more efficient system. The system I created then turned on me. I had no evidence, but I knew."

Lillian threw back her whiskey in one gulp. She knew how James was. He was building a case, just as he had done to the poor mathematics professors back at Oxford right before he laid out the answer they couldn't see.

"Things got so bad," James continued, "that some of our friends gave us the cold shoulder. Not in any bad way, but ever since Poland, there has been a distance between us and them. Dinners planned that were cancelled at the last minute. Invitations given but declined. All the reasons were legitimate, but there started to be an isolation, a distrust. I didn't want that. I started to think of a way to change our situation."

James turned to Elsa. "I'm sorry, my love. This was the only way the three of us could truly be safe."

Lillian raised her head. "Three of us?"

James put his arm around his wife. "Yes. Elsa is pregnant."

38

Something in Lillian's stomach lurched. She wanted to throw up. Instead, she stared at James in disbelief.

"I can't believe this. You contact me—*me* of all people—to come all the way here with the promise of a Nazi codebook all the while you planned on dropping this little bombshell? Why? Why me? Why not Frank? Wait, did he know about this?"

"Not at all," James said. "Even Elsa didn't know until just now. That's how secret I kept it."

"Brilliant. You're so damned perfect when it comes to keeping secrets. But again, why me?"

James grinned. "Because of who you have become."

Lillian frowned at that. "What the hell does that mean?"

"Lil, you're a soldier now. And, more important, you're an American soldier, one that the spies in Germany don't know about." He spread his arms, palms up. "What better person to help us escape Europe than a soldier from a country with which Germany is not at war? And from a neutral city."

Lillian narrowed her eyes and jammed a finger in James's chest. "You played me! My brother's killer. That just another carrot you dangled in front of my eyes?"

James shook his head. "I know his name. Get us to Britain and you'll get his name."

Lillian reached out and grabbed his lapels. She hauled him directly in front of her face. "Tell me now. I'm in no mood to help you do anything." She ground her teeth and snarled at James. "You like that I'm a soldier now. That means I've learned ways to make people talk. Want me to show you?"

"You wouldn't."

"Try me."

Henry moved next to them. With his powerful grip, he unclenched Lillian's fingers from James's jacket. "This isn't the time or the place."

"Why the hell not? He lied to you, too."

"No. You did."

Lillian started. "What are you talking about?"

Henry gave her a steady gaze. "In all the talk about the codebook and avenging Ludlow, never once did you mention anything about getting the name of your brother's killer."

"That's because it's personal."

"Maybe, but it became something more when I got involved."

He pulled her arm away from James. She wrenched it out of his grip and walked across the room. She put her back to everyone in the room. She wanted to make sure none of them saw how angry and bitter she was. She listened instead of saying anything.

Henry said, "In case you haven't figured it out, I do work for the British government, but I'm not an accountant."

"I know," James said.

Lillian turned. "What?"

Henry's head was cocked. "How?"

"You were part of our group in Liverpool," James said. "One of our agents, Johannes Bauer, sent us a photograph of you. We didn't suspect you were British Intelligence, but it was obvious when I saw you sitting at the table downstairs." He took Elsa's hand in his. "It's why I am formally requesting asylum in your country. I can work with your government and tell everything I know about Nazi codes. In exchange, I want safe passage to America where my wife and I can raise our children in peace."

Elsa yanked her hand away. "James, you never asked what I wanted."

He took her hand in his again. "Elsa, it's too dangerous here. The war has started. The invasion is imminent. Let's flee to safety before something goes wrong."

At the door came the sound of a key entering the lock. The key turned, the lock chunked back into place, and the door opened. All eyes turned to the person who entered the room.

Henry Clark drew his gun and had it at the ready.

James and Elsa Geiger turned to face the door. They still held hands.

Lillian Saxton plunged her hand into her purse. Before she withdrew her gun, however, she saw who stood in the doorway. Her jaw dropped open.

39

"Professor Graf?" Lillian Saxton stared at the man in the doorway. He looked like her old history professor from her semester abroad in Berlin. James and Frank had both gone with her. It was the time in which she chose James over Frank.

The man standing in front of her was older and grayer, but still possessed a light in his eyes. This man, if it was Graf, wore a Nazi uniform. He also held a gun aimed at the room.

"I'm so pleased you remember me, Miss Saxton," the man said in near-perfect, lightly accented English. "I'll admit I'm very surprised that you are the mystery woman my agents have been talking about these past few days." He gave a slight shrug. "I guess I should have assumed it might've been you considering Frank Monroe and James here are involved. But seeing as how it ended those years ago, I didn't think James would have the stupidity to call you. But call you he did, and now you're here."

Graf whistled. Two men and one woman entered the room. All of them wore Nazi uniforms. All carried pistols.

"Agent Clark," Graf said to Henry, "it would be advisable if you hand over your weapon."

"What if I don't want to?" Henry still had his gun aimed at Graf. "I could drop you where you stand."

"And my people would drop you. Is that what you want?"

"One less Nazi colonel in the world would make the sacrifice worth it."

"Maybe," Graf said. "But I could say the same thing about one less British Intelligence officer." Raising his voice, he called, "Get your hand out of your purse, Miss Saxton."

Lillian's hand froze. She weighed her options. It didn't take long. She had none. Graf's partners all had their guns trained on her, Henry, James, and Elsa. Henry had two aimed at him.

Not now. There will be another time.

"If you're the soldier James says you are," Graf went on, "then you will have determined your position is hopeless. Same for you, Agent Clark. Make your decision."

Henry and Lillian exchanged a glance. She nodded. "Removing my hand," she declared. Slowly, she lifted her hand out of her purse. The woman Nazi snatched the purse from Lillian's grasp.

Spreading his hands wide and lifting his pistol high into the air, Henry surrendered as well. One of Graf's men took the pistol while the other one frisked Henry. The Nazi was thorough and found Henry's knife. He took the blade and pocketed it.

"What about them?" the woman soldier asked. She spoke German.

"I don't think they're carrying," Graf said, also in German. "Search them anyway."

The woman soldier did the honors for both James and Elsa. James was decidedly uncomfortable at the thoroughness of the search. The woman soldier grinned maliciously.

"They're clean," the woman said. She came to stand next to Graf as did the other two soldiers.

Graf relaxed. He holstered his pistol and smiled. "This is like a class reunion. Who knew I'd have the chance to see you again, Miss Saxton."

"It's Sergeant Saxton," Lillian blurted.

Graf raised his eyebrows in mock surprise. "Sergeant Saxton, then. As such, of course, that makes you a prisoner of war. A valuable one at that. Are you here in a military context?"

"No. Just seeing an old friend."

Graf's features took on a mock doubting appearance. "Secret Nazi codebooks, the promise of asylum for a German citizen and her traitorous husband? That is the very definition of a military operation. We're already at war with you." This last Graf said to Henry. "But you, Sergeant,"—he turned back to Lillian—" here, in Europe. That is something *der Führer* can use in his propaganda."

After her initial surprise and shock, Lillian finally started thinking like the soldier she was. It was clear to her that this was neither the time or place to make a stand. Instead, it was time to gather some intelligence.

"So James was correct when he feared he was being watched. Why?"

"He said so himself. He is an American. No matter how much he professes his loyalty to *das Veterland* and *der Führer*, some in my government didn't trust him. I told them Herr Geiger could be trusted. Look who's the fool now."

Lillian kept her hands in view, but walked over to the desk. "Whiskey?" She poured herself some, then added some of the brown liquid in another glass. She carried it over to Graf and offered it to him.

He took it. "Thank you." They both sipped while everyone in the room watched. Graf said, "Who would have known you would turn out to be a soldier? I thought you were destined to spend your days as someone's little wife."

In her mind's eye, Lillian saw herself tossing her whiskey in Graf's face. With a comment like that, Graf deserved that and more. A few strategic punches to the face and weak spots would easily have Graf sputtering on the ground.

But he wasn't alone. Even with Henry helping, Lillian knew she couldn't take out these four Nazis and escape. Who knew if there were any more around? Even if she and Henry fought their way out, what would the next move be? Go back to Britain without the codes? Without the name of her brother's killer? That was not an option. Not here and not now.

Instead, she merely smiled.

"What's so funny?" Graf asked.

"The idea that people don't change."

Graf himself laughed out loud at that. "Sergeant, in all my years of teaching, if there's one thing I have seen is that people, by the time they are in university, have pretty much been set in their ways. I am basically the same man I was twenty years ago."

Lillian finished her whiskey. She took Graf's glass from his hand and returned both to the desk. "So, what happens now?

We're in a neutral country. You have no jurisdiction here. You'll just have to figure out a way to get us out of here."

"That part is already taken care of."

"How?" Henry said.

"Simple. We merely have to wait for the Wehrmacht to get here."

It was Henry's turn to laugh. "What's that supposed to mean?"

Graf checked his watch. Lillian noted the time on the clock on the wall behind him. "Eleven p.m. An hour before midnight." He spoke with deadly seriousness. "It means the invasion starts in five hours."

40

"How can you think of sleep at a time like this?" Lillian Saxton demanded of Henry Clark.

It had been half an hour since Colonel Graf and his minions had stormed into the room and taken them all captive. After the colonel's bold declaration that the invasion was soon to start, he had told his prisoners they would be confined in the Geigers' suite until the Wehrmacht arrived.

"I suspect it will be days," Graf said. "I mean, it's only the Belgian Army that stands in our way." He and his staff had chuckled at that. The four prisoners remained stoic.

The suite was simply a large hotel room. The full-size bed sat on the east wall, with a writing desk and chair on the south wall and a closet and bathroom on the west wall. The north wall housed the only door out of the room and a small coat closet. The south wall also sported the only window. Patrons could open the window to let in air. A small wrought-iron barricade covered the lower third of the open space that led to the concrete ledge outside.

Soon after the Nazis had left, Henry started giving orders. "You have any weapons in your bags?"

James shook his head no.

To Elsa, he said, "How far along are you?"

"Six weeks, maybe seven."

"Good. That'll make it somewhat easier when we escape." He nodded. "Okay, we need to get some sleep. The Geigers get the bed. Lillian and I will sleep on the floor."

Lillian, who had watched this display of leadership, finally asked her question.

"First order of warfare: be as rested as possible." Henry held a blanket from the coat closet. "Shall we share this?"

"That's not the point," Lillian asserted. "We've got to get out of here."

Henry indicated the door with a slight nod. "Not tonight."

Lillian pointed at the window. "What about that?"

Henry spread his arm out to indicate James and Elsa. Fear at their situation and anger at her husband clouded Elsa's face. James appeared impassive.

"Not with them."

Lillian frowned. "What?"

"They are the mission now. Well, James is. Look, before Ludlow died, he didn't entirely trust you. Turns out his instincts were correct." He let that insult sting Lillian for a few moments. "The last thing he told me was the only thing that mattered was the codebook. Well, we don't have a codebook, but we have his brain and knowledge. Thus, the only mission is him."

"So." Lillian stepped to Henry and put her face in his. "What are we going to do about it?"

"Right now, Sergeant, we're going to get as much sleep as possible." He cracked a half grin. "Do you want to share the blanket or not?"

Lillian sighed and stepped away. "Not." On second thought, she walked to the door and opened it.

The woman Nazi and one of the men sat in chairs in the hallway. They both stood at Lillian's approach. Both held guns at their sides.

"Listen," Lillian said to them in German. She hadn't spoken the language for a bit and hoped she could be understood. "I'm pretty sure you're not going to let me go downstairs and get my clothes, but I'd still like to ask."

The door to the opposite room opened. Gunter Graf stood in the doorway. He had removed his uniform jacket but still wore his pants. "What seems to be the problem?"

"The woman wants to change her clothes," the female Nazi said sarcastically.

Graf gazed at Lillian from head to toe. "Miss Saxton, you look positively stunning. Why would you want to change out of those clothes?"

Lillian stifled her disgust at Graf's look. "To get more comfortable. If what you say is true, we'll be taken captive in a few days."

"You're already a captive," Graf cut in.

"All the more to the point. I'd like to get my clothes and that of Mr. Clark. Would you like to accompany me?" She stepped out of the room. The guns in the Nazis' hands rose to aim at her.

"Excuse me a moment." Graf retreated into his room and returned a moment later. He had slipped on his uniform jacket and buckled his gun belt to his waist. "Ursula will come with us." He held out his arm. "After you."

"My purse." Lillian indicated it on the floor. "I need the key."

The male Nazi picked it up, rummaged inside, and pulled out the key. He handed it to Graf.

With her head held high, Lillian led the way to the end of the hall. She had nearly opened the stairwell door before Ursula jumped ahead of her and blocked her path.

"I go first," the Nazi muttered. She opened the door and verified no one was in the stairwell. Satisfied, she nodded to Graf who held the door open for Lillian. The three of them descended the stairs to the sixth floor. Again, Ursula scanned the hallway ahead of them.

The closer they got to her room, the more Lillian thought about her situation and what Henry had just told her. True, they had been deceived by James, but he was still willing to help the Allies provided she and Henry could get him to Britain alive. Evidentially, Ludlow had not trusted her, but had trusted the mission. Now, the mission had changed. No longer was it a small codebook that could be hidden away or otherwise surreptitiously sent back to England. Now it was a man.

And his pregnant wife.

The thought of that fact stung Lillian more than the betrayal. Six years ago, before Paris, thoughts of making a family with James were paramount in Lillian's mind and fantasies. She had imagined the life she would lead once they both graduated from college and James took a job back in America. She even had potential names picked out for their children. She had talked it over with James one night. Now, walking the hallway to her hotel room, she decided she would ask him if he and Elsa had selected any names. If he had the gall to choose one of the names Lillian had picked out, she would punch him.

"We're here." Graf stopped. His hand went to his holstered gun. "Miss Saxton…"

"*Sergeant* Saxton, Professor."

"Well, if that's the way you want it, then address me as Colonel. You made a compelling case upstairs about getting more comfortable. We'll be here for a few days. It won't take long for *der Führer's* men to arrive. Now, when we go in, I would advise you not to try anything. I will shoot you without a second thought. So will Ursula. Understood?"

The tone he took reminded Lillian of her time in his class. It was the tone of an older man to a younger woman whom he thought inferior. It nagged at her then and it sure as hell nagged at her now.

"Understood."

Graf unlocked the door and Ursula again went in first. Lillian bided her time, waiting for the go ahead. The Nazi signaled Graf and he and Lillian entered the room.

"Hurry it up," Graf said.

Lillian eschewed her make-up on the dressing table. Instead, she grabbed her valise and Henry's bag. She checked the bathroom to see if he had left anything in there. He had a few toiletries that she slid into his bag. Snapping them both closed, she turned to Graf. "Can you carry a second blanket? There aren't enough upstairs."

Graf eyed her. A pitying smile broke through his severe stare. "I find it hard to believe that the reports I read out of England of a mystery woman traveling with Frank Monroe who took out some of our men is the same woman standing in this room. You seem so"—he searched for the word—"submissive. I find it hard to believe that the Americans, soft though they are, would entrust a mission like this to a woman so meek and mild. Even your British partner has already seen your weakness and taken command."

Lillian's blood boiled at the rebuke. She got enough talk like that from the men in her unit and, sometimes, even her commanding officers. It was why she spent long hours training and preparing for the missions to which she was assigned.

But her time with Tanaka had also prepared her mentally. He had trained her to channel her mind and her energies to recognize a particular situation, its strengths and weaknesses, and figure out the best time to strike. It was clear that now wasn't the time to act. Henry had been correct. That didn't make it any easier to stand there and take Graf's abuse.

Lillian put both bags in one hand and stripped the blanket off the bed. "Fine, I'll carry it myself."

Ursula snickered.

Lillian put a shoulder into the German and knocked her sideways.

In retaliation, Ursula swung her fist at Lillian who avoided the fist striking her face but not far enough to avoid the blow entirely. The fist collided on her upper arm with surprising strength. With her hands full, however, Lillian was unable to avoid the elbow into her midriff.

Air huffed out of her lungs. Lillian sank to her knees. Her aching muscles heaved, trying to replenish the lost air.

"Enough of this. Get up." Graf nudged Lillian with the toe of his boot.

Whirling on him, Lillian spat out venomous words. "Whatever happened to the kind, thoughtful professor back at university? You were my favorite."

"Things change, Sergeant. This is war and you are my prisoner."

With a curled lip, Lillian stood up and steadied herself. "I don't have to like it."

"Who asked if you liked it? Move."

Ursula slapped her free hand on Lillian's shoulder and

marched her out the room and back to the stairwell. Her lungs still recovering, Lillian merely breathed steadily. She hoped other hotel guests might come by, see them, and raise an alarm. But she didn't think that would happen. It was nearly midnight. Those people who weren't already in bed were downstairs at the bar. They were effectively alone.

No words passed among them on the climb back to the eighth floor. Lillian struggled with the bags and blanket. The Nazis made no move to help.

Upon reaching James's room, the male Nazi stood. He opened the door and Lillian trundled in. The door closed behind her. The lock fell into place.

James, Elsa, and Henry looked up at her. Something on her face must have betrayed her troubles because Henry leaped to his feet. He took the bags. She let the blanket drop to the floor.

"What happened?" The concern in James's voice seemed genuine.

"I took a swing at Ursula. She hit back." Lillian shrugged. She beckoned her three friends closer to her. In a whisper that was barely audible, she said, "I confirmed the room is bugged. Watch what you say." Then, in a louder voice, she said, "But I got a second blanket so I don't have to share." She laughed. So did Henry.

"Well," Henry said, "now that that's settled, I say we get some sleep."

"I'm going to change." Lillian took her bag to the bathroom. A few minutes later, she emerged. She wore a traveling suit consisting of a khaki skirt and cotton blouse. The accompanying jacket she slung over her arm. She dropped her valise. "You're turn," she said to Henry.

He grinned. "I'm fine." He walked over to the wall and turned off the light. Ambient light came through the window, but otherwise, the room was dark. James and Elsa climbed into bed and settled in.

Lillian and Henry made their beds on the floor next to the window. His only concession to comfort was to remove his shoes.

Out of the darkness, James said, "I'm sorry, Lil."

She didn't reply. What could she have said?

Henry leaned in close to her. "Good work determining we were bugged. How'd you do it?"

"They commented about your taking command of the situation. They also questioned my military prowess."

Henry grinned. "Which did you hate worse?"

Despite herself, Lillian grinned as well. "Not sure. They both stink."

Reaching over to his side, Henry picked up his left shoe. He sat up on his elbow and showed it to Lillian. She studied it in the light from the window. "Nice shoe. Why are you showing it to me?"

Turning it over, Henry used a fingernail on the heel. There was a soft click. He twisted the heel. It turned and dropped away. Inside was a small device with a single button. Henry pressed it.

"You didn't really think I went rogue, did you?"

41

Their fitful sleep was interrupted just before dawn by the sound of bombs.

The bombs and the anti-aircraft fire came from the east, the direction of the Belgian/German border. The targets were across Brussels from the Hotel Le Plaza.

Henry and Lillian woke. They both stood and gazed out the window. Directly east were the train tracks that led to Antwerp. Also to the east, barely visible through trees and buildings, was the main road east out of Brussels to Louvain. Considering the direction of the bombs, Henry surmised the Nazis were attacking eastern Brussels or Louvain.

"What's the plan for the B.E.F. and the French now?" Lillian asked. She used the abbreviation for the British Expeditionary Force.

Henry sighed. "Not sure. King Leopold wouldn't let us into Belgium for fear Hitler would see it as an aggressive move. Our forces will have to march all the way from France just to meet the Wehrmacht here."

"Think they can do it?"

"Of course."

Throughout the next hour, the citizens of Brussels awoke to the realization that their city was under attack. Sirens blared, emergency personnel drove through the city. The Belgian army, who yesterday seemed so lackadaisical, now reacted. By the time the sun broke above the horizon, Brussels found itself at war.

Lillian, Henry, James, and Elsa were still prisoners. At seven, Henry requested breakfast from their Nazi captors. An hour later, cold food from the downstairs restaurant arrived. They all ate in silence, listening to the sounds of a city at war.

After the meal, James and Elsa lay together on the bed.

Lillian and Henry stood at the closed window, watching.

"What's the distance of your little shoe transmitter?" Lillian whispered.

"A few hundred yards up to half a mile." He whispered as well, although they both agreed any bugs would likely not be near the window.

"So you have other agents stationed here."

"We have agents all across Europe. Ludlow was the one who radioed ahead to alert the Brussels office we were on the way. I didn't know it at the time, but that was one of the last acts he did."

"So, what's the plan?"

"We wait."

"That's not a good plan."

"It's the only one we've got." Henry nodded back to the door. "There's no way we can blast out without help. The transmitter only broadcasts an SOS. The other agents can pinpoint our location, but it'll only be this hotel. We need to alert them where we are and wait for instructions."

"How do you plan on doing that?"

Henry reached down and plucked his red handkerchief from his formal jacket. "With this." He walked over to the desk and hefted the small paperweight. He plopped it in the middle of his handkerchief and tied the cloth together.

"What's that?" James walked over to see what Henry was doing.

"A signal." Henry pointed to James. "When I open the window, our friends outside will likely barge in. James, go open the coat closet and delay them if they come in. Lillian, you need to move the chair away from the window after I get up on the sill. For all intents and purposes, all we were doing is opening the window to let in some air. Got it?"

Lillian and James nodded. He took his position and opened the coat closet. Henry and Lillian quietly moved the chair next to the window. Elsa sat on the bed and watched.

"Where are you going to put it?"

"Above the window. You noted how this hotel is built? There

are cascading layers of concrete and marble on each floor. If we had the chance, we could merely walk the ledges and climb out that way. The Jerrys won't allow that. Ready?"

Lillian and James nodded.

Henry stepped on the chair and situated himself in front of one of the closed windows. Lillian moved the chair back to the desk and returned. On a silent count of three, she swung open one pane. Henry quickly leaned out. With the paperweight and handkerchief in his hand, he extended his arm up and out of view.

The key to the door tuned into the lock. In another second, the door swung open.

And banged into the open closet door. The Nazi guard cursed and pushed harder.

Henry kept his hand above the window, trying to find the perfect place. He brought his hand back inside. A red shape fell from where his hand had been. In a deft move, he caught the paperweight and tried again.

The Nazi at the door reached a hand around the door and grabbed the knob of the closet door. He shoved it back, clearing his path.

Henry, out of time, swung himself back inside. He landed right next to Lillian. They both faced the window and waited.

"What's going on?" Graf charged in behind one of the Nazi guards.

Lillian turned. "We wanted some fresh air. It's pretty stifling in here."

Graf looked at each of his prisoners in turn, weighing what he saw. "No." He turned to another guard outside. "Bring the handcuffs."

While he waited, Graf strode over to the window and looked out. A breeze kicked up, bringing in welcome fresh air to the stale room. He looked at Lillian and Henry, then James and Elsa. He snapped his fingers at James and Elsa. "You two, come with me."

"Where?" James said.

"Out of this room."

"Why don't we go?" Lillian asked.

"Because you want to. Gather your things," Graf commanded James. "We don't want to put any burden on your delicate and pregnant wife."

James looked at Lillian. She nodded.

"Don't seek her permission," Graf snapped. "I'm in command here. Do it."

James Geiger busied himself with filling the common suitcase with everything he and Elsa had brought. Once he finished, he and Elsa were led out of the room. The Nazi who had gone to get handcuffs had returned. Graf directed him to lock the window handles closed.

"You'll just have to suffer," Graf murmured. "The two of them are more important than you. Good try, though." He winked at Lillian.

She remained impassive.

"Can we get a radio or a newspaper in here?" Henry asked. "We'd like to know what's going on outside."

Graf sniffed. "What's going on is the subjugation of western Europe." He turned on his heel and exited the room. The Nazi guard closed the door behind him and locked it.

"Now what?" Lillian whispered.

"Now, it's more difficult." He walked over to his bag and withdrew a small box of playing cards. "In the meantime, want to play gin rummy?"

42

The one good thing about having a set of handcuffs over the window handles was that Lillian could actually crack the window to let in some fresh air. She and Henry dragged the writing table over next to the window and whiled away the rest of Friday, 10 May, playing cards, talking, and listening to the distant sounds of war. Their lunch was late and cold again, but Graf delivered a newspaper along with the sandwiches. The two agents pored over every detail, sketchy as the fog of war.

The Wehrmacht landed parachute troopers to secure the bridges along the Belgian/German border at the town of Maastricht. The late Friday editions of the newspapers had not printed an update, but Henry commented that the Belgian Army of a half million would likely fall before Hitler's million-strong Wehrmacht.

Saturday dawned as clear and bright as Friday. Most of the day, Brussels experienced few effects of the war. Off to the east, barely visible from their window, huge columns of British soldiers marched east toward the battle. Not too long after the last man and lorry disappeared from sight, Lillian and Henry heard more bombs being dropped from the very direction the soldiers marched.

"That's not good," Lillian said.

"Not in the least. If only the king had let us come in sooner, we might have had a chance."

Darkness fell on Saturday night. Supper arrived. They ate in near silence. By bedtime, they agreed to flip a coin to determine who slept in the bed. Lillian lost. Henry climbed into the bed.

Lillian lay on the floor near the window. Soon, she heard his easy breathing. She stared up at the ceiling and at the stars that shone through the window. So many stars, worlds spinning around them. She wondered how many of those worlds were at war. Did other civilizations fight each other or had they advanced to such a place where war was passé? She wondered if this world would ever get there.

It was during these ruminations and through half-lidded eyes that she first noticed the movement above the window. Her eyes popped open. Had she imagined it? No, there it was again. A slight crunch of gravel on the roof. Another swish of clothes. Then an object appeared in the window. Lillian had not figured out what it was before a flash of light blinded her.

"Ow," she murmured.

Henry sat up in the bed. "What is it?" he whispered.

Despite being heavy with sleep, Lillian remembered the room was bugged. She snapped her fingers. In the next moment, Henry came to her side.

The light flashed again.

"It's the cavalry." Henry crept to the writing table and jotted a quick note. He returned to the window and stuck his hand out. The person holding the flashlight took it.

Henry and Lillian waited. After a minute, the person on the roof stuck out his hand. Henry yanked the paper from him. Lillian crowded next to the window to read the message with the ambient light. At the top, she read Henry's note: "Room bugged. What's the plan?" At the bottom, in messier handwriting, was the response: "Still working. If necessary, deliver codebook and we'll come back for you."

"Figures," Henry murmured.

He used the windowsill as a desk. "No codebook. Have to get asset and wife out of Belgium. He will tell all once in UK." He stood on the sill and passed the message back to the agent on the roof. They heard him swear under his breath. A minute later, his hand reemerged and passed the paper back to Henry, who spread it on the sill for them both to read. "Brilliant. Requires more planning. Will be back later tonight with new plan. My name is Arnold."

Henry wrote a last response: "Understood. Name's Henry Clark. Have American with me. Lillian Saxton. Asset is James

Geiger and his wife, Elsa." He passed the note back to Arnold.

The next thing they knew, Arnold's arm was back in their view. In his hand was a shape they both knew all too well: a pistol. Henry gripped the weapon and pulled it through the window, carefully avoiding scraping it against the windowsill. He turned it over. The barrel was long, about twelve inches.

"It's a Welrod," Henry whispered. "The barrel acts as a suppressor."

Lillian nodded. She wondered if Arnold was going to pass down another gun. They waited another five minutes before assuming the British agent had left to form a new plan.

"Well," Henry whispered, "you get the bed. I'll keep watch here."

Lillian didn't argue. She climbed into the bed, but sleep didn't come easily.

43

Turned out, Lillian slept soundly enough that she didn't wake until one of the Nazi guards banged a cart into the room to bring breakfast. Lillian sat up in bed and whirled on the Nazi. The gun he raised and aimed at her heart froze her.

"*Guten morgen.*" Henry stood across the room, leaning on the writing desk.

The German sniffed and unloaded the food. Eggs, toast, and water. A newspaper was folded on the cart.

At the door, Colonel Graf stood. "It won't be long now. Our troops are making excellent progress. They've broken through at Maastricht. Louvain is next. Then Brussels." He strolled into the room, admiring the decor. "I rather like this hotel. I'm having a splendid time. I think I might suggest we make it our headquarters when Brussels falls."

"It even has a movie theater," Henry commented. "That way, you can enjoy your Nazi propaganda in an intimate setting."

Graf regarded the British agent with a cock of his head. "Your tune will change when we put you in a camp." To Lillian, he said, "I've not determined what to do with you. I'm thinking you would make an excellent prisoner of war for a country that's supposedly neutral."

"Like hell I will," Lillian blurted.

"You won't have a choice. Come on, Kurt. Let's let the prisoners eat in peace. It might be their last day of relative freedom." Graf led the way. The Nazi guard named Kurt wheeled the cart back out of the room and locked the door.

Henry said, "Well, that was cheery, wasn't it?"

Lillian chuckled. She liked the way Henry kept up his humor even in the midst of their current situation.

They sat on the floor, ate, and placed the newspaper between them. They read the latest. Henry used a map printed in the newspaper to illustrate the dire situation the Belgians faced. Maastricht was located about 125 kilometers from Brussels. Louvain was just about thirty. If the Nazis were covering almost a hundred kilometers in a day, then Graf's words would prove to be accurate. To punctuate the newspaper story, air raid sirens sounded throughout Brussels. Lillian and Henry got up and watched the people on the ground. There was a combination of panic and disbelief. Up on the eastern horizon, billows of black smoke snaked into the sky.

As Sunday, 12 May, wore on, the more they watched the city prepare to make a last stand against the blitzkrieg of Nazi Germany. Troops scurried through the streets, setting up installations for combat. Civilians lined up in front of banks which had opened despite the day, trying to get their money before they fled. Street vendors sold food to anyone who would buy. By the end of the day, the sidewalks had become clogged with people.

Lillian wanted to *do* something, but she was powerless. Every military mind knew the best time to escape an approaching army was long before they breached your defenses. If Henry's friends took too much time to form a plan, the Wehrmacht would end up in the Hotel Le Plaza lobby.

"You know," she whispered, late in the afternoon as they watched all the people and the preparations, "if we could just get down there, amid all of that, we could blend in. Graf would have a terrible time finding us."

"You may be right. How do you propose to get down there?"

"We've got the one gun. We take out one or two of the guards. I'll get their weapons. After that, we don't need to bother with a suppressed weapon."

Henry gave her an amused look. "Sounds like one of the cowboy movies out of Hollywood where the heroes blast their way out of a saloon."

"Beats the hell out of just sitting here."

Henry put his hand on Lillian's arm. "We're sitting here to bide our time and gather our energy. Once we escape, we'll be hunted mercilessly."

Lillian put her hand over his. "I know. I just hate waiting."

Dusk fell but the tension in the streets didn't. Half the city was in blackout, fearing more air attacks. The air raid sirens stopped. A silence descended over the city.

Lillian and Henry remained on alert into the night. They waited for Arnold to return. Shortly after midnight, he did.

Just like the previous night, Arnold flashed a light into the room. Henry already had his message ready: "Asset and wife likely on this floor. All guards still in hallway. Can you verify? Do you have another gun?" He slipped the folded piece of paper up.

Arnold snatched it. He also delivered one to Henry: "B.E.F. otherwise engaged vs. Jerry. Only three of us to help. Determined you four and Nazis only people left on eighth floor. Will attempt roof escape."

Henry and Lillian exchanged glances.

Roof escape? Lillian mouthed.

Henry nodded and slipped the paper into his pocket. He had changed into trousers and shirt more accustomed for the streets than his formal wear. Lillian picked up her jacket and slipped it on. Graf had taken her gun, but she still had the gun belt and holster.

"This is the top floor," he whispered in her ear. "Our window's already open. We can snip the cuffs and open it all the way. The trick will be getting the Geigers' window open without the Nazis hearing."

"You think they bugged their room?"

"Have to assume yes."

Off in the distance came the sound of bombs.

"Or," Lillian whispered, "the war could camouflage our movements."

Arnold's light flashed again. He handed down another message: "Asset and wife in next room. Suggest we get you out, then get them. Yes?" The next moment, Arnold handed down another pistol. Like Henry's it was a suppressed pistol.

The feel of a gun in her palm soothed Lillian's fast-beating heart. She was ready for action.

In the long hours of waiting, Lillian and Henry had worked out strategies for escaping the room. Naturally, a roof attempt was in the mix. The top two floors of the Hotel Le Plaza were set back from the main facade of the first six floors, with the eighth floor set back even farther than the seventh. The end result was that the top three floors resembled a tiered wedding cake. Each floor had a small ledge ringing the building. It was enough to scoot around provided you kept your back to the building.

Getting up to the roof might prove problematic. Without additional resources, Henry had devised a plan where he would boost Lillian to the roof. She would carry sheets tied together and help Henry up on the roof. Then they'd have to repeat the process with the Geigers. Knowing James and Elsa were not trained for situations such as this, Lillian would climb back down to the eighth floor and boost them up before rejoining everyone on the roof.

Now that they had other assets, it might be easier. Henry hurriedly scribbled that plan on another piece of paper and handed it up to Arnold. A minute later, two flashes of his light indicated approval.

The long-barreled pistol would not fit into her holster so Lillian stuck the gun inside her belt. Henry put his in a front pocket. Next they needed to prepare the room for the eventual entrance of the Nazis. Together, they lifted the writing desk and scooted it across the room. The trick was not to make a sound to alert the listeners.

Lillian was strong, but the desk was heavy. Twice she nodded at Henry to set the desk down and allow her to catch her breath. On the third try, they managed to navigate the small entryway without banging into either wall. With her back almost to the door, Lillian signaled a halt. She slipped under the table, barely swishing her clothes on the door. She froze and waited.

Outside in the hallway, no one moved.

Satisfied, Lillian crept back under the table and emerged in the main room. The first step was done.

They walked back to the window. Arnold's head appeared above them. Henry gave a thumbs up sign. Arnold passed down a pair of metal clamps.

In the plan Henry had delivered to Arnold, it was suggested he and Lillian escape out the window by clipping the handcuffed chain. To dampen the sound, Lillian brought the blanket from the bed. Henry took the clamp in his hand and positioned it across the chain. Next, Lillian took the blanket and wrapped both Henry's hand and the chain three times. She held one of the two panes. Henry, with his free hand, held the other. That was going to have to do.

Henry looked up at Arnold who gazed over the top of the building and nodded. He looked at Lillian. They both nodded. None of them knew how loud the sound would be. She held her breath.

Squeezing the clamp, Henry broke the chain. A muffled snap was barely audible. Henry adjusted for the weight of the blanket and slowly lowered his blanket-covered hand to the floor. He released his grip on the clamps. Together, he and Lillian opened wide the windows. Earlier in the day, Lillian had taken some of Henry's hair cream and coated the hinges to dampen any potential squeaks.

Now, came the difficult part: stepping outside. Lillian examined the ledge. She looked for loose gravel or anything that might make a sound. She wiped the area free from debris.

To avoid making any sound directly near the window, Henry's plan called for them to step out onto the ledge and climb up the side of the building away from the window. That meant scooting about six feet away from the window on a ledge that proved to be about seven inches wide. Lillian wasn't scared of heights, but there was a much better plan than that. An idea struck her. She leaned in close to Henry.

"Shoes off. Less sound and more grip on the ledge."

"Lillian, are you saying I'm a monkey?"

She cracked a grin. "It would certainly make this part of the escape easier."

Lillian removed her shoes and emptied her purse. There wasn't anything she needed in there any more. She put her shoes in the purse and slung the bag over a shoulder.

Henry took off his shoes and managed to cram them in his pockets after he transferred the pistol to his belt.

The moment of truth was at hand.

Using the chair as a step stool, Lillian got up on the sill. The wind kicked up and the breeze blew through her hair. The smell of gunpowder and burning wood mixed with the fragrance of flowers and trees. She didn't particularly like the combination.

On impulse, she decided to face the building and use her toes rather than her heels to traverse the ledge. Glancing to her left, she noted the position where the rope hung over the top of the hotel. Never had six feet seemed so far away.

Lillian moved, only about six inches, then brought her feet together. She looked down. She noted that, even though the seventh floor jutted out from the eighth, there was nothing to grip and hold on to. If she fell, that was it.

Her purse put her slightly off balance, but her prescience about bare feet providing better control was accurate. She kept her big toes up against the building, using them as guides. The exterior was fairly smooth, something she thanked the architects for.

Finally, she reached the rope. She gripped it with her left hand and pulled down on it. The rope was solid. She took a deep breath. To climb the rope effectively, she was going to walk up the side of the building. That meant she was going to have to put her back to the ground. Her stomach flipped at the thought of it, but she got it under control. Gripping the rope now with both hands, she swung out.

The rope moved. Her position sank lower to the ground. She cursed to herself and clung tightly to the rope.

A single small yelp escaped from Lillian's mouth.

44

Wilhelm Lang's assignment was listening. Not being an expert in hand-to-hand combat, he was a natural choice to be the man to listen in on the room where Lillian Saxton and Henry Clark were staying. He had a notepad at hand and a sharpened pencil. Other than the weather or random talk from the prisoners, Wilhelm's pad was mostly blank.

Saxton and Clark just didn't talk much.

Wilhelm fancied himself an important member of Colonel Graf's team. He would be the one to alert everyone if something happened.

But nothing had happened yet.

Sitting in the room across the hall from the bugged room, Wilhelm wore headphones while he listened. The prisoners were often very quiet. He was sure they weren't sleeping. He wouldn't be able to sleep if he was in their position. Sometime during the day on Saturday he got the idea that Saxton and Clark might be whispering. To test his theory, he turned up the volume on his receiver.

Still nothing for the rest of the day and into the night. When they were fed, he had to turn down the volume since Kurt often banged his way into their room. Once night fell, he turned up the volume again and waited.

He waited so long with nothing but static and hiss on the line that the ambient sounds lulled him into a semi-doze. Kurt Schmidt typically assumed a position on the bed and read the newspaper. His job was to make sure Wilhelm stayed awake or they took turns listening in.

Kurt Schmidt was fast asleep on the bed.

Wilhelm's semi-sleep phase was punctuated by a single, sharp cry. Distant but clear.

He sat up straight and rubbed his eyes. He glanced over at

Schmidt to verify his fellow team member hadn't caught him napping. Still asleep.

Wilhelm leaned forward and operated the dials on the receiver. He turned up the volume still more, to its highest setting. He stared into the middle distance, seeing nothing, trying—no willing his ears—to identify the sound.

Had he imagined it? In his near-sleep state, had his own foot or some perfectly normal hotel event caused the sound? He couldn't say.

The noise didn't repeat.

But something else came through. It made no sense. The sound he heard resembled scuffling feet on pavement. It was so faint that Wilhelm nearly attributed it to the hotel staff coming up to check on the rooms.

But the hallways were carpeted. All footfalls in the hallway were silent.

What could be making those sounds?

"Kurt." Wilhelm repeated the name until Schmidt woke.

"What?"

"Check the room."

"Why?"

"I think I heard something."

"You probably heard your own snoring."

"No. I heard something from their room."

Schmidt grinned. "Maybe they're spending their last night together with a little beischlafen."

Wilhelm shook his head. "They didn't strike me as intimate. Go check."

"You go check. I'm tired." Kurt closed his eyes again.

"If I check, you have to listen." Wilhelm knew that would get Schmidt moving. The other man hated manning the headphones.

Sure enough, Schmidt, grumbling, sat on the edge of the bed. He put on his boots and gun belt. He gave Wilhelm the middle finger and left the room. Wilhelm picked up the pencil to write down anything he heard from the room.

He heard the key go into the lock. The doorknob turning.

The door opening.

And hitting something heavy.

***

From his vantage point, Henry could do nothing to help Lillian. She had swung herself out on the rope to get her feet up on the side of the building. Unfortunately, whatever was holding the rope up on the roof moved. The end result was that Lillian's stomach slammed into the ledge which her feet had just left.

And she let out a small yelp of surprise.

Damn. Henry wondered how well attuned the microphones in the room were. If they caught a break, the bugs wouldn't even pick up the sound. Better yet, if they did, the Nazis might think the sound was ancillary or exterior to the hotel.

From the roof came a low voice. "Bloody hell. What does she think she's doing?"

Henry dared not answer vocally. And Lillian was too far away to help without making noise. Plus, the exterior of the wall had nothing with which to help her. Lillian was on her own.

Her bare feet found the side of the hotel. For a few seconds, she scrambled into a better climbing position. The problem was that her feet scuffed against the wall.

Henry looked back inside the room. He could hear her feet. He wondered if the microphones could.

From out in the hallway, he heard the sound of a person grumbling. Someone was approaching the room. He needed to act fast.

He frantically gestured to Lillian to get to the roof. She nodded and redoubled her efforts. Henry ducked inside the room. He had only seconds.

As soon as the person in the hallway opened the door to check on Lillian's yelp, he would bang into the door. Moments after that, all hell would break loose. Henry needed a distraction.

In preparation for the night, Lillian had tied the sheets and blankets together. With the rope, the sheets weren't needed. But they were available. An idea came to his mind when he heard the sound of the key jingling on the keychain.

He lunged for the chair and dragged it to the window. He hurriedly tied one end of the sheet-rope to one of the legs.

The key chunked into the lock.

Henry picked up the chair, the sheet-rope dangling at his feet. He grabbed the empty end.

The lock turned.

Henry hurled the chair out the window. It flew in a nice, graceful arc until the slack of the sheet-rope jerked the chair back to the hotel facade. Henry gripped the other end of the sheet-rope and hoped the chair would have its desired effect.

The door opened.

And immediately banged into the writing table.

***

Colonel Gunter Graf rather enjoyed this mission. So far, it had proven to be quite simple. With the Wehrmacht on the move and arriving any day now, all he had to do was while away the days and hours in this sumptuous hotel.

The food was excellent. Not as good as Wilma's, of course, but good enough that he didn't have to subsist on rations or dried meat. The soldiers under his command seemed smitten with the good food and excellent accommodations as well. Each of them allowed—or tolerated; Graf couldn't tell which—his giving mini-lectures on the types of food and their origins.

The wine available to consume was also in Graf's wheelhouse. He opted to pay for the few bottles he wanted before the Wermarcht arrived. He didn't want to raise too many suspicions on what was happening on one wing of the eighth floor. He had enjoyed enough wine that night to put him in a comfortable snooze.

The tremendous sound of something heavy smashing into a window jolted him out of his slumber.

"*Gott in Himmel!*" The half-empty wine glass smashed to the floor as Graf flailed about. "What the hell was that?"

The next thing he heard was one of his men yelling and banging something. Always ready at a moment's notice, Graf grabbed his pistol. He hurried to the door and flung it open.

Downstairs, people were screaming and yelling. He didn't smell any smoke so the sound was probably not a stray bomb. Besides, if it was, he wouldn't be here to ponder the question.

He looked over at room 809. One of his men, Kurt by the looks of him, was shoving with all his might against the door. It was barely moving. The prisoners must have put something in the way. But why?

Escape. They were trying to escape.

Ursula, Adolf, and Dieter rushed out of their adjacent rooms. "One of you check downstairs. The rest, help Kurt open that blasted door."

Dieter rushed down the hallway and to the staircase. Ursula and Adolf stood next to Graf and Kurt.

"Just a little more and I can get in." Kurt grunted with the effort.

Adolf hurried next to Kurt. He put his shoulder to the door and the two of them pushed as one. The door opened and Kurt stuck his head and shoulders around the door.

Two bullets slammed into his head. It jerked back, sending blood splattering on the wall. Kurt Schmidt was dead before his body even touched the floor.

Graf saw what had happened and brought his pistol to bear. He crouched, putting the wall between him and the shooter. How did Clark or Saxton have a gun?

They didn't. There was only one explanation.

Graf grabbed Adolf's shirt. "Keep this door secure. Shoot whoever's inside if you can. Ursula, with me." Graf stood and made his way to the Geigers' room. He fumbled for the keys. They got caught on his pants and fell to the ground.

Another door opened. Wilhelm stuck his head out into the hallway. "Who's shooting?"

"The prisoners!" Graf yelled. "Get your gun and help Adolf."

Wilhelm ducked back inside and reemerged with his gun in hand.

Graf stooped and snatched up the keys. He had put all the sets of key on a single ring. Each key had the room number carved into the brass so it only took seconds for Graf to find the right one. He slammed it into the lock and flung open the door.

45

Halfway up the side of the building, her bare feet slipping on the smooth exterior, Lillian almost wished the architects hadn't been so pristine with their craft. She found it difficult to get purchase.

Henry had ducked back inside the room. The next thing Lillian knew, he threw the desk chair out of the window. Behind it, tied to a chair leg, was the sheet-rope they had fashioned. She had only a few seconds to wonder why before the chair swung back to the side of the hotel and smashed into a window on the seventh floor.

"Well, there goes the need to be quiet."

Without the need for silence, Lillian used her knees and shimmied up to the roof. Only then did she realize why the rope had dropped when she got on it.

Three men held onto the rope.

Her heart skipped a beat. Wasn't there anything on which to secure the line?

"We've got problems," she said. Immediately she sat and started putting on her shoes.

"Where's Clark?" a man asked.

"Still inside. You Arnold?"

"Aye. And you're the American."

Lillian stood. "I am. Now, lower me back down."

"What the hell?"

Already moving to the edge, Lillian looked down. "Which room are the Geigers in?"

"Eight zero eight best we can tell."

"That's where I'm going. Be prepared to pull all four of us up."

One of the men groaned. "Don't swing on the rope. The force makes it too heavy."

"Noted." Lillian put both hands on the rope. "Ready?"

"Aye," Arnold said. "And hurry."

Without gloves, Lillian knew she wouldn't have the added padding to slow her descent were she to rappel down the side. She would just have to make her best guess on the angle and trajectory and hope her feet found the ledge.

She dropped over the side and slid down the rope. Before she knew it, her feet landed on the ledge right next to the window of room 808. She shifted her grip and drew her gun.

And smashed the window.

Inside, a woman screamed. Lillian hoped it was Elsa.

Knocking shards of glass out of the metal frame with the pistol, Lillian stepped inside and had to duck immediately as something came swinging for her head.

"Damn it, James, it's me."

"Lillian?"

"No, Tarzan."

"I'm sorry about that. I…"

"Be sorry later. Help me drag this desk in front of the door." Lillian moved like lightning. She had already started dragging the table before James reacted. He lunged for the other end and picked it up.

The key slammed into the lock.

Her back to the door, Lillian turned and fired one shot at the opening. Her bullet ripped into the wood next to the door frame. The door stopped moving inward.

At the last moment, as she had in her room, Lillian ducked under the desk. Needing no pretense of silence, she used her back and legs to lift her end of the desk and rammed it flush against the door.

Two shots rang out from the hallway. They made new holes in the door where Lillian's torso should have been.

Not wanting to waste her limited ammo on return fire, Lillian crawled on her hands and knees back into the room.

James and Elsa stood frozen in place.

"Didn't you hear me?" Lillian hissed. "Out the window. To

the roof."

"You can't be serious," Elsa replied.

Two more gunshots cracked the wood.

"Very." Lillian pointed to James. "You first."

"Why me?"

"Because we need what's in your head."

James's face took in an angry visage. "You get nothing if we both don't make it." He gestured to Elsa. "Go."

"I can't."

"Go! Now!"

He helped his wife up on the sill. The rope dangled just to the side. James helped Elsa grab the rope. He laced his hands together and provided her a step up. With a heave, he all but threw her halfway up to the roof. He glared at Lillian, then followed his wife up the rope.

More gunshots erupted. This time, they came from the room Henry was in. In a flash, he leapt up on the ledge, staggering to catch his balance on the edge of the window.

"C'mon," Lillian cried. "I'll cover you."

The British agent shoved his pistol into his belt. As she had done, Henry faced the side of the building and used his toes to move. More than half of each foot hung over nothing.

A bullet pinged off the ledge a mere inch from Henry's left foot. He jerked it away suddenly. The movement caused him to lose his balance. With no purchase to grab, the only place for him to go was down.

In a move Lillian almost couldn't believe, Henry jumped up off the ledge and plummeted to the ground. Except he grabbed the ledge with his hands. His body slammed into the side of the building. He audibly groaned but held fast.

The shot came from below. Lillian saw the head and torso of someone sticking out the window a floor below. More gunshots blasted in the night. Her angle didn't give her a good view of the shooter but the shooter had an easy aim at Henry.

Time to change the angle. "Hold on up there!" she called. Without waiting for an acknowledgment and keeping her feet on the ledge to act as a pivot, Lillian leaned out over the ledge. She almost achieved a ninety-degree angle from the side of the building.

The shooter reemerged to resume his barrage. Lillian put three slugs into him. He jerked, dropped his gun, and slumped across his windowsill.

Lillian bent her knees, changed her angle, and crouched on the ledge. She scooted a few inches to where Henry clung to the ledge.

"More weight," she called up to the roof. This time, she gave the men a moment to adjust. She positioned herself on the ledge and merely held on to the rope for support.

Henry grabbed the rope with one hand, then both, and hauled himself up to the ledge.

"Thanks," he said, breathing heavily.

"Don't mention it. Now let's get the hell off this ledge."

Henry, still holding on to the rope, bent his knee. "Need a lift?"

Lillian didn't hesitate. She used his knee as a step and launched herself up. She shimmied over the top and looked back to Henry. "Come on!"

Henry started up.

A mighty crash sounded from room 809. The Nazis had broken through the door.

"Hurry!" Lillian shouted.

"It's not like I'm taking my time," Henry retorted.

Lillian pulled her gun out of her belt and aimed at the windowsill. A head stuck out. She let a bullet fly. It missed the person, but forced the Nazi to withdraw long enough to get Henry up and over the side.

The three British soldiers all collapsed in relief. "Mate, you need to lay off the food," Arnold said.

Henry, breathing heavily, sat on the roof. He quickly put on his shoes and stood. "How'd you get up here?"

"Theater entrance," Arnold said.

"That the only access?"

"It's the easiest one."

"Let's go."

All seven people sprinted across the roof. Surprisingly, the roof was pretty flat with hardly any protuberances to trip them.

"Why'd it take you so long to come back for us?" Henry asked.

"There's an invasion going on, mate," Arnold said. "You weren't our first priority."

"What is?"

"The embassy."

"That where we're going?"

"Aye." He jerked a thumb over his shoulder at James. "He the one?"

"Yes."

"Need them both?"

Henry and Lillian exchanged glances. She wondered if James had heard the British agent ask the question.

James stopped dead in his tracks. "I want to make something perfectly clear. The only way I say anything is if my wife and I both get to Britain."

Lillian wondered what her new British allies thought of the inflected German accent James now sported.

"Is that understood?"

"Yes." Lillian grabbed his arm and pulled him along with her. "Now let me make something perfectly clear to you. You are the asset. Elsa is one, too. Do what we say and we might get out of this alive. Delay like you just did and it could cost us."

One of the unique features of the Hotel Le Plaza was that it housed its own movie theater. Situated in the rear of the building, the area could show movies or newsreels or feature live entertainment. The requirement for a large screen meant that the roof of the theater rose above the roof of the hotel itself. An access door led down into the hotel. The door was open. As they neared it, a figure suddenly appeared in the doorway. The figure started shooting.

Without thinking, Lillian dived to the ground. She brought

Elsa Geiger with her. Henry, who had been running alongside James, did the same for the mathematician. Both Lillian and Henry used their bodies as shields but both came up with pistols in their hands.

One of the assailant's bullets spun one of the agents around. The Nazi tried to duck back inside but failed as a hail of bullets from four guns pounded into him. He fell where he stood.

"Clear," shouted one of the Brits.

Henry stood and hauled James to his feet.

Lillian looked down at Elsa. In the ambient light, she saw a mixture of fear and relief wash over the German's face.

"*Danke*," Elsa said.

"*Bitteschön*," Lillian stood and helped Elsa to her feet.

A quick assessment of the agent who was shot revealed it was only a graze. All four people with guns ducked and covered each other as they descended the stairwell, ending at a door at the rear of the theater and hotel.

Arnold peeked out the door. "Clear."

The other two agents scurried to two cars parked in the alley. They each got behind the wheel and signaled.

"Let's go," Arnold said. "One asset per car."

James tried to object but Henry was already moving him to the rear car. Lillian guided Elsa to the front car. Arnold accompanied Henry. Lillian shoved Elsa inside the car and jumped in beside her. "Go!" she shouted to the driver.

He needed no other directive. He threw the machine into gear and floored the gas pedal. The car lurched forward. The trailing vehicle matched speed. Together the two cars raced across the empty streets and headed for the British Embassy.

***

Colonel Gunter Graf stood in a hotel room on the seventh floor and gazed at the slumped body of Adolf Richter. The young man had two holes in his head. The blood that had leaked out formed a congealed stain on the hotel's facade. Graf hadn't known Richter very long, but he was a fallen comrade. More important, he was a member of the team Graf now commanded and he had lost him.

A knock at the door. Wilhelm Lang entered. He studiously avoided the sight of the man and woman dead in the bed where Richter had shot them. "Sir, we've also lost Dieter. He's up on the roof. He had cornered them but took many shots and died."

Graf pursed his lips. Make that two casualties from his team. He inhaled deeply and sighed. He found, at that moment, that he much preferred teaching military history than participating in it. If a student failed an exam, he had a chance on the next one. Here, when death was the result of failure, it was permanent.

"The hotel staff. What are they doing?"

"They've called the police, but with the invasion coming, they are preoccupied. But they will come."

"I know." Graf flexed his jaw muscles. "And we will still be here. We've paid the hotel well. They will play their part." He waved his hand in the air as if to swat an invisible fly. "Besides, it won't matter soon anyway. Once the Wehrmacht arrives, we can do what we please without resorting to pleasantries." He indicated Richter's body. "Did you know him well?"

"Yes, Herr Colonel. We served in Poland together."

"And Wolf?"

Schmidt cleared his throat. "Yes, Herr Colonel. He was like a brother to me." His voice cracked with emotion. "Also in Poland. He saved my life. I owed him."

Graf looked at Wolf's body, still slumped over the windowsill. The head, hanging outside the window, had bullet holes in it. Precise bullet holes. He wondered who had shot Wolf: Saxton or Clark? He thought about what he knew about Lillian Saxton.

Back in university, Lillian Saxton was a smart girl but prone to learning everything by rote memory. She demonstrated little in the way of creative thinking. Graf had the impression, even when she was his student and he her professor, that she was using her university education as a means of escaping her upbringing. He remembered her running around with James Geiger, Frank

Monroe, and others. She had dated Geiger for a long time.

Graf had lost track of them after they finished their semester abroad. Geiger had decided to stay in Germany and offer his mental abilities to *der Führer* by helping with the codes. Geiger had displayed all the traits of a man committed to *das Vaterland* despite his country of origin. He had become well respected in Berlin. His marriage to Elsa Stein further solidified his stature in society.

But something had happened to Geiger. It was the only explanation for his sudden turn against the Third Reich and *der Führer*. The event must have been significant for Geiger to put his pregnant wife at risk.

"Herr Schmidt," Graf said, looking at the dead eyes of Adolf Richter, "you will have the chance to make good on your debt."

"Sir? What do you mean? They're heading to the British Embassy. It's the most likely destination."

"I know. And it's a good thing."

"I don't understand. How can that be a good thing?"

Graf reached out and closed Richter's eyes. "You forget I'm a history professor. The embassy may be a castle to them, but I know a thing or two about sieges. They'll have to come out sooner or later. When our soldiers are marching down the avenues of Brussels, they'll try to avoid capture. And when they do, we'll be waiting. In the end, they'll simply fall into our nets."

46

"What do you mean we have to leave today?" Lillian Saxton asked. "I thought we were safe here."

She rubbed her eyes. Her body ached, partly from the exertions in escaping the Hotel Le Plaza and partly as a result of sleeping on the floor of the British Embassy. It was an office building without any proper sleeping facilities.

When they had arrived the previous night, they all ran inside the building. The car were parked haphazardly on the street in front of the embassy. The building encompassed an entire block. The structure was four stories tall, with windows all around. There was the front door, now barred at night, and a back door on the opposite street.

Lillian found herself surprised when she noted so few people in the embassy. Arnold, chief security officer, told them most of the personnel had already evacuated. A skeleton crew remained, but they showed all the signs of impending flight.

Arnold turned out also to be in charge of the embassy itself. He told Lillian, Henry, James, and Elsa to make themselves as comfortable as possible and get some sleep. He posted sentries on all four corners of the building and lookouts on the ground floor and roof. That wasn't just to keep an eye out for Graf, but also to make sure no enemy agents tried to storm the embassy.

James and Elsa found a spare office in the center of the building and secluded themselves from everyone else. Lillian knew they had lots to talk about, starting with James's decision and how it affected the two of them. More than once, she heard their raised voices arguing. They quieted down soon, however. The last thing he heard from the room was soft crying.

It wasn't as though Lillian couldn't appreciate their predicament. She'd faced it herself when she won a scholarship to go to college as far away from San Diego as possible. She was happy to leave all that she knew in favor of something—anything—better. Elsa now faced a similar situation, albeit one that was forced on her by her husband and not of her own choosing. Lillian wondered what she would do were she in Elsa's shoes. Would Lillian acquiesce and go with her husband even though he had made a decision without consulting her? The independent streak Lillian had developed in the years since Paris made her realize the answer would be no. Back in Paris, the answer would have been an unequivocal yes. If James had wanted to take her to Antarctica, she would have gladly left that very day.

Sitting by herself in the embassy less than an hour after they had arrived, Lillian visibly sagged in relief and exhaustion.

Henry approached and offered her a glass of water. "They don't have much else. The ambassador took his stash of whiskey with him when he left." Lillian took the water and offered a meek toast. They both drank.

"Thanks for taking out that shooter on the seventh floor," Henry said. They sat in office chairs in a vacated office on the east side of the building. The blinds were open and starlight streaked inside.

"You're welcome." Lillian placed the cool glass on her forehead. "I have such a splitting headache. Any aspirin around here?"

"I'll go find out." Henry left the room. He returned five minutes later. He dropped a small package in her lap. "Aspirin powder." He held up a bottle and grinned. "And gin. Found it in one of the desks. If I were evacuating, I'd certainly take my gin with me."

Lillian chuckled. "Think I'll mix the powder in gin." She poured the powder in her water glass, stirred, then gulped the water down. Wiping her mouth with the back of her hand, she held out her glass. "Now, for the gin chaser."

Henry poured some gin in her glass and into his. He toasted. They both drank. The gin burned as it snaked down Lillian's throat. She thought, considering the evening and the narrow escape from death, that gin was the best she'd ever tasted. The warmth of the liquor almost immediately soothed her. She started to relax. She savored the gin, finishing what Henry had poured.

Told there were no beds in the embassy, she wondered how she might sleep. After the gin, she didn't think she'd have a problem sleeping on the floor. Turned out, she was correct.

The only problem she now had was waking up. The bright spring sun glared in her eyes when Henry opened the curtains and told her they'd have to leave today. She repeated her question.

"Because of the speed of the invasion," Henry answered. "The Nazis are faster than we expected. They're already at Louvain."

Lillian pulled an image of a Belgian map in her mind. Louvain was only thirty kilometers from Brussels. "Oh my."

"That's one reaction. Another might be panic."

"Panic? We can still get out, right?"

"That's the thing we're about to find out."

Lillian put her shoes back on and stood. She swayed for a moment. *How much did I drink last night?*

Henry reached out a hand and steadied her.

"Hangover after only one drink?" He grinned at the joke.

"And the adrenaline crash." Lillian shook his arm away. "I'm fine. What's the situation?"

"We have to leave today. Preferably as soon as possible. Arnold says he knows the guy who runs the trains. They're running late and full. We can hop on the last one out of town if we hurry."

Lillian tried to process what she had just heard. "Only one train out of town?"

Henry nodded. "No trains leaving going east or south. The Nazis are already there. That only leaves Antwerp to the north. Not much to go to out west. Almost everyone is going to Antwerp, trying to catch a boat off the Continent. I think that's our best option. The Royal Navy's got the Channel tied up. We get on a boat, we're home free."

Lillian nodded. "Sounds like a plan." She peered outside. "What time is it?"

"Ten."

"Ten? I slept that long?"

Henry shrugged. "I closed the curtains. Made it darker in here." He grinned. "It also made it easy to wake you."

"Where'd you sleep?"

"Next room. I gave you some privacy. Of course, I heard your snoring through the wall." He winked.

Lillian playfully punched his shoulder. "Shut up." She again marveled at his ability to bring lightness to dire situations. "You tell James yet?"

"They're already awake."

"Really? You let me sleep past them?"

"They're just the assets. We're the ones to protect them. They don't need as much sleep as you do."

"I've had enough. Let's get moving."

"Hold on." Henry actually raised a palm at her. "We need to call London. Let them know what's going on, what we plan to do. It's protocol."

Lillian frowned. "It's protocol always to call in? What about on the fly decisions?"

"They're made on the fly," Henry conceded. "But that's not the situation we find ourselves in. We have a moment to breathe."

"I thought you said we need to leave today. Why not now?"

"Because we don't have plans yet. We're calling London. They may want to talk to you. Be ready. There's coffee and some food down the hall."

He turned and left but stopped. "Oh," he said, reaching over to a table. "This is yours." He picked up a holstered pistol and handed it to her. The leather belt and holster also housed two additional clips.

Lillian took the belt and strapped it on. She withdrew the pistol and put a round in the chamber. "Thanks."

Satisfied, he turned and went to make the call.

Lillian hefted the pistol in her hand, weighing it. She wanted to let her mind and hand and arm feel what it was like to hold that particular weapon. Her preferred gun had been lost at the hotel. She was grateful to be armed again. She shifted the gun from hand to hand. Finally, she holstered it and moved around the interior of the embassy looking for the kitchen.

The embassy itself was nearly in shambles. In peacetime, she imagined this office environment to be refined and stoic. Now, in war, it showed the wear and tear of improvisation and desperation. Drawers in desks were pulled out, emptied, and left open. Many of the desks had their office supplies scattered. Book shelves that lined one wall had lost many of their books. There was an odd smell, too. She couldn't place it. Strangely, it got stronger as she got closer to where the food was.

The little kitchen wasn't a real kitchen, but another office, albeit one with a sink and a refrigerator. The smell was strong. It was rotting food. Lillian wondered what had spoiled and why someone didn't just take out the trash.

A man stood at the sink, washing something. Lillian came into the kitchen and went for the percolator on the stove. She grabbed a cup and poured herself a cup of coffee. She looked around for a lump of sugar. Finding none, she sipped the hot brew. It was bitter but good.

Then she noticed who the person was: James Geiger.

It was the first time she'd actually been alone with him since they had met again. A thousand questions flooded through her mind. She settled on, "Would you like some coffee?"

James turned when she spoke. The running water had drowned out her approach. Their eyes met. He turned off the water and placed the coffee cup he held on the counter. He picked up a towel and dried his hands. "No, I've already had some. There aren't enough cups to go around so I was washing mine for Elsa." He half smiled. "But thanks."

"You're welcome." Lillian enjoyed holding the cup because it hid her shaking hands.

"Hey, and thanks for all you did last night." James shook his head in admiration. "You have certainly changed since our time at the university."

Lillian shrugged. She was proud of her proficiency in martial arts, espionage, and handling weapons. She enjoyed the thrill of the chase. She could do with a little less of the daring escapes, but, deep down, she knew there was a part of her that thrived on that kind of action. Idly, she asked herself if he knew his decision to break up was what had led to how she was. From a certain point of view, he was the one who had made her.

"Yeah, well, I kind of had to."

He frowned. "What are you trying to say?"

Lillian sipped her coffee. "You know, after Paris, after Frank and his ill-timed question, I had to do something. I wandered around a while until I found my way. I guess in some respects I have to thank you for that."

"Thank me for that? What the hell is that supposed to mean?"

She put some sternness in her voice. "It means exactly what I say it means. After you broke us up in Paris, I had to figure out something to do."

"I broke us up? I think it was actually you that broke us up."

"How do you figure that? You are the one who insisted on staying in Germany. I didn't want to stay in Germany."

James broke into a wide grin. "Exactly. You didn't want to stay in Germany. That means you are the one who broke us up."

Lillian set the cup down. She took a step closer to him, getting into his face. "I don't see it that way. I don't think you realize how much Paris broke me. I was in complete shambles when you sprang your choice on me. I had no way to prepare. It didn't help matters that Frank posed his question. Can you believe he actually proposed to me mere hours after you and I broke up? No, James, you are the one that broke me in Paris." She spread out her hands. "Actually, I sometimes wanted to thank you and these past six years. I found that I'm a pretty good Army soldier, and I like what I do. Do you like what you do?" She play-acted, putting a finger to her chin and rubbing it in thought. "What do you do exactly? Besides lying to bring me here all the way from America? And getting Frank killed in the process?"

James cut the air with his hand. "Listen, I had no idea that anything was going to happen."

"Of course you didn't. This isn't your realm. It's mine, and I know the dangers. You sent Frank into this mission not knowing how dangerous it actually was. That's what got him killed. That's what you have to live with."

He looked down at the floor. "I know," he whispered. "It's something I'll be living with the rest of my life."

Lillian picked up her coffee cup again. The brew tasted even more bitter than before. She still drank it.

James looked up at her and met her eyes. In a soft voice, he said, "I don't think you realize how much Paris broke me. There's a part of me that's still there. Still there willing you to say yes to my proposal. I so wanted you to say yes. I so wanted you and me to live together for the rest of our lives. Why'd you have to say no?"

The word stung Lillian, but she hoped her outward appearance didn't betray her. She didn't want James to know how much it hurt, even now, to look at him, much less to look at him with his wife.

"I didn't want to live in Germany," she said. "I could see what kind of country it was becoming. I didn't like it. I wondered what you saw in it. I thought about it, and realized that if you saw something in Germany that you liked, we could never be together. So I had to say no."

James inhaled deeply, and sighed. "Just imagine if you had said yes."

"Just imagine if you hadn't insisted that Germany be our home."

From the door came a shuffling sound. Lillian and James both looked over and saw Elsa standing in the doorway. From the corner of her eye, Lillian noted that James blushed. He cleared his throat, and then excused himself to go down to the men's room. That left Elsa and Lillian standing alone in the kitchen, contemplating each other.

"Coffee?" Lillian asked.

Elsa brushed by her. She picked up the cup James had washed and poured coffee into it. She didn't even bother looking for cream or sugar. She sipped the near-scalding liquid and didn't flinch. She regarded Lillian over the coffee cup.

"I've known about you for as long as I've known James." Elsa spoke these words in such a declarative way that it came across as fact. The statement took Lillian aback. Elsa noticed. "That's right. Those many years ago—six, wasn't it?—you broke my husband's heart. You refused to stay with him after giving every indication you would." She cocked her head. "Why was that?"

Lillian drank some coffee. Ever since she had laid eyes on Elsa, Lillian had wondered about her. The trained army sergeant in her sized up Mrs. Geiger in a glance: tall, lithe, blonde, strikingly beautiful with an aristocratic air about her. Even now, when Lillian wore clothes that showed evidence of last night's action, Elsa Geiger looked little the worse for wear. Seeing her looking like that and having the German woman question her made Lillian more than a little peeved. "He caught me off guard by his plan."

"Much like he caught me off guard with this foolhardy adventure we now find ourselves in. I might even have it worse. People are shooting at us." She scoffed and flippantly waved her hand at Lillian. "Well, let's be honest: they're shooting at you. I know Colonel Graf…"

"So do I," Lillian cut in. "He was my professor while at the university for a semester in Berlin."

Elsa mocked being impressed. "Oh, so he was your professor. I bet you really got to know him. Was that during office hours or after hours?"

Lillian tightened her jaw. "As a professor. I was with James at the time. And I would never do something like that."

"I suppose not. I know Colonel Graf as a military strategist. He was specifically brought into the Wehrmacht because he thought differently from others. He's had some adjustment to deal with, but his mind is quite sharp. I highly doubt we will leave Brussels without manacles around our wrists. No, around your wrists. Or you might just die in the streets with a bullet in your brain."

Lillian had had enough. She slammed the cup onto the counter, sloshing the dark liquid on the surface. "Listen here." She could barely hold back her growing rage. "I have a job to do. And since *your husband* lied to me regarding the codebook, I now have to get him and you to England. If I thought he would talk without you, I'd leave you here in Europe where you can slink back to Berlin and be cheerleader for *der Führer*. But I can't. He wants you with him, although I can't see what he sees in you."

"He sees a woman who loves him, a woman who is having his baby, and a woman who will do anything for him." Elsa arched an eyebrow at Lillian. "More than you ever offered."

The impulse to punch Elsa in the face was so strong it took all of Lillian's willpower not to strike. Instead she breathed, clamping her lips together so no inappropriate words would come out.

"While I've got your attention," Elsa continued, "I wanted you to know one thing: we love each other. We're devoted to each other. Make no mistake. I could walk over there, pick up that phone, and call Berlin right now. I could talk with my father and tell him the situation. James and I could be back in Berlin before you get to England. And my husband would come with me. He might not want to, but he would. He would apologize and beg forgiveness and my father would accept it. James, of course, wouldn't have as high a stature as he did before, but we'd live our lives and raise our children. When the Wehrmacht came to fetch us, they'd probably kill you and everyone else here." She sipped her coffee and smiled over the rim. "All it would take is a phone call." She let the threat hang in the air.

Lillian narrowed her eyes, then bolted across the room. She picked up the phone and yanked the cord out of the wall. Throwing it down, she gave Elsa a satisfied look.

Embassy staffers, hearing the sound, came running, Henry and Arnold among them. Lillian pointed an accusing finger at Elsa. "Make sure she does not get near a phone. This Nazi just threatened to call the Wehrmacht on us."

The staffers looked at each other, brows furrowed.

James rushed into the room. He looked at the anger in Lillian's eyes and the self-satisfied grin on Elsa's face. Lillian jabbed a finger into James's chest. "You make sure to keep a leash on your wife. If she steps out of line again or threatens this mission, we will leave her behind."

Hurrying over to Elsa, James turned. "Then you'll get nothing from me, and Frank will have died in vain."

"Frank already died in vain because of your stupid lying!"

Henry put a soothing hand on Lillian's shoulder. She viciously shrugged it off and stormed out of the room. She wanted to get as far away as possible before the tears streaked down her cheeks.

***

Henry Clark looked at the departing Lillian Saxton. For a moment, he didn't know what to do. He had only known the fiery American sergeant for less than a week, but he had a pretty good handle on how she viewed military and mission matters. He had begun to get a sense of her on the Channel crossing. It was reinforced during their captivity in the hotel and the long hours before their escape. They had talked about life and the events that had landed them there, together, in a hotel room in Brussels. He knew she wouldn't stop this mission until it was over, but that didn't mean she wasn't right about something.

He turned to one of the embassy staffers who carried a side arm. "Follow the sergeant's orders." He eyed the Geigers. "Keep watch on both of them until we leave."

James Geiger took offense. "We are not prisoners. We are defectors."

"Exactly. And I'm an official representative of His Majesty's government. I am willing to get you both to England where you can divulge all your secrets. But, until then, am I not obligated to treat you as enemy spies? What if this is all just a trick?"

Geiger gave him a look that told Henry he was being preposterous. "For what purpose? To capture or kill a handful of British agents and an American? The Wehrmacht is practically at the doorstep of Brussels. If we don't move soon, we'll all get swept up in the invasion."

"I'm fully aware of the situation." Henry walked to the counter and, with a towel, wiped up the mess Saxton had made. "We have a plan. We leave today. In the meantime, however, the two of you are confined to this room since the sergeant took great pains and, dare I say it, pleasure in removing any source of communication from this room." He grinned.

"I will not accept that," Geiger said.

"You don't have a choice."

***

Gunter Graf sat in the Hotel Le Plaza and dreaded the call he had to make. Wilhelm was right: he needed to report to General Siegfried. Despite all the calm assurance he had showed to his adjutant, Graf knew he was on the precipice of failure. He had lost two members of his team. His prisoners had escaped. They now had additional resources at the British Embassy while he had fewer.

Graf sat in contemplation, a finger idly rubbing his lips. A glass of brandy rested on the side table. What would they do? How would they get out?

He thought about all he knew about the British and they way they fought wars. They were rigid in their protocol. They followed orders. They liked order over chaos. Why was the embassy still open in the face of the Wehrmacht onslaught?

Because they wanted to keep everything normal until the last possible moment. If that was the case, they would likely seek an orderly way out. A normal way of escaping.

The proper British means of escape would be the thing that's still running. Graf smiled.

The trains.

He had mentioned to Schmidt that they would lay siege to the embassy, but Graf had had time to ponder the question and rejected it. He only had four men, including himself, to use. Graf had to pass some standard gun-handling exams but he was far from an excellent marksman. Now that Richter was dead, Ursula was the best. Schmidt was good and Wilhelm could hold his own. That meant Graf was the weak link when it came to arms.

He wasn't the weak link when it came to strategy.

The trains would be the most logical means of escape. The only thing Graf had to do was get on and the traitor Geiger and his new allies would be trapped.

With a lightness in his heart, Colonel Graf picked up the telephone to call his superior.

47

The plan to evacuate the embassy was extraordinarily simple: buy a ticket and get on the train. Actually, Arnold said, they had a standing agreement with the engineers at the train station that embassy personnel didn't need a ticket as long as they showed the proper identification.

"So we're just going to ride the train out of Brussels?" Lillian asked for the third time. Henry had briefed her on the plan, yet she still struggled with its simplicity.

"Yes. It's that simple."

"Great. Now, tell me how we're going to get there. Colonel Graf is still out there. He knows where we are."

"He likely does," Henry conceded. "But with no action against the embassy up to now, that likely means he's working with a small team. A team that's down two if you recall."

"Yeah, I remember. It was only hours ago. What about the Geigers? They don't have tickets and neither do we."

"Arnold has it arranged."

Lillian walked over to the window and looked out. From four stories up, if she looked directly out, everything looked peaceful. She could almost forget there was a war on. When she craned her eyes down to the crowded streets, she remembered where she was and what she was doing.

"I'll still be much happier when we're on the train."

"I'll be much happier when we step foot on British soil." Henry stood. "Ready?"

She looked once again at the people down on the street. Somewhere, among them, Colonel Graf and his team waited for them. Would the Nazis hesitate and show mercy to the innocent civilians? Probably not, which all the more reason Lillian wished she knew where Graf was.

"As I'll ever be."

"There going to be any issues with the Geigers?"

Lillian bit her lip. When she had stormed out of the kitchen, she managed to escape to a room far enough away from everyone where her sobbing couldn't be heard. The cry cleansed her of the tension, the fatigue, and the memories. She emerged refreshed and rededicated to the mission. What happened once they got James and Elsa to Britain was another matter.

"Nope."

She and Henry walked downstairs to the ground floor. Arnold and his men waited. James and Elsa waited with them. The two of them avoided eye contact with Lillian.

"Ready to give this a go?" Arnold asked.

"As rain," Henry replied.

"Everyone remember our plan? My men head out first and secure the perimeter. Clark and the sergeant come next with the assets. If there's trouble, the Geigers stay inside until the trouble is gone. Otherwise, we get to the train station and get the hell out of Brussels."

The men nodded.

"Let's go."

Arnold, his men, Lillian, and Henry all drew their weapons. James and Elsa waited. Other than a few of the unarmed employees from the embassy, no one carried any luggage.

One of Arnold's men opened the back door but didn't go out. On a signal from Arnold, three men ran out and got behind each of the three cars parked along the street. They waited a few moments. When nothing happened, they climbed into the vehicles and started the engines.

Among Henry, Arnold, and Lillian, there had been some discussion about distribution of personnel. Henry wanted to separate James and Elsa, but Lillian vetoed the idea. "He won't do it," was all she said. It was agreed that the Geigers would be in the middle car in case the worst happened and the lead car was damaged.

On the count of three, everyone else ran out of the embassy. They all kept their heads down. Lillian led the way with James and Elsa close behind. They piled into the middle car and slammed the rear door shut. Henry climbed into the front seat next to the driver.

Nothing happened.

"I don't like this," Henry said.

"Me neither," Lillian replied. "I'm feeling like we're just walking into an ambush."

James said, "You should have given me a gun."

Without turning to him, Lillian said, "Your only job is to stay alive. It's our job to protect you." She tapped the driver's shoulder.

The driver stuck his hand out the window and gave a circular motion. With that, all three drivers put their respective vehicles in gear and pulled out.

The closer they got to the edge of the embassy, the faster Lillian's heart beat. If ever there was a position in which to attack, it was at the edge of the street.

Henry covered the side facing the embassy.

She covered the opposite side. "Get down," she commanded the Geigers.

They complied.

All three cars burst through the intersection and took an immediate left. Tires screeched and people along the sidewalks turned and watched.

From somewhere along the roads, gunshots rang out. Lillian turned in her seat. The sounds came from behind them. The third car lurched on the road, losing control. No, the driver took evasive action. He was steering the car in an erratic way to avoid more gunshots.

Lillian wiped the perspiration on her forehead with her sleeve.

While the sidewalks were jammed with people, the streets were relatively empty of traffic. All three drivers poured on the gas and raced through the streets of Brussels down to the train station. They encountered no further action against them.

Instead of parking in front of the station, as planned, the

three drivers parked in the rear. "It's part of our agreement with the engineers that we can go through the back," Arnold had said. As they approached the narrow alley behind the station, Lillian wondered if Graf had planned for this. They would be sitting ducks in here.

Nevertheless, everyone parked. Almost the instant the cars came to a halt, the doors were flung open and the occupants escaped and lined up against the side of the station. With nervous looks among Arnold's men, they all made their way around the back corner to a door. Arnold holstered his gun and knocked. A moment later, the door opened and a gun pointed in his face.

"We're from the British Embassy," Arnold said, hands up, palms out.

The pistol disappeared. "Come on," a man said in French.

The door opened all the way and everyone went inside. It turned out to a service hallway with unpainted cement walls. The man who had opened the door signaled the new arrivals to follow him. They did. At the end of the hall, he used a key and unlocked another door. When it opened, Lillian was aghast at what she saw.

***

They were inside the station, but on the service side. No platforms existed where they stood. On the far side, where the passengers normally boarded, throngs of people waited to get on the trains. Some had luggage, others held children in their arms. All had the look of desperation in their eyes.

"This way," said the man who had unlocked the door. "You get on the last car."

They trundled along the side of the station. Debris and trashed skittered along with the breeze. The smell of diesel and exhaust filled the air.

Lillian sidled up to their guide and spoke to him in French. "Will all those people be able to get out?"

"Probably not," he replied. "But we'll keep the trains running until the Nazis get here."

Lillian looked at the people. Women, children, the young, the old, husbands, wives. Those on the platform who caught sight of the small band watched as Lillian and her party skirted the lines and went to the trains unencumbered. A sense of shame washed over her. Why should she have it free and clear when so many had to stay behind, potentially never to get out before the Wehrmacht swept through the city?

But then she looked behind her and caught sight of James and Elsa. That was why she was here. Lillian needed to stifle her personal feelings and move forward. She noted a smugness in Elsa's face. This must have been the type of special privilege the German was used to. The thought turned Lillian's stomach.

Their guide reached the lead passenger car and whistled. Another man responded and opened a side door just next to the bellows that connected the first and second car. Everyone climbed aboard and found seats. A number of passengers were already seated and the embassy group had to split up. The embassy personnel and some of Arnold's men went forward while Lillian, Henry, Arnold, and the Geigers moved to the second car. All the seats faced the front. The Geigers sat in one bench seat. Arnold took a spot ahead of them while Lillian and Henry took the seat directly behind them.

They waited. Upon a signal, the doors opened in all the train cars and the people on the platforms stormed forward. Lillian watched in horror as people pushed and shoved to get closer and get inside for a chance of freedom and escape. Her heart went out to everyone outside the trains.

Not able to resist herself, Lillian leaned over the seat. "That's the kind of desperation your *Führer* makes," she said to Elsa and James.

Henry pulled her back before either Geiger could respond. "You don't have to antagonize them."

"Why not? I just wanted to point out that all those people are in that state because of the Nazis."

"Everyone knows what's at stake. Now, keep your eyes peeled. Just because our friend Graf didn't get to us outside the embassy doesn't mean he won't try here."

"How?" Lillian blurted. She gestured outside. "How could he and his team possibly get through that?"

Henry shrugged. "Just keep watch."

Fifteen minutes passed by. More and more people flooded into the train. In the car behind theirs, Lillian noted the stevedores were allowing people to stand in the aisles two and three deep. In their carriage, however, fewer people were allowed. In fact, a stevedore stood guard at each of the doors that led into their car. She couldn't stand it. Lillian got up and strode over to one of the guards. "Why aren't you letting people in?"

"This is first class." The man spoke the words like he was commenting on the color of the sky.

"There's room for people to stand in here."

"No, madam. Not in this car."

She put her hand to the holstered gun. "I could make you."

With level evenness, the stevedore said, "And I could throw you off this train."

The next moment, Henry stood beside her. "Let it go."

Lillian gazed out the window at the people who could not get on the train. "I can't."

"You will." Henry placed a hand on her shoulder. He guided her back to their seat. "You have a job to do. It's only those two people you should care about."

"What about them?" She gestured toward the people on the platform. "Don't you care about them?"

"In war, we have to make choices. Our choice was made for us when we took this mission. All other things fall by the wayside."

The whistle sounded. The character of the throng outside changed. Desperation set in. There was more shoving and pushing. A few people fell to the ground from the platform. Belgian police and military struggled to keep the crowd at bay.

With a lurch, the train began to move. It pulled out slowly.

Lillian turned away from the platform and stared out the window on the service side. It was a good thing she did.

At the end of the tracks, right before the train left the station, she saw something and gasped.

Henry turned. "What is it?"

Lillian pointed.

Four bodies lay strewn in a haphazard line. All had bullet holes in their heads. Each body wore only undergarments.

"I can think of only one reason those people are dead and hidden from sight," Henry murmured.

"Yeah," Lillian replied. "It means Graf and his team are on this train."

48

Colonel Gunter Graf experienced a moment of hesitation when he told his remaining team members of the new plan to infiltrate the train. It wasn't that the plan was wrong. In fact, it proved to be quite easy. It was the details. Namely, the need to get on the train without being detected. In order to accomplish that, he realized they needed to blend in, and what better way to blend in than with the clothing and accouterments of railway workers?

He charged them with that task. They had returned, in a surprisingly short amount of time, to the building across the street from the train station. Schmidt, Lange, and even Ursula wore uniforms of the railway. They handed a folded wad of clothes to Graf.

"Dare I ask how you obtained these uniforms?"

Ursula shrugged. "The men who wore them refused to hand over their clothes. Now, they no longer need any."

The nonchalance of the statement and the action behind it still chilled Graf's spine as he sat in the lead passenger car. The train was moving now, building up speed through Brussels. The clickety-clack of the wheels had already started to mesmerize him. He was tired. He had a headache likely caused by drinking too much and eating food of a caliber far inferior to his wife's cooking. He was looking to putting an end to this mission and returning to Berlin a vindicated man. Siegfried could shove his doubts up his ass for all Graf cared. He would have proven himself in the field, leading a team. With that kind of clout, Graf assumed he could parlay any additional assignments in the field to someone else.

The last call he had made was to Siegfried. The general had informed the colonel that the Wehrmacht was on the move near Antwerp. It was likely that the German Army would sweep through the port city before the train from Brussels could arrive. In effect, Siegfried had told Graf, the last train that left the free city of Brussels would arrive in Nazi-controlled Antwerp.

Which meant to Graf only one thing: get on the train, make sure the Geigers are on the train, and lead them into the trap.

Graf smiled to himself. He had directed Ursula, Wilhelm, and Schmidt to pose as the stevedores for the first two cars. Graf had suspected the embassy would have some sort of backdoor deal with the trains to get their people out without any unnecessary encumbrances. He was correct. Now, the Geigers, Saxton, and Clark were on the second car. The only members of the British team he had noted carrying weapons were seated a few seats from the rear. Thankfully, there were only two of them. Ursula could easily take care of them.

Looking out his window, Graf noted the urban sprawl of Brussels slowly faded into the springtime of the country. Refugees and stragglers clogged the streets trying to avoid the approaching German Army. Graf had little use for them. The Belgians had defied the Allies' attempt to create a united front by joining with Britain and France. King Leopold III thought he could stay out of the war or, at best, defend his little country. According to the latest reports, the Germans were having little resistance moving toward the English Channel and crushing both the British and French Army.

Fifteen minutes out of Brussels and halfway to Antwerp, Graf stood. He moved to the front of the car. He turned and faced the rear. Ursula stood by the door. With her hair pulled up into the hat she wore and the large, ill-fitting uniform, her gender was effectively concealed. The murmur of the passengers dimmed as each of them noticed Graf standing. They waited for instructions on what to do next.

What they heard was gunfire. The two reports proved surprisingly loud in the car. Women screamed and men yelled as they turned to look at what happened in the back of their train car.

Ursula stood there, her smoking gun in her hand. Two men

slumped in their seats and leaned against the window. Blood splatter coated the window.

"Ladies and gentlemen," Graf spoke in French, "please remain calm. I would hate to have my friend shoot you."

49

Lillian and James had been racking their brains trying to figure out a way to identify Graf and his men. They assumed he might have commandeered the engine and were driving them straight to capture at Antwerp.

Now, however, as the outskirts of that port city came into view, Lillian wasn't so sure. Out the right window that faced northeast, the signs of war filled the vista. Huge plumes of smoke snaked into the sky. Even over the train engines and wheels on the tracks, the bombardment by the invading Nazis could be heard. She looked at Henry. The concern in his eyes mirrored hers.

The other window, however, the one that faced southwest, showed a nearly opposite vista. With the fighting armies still to the north, the south looked downright pastoral. Plowed fields were starting to show signs of new spring growth. The trees that dotted the landscape looked like something a French impressionist might paint. But what caught her eye most of all was a wide space off about a mile or two.

She tapped Henry's arm to show him, but before he could follow her pointing finger, two gunshots sounded. The passengers in this car gasped and murmured in alarm. James turned around in his seat. "What was that?"

"That came from the lead car." Henry pulled his gun and rose to see what had happened.

"Sit down," said the stevedore.

Lillian caught a quick glimpse of something slicing through the air the second before the stevedore banged his gun down on Henry's head. The Englishman doubled over in pain, but he didn't drop his gun.

Lillian reached for her pistol but the other stevedore, the one from the front of the car, approached. A gun was in his hand

and he aimed it at them.

"Your weapons." The stevedore from the front swung his gun. "Give them to me. You first," he said to Arnold.

With defeat in his posture, Arnold surrendered his gun, butt first, to the stevedore. No one else in the car moved, so rapt with astonishment were they at what was happening in front of them. The stevedore from the rear yanked Henry's gun from his hand and slipped it into a pocket. He extended his open palm to Lillian. "Your gun, Fräulein, bitte." Seeing no choice, Lillian complied. The Nazi—for that's who he was—took her gun and slipped it in another pocket.

A knock came from the front door of their car. The Nazi in front—a blond man who appeared to be the epitome of the Aryan race Hitler favored—moved aside. Colonel Gunter Graf entered the train car. He wore a smile as big as his face. His eyes swept across the passengers and landed on Lillian. "Sergeant Saxton, we meet again."

Lillian held her tongue. To occupy her time, she assessed Henry. He had a gash on his scalp that seeped blood. It was already staining the back of his collar. "Does anyone have a handkerchief?" she asked in French. "This man needs medical attention."

Graf chuckled as he moved along the aisle. "He'll need more than that, Sergeant. But, if it'll make you feel better in the near term…" He turned to the rest of the passengers. "Can anyone fulfill the *Fräulein's* request?"

The other passengers were too scared to move. One man finally held up a handkerchief. Graf took the cloth and gave it to Lillian. She immediately dabbed Henry's head with it.

The Nazi colonel turned his attention to James and Elsa Geiger. "Ah, the traitors." He smirked and leaned on the back of the seat in front of them. The passenger in that seat, an old woman wearing an absurd headdress as if she were going for a stroll in the country, recoiled. "That is what the two of you are. Traitors." He pointed at the two of them, waving his finger back and forth. "You, sir, I assumed to be a traitor from the outset. Anyone not born in Germany should have his loyalty questioned and proven over and over again. Am I right?"

"No," James said. "I have been loyal to the Reich up until recently."

"Which means you've never been loyal to the Reich," Graf corrected. "If you're loyal, you don't make the choices you have made." He leaned closer to James who sat by the window. "Why?"

James remained mute.

"Why," Graf went on, "did you turn your back on the country that has offered you so much? That has offered you one of the finest women of her generation?" He gestured at Elsa as if he were presenting the winner of a beauty contest. "Why did you disgrace her family by bringing her along?"

"Because of what the Reich is doing."

"We are merely consolidating our strength on the Continent to rule it as the great power we are."

"But you're murdering innocents!" James's voice rose in fury. "The camps, Colonel. Why does Hitler need the camps?"

"To weed out all undesirables." He spoke the words matter-of-factly. "It makes our dominion of the Continent all the easier. It also clears out the clutter. Think of them like the underbrush in a forest. From time to time, you have to clear it in order for the oaks to grow strong and tall."

He bent low to look out the windows. "Over here, you have the fire of purity in the form of our Wehrmacht burning through the underbrush of Belgium." He directed his gaze to the other side. "And over here, this land awaits the purity to come. We'll keep what's best and eliminate the clutter."

"But who determines what is clutter and what isn't?" Lillian blurted.

Graf gave her a look. It was the same look he had given her back in her university days when she answered a question wrong. "Sergeant, our *Führer* determines that. And he has made his judgment. It is our job to follow his orders."

The colonel turned his attention to Elsa. "Frau Geiger,

what is your opinion on the subject? Are you here on your own volition?"

Lillian couldn't see Elsa's face from this angle, but she saw the muscles in her jaw flex and tighten. "Colonel Graf, I stand by my husband."

"Even if what he is doing is a mistake?"

"I stand by my husband. I am in the process of talking him out of this foolhardy action. I was making progress, too. As much as I stand by James, he will stand by me. And let me tell you something, Herr Colonel. I may be here, but I still am my father's daughter. You know him and his reputation. When we get back to Berlin, I will have a word with him. You won't like the outcome."

For once, Lillian admired the snottiness of Elsa Geiger when it wasn't directed her way.

Graf stood and waved his hand dismissively. "Your father will have a hard time saving your husband. You, on the other hand, will soon be free to marry a true German." He winked at her. "A widow often makes an excellent wife to an army officer." He made his way to the front door and stopped. "Enjoy your last train ride. We'll be in Antwerp soon." With that, he exited the train car and closed the door behind him. Blond Nazi assumed his place guarding the door. The other Nazi stood guard at the rear door. Both held their guns.

Henry leaned forward. Lillian did the same. "That didn't go well," the British agent whispered.

"Nope. How long do you think we have?"

"Five, ten minutes. We have to get off this train."

"There's an airfield off to the southwest. Did you see it?"

Henry nodded. He winced and touched his head. His fingers came away bloody. He wiped them on his pants. With his bloody fingers, he smoothed out the fabric.

Lillian watched as the blood soaked into the fabric. The blood began to reveal the shape of something in Henry's pocket.

A knife blade.

"Listen," Henry said, "I've got a plan."

50

After a few harried minutes of planning, Lillian and Henry had the strategy fixed. Through the narrow gap in the seats in front of them, Lillian whispered, "James."

"I heard," came the reply. "We're ready."

"Tell Arnold."

James leaned forward and whispered. From over the seats, Lillian saw Arnold's head nod once.

While they were talking, Lillian had wormed her leather belt off her traveling suit. At the same time, Henry had worked the knife out of his pocket. In order to avoid attention, he moaned loudly and leaned forward. That left his left pocket exposed for Lillian. Swiftly, she snaked her hand into his pocket and slipped out the knife. She played nurse and brought him back to her, tending to his head wound. She glared at the Nazi standing one row behind them at the rear door.

The train engineer deftly applied the initial brakes. The train began to slow.

Lillian whispered to James. "It's time. When we move, lean down and avoid the bullets if either Nazi starts shooting."

"Won't that bring the others?" James asked.

"Yes. Be ready."

Henry had taken Lillian's belt and wrapped the non-buckled end once around his hand. The rest of the belt and the brass buckle rested on his knee. He looked at Lillian.

She looked back at him. He nodded once.

They moved.

Henry stood in the aisle and turned to face the Nazi in the rear. As expected, he brought up his gun to shoot. Henry lashed out with the belt. The weighted buckle found its mark on the Nazi's arm. It wrapped once. Henry yanked. He pulled the Nazi forward and planted a massive punch in his face. Dazed, the

Nazi fell to his knees.

While Henry was concentrating on the Nazi in the rear, Blond Nazi was Lillian's concern. When Henry moved, Blond Nazi noticed. He started to move forward a step, yet only then did he think to raise his gun. That hesitation cost him.

Lillian stood up and threw the knife at Blond Nazi. The blade thunked into his chest. He stood a moment, dazed at what had just happened. He coughed once. His gun hand fell to his side, the weapon skittering across the floor. He sank to his knees and fell face first in the aisle.

They had completed their task without any gunshots. For that, Lillian was thankful. She hadn't anticipated any of the passengers screaming.

One did. The sound was earsplitting.

Through the windows in the doors that connected the first and second train cars, a woman standing guard in the first car turned. Her eyes widened. She began to move.

"Let's go!" Henry yelled. He kicked the fallen Nazi and picked up his gun.

Lillian hustled James and Elsa out of their seats and to the rear of the car. Henry had already opened the rear door. The smell of exhaust flooded into the train car.

Arnold had moved from his seat, too. He bent down and retrieved Blond Nazi's gun. "Go!" he yelled at Lillian. "I'm right behind you."

Lillian shuffled right behind Elsa to the rear of the car.

Two gunshots rang out. The first took out the connecting windows of both doors between cars one and two. The second slammed into Arnold's back, pushing him forward. He caught his balance on the backs of two seats. He remained standing.

Lillian turned. "Arnold!"

He tossed her the gun. "Get them out alive." He smiled. Blood coated his teeth. "I'm your shield."

As if in answer, two more gunshots erupted. Both landed with wet sounds into Arnold's back. He fell forward, but Lillian was already moving to the rear door, keeping her head down as more bullets pinged off the interior of the train car.

She reached the bellows connecting cars two and three. No one was there. She glanced out and behind them. Henry, James, and Elsa were already getting to their feet and running away. Trying to judge the speed of the tracks, Lillian leaped into the air.

She landed hard on the ground and rolled twenty feet. She held onto the gun for dear life. Finally, she stopped. She saw stars and wondered if she had a concussion. Shaking her head to clear it, she rose to all fours. The rear of the long train was approaching, which meant the first train car with Graf and the woman Nazi was far enough away that Lillian didn't have to worry.

A new sound screamed through the stillness. It was the sound of the emergency brakes being applied. The train lurched forward and slowed.

"Great," Lillian murmured. She got to her feet and ran.

51

When Gunter Graf heard the screams from the second train carriage, he pretty much knew what was happening. The prisoners were trying to escape. He stood from his seat at the front of the car and walked to the rear.

He watched as Ursula pulled her gun and fired through the two door windows. The first bullet cleared the glass. The second bullet hit a man standing in the aisle of the second car.

Graf hurried forward, drawing his own gun.

Ursula opened the door from train car one and stepped through the opening. Before opening the second door, she let loose two more shots.

The man standing in the aisle fell forward. He tossed an object at another person at the far rear of the aisle. The person was Lillian Saxton. The object was a gun.

"Keep at it," Graf ordered.

He didn't need to waste his breath. Ursula was already opening the front door to train car two and moving forward. She fired more shots at the fleeing American soldier. The bullets ricocheted around inside the car. One of them found a home in the neck of a passenger. The man pitched forward, blood spurting from his wound.

Ursula stepped over the prone form of Wilhelm and jumped into the bellows. Through the window, Graf saw the prisoners who had been so recently in his grasp. His temper flared.

A passenger tried to reach up and take the gun from Graf. With a vicious punch, Graf struck the man, then turned his gun on him. One shot to the head ended that short battle.

Without missing a beat, Graf leaned over and yanked the emergency stop cord. He held on while the train's emergency brakes engaged and the train slowed to a stop.

Graf righted himself and bent to see if Wilhelm was alive.

The colonel found the younger man's pulse. He slapped his assistant numerous times before Wilhelm awoke. He looked up at Graf, his nose bloody.

"Sir? What happened?"

"The prisoners have escaped." He stood and lent a helping hand to Wilhelm. "We're going after them." He shoved Wilhelm to the rear door and out into the bellows. Ursula was already on the ground.

"Move it, Lieutenant."

Wilhelm jumped to the ground and immediately fell.

Graf noticed that the passengers in train car three were looking to see what had happened. He held up his gun. The people fell back. Graf smiled at the power he possessed.

Making his way to the ground, he joined up with Ursula and Wilhelm. "You see where they went?"

"That way." Ursula pointed at a pasture that bordered a small stand of trees.

Graf pulled a map of Belgium in his mind. He merged that with the landscape he had seen from the train. "The airfield. Did you see it?"

Ursula nodded. "Down to the south?"

"That's the one. Take Wilhelm. Lieutenant, are you armed?"

Wilhelm took both confiscated pistols from his pocket. Anger seethed across his face. "Double."

Graf nodded. "Try to take them alive, if at all possible. If any has to die, let it be the British. I want the Geigers and Sergeant Saxton."

"Why?" Ursula asked. "Why not kill them all and be done with it?"

"You have your orders. Alive. They are worth far more alive than dead. They'll be dead enough when the invasion's complete. We can make better examples of traitors when they are captured alive. And to have an American army sergeant also captured will enable *der Führer* to use her as he sees fit."

"What are you going to do?" Wilhelm wiped blood and mucus from his shattered nose.

"Flank them. You both, get to the airfield!"

Ursula and Wilhelm scurried away. Graf turned and started walking back to the head of the train. The big locomotive had stopped near a street. In fact, it blocked all traffic. Cars and motorcycles were halted in a haphazard fashion. Horns blared and shouts were heard.

Graf stormed to the train's engine car. An engineer had climbed down from the cockpit. Seeing the uniform Graf wore, asked in French, "Do you know why we stopped?"

The bullet Graf put in the engineer's head ceased all conversation.

A few of the drivers saw what had happened. Some tried to drive away, but got caught between other cars, signs, and buildings. Others merely evacuated their vehicles and fled on foot.

Again, Graf relished the power he possessed. He strode purposefully to an abandoned car and climbed in. The engine was still running. Not caring about damage to anything, he threw the car into gear. He scraped the bumper of one car while shearing off a quarter panel of his own car. He didn't care. His entire focus was to get to the airfield.

He eased the car enough to gain clearance. Then, he slammed the gas pedal to the floor. The car shot forward. Pedestrians leapt out of the way. He came around the end of the street, passed right next to the stalled train, and headed back to the airfield.

Gunter Graf was going to have his victory.

52

Part of the official U.S. Army training program is long-distance running. Lillian Saxton excelled in that category, even besting her male counterparts. She attributed her ability to run for a long period of time to the training she had received from Kenji Tanaka. In her time at his compound, she had learned proper breathing that enabled her to channel her energies when she ran.

The moment Lillian passed the threshold of the forest, she halted, barely breathing hard. Henry, James, and Elsa stood still. The trio had stopped to catch their breath and wait for Lillian.

"Why'd you stop?"

"Waiting for you," Henry said.

"I'm fine." Lillian pointed at the stopped train. "They're coming. Let's get a move on. Stay in the woods as long as possible. Only cross empty fields when you have to. Keep bearing southwest to the airfield."

All four set out at a run. Of all of them, Elsa had it the hardest. Her heeled shoes were taller than Lillian's more sturdy practical ones. Elsa slipped and fell. James was there to help her. Before Elsa stood up, Lillian stopped her.

"Your shoes. Take them off."

"But I won't be able to run as fast." Elsa was breathing heavily, gulping lungfuls of air.

Lillian gave her an even stare. "If you want, we can let them get closer. Then you'll run like hell."

James slipped one of Elsa's shoes off her foot. "It's the heels." He banged the shoe against a tree. He banged again and again.

"Keep it up," Lillian said, lacing her voice with sarcasm. "I'm not sure they have a direct line on us."

Henry ran back. "What's going on?"

"High heels are slowing her down." Lillian sighed. "She won't listen to me. You tell her."

Henry gave Elsa a warm smile. "She's right. And stop that banging."

The last strike by James resulted in a crack. He brought the shoe up triumphantly, expecting to see a shoe without a heel. What he held was a shoe broken in the middle.

"Brilliant," Lillian said.

Elsa tore off her other shoe and threw it at her husband. He blocked the shoe.

Lillian laughed.

A bullet whizzed by them and struck a nearby tree. Then they heard the gunshot.

They all ducked low.

"Where'd it come from?" Lillian asked.

Henry peered through the forest. "Can't tell. But they had a line on us."

Lillian shot an I-told-you-so glance at James. "Let's move. Stay low."

They stood. Elsa gingerly started stepping with her now bare feet. Another bullet sailing through the air made her run faster.

But they still weren't as fast as Lillian would like. "I only saw two behind us. The woman and the man you decked."

Henry concurred.

Lillian grinned. "Let's even the odds."

James said, "Do you think that's wise?"

"You want them to catch us?"

Up ahead, the forest got thicker. A few trees lay fallen on the ground, rotting. Lillian saw the way. She stopped. The other three did likewise.

"Listen, James, you and Elsa keep going. You'll be our bait."

"What the hell?" James blurted.

"They're not likely to kill you. Graf said so. Me and Henry, not so much. We'll stop, hide, let the Nazis get past us and we'll ambush them from behind."

James opened his mouth to reply but Henry cut him off.

"This isn't a discussion. It's our best option."

"Keep going until you see the airfield." Lillian continued. "We'll be right behind you soon. Stay inside the woods. Don't cross the airfield to the aerodrome alone. Understand?"

Nodding, James helped Elsa back into the path they had just left and started off.

"Think this will work?" Henry took a position behind a large tree.

Lillian gave him a grim smile. "It's our best option."

"I'm beginning to like the way you think, Miss Saxton."

"Why thank you, Mr. Clark."

They hushed. Not wanting to look around the tree for fear of giving away their position to the approaching Nazis, Lillian and Henry ended up craning their ears for upcoming footfalls. And they did so by looking at each other. Lillian regarded the tall British agent leaning against the tree. His clothes showed the signs of the action: torn sleeve, bloody collar, shirt half tucked in. The dark hair had fallen over his brow. He constantly swept his hands through it only to have it fall over his forehead again. His shirt was open, revealing the top of his broad chest and the dark hair that covered it. Despite their situation, she found the sight of Henry Clark quite appealing.

He frowned at her and she suddenly looked away. What kind of look had she been giving him?

She didn't have time to think of it any longer. Footsteps approached. In another moment, a figure raced by them.

Henry leaped through the air. He landed on the running man. Both crashed to the earth in a heap. Henry recovered first. He landed a massive fist on the man's face.

The man brought up his gun to shoot Henry. The Englishman grabbed the Nazi's wrist and wrung the gun out of his grip. On his knees, Henry turned the gun around and made ready to shoot.

"Don't!" Lillian hissed.

Henry twisted his head to her. "Why not?"

"The sound will bring the other one. Also, we're supposed

to be better than they are. We've bested him. You kill him now, it's murder."

"But he was about to murder us!"

"Doesn't matter. Take him out but don't kill him."

Henry grunted in frustration.

A soft footfall sounded from nearby.

Lillian whirled to see what had made the sound, but she was too late.

The female Nazi stood there, gun drawn.

She fired at Henry.

53

Henry tried to move out of the way, but spun with the impact of the slug. He fell to the ground, clutching his arm. He grunted in pain.

Lillian raised her gun but the Nazi already had a bead on her.

"I'm supposed to keep you alive," the Nazi woman said in heavily accented English, "but that doesn't mean uninjured."

Lillian and the woman stood in the forest, each with their guns aimed at the other. "I could shoot you now," Lillian said, "and be done with it."

The woman angled her head in the direction she had come. "What about them? Aren't you supposed to get them out of Belgium?" Louder, she said, "Come out."

James and Elsa emerged from the darkening woods. James had a gash on his temple. The blood streamed down his cheek and into his eye.

"Sorry," James said. "She caught up with us. Came from the side."

"It's okay." Lillian assessed her predicament. She saw no way out. "What's the play?" she said to the female Nazi.

"I shoot the British one and then bring the three of you to the airfield. That's where you're going, right?"

"You can't."

The Nazi frowned. "Can't what?"

"Shoot him."

"Why not?"

Lillian's mind raced for an answer. It came with surprisingly speed. "Because he's a double agent."

The Nazi stared at Lillian. "You lie."

"No," James said in German, "she doesn't." He took a step forward. "Ursula, you know me and what I do for *der Führer*. This man is one of our agents. He worked undercover at our ring in

Liverpool. He's been there for nearly a year. His codename was Becker. This entire operation was ordered by Siegfried."

"You lie!" she repeated.

"Maybe," James said. "But don't you think you ought to check with Graf first?"

"He never said anything about the British one being Becker."

James shrugged. He stood a little taller, some swagger coming into his features. "Suit yourself. Makes no difference to me. You're going to take us to Graf who will then take us back to Berlin. The American's coming, too, I assume. She's going to be a wonderful piece of propaganda Goebbels can use to shame the United States." He took another step to Ursula. "What's the problem with just waiting to see what Graf says?"

James gestured down on the ground to Henry. "He's injured. He's not in any state to fight back." He then stepped slowly over to Lillian. He reached out and gently put his hand over her gun. "And we want this one alive. It's the only way we can use her."

Lillian looked into James's eyes. What she saw there confused her. On the one hand, he spoke as he always had to her, back when they were dating and in love. Now, that look was laced with something else. Was he trying to take over the situation?

Or was it merely his way of guaranteeing her survival?

Slowly, Lillian let James take the gun from her. In her mind's eye, she wanted him to turn the gun on this Ursula woman and shoot her between the eyes.

What he did was empty the cartridge into his hand. He threw it away. He then ejected the round in the chamber and let the bullet fall to the ground. Last, he threw the gun in the opposite direction of the cartridge.

"Can we go now?" James walked over to Elsa and put his arm around his wife. Together, they started walking to the airfield.

Ursula was attuned to the changing situation. The Nazi kept her eye on Lillian as she stepped over to Henry. She found his gun and kicked it away.

"Up," she commanded. When Henry groaned, Ursula said, "Help him."

Lillian, hands in plain sight, walked over and helped Henry to his feet. He wobbled unsteadily for a step or two, then got his legs under him. They looked at each other in the growing twilight of the woods.

Ursula got in position behind Lillian and Henry.

"What about him?" Lillian pointed down at the sprawled form of the Nazi Henry had struck.

Ursula nudged the prone man with her foot. He didn't respond. She shrugged. "We'll come back for him."

"Are you serious?" Lillian asked, perplexed.

"Go."

They went.

54

Colonel Gunter Graf walked around the hangar of the aerodrome and waited. The sign painted on the facade was too difficult to read in the gathering twilight. Upon entering the structure and seeing what was inside, he remembered why this was one of the few airfields in Belgium the Luftwaffe had spared.

Lined up inside were six fixed-wing biplanes. He flipped on a light switch. Lights high atop the ceiling came on, illuminating the planes. He recognized the style. Stampe et Vertongen SV.4. They were trainer planes used to teach people how to fly or to take tourist up for a short flight. Hermann Goering didn't consider small planes like the Stampe to be a threat, and airfields such as this one could be converted for the Reich's use.

He strolled up to one of the planes. It was painted yellow. He ran his hands over the smooth fuselage, admiring the craftsmanship and attention to detail. He idly wondered where the designers were in Belgium and if they were to be captured, how much good they could do for the Reich.

With no active battle nearby, crickets chirped the twilight songs. The sound was cut through by Ursula's call. "We're here." Her words echoed in the hangar.

Graf spun on his heel and strode forward. Across the hangar, about fifty yards away, five figures emerged from the twilight outside. He recognized James and Elsa Geiger leading the way. Lillian Saxton and Henry Clark followed. Graf took pleasure in noting the British agent held one arm. Blood had soaked his coat and shirt. Ursula brought up the rear.

"Where's Wilhelm?" Graf asked.

"Back in the woods. This one"—Ursula lashed out and slammed her gun against Clark's injured arm—"overtook him."

"Dead?"

"*Nein.* Just knocked out. This stupid American convinced her ally to spare Wilhelm's life."

Gunter Graf laughed. "You Americans. Always thinking with your hearts." He came to stand in front of Sergeant Saxton. He reached out and slapped her. "This is war! There is no room for heart in war. Didn't I teach you anything when you were my student? Winning a war requires total commitment. Everything is on the table, ready to be sacrificed. Even your precious morality."

"I saw enough of your morality on the train platform back in Brussels," Saxton shot back. "All the people in the streets. The untold number your army has already killed in the invasion. At what cost victory?"

"Any cost. Any price."

Graf looked down into Saxton's eyes. He saw fury in them. Rage. He also saw defiance. Her jaw set, her chin forward, even now, captured as she was, his former student wasn't backing down. He had been so used to having his underlings cower around him or soldiers such as Ursula who answered to someone else that it took Graf by surprise to see someone so actively standing up to him. Truth be told, it unnerved him a little.

She will make a great capture. The idea of using this foolish American to shame and humiliate President Roosevelt was too good to be true. "And you." Graf turned his attention to Clark. "You've not fared very well. What have you to say for yourself?"

In German, Clark said, "It doesn't matter if I lose today. The British Empire will never surrender and never fall."

Graf chuckled. "Have you heard the reports from the front? We've been active for less than a week. We've nearly driven your precious B.E.F. to the sea. We've nearly split the French and the English lines. Your precious armies have nowhere to go. We will crush them on the beaches and then *der Führer* will dictate terms." Graf's voice rose in pitch and echoed through the hangar. "I've already alerted my commanding officer where we are. Once the Wehrmacht overtakes Antwerp tomorrow, he'll arrive and I'll present him his gift. And that includes the two traitors."

James and Elsa Geiger faced him. Unlike on the train when James was stoic and Elsa afraid, now both of them looked scared but firm.

Graf wondered if Elsa could be turned now. Chances were small.

"Professor Graf," Saxton began.

Graf whirled on his heel. "*Colonel* Graf, Sergeant."

Saxton smirked. "Colonel Graf, then. I remember all your lectures. I used to love how organized you were. More than just about any other professor I had. Your teachings about military campaigns and strategies really came back to me when I joined the United States Army. You praised the military organizations and formalities of Germany, Britain in the Napoleonic Wars, and the Romans."

"I'm pleased. It seems that my education didn't go unnoticed."

"You're right," Saxton said. "But you always left out us Americans."

Graf gave her a mocking look. "That's because you Americans usually stumble into victory. There's little to be learned from your history."

"Not true. You know what makes us formidable? We improvise."

Graf opened his mouth to respond. He stopped when he saw something glint in Saxton's hand. In the split second it took for his brain to process what it was, Saxton acted.

55

One of the main lessons Kanji Tanaka taught a young Lillian Saxton was the art of biding one's time. There will always be an adversary who will be impatient for victory. That will be his undoing.

After Ursula had captured them, Lillian bided her time. All through the forced march to the airfield and into the hangar, Lillian bided her time. She tripped once, but that was on purpose. Henry reached down to help her up. Unknowingly, he shielded from Ursula's view the subtle movement of Lillian's hand to her dress pocket. When she stood again, Lillian thanked Henry and kept walking.

Upon reaching the hangar, she still bided her time. It was fairly simple, what with Graf reverting back to professorial mode. When he started his lecture, Lillian knew the time was close.

She stood facing Graf while he lectured. Henry was to her left and the Geigers were to the British agent's left. Ursula stood immediately behind Lillian. *Close enough.*

In his arrogant tone and posture, Graf said, "That's because you Americans usually stumble into victory. There's little to be learned from your history."

"Not true." Lillian extended the fingers of her right hand. "You know what makes us formidable?" The knife she had taken from the kitchen in the embassy slid down her sleeve and into her palm. "We improvise." Lillian turned the blade behind her and jammed it into Ursula's thigh.

Everything happened at once.

Ursula screamed and staggered back a step.

Graf, who saw the blade a second before Lillian drove it home, unholstered his gun.

Henry, unarmed, dove on top of James and Elsa, shoving

them to the ground and covering them with his body.

Lillian pivoted and ducked the expected blow from Ursula. The Nazi's gun hand swung through empty air. Lillian rose and grabbed Ursula's wrist and gun. She continued her upward thrust into Ursula's body. The strike caught the Nazi off guard. Both crashed to the floor on their backs, Lillian on top of Ursula.

The move saved her life.

Graf fired half his magazine. All the bullets sailed overhead.

With her hand still on Ursula's gun, Lillian brought the weapon around and aimed it in Graf's direction. Forcing down Ursula's trigger finger, Lillian managed to get off a few shots. They didn't hit the Nazi colonel, but they forced him to duck and retreat behind one of the nearby airplanes.

Lillian needed to disarm Ursula quickly. To accomplish that, she brought Ursula's wrist to her mouth and clamped down. A part of Lillian was happily satisfied with the howl of pain that came from the Nazi agent. The gun dropped on Lillian's chest. She grabbed the pistol and tossed it to Henry. It skittered across the hangar floor. "Go after Graf."

Henry, now sitting up, dove for the gun as Graf fired in their direction again. Henry snatched up the pistol and put two rounds into the fuselage behind which Graf hid.

"On it," the British agent said. To the Geigers, he said, "Find cover."

They obeyed without question.

Lillian heard a metallic rasping. The next thing she knew, a wire wrapped around her throat. If it hadn't been for the collar of her blouse and jacket, Lillian's throat would have been sliced open by Ursula. As it was, Lillian, gasping for breath, fell back on Ursula.

The Nazi pulled hard.

Lillian didn't even have breath to gasp or try to call for help. Not that there was any help. Henry pursued Graf somewhere in the hangar and the Geigers were hiding. Lillian was able to snake a couple of fingers in between the wire and her neck, but they did little good. Ursula just yanked and pulled harder. Lillian's vision blackened around the edges.

This was it. This is where I die. Voices in her head warred with each other. *No, it's not. Not here. Not today. And sure as hell not like this.*

Lillian's free hand flailed. She tried to punch Ursula. Her hand met only air.

Ursula tugged harder. One of Lillian's fingers holding back the wire sliced opened. Her blood poured out of the wound. She knew she only had seconds to live or die.

Her hand hit something. It was the knife she had plunged into Ursula's thigh. Lillian gripped the handle. She shoved downward. Ursula grunted in pain but didn't let up on her efforts to choke the life out of Lillian.

In a last desperate maneuver, Lillian withdrew the blade. The blade still pointed downward. Lillian flipped the knife in the air and caught the handle again. Now the blade faced her. Moving aside as much as possible, Lillian jammed the knife past her face and into Ursula.

There was a gurgling sound, then a gasp. With a jerk, the wire around Lillian's neck slackened. Lillian fell onto the floor and scooted away from Ursula as fast as possible. It was only then she looked back at her handiwork.

The knife protruded from Ursula's eye socket.

Lillian gulped, her lungs craving the luscious sweetness of fresh air. She coughed and spat on the ground. The blood still flowed from her injured finger. All she was aware of at that point was the floor of the hangar and her breathing.

Before she knew it, James and Elsa rushed to her side. "Lil, are you okay?"

Lillian could only nod. Through a rasping voice, she asked, "Henry?"

As if in answer, gunshots rang out at the back of the hangar. A man's guttural yell echoed through the empty chamber.

Trying to stand, Lillian stumbled once.

"You should take it easy," Elsa said.

"When we're safe," Lillian said, using James's shoulder for

leverage to stand, "then I'll take it easy." She looked around, swaying and unbalanced. "Any weapons?"

"No." James put his arm around her. Elsa stood on the other side, steadying her.

Lillian looked at James. She focused on his face, the familiar lines now deeper than they were in their university day. She used him to center her mind, reminding her what was at stake.

An idea formed in her head. "Find the keys to the planes. Just two."

"What?" James asked, shocked.

Lillian grabbed his lapel. "Do it. Fast. I don't know if Graf called in reinforcements." She stumbled away from them, heading to where Henry went.

"Can you even fly a plane?" James yelled after her.

"Sure." Under her breath, she said, "I'm learning tonight. How hard can it be?"

With steps that steadily got more sure, she ran across the hangar. She skidded to a halt when she smelled gasoline.

56

"Over here," Henry Clark said to Lillian.

She looked around and spied the British agent hunkering down behind one of the biplanes. She ran over to him.

Someone fired a bullet in her direction. It pinged off the concrete.

"What's going on?" Lillian asked.

"Graf," Henry said. "He's holed up in one of the offices. I spread gasoline across the front of it. Now we're negotiating."

"Negotiating what?"

Henry pointed with his finger, tracing a line from the office to the planes. "He's got a direct line of sight to the planes. We try to get in one or two, he just takes careful aim and shoots us or the tanks. Isn't that right, Graf?" These last words he shouted at the closed door.

The office where Graf had taken refuge had glass windows that faced the hangar. One was already shot out. Broken glass littered the ground.

Across the hangar, James smashed through the window of the main office. He reached around the window and opened the door. He ducked inside and emerged a minute later with a handful of keys. He held them up to show Lillain.

She nodded. "Okay, we got the keys to the planes. Now what?"

"Convince your old professor to let us go." Henry spread his palm and indicated the office.

Lillian, her voice still raspy, shouted, "Colonel Graf?"

"What?" His voice sounded small from the office.

"You've been beaten."

"Not really," came the reply. "I've already alerted the Wehrmacht. They're on their way."

"No, sir," Lillian called. *God, it hurts to yell.* "You're bluffing."

No response came.

Lillian racked her brain trying to remember details of what Professor Gunter Graf was like. One came to mind. "Your wife; she was a good cook."

No response.

"She made dinner for some of your favorite students. I was one. I remember how good her food was."

In answer, a gunshot. "Leave my wife out of this!"

Lillian smiled grimly. She had her edge. "What do you think she would tell you were she here?"

"To fight on."

"No, sir. She would want you to be safe. To stay alive. We've won. You've lost. All you have to do is let us go."

A moment of silence. Then, "I will fight you until the end!" A gunshot punctuated the response. It flew harmlessly into one of the planes.

Henry whispered, "We're getting nowhere. What's your next play?"

Lillian Saxton thought about the situation. Gunter Graf was her old history professor, but that was a lifetime ago. Now, he was the enemy. She hated taking life, but understood it was part of her duty at times. *Is this one of those times?*

"Colonel, are you going to let us leave without incident?"

"Never!"

Lillian took the gun from Henry. "This is your last chance. Let us go or die."

"You don't have the stomach for such a decision!"

Without another word, Lillian raised the gun and fired at the cement floor coated with gasoline. The bullet caused a spark which ignited the fluid. Almost instantly, huge flames surged up. They followed the line Henry had drawn, almost to the door of the office. More important, there was a line of flame in front of the broken window. The flames gave Lillian and Henry the camouflage they needed to scurry back to James and Elsa, climb into two planes, and taxi out of the hangar.

Keeping back tears of rage, Lillian shoved the gun back into

Henry's hand. "Let's go."

57

Colonel Gunter Graf heard the last words of Sergeant Lillian Saxton. "This is your last chance. Let us go or die."

He chuckled. The student he knew from the university was too timid to make such an idle threat. He remembered her constantly hounding him during office hours, asking him a million questions, all in the vain hope she could answer his questions exactly as he wanted them answered on tests. Lillian Saxton was a fool, a woman whose only ambition as a young woman seemed to be to land a husband such as James Geiger.

A person like that would never knowingly, and in cold blood, do anything so drastic as light the gasoline.

With confidence in his voice, Graf responded. "You don't have the stomach for such a decision!"

A few seconds later, Gunter Graf was proven wrong.

A single gunshot ricocheted off the cement floor of the hangar. The spark lit the gasoline. Flames rose up almost instantly.

Graf smelled the smoke first. Then he saw the flames run across his field of view out the window. He stood up, knowing for a fact that Saxton and Clark would be making their way across the hangar floor to the planes that would deliver them to safety.

Vaguely, through the orange fire, he saw two figures running. In defiance, he fired at them. He couldn't tell if his bullets reached their targets. In the next instant, he lost sight of them.

The flames in front of the window grew. They found the wooden crates directly in front of the office and fed on them. The fire consumed the crates and craved more.

Gunter Graf opened the office door. Raging fire blocked his escape.

He closed the door. He looked around the room. It was an

interior office. No windows provided an exit. He was trapped.

The smoke curled into the office. Graf coughed. The black smoke clogged his lungs. He coughed harder. With no alternative, Graf slid to the floor where the smoke was not as dense. He still coughed.

His mind wandered back to Wilma. He brought to his vision her lovely face. It was there, right in front of him, amid all the smoke. Her face shone bright amid the darkening office. He thought of her cooking and their lovemaking, how they both fulfilled him beyond all measure. Tears crested his lids and streamed down his face.

"*Meine Ehefrau,*" he whispered. "*Ich liebe dich für immer.*"

He put the gun to his head and pulled the trigger.

The hammer clicked on metal. Nothing happened. It was empty.

"Oh my." Colonel Gunter Graf lay on the floor and awaited eternity.

58

"The fire's giving us camouflage," Henry said. "I'll cover you just in case. Go."

Lillian needed no more prompting. She got up and ran across the hangar.

Henry ran close at her heels.

Graf shot at them. They ducked, but his aim must have been off for she couldn't tell where the bullet landed.

The two of them rounded a plane and nearly plowed into James and Elsa. "Whoa, there," James said. "We're here. We have all the keys. That's so no one can follow us."

"That won't be a problem," Henry muttered.

James looked at Lillian. She only nodded.

"Okay," Henry said, command in his voice, "here's the plan." He put a finger in James's face. "No discussion. James goes in one plane with Lillian. I'll take Elsa."

"Then what?" James asked.

"We fly to the Channel. As far as we can. His Majesty's Navy rules the Channel. They'll pick us up."

"What if the Luftwaffe find us?" Elsa asked.

"They won't."

"How do you know?" she pressed.

Henry didn't respond to her question. "Where's the office?" James pointed.

Henry took off running.

"Can you fly a plane?" James asked.

Lillian gave him her best assured smile. "Sure."

He cocked his head to her, the same gesture he used to make when he was trying to get a secret out of her back in their university days. "Lil, I know you."

She gave him a firm look. "No, you *knew* me. I'm different now." A slight smile curled half her mouth. "As you can see now.

And yes, I can fly a plane."

Elsa said, "Your hand. How is it?"

Lillian clamped her bleeding fingers into her dress. "I'm fine."

Henry whistled and gestured that they all come to him. They ran, stopping in the office. Smoke now started to fill the hangar.

"Here," Henry said, "I didn't feel like lugging them across the hangar." He tossed a life vest to each one of them. "They call this a Mae West. You'll see why when we ditch in the Channel."

Lillian frowned. "Ditch in the Channel?"

Henry nodded. "I don't know the range of these planes. I'm not sure they'll make it all the way across the Channel. The plan is to fly directly northwest, toward England. As soon as you see a ship, light a flare"—he showed them the box on the desk—"jump out of the plane, and parachute to the water. The good guys'll pick us up. Now, put these parachutes on. Hurry!"

They all set about donning the parachutes. Lillian had parachuted out of planes before. Unlike traveling by sea, she had little issue with a smooth plane ride. She and Henry cinched their parachutes quickly, then helped the civilians with theirs.

The acrid smell of smoke and fire became thick and heavy. They didn't have much time. Everyone picked up a flare. In short order, Henry showed them how to ignite them.

Henry pointed through the office window and across the hangar. "Lillian, take James in the yellow one. Elsa, climb into the rear seat of the white one. Go! Now!"

"What are you going to do?" Lillian asked.

"Make a phone call." He gave her a lopsided grin and winked.

At that moment, Lillian wanted nothing more than to kiss this handsome British agent. Instead, she burst out laughing.

Henry kept grinning while he frantically gestured to them to follow his orders.

They did. After James and Elsa exchanged a tight hug and a kiss, Lillian and James helped his wife into her seat. Next, they ran to their yellow plane. James offered to help her up, but she refused. "I got this." She climbed into the front cockpit, James into the rear one. Scanning the dials and knobs, Lillian found the starter. She jammed the key into it and cranked up the engine. She bit her lip, willing the propeller to spin.

It did.

The sudden wind current in the hangar dissipated the thick smoke now clogging the entire hangar. It helped Elsa who was all but in the dark cloud.

Lillian released the brake. The biplane slowly moved forward. Hers was the plane nearest the hangar door. In seconds, she had cleared the hangar and taxied to the runway. The last vestiges of sunset enabled her to get her bearings. The runway faced west. The runway was the direction of safety.

She looked behind her and verified Henry's white plane was moving. It was.

"Hang on!" she yelled to James. "Here we go!"

Lillian engaged the throttle and the plane surged ahead. The runway was little more than a dirt road, but the rocks had been cleared. The plane picked up speed and Lillian prayed that her little training behind the control stick of a plane while it was on the ground would serve them today. She pulled back on the stick, and the plane lifted into the air.

She let out peals of laughter at her achievement.

"Why are you laughing?" James called to her.

"I did it! I actually did it!"

"You really can't fly a plane, can you?"

"Nope. But I can now."

Flying directly west, Lillian looked back over her shoulder to Antwerp. She literally saw the line between the approaching Wehrmacht and the B.E.F. Fires all along the front and into the buildings of Antwerp lit up the ground. Behind them, the hangar was now engulfed in fire. It was like a single beacon on the dark land.

Soaring above the war-torn Continent, Lillian felt free. The fresh air cleared her lungs of the smoke. It also cleared her head of all the worry about this mission. They were headed to safety. They had won.

After about an hour, the vast darkness of the English Channel loomed ahead. Up until then, flying over land, Lillian knew that if anything happened, all she had to do was land the plane or jump out with the parachute. Looking down, she saw no evidence of ships at all.

She trusted Henry. They flew on.

Another hour later, the engine started sputtering.

"Great," she muttered.

A second later James yelled, "That doesn't sound good."

"We're out of gas," Lillian said. "Get ready to bail out."

"I'm not sure I can do that."

"Yes, you can. Light the flare!"

She banked the plane higher, hoping to keep the nose up as long as possible. The bright red glow from behind her told her James had ignited his flare.

"Unbuckle the seat belt and jump."

"Together," James yelled. "I can't do it without your help."

Lillian bit her tongue on a retort. She unbuckled her seatbelt. Still holding onto the control stick, she stood on her seat. She pulled one of two flares. One she lit and tossed it onto the floorboard. She looked at James. He also stood on his seat.

In the glow of his flare, all of his aging disappeared. He looked just like he did six years ago: young, vibrant, handsome. The scene calmed her. She smiled.

"Okay," Lillian called. "On three, I'm releasing the stick and we're jumping." She put a foot on the side of the cockpit. He mirrored her.

"One."

He reached out his hand to her. She took it.

"Two."

James opened his mouth to say something, then closed it.

"Three!"

Hand in hand, Lillian and James leapt into the darkness.

59

Lillian fell. She yanked her hand from James's grasp. "Open your chute!"

James used his flare to see the toggle. He pulled it. The chute deployed. He stopped falling. Lillian continued for a second more, then pulled the ripcord. Her chute bellowed and she, too, stopped her descent. Below them, the ink-dark English Channel roiled.

Overhead in the darkness, she heard the sound of the other biplane. Henry's plane must have had more petrol. Her plane, the other flare igniting something on the floorboard, burst into flames as it plummeted to the sea. She watched it pitch, gracefully roll, and plunge into the Channel.

She had no power to steer her chute so she watched the progress of James's flare. It lit up his translucent chute like a Japanese lantern. Ironically, she realized it was the first true moment of relaxation she'd had in days. She enjoyed the feel of the sea breeze on her face and through her hair. It calmed her. She breathed in deeply, refreshing her tarnished lungs with clean air.

James's chute deflated when it hit the water. Within a few more seconds, she plunged in the water. Holding her breath, she released the straps and swam free from the entangling lines of the parachute. James's flare still sizzled on the Channel surface. Lillian toggled her life preserver and swam to him.

"I see why these things are called Mae Wests," James said when Lillian reached him. He held his hands over his chest. The inflatable material resembled a woman's breasts.

Lillian laughed. A good hearty, from-the-gut laugh. More tension released from her system. James joined in, even slapping the water. It splashed in her face, but she didn't mind.

Overhead, Henry's plane circled. Elsa, in the aviator seat,

held her flare aloft. From the distant darkness came the sound of a ship plowing through the waves.

"Listen," James said "I want to apologize for lying to you about the codebook. I was desperate to get out of Germany before it got bad. I wanted my wife and child to be raised in peace and safety."

Lillian regarded him as they bobbed up and down in the waves. His decision was hugely selfish. It had cost Frank his life, and loads of grief and pain for her and Henry. She wanted to tell him that. She wanted him to promise to visit Frank Monroe's parents and tell them their son's life was less important than his or his wife's. She wanted to say this and more. Instead, she said, "the information you give the British better be damn good, save lives, and end this war quickly. Cooperate fully. No questions asked. When this war's over, then you'll be able to go back to America. Understand?"

James nodded.

"Promise." She laced her voice with command.

"I promise." He smiled and floated in the water, saying nothing but just looking at her. "You really have changed."

Not wanting to let the comment go unchallenged, Lillian said, "I had to move on. I found a new path in life. I like it."

"You ever wonder what might have been? If you'd stayed with me?"

"Or if you'd returned to the U.S.?" she countered. "I used to, yeah. But then I met a great teacher, one who showed me another way. He helped me get out of the hole I found myself in six years ago. Don't take this the wrong way, but I rarely thought about you and me for the past five years. It wasn't until your message came that those thoughts all flooded back. When this assignment started, I wasn't prepared to deal with the emotions. Now, seeing you, Elsa, and the two of you together, I'm good. My hand hurts like hell and I'm ready for a bath, but I'm good."

"Lillian Saxton, you are a remarkable woman."

The genuineness of James's comment warmed her. "You owe me something." She changed her tone. "The name. Who killed my brother?"

James said, "Christoph Dombacher. He's an agent for the Reich. His commanding officer is General Hans Siegfried."

The name meant nothing to her now, but she knew it would mean everything in the future.

The engine of Henry's plane sputtered. Elsa threw the dying flare. It pinwheeled through the sky and landed with a plunk in the water. The starlight showed the shadow of the plane, then it dived in the distance. Two plumes blocked the stars.

Lillian and James watched as Henry and Elsa floated to the sea. They splashed about fifty yards away.

James started to swim in that direction but Lillian held him back. "Let them come to us. It'll make it easier for the boat to find us."

They waited in silence for a few minutes. The lapping of the water around her began to lull Lillian. She hadn't realized how tired she was, how hard the exertions she had just undertaken.

"Lil," James said.

"Yeah?"

"I want to tell you something before they get here. I assume we'll be separated once we get on land, seeing as how I'm a war asset now."

Lillian's relaxed state suddenly left her. "Okay."

"I never got over you. I only tried to replace the hole you left in my life. For what it's worth, I'm sorry for forcing that decision on you back in Paris."

He swam closer to her. The dying flare bobbed in the water, but it was enough light for Lillian to see the look in his eyes. She knew what he was going to do.

James leaned in to her, meaning to kiss her. She put her hand on his lips, preventing him. Instead, she put her arms around him. The life jackets prevented a good, solid hug, but the emotion was there. She hugged him tightly, all the emotions and the years surging through her. He reciprocated. Lillian knew this was the last time she'd have with James, alone, all to herself.

They parted and looked at each other. She saw into his soul.

She wondered if her soul was open to him.

Henry and Elsa neared. "Hey!" The British agent called.

"We're here!" Lillian gently pushed James away. He kept his gaze locked on hers. "Watch your eyes," she said. She lit her flare and tossed it nearby.

The water boiled near the burning flare. Henry, pulling Elsa along, emerged from the darkness. His smile was big and contagious.

"Does the Navy come by here?"

Lillian laughed.

Elsa, seeing James, paddled over to him. The Geigers embraced each other, Elsa softly sobbing.

Henry treaded water next to Lillian. He patted her on the back. "For a Yank, you did pretty good."

She splashed water at him. "Glad you could keep up."

He splashed water back at her.

A Royal Navy cruiser, its engine churning the water, sliced through the waves. She steered clear of the four people in the water. From the deck, a bright spotlight illuminated the night.

Lillian clamped her eyes shut and held her hand up to block the light.

"Friend or foe?" came the call from the deck.

"Friend," Henry replied. rattling off the coded message.

The crewman on deck replied in kind.

The ship slowed. In the new light, Lillian watched a lifeboat lower to the water level. Two men were in the boat. They rowed toward the quartet bobbing in the water. Together, they hauled Elsa up first, then James.

Henry, ever the dapper English gentleman, said, "After you, my lady."

This time, Lillian didn't mind going first. Henry's powerful hands helped her into the boat. He climbed in after her. She planted herself on one of the benches. Henry sat next to her. Right next to her.

After all they had been through together, the talks they had in the hotel, Lillian felt comfortable with Henry Clark. She leaned against his shoulder. He put his arm around her. Together, they let someone else take control.

60

The *H.M.S. Delhi* steamed back to England throughout the night. The Geigers stayed in a room to themselves. The bunks were one over the other so they didn't get to lie together. As expected, a guard stood out in the hallway. He was armed.

Henry Clark headed straight for sick bay. The doctor got the agent on the table and stitched up both wounds, the scalp as well as the arm. Henry got a nice dose of morphine to dull the pain and sank into an empty bunk.

Lillian was given her own bunk in her own room. She peeled off her wet clothes and donned a spare uniform. The medic attended to her injured hand and neck. Cleaned up, she crashed into the bunk and was asleep in seconds.

She woke and stared at the gray ceiling of the room. This was her last day on this mission. An odd feeling always crept into her soul when a mission reached its conclusion. In almost all cases, it was a job well done. She prided herself on her professionalism. In those cases in which the job didn't end well, she looked for the debriefings where the issues were analyzed and lessons learned were internalized.

This mission, despite the glaring lie at the center of it, was a success. She had brought James Geiger out of Belgium and into the custody of the British government. His wife was with him. He would divulge all he knew about the Nazi codes and, with any good luck, that information would help the Allied war effort until the United States joined the fight.

And she had the name. Christoph Dombacher. Her brother's murderer.

But there were costs. Frank Monroe topped the list. His loss wrenched her gut. He had been out of his element. She knew it, and James should have known it, but he insisted Frank deliver the message to Lillian. Frank did so, and it cost him his life. She vowed she would make a pilgrimage to see Frank's parents and express her personal sorrow. She also made a mental note to check on where his body was.

Tired as she was, she couldn't keep her mind from racing. She needed some time off, but a part of her was antsy for the next mission. The only problem was that she would have to travel by sea to get back to America. That was a prospect she didn't relish.

With her red hair pulled back in a semiformal style, Lillian sauntered down the narrow halls to the mess. Being one of two females on board—and the only single one—she received lots of looks from the men. She tried to let their stares roll off her shoulders, but she liked the attention. Not that any of these blokes would have a chance with her. Back in the U.S. Army, she strove to be one of the guys. Here, she was the anomaly. She fancied it.

James, Elsa, and Henry were sitting at one of the tables, eating. Lillian got some food and sat next to Henry. "Good morning."

"*Guten morgen.*" Elsa reached her hand across the table and grasped Lillian's hand. "I want to thank you for risking so much in getting us here. I know my husband lied to you, but I admire your resilience and courage. I might not have made the same decision as he did, but I'm glad you were there to help us."

Lillian tightened her fingers around Elsa's. "*Gern geschehen.*"

They ate and talked about nothing and everything. Lillian wondered if James had mentioned his attempted kiss while floating in the Channel, but then realized she didn't care. The two of them were married. Who cared what they said to each other?

"We're expected at MI-6 when we dock," Henry said. "You'll be expected to deliver a report. In writing." He rolled his eyes. "Do you have this kind of paperwork back in America?"

Lillian nodded. "Except for those times I'm off-the-books, like this one. I expect I'll be one of those footnotes in the history of this war: American sergeant helps German defector escape Nazi clutches."

"If you win the war," Elsa said.

"Oh, we'll win it," Lillian assured her. "It won't be pretty. It may not be short, but we'll win. Because I want a seat at the peace table. I want to ensure America has a hand in creating the postwar world."

Elsa opened her mouth to respond, then closed it. "We'll see."

"We will."

They finished their breakfast talking about other subjects. The captain, a tall man with a weathered face and mustache, came down to the mess. He told them they'd dock in ten minutes and to be ready on deck. He signaled a crewman with a side arm to lead the Geigers up to the deck.

"That won't be necessary," Lillian said.

"Orders from MI-6."

Lillian shook her head. "This started as an American mission and it'll end as one. When we get ashore, I'll hand over the Geigers to the British government. Until then, they're with me. And we don't need the guard." She leveled her gaze at the captain, five inches taller than she was.

His steely eyes softened. "As you wish, Sergeant."

Lillian saluted him. "Thank you, sir. Permission to disembark."

He returned the salute. "Permission granted."

With that formality out of the way, Lillian led James and Elsa on deck. Henry trailed behind. The new morning was warm and sunny. The harbor was alive with activity. From this side of the Channel, Lillian couldn't tell there was a war raging only thirty miles away.

The *Delhi* docked. With the gangways lowered, Lillian, Henry, James, and Elsa disembarked. The men waiting for them were not hard to discern. Dressed in identical brown suits, they approached the quartet and identified themselves as Elliot and Raslo. They were to escort the prisoners to MI-6.

"They're not prisoners," Lillian corrected. "They are defectors from Hitler's Germany and important war assets for the British government. They should be accorded proper courtesy."

When Elliot mumbled something about taking them into custody, Lillian cut in. "Where's your car? Until we set foot in MI-6, they're with me. Understand?"

Both men nodded. "This way."

Elliot and Raslo led them to a dark sedan. Everyone piled in. Elliot drove through London. Elsa stared out the window. She was viewing London for the first time. In short order, they arrived at the headquarters for British Intelligence. Lillian led the way into the building, the others trailing her.

Admiral Charles Hastings stood inside the entryway. Flanking him were four other people, all severe-looking men. Hastings beamed at Lillian.

"Sergeant Saxton, so good to see you." He reached out and shook Lillian's hand. "Agent Clark, glad to see you in one piece." Likewise, he shook Henry's hand.

Then he turned to look at James and Elsa Geiger. "Mr. Geiger?"

"Yes."

"I'm looking forward to some long talks with you."

James Geiger raised his chin. "And I'll willingly provide you with all that I know. I only ask we be treated with the proper respect."

A muscle in Hastings's cheek twitched. "As long as you provide details, you'll be accorded the utmost respect." He indicated the men standing with him. "These men would like to begin as soon as possible. The situation on the Continent is, unfortunately, quite desperate."

James nodded. He faced Henry. "Agent Clark, thank you for helping us escape." The two men shook hands.

Elsa performed a small bow, like a dancer at the end of a stage play.

To Lillian, James also offered his hand. He also gave her the look in his eyes. They had had their personal moment in the Channel. This was purely for show.

Lillian took his hand and shook it.

"Thank you, Lillian."

"You're welcome."

"Fräulein Saxton," Elsa said.

Lillian looked at the German woman. "Frau Geiger."

Elsa stepped forward and embraced Lillian. After a moment, Lillian put her arms around James's wife and the mother of his unborn child. All those years at the university, Lillian had desperately wanted to be in the role Elsa now held. Here, after all the years in between, Lillian Saxton was glad she was not Mrs. James Geiger.

"Thank you," Elsa said. "You are a brave woman. If your country truly does join the war and possesses fighters like you, I'm afraid the Reich doesn't stand a chance." They parted and smiled at each other.

On a nod from Hastings, the four men led James and Elsa Geiger away.

"Well, now that that's settled," Hastings said, turning on his heels. "Follow me."

Lillian and Henry exchanged glances. Silently, Henry shrugged. They followed. Hastings led them through the halls of MI-6. With Lillian dressed in an ill-fitting sailor's uniform and Henry dressed similarly, the two of them must have looked quite the pair.

Hastings led them back to his office. The last time she was here, Lillian had given the older man an earful. She wondered if he was about to return the favor.

Walking over to a side table, Hastings stood next to a contraption that looked like a phone attached to a speaker. He pushed a button. "Cedric, they're here. Please patch through the connection."

What followed was the sound of static and squawks. Finally, a familiar voice came out of the speakers.

"Sergeant Saxton, this is Captain Donnelly."

She tried to hide her shock at hearing her commanding officer's voice, but she failed. Her mouth dropped open.

"Congratulations on a successful mission. I'm sure our

British friends will find the information James Geiger delivers to be useful."

"Thank you, sir."

"And you're not the worse for wear?"

She glanced down at her bandaged hand. "No, sir. Just a few scratches."

Henry and Hastings grinned at her.

"Listen, Sergeant, I need to tell you something. And it's passed through all the brass over here, so don't think this is another incident of my going off the rails like we did in California."

"Understood, sir."

"Sergeant, I am officially placing you on detached service. You're still a sergeant in the United States Army, but for now, you'll be reporting to Admiral Hastings for further assignments in the near term."

"Sir?"

"At ease, Sergeant. The matter is simple. We're not at war. Yet. You and I both know that day is coming. Sooner or later. Until that time comes, I feel you will better serve the war effort working with those who are already fighting that son of a bitch Hitler. I'll still expect regular reports, and Admiral Hastings will keep me up-to-date as well. I'll pass on your reports to the upper brass. All commendations you receive over there will be on your official record. From what Admiral Hastings tells me, you'll be paired with Agent Clark. From the details the admiral has given me, you two make quite the team. Do you understand, Sergeant?"

It took Lillian a moment to respond. "Yes, sir. And thank you."

"You're welcome. Now take the war to the Nazis. Make us proud."

The signal ended. Silence emanated from the speaker.

Lillian Saxton looked at Henry Clark. He seemed as surprised as she was, but there was a sparkle in his eye. He winked at her.

"Did you have anything to do with this?" she asked.

"Not a thing," he replied. "You're actions in the field earned this. I'm just happy you're on our side. I don't know what we'd do if you worked for Jerry."

Admiral Hastings eased himself around to his desk and sat. "Sit."

They complied.

He folded his hands and looked at each of them, then turned to Lillian.

"Sergeant, have you ever been to Rome?"

ACKNOWLEDGEMENTS

The origin story of *Ulterior Objectives* starts in another book, *Wading Into War*. In that tale, private eye Benjamin Wade is hired by Lillian Saxton to locate a missing reporter with information regarding the death of her brother. The last chapter of *Wading Into War* is the opening chapter of *Ulterior Objectives* but from her point of view. The more I thought about the big reveal that Lillian Saxton actually worked for the US Army, the more I wanted to tell a story with her as the featured hero.

Ulterior Objectives is the result.

But getting the story developed was another thing entirely.

I wrote my initial thoughts in May 2015. The first sentence I wrote was this: "Lillian Saxton is told to go get a friend of a high-level politician out of Europe days before France falls." The second sentence I wrote was the opening line of *Ulterior Objectives*. I had lots of ideas, and the basic story started to take shape as I planned it during the summer of 2015. A key component, even from the beginning, was the idea that Lillian would have to help a person escape Europe and not just a codebook. But many of the ideas were scattered, not streamlined. I needed an assist.

My Dad was just the one to help me zero in on the story. On a trip back to Houston from Dallas, he and I hashed out the entire story. I was driving and he was in the passenger seat, my notes laid out in front of him. For the entire trip, we ironed out the story, the pacing, and the order of scenes. By the time we got back to Houston, I couldn't wait to get started.

The ease by which this story unfolded through my keyboard is largely attributed to the help Dad gave me. He's a lifelong reader, steeped not only in the westerns of Louis L'Amour but also the thrillers of Alistair MacLean. He knows what works and what doesn't. He helped make *Ulterior Objectives* the novel it is. For that, Dad, I give you a wholehearted thank you. Without you, this book doesn't exist.

When it came time to design a cover, I wanted *Ulterior Objectives* to stand out from the other three novels to date. I wanted a cover that would mirror this book's big action.

When I got to thinking about what kind of image I wanted on the cover, only one sequence came to mind: the car chase. It had all the components: danger, excitement, explosions! Not only did I have a scene I wanted to showcase, I also had inspiration. In short, I wanted a Clive Cussler cover. No matter the series, if you look at nearly all of his modern covers, there is a commonality to them. You've got the title, his name, and the subtitle of whichever character is featured. That is what I wanted.

I conducted a contest at 99Designs.com. I wrote out a lengthy brief detailing what I wanted, including color schemes, and other things that inspired me. I also had a crude pencil sketch that I uploaded. I have to say that it's a little bit nerve-racking when you push the save button and the contest launches. You don't know how many designers are going to show up or even bother to submit designs.

Bob, from B&J, was the first artist to submit a cover. And it was all but perfect. The only change I had him make was change it from night to day and make sure that the background looked like the English countryside. He did and, well, you've seen the result. I love the little details Bob drew. Lillian's hair flying around as her car speeds down the road. Tire marks on the road. The bad guy driver, visible, but in shadow. Cool explosion of one of the motorcycles. Needless to say, when Bob presented me with this cover, I was ecstatic.

So, to Bob: thanks for helping me bring to life the cover for *Ulterior Objectives*. You knocked it out of the park.

Regarding the words, I can write them, but I can't make them shine as well as they without the help of my editor, Anna Marie Flusche. As with all my 1940s-era stories, she called me out on a few phrases that were too modern, verified my historical accuracy in other cases, and generally tightened up the prose.

Every page had marks, of course, but I always look for the little checkmarks near certain passages. It meant she enjoyed parts that I hope all readers enjoy. As always, any issues with the novel now are all on me.

Thank you again, Anna Marie, for making this a better book.

Lastly, thank you, dear reader. Thank you for taking the time to read this book. I hope you enjoyed *Ulterior Objectives*. If you did, I would certainly appreciate you telling your friends and family about it. And, if you are of a mind, I would greatly appreciate you leaving a review at the bookstore of your choice. Word of mouth and reviews can help other discover *Ulterior Objectives*. Thank you.

READER RESPONSE

Thank you, dear reader, for reading *Ulterior Objectives*. I'd love to hear what you thought of the book. Your feedback is important to me and for helping other readers find books they like. In this new age of publishing, word of mouth is just as important as it has always been in spreading the news about good books. Online reviews are a new form of word of mouth.

If you enjoyed this book, I would appreciate you leaving an honest review over at Amazon or any other review site. It really helps other readers find this book.

And if you'd like to know about upcoming titles, please sign up to my mailing list.

OTHER BOOKS BY
SCOTT DENNIS PARKER

WADING INTO WAR
A Detective Benjamin Wade Mystery

Benjamin Wade's first case!

Houston, 1940

Benjamin Wade is a laid back private investigator whose jobs are so mundane that he doesn't even carry a gun. He thought his latest job was going to be easy.

He thought wrong.

Hired by beguiling Lillian Saxton to find a missing reporter with knowledge of her brother's whereabouts in war-torn Europe, Wade follows a lead and knocks on a door. He gets two answers: bullets and a corpse.

Now Wade must unravel the truth about the reporter's death, Lillian's brother, and the whereabouts of a cache of documents that uncovers a shocking story from Nazi-controlled Europe and an even more nefarious secret here at home.

ALL CHICKENS MUST DIE
A Detective Benjamin Wade Mystery

Benjamin Wade Returns!

May 1940, the last days of the Great Depression, and private investigator Benjamin Wade isn't exactly rolling in the dough. He doesn't even have a secretary. So he's in the unenviable position of taking any client that walks in his office.

Elmer Smith, a local farmer, has a problem: all of his chickens are scheduled for slaughter. He's desperate to save his livelihood. He got a court injunction to slow the process, but time is running out.

Instead of laughing Smith out the door, Wade suppresses his pride to take the case. It seems like a simple, straight-forward paycheck. He zeroes in on a central question: What really happened the night police chased someone through Smith's farm? Wade isn't the only one asking that question, but he could be the only one who might die for it.

THE PHANTOM AUTOMOBILES
A Gordon Gardner Mystery

You met him as a co-star in *Wading Into War* and *All Chickens Must Die*. Now, Gordon Gardner stars in his first feature story.

Gordon Gardner, Ace Reporter!

There's not a story he can't crack. He's got his finger on the pulse of his town. His dogged tenacity means no politician is safe. Even the U. S. Army keeps tabs on him to ensure he safely harbors national secrets. And he looks smashing in a tux.

His latest assignment is a basic police blotter piece: a pedestrian struck dead by a car. As a reporter who is second to none, Gardner's disappointed. How could a simple accident be worthy of his considerable talents when there are so many other more interesting stories to cover? Even his pairing with a beautiful photographer doesn't lighten his mood.

His editor wants the piece yesterday. The police already closed the case. But then Gardner asks a simple question: why would a seemingly normal person willingly dive in front of a speeding car? Witnesses said the man went crazy just moments before he leapt to his death. What he alleged made no sense: he said the cars on the street didn't exist and there was only one way to prove it.

He was wrong. Dead wrong.

Now, Gordon Gardner, in defiance of his editor and the police, resolves to investigate the mysterious circumstances behind the dead man's life and uncover the real truth behind the phantom automobiles.

ABOUT THE AUTHOR

Scott Dennis Parker lives and works in his native Houston, Texas. He is the Saturday columnist at DoSomeDamage.com. He is the founder of Quadrant Fiction Studio, an independent publisher that specializes in stories that will amaze, excite, and, most importantly, entertain you.

Official author website and blog: scottdennisparker.com

Twitter: https://twitter.com/sdparker7

Official author page on Facebook:
www.facebook.com/scottdennisparker

Email: scott@scottdennisparker.com

Monthly Newsletter

Sign up for the monthly Scott Dennis Parker email newsletter to receive exclusive sneak peeks at upcoming titles, behind-the-scenes of the book making process, and more.

Plus, you can get a free copy of *Wading Into War: A Detective Benjamin Wade Mystery*. Sign up at the official author website.

WESTERNS BY S. D. PARKER

You've got a lot of choices in what you read. So do I.

That's why I specialize in Western stories that will amaze, excite, and, most importantly, Entertain You.

I call it Old-Fashioned Escapism for the 21st Century.

The westerns I write, under the pen name of S. D. Parker, draw their inspiration from classic novelists from Louis L'amour, Luke Short, and Bradford Scott to modern authors like James Reasoner, Robert J. Randisi, and Peter Brandvold. Classic television shows like The Wild Wild West, Maverick, and The Adventures of Brisco County, Jr. also spur the imagination.

The westerns Scott writes using the S. D. Parker pen name draw their inspiration from classic TV shows like Maverick, The Wild Wild West, and the Adventures of Brisco County, Jr. and authors such as James Reasoner, Robert Randisi, and Louis L'amour.

Official S.D. Parker - West Author website and blog:
 scottdennisparker.com

Official author page on Facebook:
www.facebook.com/SDParkerWesternAuthor/